MW01093562

GOAT SONG

KONSTANTIN VAGINOV (1899–1934) was born in Saint
Petersburg. His mother came from a wealthy family and his father
was a high-ranking official, descended from German immigrants
whose name had been Russified from Wagenheim. During the
Civil War, he served in the Red Army. Active in Nikolai Gumilev's
Acmeist movement and the Guild of Poets, he was a core member of
the avant-garde group OBERIU and well acquainted with Mikhail
Bakhtin and his intellectual circle, who partly inspired his fiction.
Vaginov wrote four novels before his death from tuberculosis at the
age of thirty-four.

AINSLEY MORSE teaches literature and translation at the
University of California, San Diego, and translates from Russian,
Ukrainian, and Bosnian-Croatian-Serbian.

GEOFF CEBULA has a Ph.D. in Slavic languages and literature
from Princeton University. He is the author of the novel *Adjunct*
and has published several articles on the avant-garde collective
OBERIU. He lives in Indiana.

EUGENE OSTASHEVSKY is a poet and translator. His books
of poetry include *The Pirate Who Does Not Know the Value of Pi*
and *The Feeling Sonnets* (both published by NYRB Poets). As a
translator, he works mainly with avant-garde and experimental
literature in Russian.

GOAT SONG *and*
THE WORKS AND DAYS
OF WHISTLIN

KONSTANTIN VAGINOV

Translated from the Russian by
AINSLEY MORSE
with **GEOFF CEBULA**

Introduction by
EUGENE OSTASHEVSKY

NEW YORK REVIEW BOOKS

New York

THIS IS A NEW YORK REVIEW BOOK
PUBLISHED BY THE NEW YORK REVIEW OF BOOKS
207 East 32nd Street, New York, NY 10016
www.nyrb.com

For Vladimir Earl and Dina Gatina

Library of Congress Cataloging-in-Publication Data
Names: Vaginov, K., author. | Vaginov, K. Kozlinaia pesn̂. English. | Vaginov, K.
 Trudy i dni Svistonova. English. | Cebula, Geoff, translator. | Morse, Ainsley,
 translator. | Ostashevsky, Eugene, writer of introduction.
Title: Goat song: The works and days of Wistlin / Konstantin Vaginov;
 translated by Ainsley Morse, with Geoff Cebula; introduction by Eugene
 Ostashevsky.
Other titles: Works and days of Wistlin
Description: New York: New York Review Books, 2025. | Series: New York
 Review Books classics |
Identifiers: LCCN 2024008814 (print) | LCCN 2024008815 (ebook) | ISBN
 9781681378886 (paperback) | ISBN 9781681378893 (ebook)
Subjects: LCGFT: Novels.
Classification: LCC PG3476.V285 K6413 2025 (print) | LCC PG3476.V285
 (ebook) | DDC 891.73/42—dc23/eng/20240226
LC record available at https://lccn.loc.gov/2024008814
LC ebook record available at https://lccn.loc.gov/

ISBN 978-1-68137-888-6
Available as an electronic book; ISBN 978-1-68137-889-3

The authorized representative in the EU for product safety and
compliance is eucomply OÜ, Pärnu mnt 139b-14, 11317 Tallinn, Estonia,
hello@eucompliancepartner.com, +33 757690241.

Printed in the United States of America on acid-free paper.
10 9 8 7 6 5 4 3 2 1

CONTENTS

INTRODUCTION
Double-Voiced Words

In memory of Dmitry Golynko (1969–2023)

These were the musings of one of the few pagans,
one of the very few still left,
as he sat in his shabby room just after reading
Philostratos' *On Apollonius of Tyana*.

—C. P. Cavafy[1]

Konstantin Wagenheim was born in the fall of 1899 in Saint Petersburg.[2] In *Notes from the Underground*, Dostoevsky jeered at the Jewish dentists who were his paternal ancestors.[3] Wagenheim père, a twice-baptized police official, had married a Siberian heiress; they owned a five-story apartment building on a fashionable avenue. At the outbreak of World War I, the German-sounding name of Saint Petersburg was changed to the Russian-sounding Petrograd. Many families with Germanic names followed suit and Russified them. The Wagenheims—whose name was pronounced as Vagengeim—chose Vaginov, with the stress falling on the first syllable. It is a not-impossible Russian last name that has no relation to what was then a medical term that the police captain might not even have been aware of.

In his first novel, *Goat Song*, Vaginov bestows on the unknown poet his own memories of a privileged childhood and tempestuous youth. The sheltered boy read Edward Gibbon's *The History of the Decline and Fall of the Roman Empire* and collected ancient coins. In 1916–1917, while the Russian Empire was collapsing, young Vaginov ran around the dark streets at night, sniffed cocaine, and fell in love with a homeless prostitute. He also wrote poems. These diversions partially eclipsed the chaos and violence of the revolutionary street. His father lost his post and had to hide his past. The family was evicted from the building they once owned. With the Civil War, Petrograd turned into a "terrifying, boarded-up, empty city, overgrown with grass." Apartments emptied, stores were shuttered, transportation did not run, crime and state-encouraged class violence ruled the streets. The Bolshevik authorities failed to keep the city supplied with food, and they arrested anyone who tried to bring it in from the countryside as "speculators." Bread rations were minuscule. Famine began. Up to two hundred people died every day as a consequence, and by 1920 the city's population had been reduced by half, to seven hundred thousand. Vaginov, who had enrolled in the university to avoid the draft, was conscripted anyway. He served, apparently as a paramedic, against the Poles in the summer of 1920 and then against the Whites in the Urals.

A poem dated March 1922 remembers that period of convulsion and transition:

> I remember the last night in the home of my deceased childhood.
> Books dismembered, the lamp overturned on the floor.
>
> I ran out into the streets and the eyelashes of the bronze sun
> Toppled with a double sound into my wound-up shoulders.
>
> Bunks. Snows. I'm in the crowd of a homespun army.
> A pounce into Poland, then a bounce to the East.
>
> Oh how it glows, the Chinese dead sun.
> I remember looking forward to it in the long nights of longing.
>
> Back in the homeland. I am eating lentil stew.
> The hum of the Baltic. The mild gait of the winds.
>
> But there's no made-up Masha to undo the door chain for me.
> A pack of white humans in moonlight gnaws on a horse.

Titled "A Young Man" in one publication, the piece is at once avant-garde and antiquarian. The narrative jumps from one discrete moment to another and the syntax connects words that are hard to reconcile in meaning ("eyelashes of the bronze sun," etc.). Still, the meter loosely evokes the Greek elegy, as does the personal mythmaking. The striking close carries the memory of the recent Petrograd famine, when passersby would cut up and eat horses that collapsed in the streets. It is said that Vaginov's heiress mother used to go outside with a big knife for that purpose.[4]

Vaginov returned to Petrograd at the beginning of 1921—slight in stature, starving, with front teeth gone. Another poem, composed in the same months as the first, presumably represents his trip back from the army:

> Each has his mouth around a neighbor's leg.
> Outside, the steppe glows. The summer evening is easy.
>
> I am riding north on a dead train, to the city
> Where the dead sun gleams like ice.
>
> My way is calm. My passions are past.
> I don't know. Shall mother meet me? Shake my hand?
>
> I heard my city has become a mild friar,
> Hawks candles and bows low bows.
>
> They also say the ships are a-coming in,
> A-coming in now into the unpeopled city
>
> With foreign wines and silk in the hold.
> They ply the dead one with drink. Then they dress it in silk.
>
> Hey, quicken, stoker, hurry to the north!
> The night is clear tnight. How like a corpse it smells!

> We are dead, Ivan, the clover is over us.
> The German colonist stirs on the threshing floor.

All the furniture of this poem—the sun, the train, the riders, and the destination—is doubled, at once living and dead. "The German colonist" refers to ethnically German farmers in, mainly, the Volga region.

As the war was coming to an end, economic and literary life started to recover. The young veteran began to take part in different literary circles immediately upon arrival. He frequented an established creative writing workshop which advocated Acmeism, a modernist poetics devoted to formal excellence, economy of means, and "direct treatment of the thing." Gathering with other poets his own age in ephemeral groups, he published a jejune chapbook called *Journey into Chaos* and formed a lasting friendship with the poet Nikolai Tikhonov, who went on to become a prominent Soviet writer-functionary. Finally, he frequented the apartment that the older poet and composer Mikhail Kuzmin shared with his romantic partner, Yuri Yurkun. Kuzmin was a refined aesthete who linked three generations of Russian poets: the Symbolists, the Acmeists, and the young modernists who felt spiritually alienated from the revolution, although they were still able to publish. The circle, whose discussions ranged over different historical epochs, included brilliant translators from ancient and modern languages. Kuzmin's taste for the more exotic literature and philosophy of late antiquity and France of the classical age—he had published a book of poems set in Alexandria, and a book of fiction about Enlightenment alchemy—especially spoke to Vaginov. The circle's almanac, *Abraxas*, was named after a rooster-headed god of the Gnostics.

Vaginov's early attempt at fiction, published in *Abraxas*, refers to Philostratus, a Greek prose writer from imperial Rome. His figure still haunts *Goat Song* some years later: "All of Philostratus's being was filled with unspoken music, his lovely youthful eyes beneath their wings of lashes were laughing, his long fingers, adorned with rings, held a tablet and stylus. Philostratus often walked and seemed to converse with Balmcalfkin," the older amateur scholar who is one of the novel's protagonists. The unknown poet seeks an edition of the

Greek writer's masterpiece, *The Life of Apollonius of Tyana*, a heavily fictionalized life of a first-century mystic who travels to India, Egypt, and other places of traditional wisdom. In the novel's self-referential play, Philostratus—endowed with the androgynous sexiness of Apollonius, although in real life the prolific scholar probably bore a greater resemblance to Balmcalfkin—is the alternative author of *Goat Song*, who would have treated his protagonists with greater sympathy than the character called "the author" did. He would have shown them as "radiant," whereas the novel's author "blackened" them, as the original Russian has it, "in the eyes of posterity."

Why does Philostratus, a somewhat obscure writer at the court of Emperor Septimius Severus, appear as an alter ego in Vaginov's prose and poetry? Philostratus was a pagan. His Apollonius was said to have been not only a pagan but also a divinely inspired miracle worker. Later pagans, drowning in the rising tide of Christianity, grasped at straws by citing Apollonius as the hygienic and civilized alternative to the miracle worker from Nazareth. Interest in Philostratus and his protagonist was reborn in the Renaissance and again in the early twentieth century, themselves epochs of great cultural rupture.[5] The Greek poet Constantine Cavafy, who was fascinated by the transition from paganism and Christianity but not known to the Kuzmin circle, evokes *The Life of Apollonius of Tyana* repeatedly in the same years as Vaginov. Some years later, as an auditor in a seminar of Greek translators, Vaginov may have urged his friend Andrei Egunov to translate the book.[6]

The young poet read Philostratus in the context of his childhood exposure to Gibbon's *Decline and Fall*. The Enlightenment historian blamed Christianity, fanatical and uncivilized, for the destruction of Rome and its sophisticated, pluralistic culture. In *Goat Song*, Vaginov projects Gibbon's explanation for the fall of the Roman Empire onto the fall of the Russian Empire. He interprets the Bolsheviks and the underclasses they brought to power as the new Christian masses, teeming, unwashed, benighted, and hysterically certain of their truth. "I saw the new Christians . . . I saw indistinct crowds demolishing idols," exclaims the unknown poet, for whom the emergence of Bolshevism "resembles the first centuries of Christianity." In the novel, the figure of Philostratus serves as a figurehead to this cyclical understanding of history, in which high civilization periodically suffers death at the hands of barbarism but then is reborn like the Phoenix.

In the spring of 1924 Vaginov befriended Mikhail Bakhtin, a historian and philosopher of literary language. Interviewed half a century later, Bakhtin remembered the young man's poems by heart and could describe the novels in detail. He praised Vaginov as a "truly unique figure in world literature" and knew that the characters in *Goat Song* were partially based on members of his circle, including himself.[7] The philosopher reminisced about Vaginov's book collection with admiration and perhaps even a touch of envy. Since, after the revolution, the libraries of the dead and the fled were being sold for next to nothing, Vaginov was able to collect early modern editions with the little money he earned by writing. A friend recalled him reading an old edition of Ariosto on a crowded early-morning tram in the factory district.[8] Yet, apart from his book collection, the poet was unimaginably poor. He studied Romance languages on food lines. His room did not have electricity until the late 1920s, despite—or perhaps because of—the Bolshevik call for the electrification of the whole country.

The Bakhtin circle met at the apartment of the pianist Maria Yudina, where they heard and discussed lectures, poems, and music performances in a free-flowing unofficial seminar. In 1926, they held a release party for Vaginov's second, untitled poetry collection, whose print run was about five hundred copies, the same as that of his first book. In a letter from this time, Yudina explores a poem by Vaginov to reflect on the intellectually active listening that she, as a modern pianist, desires from her audience.[9] The poem in question is Vaginov's "Music":

> Words fly in book rotatories.
> I wander in word repositories.
>
> All of a sudden like the nightingale
> A word breaks into song. I run toward the stair.

The word is there, before me like a hallway,
A journey underneath the agitated

Moon: from dark to light, from littoral bluffs
To the indefinite shifting of the sea.

Music does not lie in sounds. It lies
In the transformation of images.

Nor O, nor A, nor any other sound
Mean anything around such music.

You're reading a book. Far off you hear
A choir of dancers circling near.

Desire for laughter comes my way
On an unforeseen spring day.

While the poet imagines poetry as music, the pianist imagines music as poetry. She demands that her listeners "decipher 'the transformation of images'" in her performance as if it were a complicated string of associations, and believes that Vaginov expects the same type of heightened attention to his writing. These adherents of the modernist value of difficulty held music and poetry to be arts of the intellect.

By the mid-1920s Vaginov was an acclaimed poet in the semiofficial intellectual culture of Leningrad. Osip Mandelstam supposedly telephoned the noted formalist critic Boris Eichenbaum with the news that "A Poet appeared!" "Who?" "Konstantin Vaginov!" When the critic gingerly ventured another candidate, Mandelstam broke into laughter. "It's a good thing the telephone girl can't hear you!" he declared derisively.[10] A public meeting in Vaginov's honor was presided over by the well-connected Soviet writer Konstantin Fedin.[11] The young formalist Boris Buchstab perceptively described Vaginov as a poet of disjunction, who "took the decomposition of the Acmeist system to its limits," and contrasted him with the less radical Mandelstam. For

Buchstab, Mandelstam builds by having one image suggest the next, whereas Vaginov breaks up, breaks off, and deviates. Mandelstam develops a personal lexicon, whereas Vaginov avoids coining his own terms; rather, he writes his derivative, alienated (*chuzhie*—strange, foreign) images in a derivative, alienated diction, which he studiously dislocates and defamiliarizes. In Mandelstam's poems the stanzas are discontinuously joined, writes the critic, but with Vaginov "each word pushes away from its neighbor." He cites alogical adjective-noun combinations such as "bald voice," "double-breasted Berlin," and "the flame of sky seas."[12]

Vaginov referred to this violation of sematic cohesion as *sopostavlenie slov*, "juxtaposition of words." He even titled his 1931 poetry collection *Experiments in Juxtaposing Words by Means of Rhythm*. He also distributes his poetics to various characters in *Goat Song*. The unknown poet regards poetic composition as putting words together that do not belong together, their slight correlation being found only afterward. For Balmcalfkin also, the act of juxtaposing words precedes intention. The words do the thinking for the poet; their obscure combinations acquire meaning only with time. The persona of the author uses the same terms and concepts to describe the creation of the novel: "No one suspects that this book emerged from the juxtaposition of words." The author believes that, by juxtaposing words, he created and subsequently came to know his own soul and the universe, saying that "a whole world emerged for me in language and rose up from language. And it turned out that this world risen from language coincided astonishingly with reality."

In the fall of 1927 Vaginov joined a group of young avant-garde poets led by Daniil Kharms, Alexander Vvedensky, and Nikolai Zabolotsky, based at the House of the Press in the center of the city. The collective name they chose was OBERIU, an acronym that feels circus-like, Futurist, and parodic-Soviet at the same time. Vaginov took part in "Three Left Hours," the OBERIU extravaganza held at the House of Press on January 24, 1928, that also featured absurdist theatrical stunts. As he recited "Music," a ballerina was dancing behind him. (He displays mixed feelings about the performance in his second novel, *The*

Works and Days of Whistlin, in which somebody rides a child's tricycle during a reading, just as the poster for "Three Left Hours" had promised.) He quit the group together with Zabolotsky in October 1928.[13]

Scholars generally consider Vaginov's association with OBERIU half-hearted and superficial. But there is some agreement in poetics. The OBERIU manifesto employs the phrase "collision of word meanings" as an umbrella term for the group's composition technique. It stands for alogical word combinations and is largely synonymous with Vaginov's "juxtaposition of words."[14] Statements of poetics scattered throughout *Goat Song* often overlap with OBERIU positions. However, Vaginov's belief that poetry of disjunction will eventually start to mean something, rather than always remain an example of what Vvedensky called *bessmyslitsa* (meaninglessness), places him with Zabolotsky on the conservative wing of the group.

The novel expresses both impatience with and admiration for OBERIU. In chapter 15, the unknown poet harangues the three "mad youths" using Vvedensky's language. He argues: "You are striving for meaningless [*bessmyslennoie*] art. Art demands the opposite. It demands that we give meaning to the meaningless [*bessmyslitsa*] . . . a meaningless selection of words organized by a rhythmic scheme" may eventually offer its readers a new way of perceiving the world. The poet-Orpheus must descend "into the hell of meaninglessness" but he also must "return with Eurydice—art." Yet the unknown poet also admires the mad youths as "real beyonsense[15] poets" who "tug new meaning out from under the dunce caps [*kolpaki*, an OBERIU symbol] of words," quite in accordance with his own practice. To the novel's mad youths it is given to cohabitate with the Muse.

An abbreviated version of *Goat Song* came out in the periodical *Zvezda* (The Star) in October 1927, and the reworked novel appeared in book form in August 1928. Vaginov then substantially revised it for a second edition, which never saw print, because reviewers and censors decried the book as ideologically alien to the Soviet project. Indeed, the protagonists of *Goat Song* are not the right kind of Soviet citizens but rather what was then called "the former people"—those who, like Vaginov's family, lost their social status with the revolution. The overarching theme of the novel is the death of the old world and the coming in of the new, in which former people and former values gradually go extinct. The work is not driven by plot, or even character; rather, it is the story of a circle of individuals being transformed under the pressure of history. *Goat Song* is a satire, and perhaps an unkind one. It was received as a roman à clef, but among the prototypes of its characters only one critic in the Bakhtin circle broke off relations with the author.

As Vaginov was teasing out the form of his first novel, he must have considered some of Bakhtin's ideas on the special properties of the novel as a genre. These ideas were not yet published, but they appear to have been developing in the open, conversational culture of the circle. The philosopher had been working on his first monograph, *Problems of Dostoevsky's Creative Art*, throughout the 1920s, and it was finally released in 1929. The title of *Goat Song* evokes Bakhtin's rejection of an earlier critic's analogy between the Dostoevsky novel and the Greek tragedy. Bakhtin regards the Dostoevsky novel as a polyphonic—even contrapuntal—composition of multiple points of view, protagonists, and plotlines (he calls it "a genuine polyphony of fully valid voices").[16] As such, it is fundamentally different from the tragedy, which tends toward unity in style, place, and action. The phrase "goat song" translates the Greek word for tragedy too literally (*tragos* in Greek is goat and *ōidē* is song), and thereby burlesques it. If tragedy flatters its characters by depicting them as "fair and radiant," charges the unknown poet, *Goat Song* depicts them as if they were "devils of some sort."

Or satyrs: Vaginov may even be anticipating some of the philosopher's later arguments. The imagery of nymphs and satyrs bookending *Goat Song* recalls the importance Bakhtin allotted to low literary genres in the picture of the historical roots of the novel that appeared in his studies of the 1930s. Bakhtin argues that the novel emerged from the burlesquing of high genres, such as the epic and the tragedy, by low genres, "saturated with a specific *carnival sense of the world*."[17]

Whereas high genres propagate traditional hierarchies and heroic values, low genres, associated with satyrs in antiquity, turn value hierarchies upside down. If high genres demand unity and loftiness of style, low genres demand variety and result in motley, patchwork compositions. Allusions to low genres do indeed permeate Vaginov's novels. They are visible not only in the way he imagines his characters but also in his decision to introduce snippets of poetry into a prose composition, as well as in his erotic, picaresque, and culinary motifs. In another interview given late in life, Bakhtin draws on his later vocabulary to describe Vaginov as "a truly carnivalesque writer."[18]

In the 1929 edition of *Problems of Dostoevsky's Creative Art*, Bakhtin argues that the Dostoevsky novel rejects ideological closure in that it incorporates opposing viewpoints without reconciling them. Such "dialogism," as he calls it, may appear not only on the level of character development and interaction but on the level of the individual utterance—as short as a single word. The word attains "internal dialogism"[19] when, by evoking a particular speaker or context which does not match that of its current usage, it represents multiple points of view ("voices") at once. The points of view stand in an ironic juxtaposition that the speaker may not even be aware of. Bakhtin calls such ideologically unreconciled utterance "the double-voiced word." An allegory of the double-voiced word may be seen in the two-sided ashtrays collected by Kissenkin: "on one side the ashtray would be perfectly decent, while the flip side was entirely obscene." In the same way, the title of *Goat Song* only works when the reader is aware of it as a translation of the invisible term "tragedy." By implication, tragedy and comedy do not describe different phenomena; rather, they are different vantage points on the same thing.

Vaginov's intertextual games offer more instances of double-voicedness. He plants an allusion when he wants the passage to be read not autonomously but as a skeptical riposte in a dialogue with an earlier work or genre. For example, the concept of "new life" appears with three different meanings in Balmcalfkin's marriage. One is Dante's book, with which the scholar inadvertently confesses his love. Two is the marriage idyll that ensues. Three is Soviet industrialization:

"factories were being built . . . the villages now had not only electricity but radios too." The reader is meant to consider the three versions of "new life"—poetic, appetitive, and Bolshevik—together, in an ironic collision. The political significance of intertextuality is, of course, that it is a sieve. Many readers will not get it. It is a secret code for the disenfranchised individuals whom the greedy and triumphant masses of new Christians accuse of elitism.

On the narrative level, Vaginov employs the double-voiced word to think about change, which takes place over time but is perceived in the moment. His novel about former people represents the unfolding of time as an occasion for irony. Momentous events, lofty passions, and great expectations are transformed into knickknacks, objects without function, remembered sayings without context, absurd fragments shored up against our ruin. What starts as a tragedy is translated into a farce. The rushing current of history empties into the marsh of the flea market. For Vaginov, the flea-market commodity is the thing version of the double-voiced word. It carries the traces of its old meaning and employment, but its meaning and employment are entirely different in the new context. Vaginov also regards the protagonists of his novel as human counterparts to double-voiced words. Thrust from the old world into the new, they are in the process of metamorphosis, which for now turns them into double people—satyrs, no longer men but not yet goats. The narrative abounds in endings that answer their beginnings only ironically. A déclassé landlady shuffles off to teach high culture to the victorious proletariat, and a former cavalry officer, now a construction worker, thinks about joining the union "the way he had once thought about the St. George's Cross."

Vaginov's protagonists are victims of the revolution—or rather, victims of industrial modernity, of which the revolution is only another symptom. Modernity has replaced the culture of individuals with the culture of the masses. The guests in the "tall tower of humanism" that Balmcalfkin has rented in a suburb of Leningrad, constitute "the last island of the Renaissance . . . in the dogmatic sea that surrounds us on all sides." Whatever little plot *Goat Song* has can be described as "the demise of humanism." Humanism implies that the human being is free to seek truth and beauty unsullied by politics or any other kind of utility. The besieged humanists wish to escape history in the pastoral, a genre of classical poetry that they see as affirming eternal, absolute values. Balmcalfkin imagines the unknown poet as "a sly Odysseus" who remains forever on Circe's island of art instead of venturing out on the swollen waters of sociology. Yet the balding young men are able to escape their historical age no more than they can escape biological aging. Time carries them toward death or conformism. Their options are to go down among the asphodels or to become one with the victorious masses, "lacking all humanist sentiment."

Goat Song is a novel about the death of poetry. There is no place for poetry in the mass culture of modernity. It expires in banality and profiteering. The success-story Asphodelov has abandoned the composition of poetry, which he still loves, in order to write propagandistic children's stories and newspaper encomia of proletarian literature, since they pay money, which he loves even more. He is "willing to stand on the side of the modern age," and accordingly Vaginov turns him into a rapist. The poets of the novel gradually lose the madness that made them poets, the Rimbaudian *dérèglement de tous les sens* that had earlier let them take language to its limit. Now, in their more rational, utilitarian state, they become dead to language, no longer able to make out the flickering indications of meaning which connect alogically joined words. At the end, the unknown poet admits that his poems make no sense at all. Orpheus rises from the hell of meaninglessness empty-handed, without Eurydice—that is, without art. When he kills himself in a hotel room, his friends steal his tie and cuff links as relics, that is to say: as eventual flea-market commodities. It is not art but kitsch that remains of a poet's life.

A year later, in 1929, Vaginov published his second novel, *The Works and Days of Whistlin.* A piece of metafiction, it shows a novelist fashioning the book we are reading by consciously transcribing and appropriating the words of acquaintances. His labor is comparable to collecting and to collage. The fictional author gathers (and his author amply quotes) sources as far apart as crime journalism and Renaissance fiction presented in delicious early spelling. The author and the author's author organize an assisted collage of quotations, "fleeting sketches, clippings, scribblings," jotted-down "phrases overheard in shops . . . and conversations," and on the street. One of Vaginov's notebooks, which has recently been published, does include overheard phrases recorded for later use.[20] *The Works and Days of Whistlin* reconstructs—or rather, caricatures—some of Vaginov's actual working techniques.

His protagonist collects and collages not only texts but also people he meets, whose traits he writes into his own protagonists. Whistlin styles himself a "fisher of souls," a phrase that infernally inverts the "fishers of men" of Matthew 4:19, as it anticipates Stalin's famous toast of 1932, to Soviet writers as "engineers of human souls." Indeed, the novel looks back to the *Dead Souls* of Nikolai Gogol, another collection of tackiness, kitsch, stupidity, and impostorship. Like Gogol's protagonist, who seeks to acquire dead serfs ("souls") in order that he may use this fictive property in future financial speculation, the Mephistophelian Whistlin collects the souls of his human specimens for translation into the other world of his novel. At the same time, *The Works and Days of Whistlin* satirizes the so-called "literature of fact," advocated by the aging Soviet Futurists and fashionable in the second half of the 1920s. Rejecting the very concept of fiction as bourgeois, literature of fact consists of nonfiction prose, which reports on real people and real events, and documentary poetry, which works with found language. Vaginov's novel burlesques both techniques and strips them of the expected ideological spin.

Vaginov cut an extremely improbable figure in Soviet letters of his time. A child of parents who had been the beneficiaries of the old regime, a writer whose writing violated Soviet proprieties both ideologically and stylistically, he somehow published another book of poems and another short novel as late as 1931, despite the swelling indignation of his reviewers. Perhaps his charm and talent for friendship helped him get by. Nonetheless, the establishment of socialist realism as the obligatory Soviet style made further publications increasingly unlikely. His third novel, *Bombocciata*, was named after a type of Baroque genre painting that showed the life of common people. Its protagonist is an endearing picaro, "entirely lacking in any feeling of responsibility to anyone or anything." A collector, needless to say, of old books and young women, he attends multiple feasts at the home of a learned gourmand and collector of candy wrappers, until diagnosed with (unnamed) tuberculosis. Dying, he travels.

The author gives the protagonist of *Bombocciata* his own illness and coming death. Vaginov had been diagnosed with tuberculosis in 1927, the same year that he married, and published *Goat Song*. As a Soviet writer, he was offered the opportunity to enjoy, if that is the word, regular stays in sanatoriums. Initially he would check into medical establishments near Leningrad, where he continued to work. He submitted his next and last novel, *Harpagoniana*, one of whose collectors is a collector of dreams, but then withdrew it to bring it "in line with the times." In late 1933, as he was hemorrhaging blood, doctors directed him to one of the tuberculosis sanatoriums in Yalta, Crimea.

It was there he wrote this poem:

> The nor'easter bowed palms, medlars, olives,
> Swayed the sequoia like a woman.
>
> The pelerines of stair steps stuck fast
> Sewn onto the shoulders of cliffs.
>
> I wandered o'er the subterranean shore,
> And saw a nightingale. It was engaged in mimicry.
>
> It recalled with its voice
> A statue awash in sunlight.
>
> I stood on the balcony of a subterranean building.
> Snow flurries flew. The moon was a boat.

> The gale cracked its glacial scourge,
> Punishing flowers and grass.
>
> I found myself in an Elysium of crystal,
> Where there's no grief, where there's no love.
>
> Where, like reflections icy and far away,
> The nightingales that make no sound, sway.

He had come to a south that had once been part of the Mediterranean world of the classical antiquity. But Crimea is not all that welcoming in winter. The landscape was estranged by the season Persephone spends in Hades, and life was elsewhere. The surroundings are seen by a visitor emotionally frozen at the approach of death. Or rather, by an act of doubling, the poem shows them as "subterranean," its point of view already that of a lifeless shade. Mandelstam, who heard it during his exile in Voronezh, called it, admiringly, "a real posthumous poem."[21]

Another poem, composed at Yalta that December, is about music, or rather about listening to music. It recalls an early Soviet talkie in the same way that "Each has his mouth around a neighbor's leg" recalls a silent montage film:

> Crimea. I stepped into a reflecting cool.
> An orchestra played love under a hail of acorns.
>
> Spectators from all reaches of the USSR
> Stood specter-like and took in *Carmen*.
>
> How beautiful love is at the time of consumption.
> I cannot suffer your familiar voice.
>
> You are eternal, like a stone carving.
> Your listener is longingly or tediously somebody else.

A blind beggar, he circuits the green garden
And horribly gropes the petals.

He longs like the prodigal son to enter
That singing amorous nightingale world.

There once was a time when Vaginov saw music as a metaphor for language which is living and loved. In this poem, however, the listener stands irremediably apart from the music and from the collective of listeners because he is dying and they are living. But Vaginov may have closed the poem with an allusion to a painting—Rembrandt's late and great canvas, *The Return of the Prodigal Son*, in which the son kneels as the father puts his hands over him in a blessing. That image of reconciliation is one of the best-known works in his city's art museum, the Hermitage.

The poet returned to Leningrad that January and died three months later, on April 26, 1934. A stranger who lived in his room during the siege of Leningrad sold off his book collection.

—EUGENE OSTASHEVSKY

GOAT SONG

FOREWORD

spoken by the author who appears periodically at the book's threshold

PETERSBURG for me has been tinted for some time now with a greenish hue, shimmering and flickering, a terrible, phosphorescent color. Houses and faces and souls quiver with a greenish flame, snickering and malignant. The flame flickers—and where Pyotr Petrovich stood, you see instead a slimy, creeping thing; the flame flares—and you yourself are worse than any vermin. And it's not people walking the streets: peek under a hat and you'll spy the head of a snake; look closely at an old lady—it's a toad sitting there wiggling its belly. And all the young people each cherish a special dream: the engineer desperately wants to hear Hawaiian music, the student wishes to hang himself with real flair, the schoolboy wants to father a child to prove his virility. Go into a shop and there's a former general sitting behind the counter, smiling mechanically; enter a museum and the guide knows that he's lying and goes on lying. I have no love for Petersburg, my dream has ended.

FOREWORD

spoken by the author who made an appearance in the middle of the book

NOW THERE is no Petersburg. There is Leningrad; but Leningrad has nothing to do with us—the author is a coffin-maker by trade, not a cradle expert. If you show him a coffin, he'll knock on it right away and find out what it's made of, how long ago, by what tradesman; he'll even call to mind the parents of the deceased. And right now the author is preparing a coffin for the twenty-seven years of his life. He's terribly busy. But don't go thinking that he's putting together this coffin with any sort of goal in mind, it's just a hobby of his. He takes a sniff—smells like corpses; so we'll need a coffin. And he loves his stiffs, and follows them around while they're still alive, and shakes their hands warmly, and starts conversations with them, and all the while he's sanding down the boards, stocking up on nails, buying some lace when he can find it.

1. BALMCALFKIN

In the city every year starry nights were succeeded by white nights.[1] In the city lived a mysterious creature—Balmcalfkin. He could often be seen walking with a teapot to the public cafeteria for hot water, surrounded by nymphs and satyrs. Exquisite groves bloomed fragrantly for him in the foulest-smelling places, and prim-and-proper statues, the legacy of the eighteenth century, seemed to him like gleaming suns of Pentelic marble. Balmcalfkin only occasionally raised his enormous, clear eyes—and then he saw himself in a desert.

A rootless, billowing desert that took on various forms. The heavy sand lifts and spirals up into the unbearable sky, petrifying into columns; waves of sand sweep up and solidify into walls; a pillar of dust picks itself up, the wind gives it a smack—and there's a person for you; grains of sand come together and grow into trees, and strange fruits glimmer.

For Balmcalfkin, one of the least stable dust-pillars of all was Maria Petrovna Dalmatova. In her rustling silk dress, to him she appeared an entity constant in her inconstancy. And when he met with her, it seemed to him that she brought the world into a graceful and harmonious unity.

But that only happened sometimes. Ordinarily Balmcalfkin believed in the profound constancy of humanity: like a plant, having once appeared, it bears flowers that transition into fruits, and the fruits scatter into seed.

To Balmcalfkin everything seemed like a fruit scattered to seed. He lived with the constant sensation of a decomposing husk, rotting seeds amid new shoots already rising.

For him, the rotting husk gave rise to the subtlest emanations that took on various forms.

At seven in the evening Balmcalfkin returned to his room with hot water and became absorbed in an astoundingly senseless and unnecessary activity. He was writing a tractatus about a certain unknown poet, in order to read it to his circle of ladies drifting into slumber and youths going into rhapsodies. A table would be placed with a flower in a vase and a lamp beneath a colorful shade. Everyone would sit in a semicircle around the table, and he would alternate between raising his eyes to the ceiling in rapture and lowering them to the pages covered in writing. This evening Balmcalfkin was supposed to read. Glancing automatically at his watch, he folded the writing-covered pages and went out. He lived on Second Rural Poverty Street.[2] Grass grew between the cobblestones, and children sang indecent songs. A tradeswoman selling glossy sunflower seeds followed him for a long time, entreating him to buy her leftovers. He looked at her but didn't notice her. On the corner he met Maria Petrovna Dalmatova and Natasha Holubets. To him it seemed a mother-of-pearl-tinted light emanated from them. Leaning over, he kissed their hands.

No one knew how badly Balmcalfkin yearned for renaissance. "I want to marry," he often whispered, when alone with his landlady, the owner of the apartment. At such times he would lie on his pale-blue knitted blanket, lanky and thin, his hair dry and graying. The landlady, by nature generous in love, a creature grown to mountainous proportions, sat at his feet, tempting him vainly with the sumptuousness of her contours. This was a dubious noblewoman, a purported speaker of foreign languages, who had preserved from that imaginary grandeur a silver sugar dish and a plaster bust of Wagner. Sporting a bob, like nearly all the women in the city, she like many others gave lectures on cultural history. But in her early youth she had taken an interest in the occult and had summoned rosy men, and naked rosy men in clouds of smoke had kissed her. Sometimes she told of how she once found a mystical rose on her pillow and that it had turned into evanescent slime.

Like many of her fellow citizens, she loved to talk about her former wealth, about how a lacquered carriage upholstered in dark-blue padded silk had waited for her at the entryway, how she had descended the red-carpeted stairway and the stream of passersby had stopped in their tracks while she was getting into the carriage.

"Little urchins gaped with their mouths hanging open," she would say. "Men in fur coats with sealskin collars surveyed me from head to toe. My husband, an old colonel, slept in the carriage. At the back of the carriage perched a footman wearing an embroidered hat, and we sped off to the imperial theater."

At the word "imperial" something poetic awoke in Balmcalfkin. He seemed to see Averescu, wearing a golden uniform, on his way to see Mussolini; he saw them conferring over the takeover of the Yugoslav state, the formation of a newly ascendant Roman Empire.[3] Mussolini marches on Paris and conquers Gaul. Spain and Portugal join Rome of their own volition. In Rome there is a meeting of the Academy for the discovery of an idiom capable of becoming the *lingua franca* of the recreated empire, and he, Balmcalfkin, is among the academics there. The landlady, meanwhile, seated on the edge of the bed, prattled on and on until she remembered that it was time to go to Politedu.[4] She shoved her broad feet into Tatar slippers and, jiggling, sailed toward the door. This was Eudochia Ivanovna Troubadorov, the widow of a conductor.

Balmcalfkin lifted his graying, withered head and malevolently watched her go.

Not a trace of noble upbringing, he thought. *She's glommed onto me like a pimple and keeps me from my work.*

He got up from the bed, buttoned up his yellow Chinese dressing gown that he'd bought at the flea market, poured some cold black tea into a glass, stirring it with a tin spoon, and from the shelf got down a little volume of Parny and began checking it against Pushkin.

The window burst open, the silvery evening rippled, and Balmcalfkin imagined: a tall, tall tower; the city sleeps while he, Balmcalfkin, is awake. *The tower is culture*, he mused, *at the zenith of culture—there I stand.*

"Where are you always hurrying off to, my damsels?" asked

Balmcalfkin, smiling. "Why don't you come to our gatherings? Today, for instance, I'm giving a report on a marvelous poet, and on Wednesday next week I'll give a lecture on American civilization. Miracles are happening in America these days, you know; the ceilings steal sounds away, everyone chews flavored resin, and in the manufacturing plants and factories an organ prays for everyone before they start work. Come, you really must come."

Balmcalfkin gave a firm bow, kissed the proffered hands, and the damsels, their heels clattering, disappeared into the passageway.

Whether he was walking in the garden overlooking the river, playing vint at a green table, reading a book, Philostratus was always right there beside him.[5] All of Philostratus's being was filled with unspoken music, his lovely youthful eyes beneath their wings of lashes were laughing, his long fingers, adorned with rings, held a tablet and stylus. Philostratus often walked and seemed to converse with Balmcalfkin.

"Look," Balmcalfkin imagined him saying, "watch how the Phoenix dies and is reborn."

And Balmcalfkin saw that strange bird, with its feverish feminine Oriental eyes, standing on a bonfire and smiling.

Let the reader not think that the author does not respect Balmcalfkin and is laughing at him; on the contrary: it could be that Balmcalfkin himself invented his insufferable last name, so as to banish into it the reality of his being, so that none of those laughing at Balmcalfkin could ever reach Philostratus. It is known that consciousness can be split; perhaps Balmcalfkin suffers from this split consciousness, and who can sort out who dreamed whom—whether Balmcalfkin dreamed up Philostratus or Philostratus dreamed up Balmcalfkin.

Balmcalfkin was sometimes haunted by a dream: he is coming down from his tall tower, exquisite Venus is standing in the middle of the pond, slender reeds are whispering, the rising dawn is gilding their tips and the head of Venus. Sparrows are twittering and hopping along the paths. He looks and sees: Maria Petrovna Dalmatova is sitting on a bench, reading Callimachus, and raises eyes filled with love.

"We are living amid dread and desolation," she says.

INTERMEZZO

ON 25 OCTOBER Avenue two well-mannered young men, Kostya Kissenkin and Misha Kittenkin, leaning against iron railings, held out lit matches to one another.[6]

In the old days, at a later hour, young men no less well-mannered would have been whirling around in a Hungarian dance or mazurka, humming along to the music. As is well known, in the old days the avenue would be completely empty after three a.m. The lanterns would go out, and subjects on the lookout and women wiggling their behinds would disappear into the appropriate establishments.

But right now it's about nine o'clock. At least, the clock on the former city assembly, now a third-rate cinema, says it's ten minutes to nine. But the young men were not standing opposite the former city duma building; they were on the bridge under the horse rearing up on its hind legs and the naked soldier—or at least it seemed that way to them.

2. THE CHILDHOOD AND YOUTH OF THE UNKNOWN POET

1916— On this very avenue, after the Western fashion, the unknown poet had spent his youth. Everything in the city seemed Western to him—the buildings and the churches, the public gardens; even the poor girl Lida seemed like an English Anna or a French Mignonne.[7]

Waiflike, with a small blond cowlick and violet eyes, she would wander between the café tables to music that was popular at the time, hesitantly taking a seat with the regulars. Some of them would treat her to coffee, brewed with cream, others to foamy chocolate with two biscuits, others to just tea with lemon. Men wearing tailcoats and carrying napkins would address her condescendingly in passing and, leaning over, whisper indecent things in her ear.

In this café young people of the male gender would go off to the men's lavatory—not for the usual reason people go to such places. There, glancing around, they would take some out, sprinkle onto their hands, and inhale; after a brief while they would give a quick shake of their heads, and, grown slightly pale, return to the hall. Then the hall would have changed. For the unknown poet it changed nearly into Lake Avernus, surrounded by precipitous banks overgrown with thick forest, and it was here that the shade of Apollonius once appeared to him.[8]

1907—The crowds of promenaders moved along unhurriedly. In snow-white, baby-blue and pink carriages children sat, lay and stood. Mooning high-school boys accompanied mooning high-school girls. Sellers offered hothouse violets, smelling of cheap perfume, and bobbing daffodils. The bourgeois were returning from their morning outing to the islands in landaus upholstered in dark-blue or brown fabric, in charabancs, carriages pulled by a single black horse or a gray pair. Once in a while a stately coach could be glimpsed, with old-lady noses and chins peeking out. They would drive up, a doorman would dash over and respectfully open the door. The unknown poet often rode around in carriages like this. His mother, a thoughtful, pale woman, sitting there; the coachman's rump visible on the box; on his mother's knees flowers or a box of chocolates. The boy was about seven years old and loved ballet, loved the bald heads of the people sitting in front of him and the universal tension and festive elegance. He loved to watch his mother powdering herself in front of the mirror before going out to the theater, fastening her sequin-covered dress, opening the mirrored doors of her dresser and scenting her handkerchief. He, dressed in a white suit and wearing white kid boots, would wait for his mother to finish dressing, to brush his curls and give him a kiss.

1913—The family sat at a round table illuminated by an icy red sun. The stove was being stoked in the next room and the sound of logs crackling was audible. Outside the windows a toboggan slide had been set up, and the neighborhood kids could be seen tearing down on their sleds from up above.

After breakfast the future unknown poet went with his tutor to the banker Kopylov's study. Kopylov published a journal, *Old Coins*. In his study stood modestly sized oaken cabinets whose sliding shelves were lined with dark-blue velvet; on the velvet lay Alexander the Great's staters, Ptolomy's tetradrachmas, gold and silver dinars of the Roman emperors, coins of the Cimmerian Bosporus, coins with pictures: of Cleopatra, Zenobia, Jesus, mythological beasts, heroes, temples, sacrificial tripods, triremes, palms; coins of every possible coloring, size, country of origin—some that once shone brightly; of every possible nation—some that had shaken the world through their conquests or their art, through their heroic personalities or their commercial acumen, but which now no longer existed. The tutor sat on a leather sofa and read the newspaper, the little boy examined the coins. Outside it grew dark. On the counter a light shone under a green glass shade. Here the future unknown poet grew accustomed to the inconstancy of all that exists, to the idea of death, to transporting himself to other countries and peoples. Here, thrust forward on its neck, was the head of Helios, with its half-opened, seemingly singing mouth, demanding that all else be forgotten. This head would probably accompany the unknown poet on his nighttime wanderings. Here was the temple of Artemis at Ephesus and the head of Vesta, here was a Syracuse chariot dashing headlong; and here were barbarian coins, pathetic imitations on which mythological figures became mere ornamentation; and here the Middle Ages, linear and fanatical, where a single small detail would suddenly call forth the scent, through some other life, of sun.

And there were ever more new drawers.

The tutor read through his entire newspaper. Streetlamps were glowing outside.

"Time to go," he'd say, "or we'll be late for dinner." The coins purchased were slipped into individual small envelopes, and these into one large envelope.

Back home, the boy would get out his magnifying glass, huge as a round window, pull an oaken stool up to the table and lay out the newly acquired coins. He would travel through time until his father in his Bukhara dressing gown would stride past on his way to the dining room, and the maid would run in to say:

"Dinner is served."

After dinner his father would proceed to his book-lined study to nap for an hour or two on the tapestried sofa. The bookshelves held the magnificent books that one might expect to see in any cultured family: appendices to *Niva*, Kryzhanovskaya's most terrifying novels, the insomnia-inducing Count Dracula, countless Nemirovich-Danchenkos,[9] foreign belles lettres in Russian translation. There were scholarly books as well: *How to Eliminate Impotence*, *What the Child Needs to Know*, *Three Hundred Years of the House of Romanov*.

At nine in the evening his father would don his uniform, perfume himself, and leave for his club.

After his father's departure, the future unknown poet would pop up in his study and sit on the sofa; a map would be spread out over the carpet while the sofa would be strewn with Gibbon and all sorts of archaeology. In the next room, the living room, his mother was playing "The Maiden's Prayer." In his room, his younger brother was reading Nat Pinkerton; in the unknown poet's room, the tutor was putting on his boots, humming a little tune—he was heading out to have some fun after the workday; in the kitchen the valet was bouncing the maid on his knee, while she hooted with laughter.

1917—The unknown poet was sixteen and Lida eighteen when they met. At that time she only rarely made appearances in the café. Sometimes she would say she was in high school and think back to that trip in a fast carriage, the night so quiet, the buildings rushing past, flickering trees and the private room at the restaurant, the officers, the clinking of glasses and how she had wept on the sofa, wiping away tears with the hem of her black apron. Sometimes she would say that she'd been in love with a university student, a dandy with nothing but scorn for the democrats and revolutionaries, and recount how he had given her over to his comrades.

Sometimes she would say that she'd been brought to ruin by a married man, a well-respected figure in the city with a long gray beard, who liked to take evening strolls in the Summer Garden.

The unknown poet tore himself away from his reading, from arranging the books on the shelves, from examining his coins. It was three in the morning. Past the tightly drawn drapes, down the back stairs he went out into the deserted courtyard, blindingly illuminated by an enormous hanging lantern. The astonished caretaker let him out the gate and saw the young man running off down the wide street toward Nevsky. A light slanting rain was falling. On the steps of an entryway, with the satin cards he'd given her the previous night laid out beside her, Lida sat leaning against the door. She was dozing, her mouth half-open. The unknown poet sat down beside her. He looked at her girlish face, at the melting snow all around, at the clock above their heads, took out something white and sparkling from his pocket, turned to face the wall. A distinct sound resembling a long drawn-out "oh" shifting into "ah"—so he imagined—went rolling through the streets.

He saw—the buildings narrowed and stabbed the clouds with their enormous shadows. He lowered his eyes and the enormous red numbers of the lampposts were winking on the pavement. Two was like a snake, seven like a palm tree.

His eyes gravitated toward the spread cards. The figures came to life and entered into a barely perceptible correlation with him. He was bound to the cards like an actor to the curtain; he quickly woke Lida up and with a strange sense of irony began playing durak with her; the sets of five cards quivered in their hands until the world began to go dark for them, the wind obstructed them, they turned to the wall; the rain turned into a fluttering soft melting snow. They were protected by the awning.

The cards seemed a horror and a void to him. Soon the city would begin to wake up.

"To the teahouse, to the teahouse, quick!" said Lida. "This cursed night has frozen me stiff! Why couldn't you have come sooner and taken me to a hotel! I'd have slept like the dead! This is my third night on the street, you know! Don't you have any money, maybe we can find an empty room."

"You're mad, Lida! At five in the morning all the hotels are full to bursting, no one would take us in!"

"Then let's get to the teahouse as quick as we can. I'm so miserably sad. My God, quickly, to the teahouse!"

He looked at her perfectly white face, at her dilated pupils; how many inner years had he been sitting here, what does this lantern signify, what does the snow signal and what does he himself mean, having appeared here on the avenue?

Flowers of love, flowers of drunken rapture . . .

Lida unexpectedly burst into song, stepping away from the entry-way. A barfly was passing by; he gave them a sardonic look. The un-known poet and Lida, through a curtain of pricking snow, set out. The cards lay forgotten in the entryway.

The all-night teahouse was roaring. Prostitutes in headscarves and calico dresses gazed with shameless provocation. The pale faces of thieves not yet caught winked with eyes that chased from corner to corner of the room; on the round tables stood tea of a color unbear-able as the dawn. The unknown poet and Lida appeared in the door-way. Night retreated.

In those days 25 October Avenue bore a different name. Adorned with round, blindingly bright electric streetlamps, while the sur-rounding streets and side streets glimmered with gas lighting, the avenue spread out its palaces, churches, and government offices among the residential buildings. Through the glass of windows and doors one could see snow-white staircases with carpets of the softest hues, drapes fluttering their silks, little tables made of every possible mate-rial, armchairs and sofas of every possible form. Sometimes in long halls beneath ceilings festooned with flying cupids young people sat the whole night through, gazing into space with dead eyes.

Sergei K. sat in his room, which had been divided in two by bookcases holding French books.[10] The dining room, which preserved traces of the eighteenth century, was quiet—everyone in the family, even his grandmother, had had their fill of evening tea and dispersed to their separate rooms. His grandmother must be taking off her headdress in front of the mirror, or perhaps spreading some kind of paste on her hands for the night, or freeing herself from her corset with the help of her maid; his mother must be writing to her friend in Paris or, perhaps, leafing through her album from before she was wed, or letting down her hair in front of the mirrored dressing table, while her maid was letting down the shades. His father at that moment was driving up to the yacht club on Morskaya, to spend the night at a green table, or perhaps walking into Cubat's restaurant to meet with one of the midnight divas.

The clock in the dining room struck eleven. The doorbell rang, the unknown poet entered, and the friends went out.

The moon and the stars came into focus above the city. Snow squeaked underfoot, trams—white with light and stuffed with Zem-city officials[11]—tooted away; cinemas offered alluring spectacles, and individuals lurking under gates offered pornographic booklets and cards; couples trotted along in cabs and taxis rolled past, ready to race off.

On the sidewalks, in clumps, women with painted faces stood, strolled and pawed the ground.

The unknown poet stopped.

"Remember last night"—he turned his face with its overhanging brow and atrophied lower half toward Sergei K.—"when the Neva turned into the Tiber and we wandered around Nero's gardens, the Esquiline cemetery, surrounded by the dull eyes of Priapus. I saw the new Christians, who will they be? I saw the acolytes, the dispensers of bread, I saw indistinct crowds demolishing idols. What do you think it means? What does it mean?"[12]

The unknown poet gazed into the distance.

In the sky before him, he saw it gradually taking shape: the terrifying, boarded-up, empty city, overgrown with grass—the two friends were walking along the well-lit, buzzing, chattering, singing, shouting, jingling, gleaming, frolicking street, among the utterly unsuspecting crowds.

1918–1920—On a mountain of snow, on Nevsky, alternately hidden by the blizzard and appearing anew, the unknown poet stands: behind him is emptiness. Everyone has long since left. But he doesn't have that right, he cannot leave the city. Let everyone else go running, let death come, but he will stay here and preserve the high temple of

Apollo. And he sees that a temple of snow and air is forming around him and that he is standing above a crevasse.

The unknown poet and Sergei K. made their way over the foyer carpets on tiptoe. For some time now they have felt a pain near the napes of their necks.

Lady police officers stood at their posts, their feet stuck out at a theatrical angle, cracking sunflower seeds and exchanging insults with the gyrating individuals under the streetlamps.

A dark night of late summer unfurled. No longer the moon and one single star, but the moon and thousands of stars—pale blueish, reddish, yellowish—illuminated the city.

These were the sidewalks and thresholds that Lida ran along, having lost by now her shoes and good looks.

"Well goddamn," she thought, "this is how life ends. Where can I rustle up enough for stockings and slippers? The way I'm going you can't even make enough for a toot."

She dashed into the teahouse.

"Get out," a man with a cloth shoved her in the chest, "you coming in here and slouching around is gonna get us shut down."

The unknown poet and his friend appeared in the gateway.

"Seryozha, let's go to the Summer Garden," he said, "we'll sit awhile on a bench."

"You!" shrieked Lida. But a second later she stepped back. "Excuse me, sirs, for bothering you."

A patrol was approaching.

Lida dashed through the gate of the neighboring building.

The young men dropped out of sight on Nevsky.

3. INTERWORD

I'M SITTING at my friend's place. A well-known artist, he's sleeping three rooms away. The room I'm in opens into a rotunda that looks out on the street. It is three a.m. The electric lightbulbs fixed to the tram pole burn brightly below. The rooftops of the buildings can't be seen from the window, they merge with the sky, while beyond the buildings, I can feel it—the Neva is flowing, a soft pale blue.

It's a dark night. Right now it's three a.m. My heroes' favorite hour. The hour of the unknown poet's zenith, and that of his faculties and visions. Once again I see: through bitter frosts, across the snowy bumps and hollows of the streets, against the horrifying wind that deadens the face, he is seeking intoxication—not for pleasure, but as a means of cognition, a way to cast himself into that holy madness (*amabilis insania*) which reveals a world accessible only to visionaries (*vates*).

The windows are closed. The buildings have been gutted. Holy madness retreats ever further away from him. There are no more palm trees, plane trees, cypresses. No porticos, no waterworks. The great freedom of the spirit is no more. No more conversations beneath the open black or golden-colored sky. I see him bidding his friends farewell amid the crumbling buildings. Here's one of them, sitting on a stone, his eyes darting like a madman's. And another one lying motionless on the ground. He feels that he has died. And a third climbing up a wrecked staircase in a building open on all sides, in order to look out over the city from up high for the last time. Here's the unknown poet leaning against a column. Its broken capital, decorated with acanthus leaves, reaches his knees; he can hear a rooster crowing in the next building. He thinks of the cats who go off to die in abandoned buildings just like this one. One of them quietly appears, stretching out its neck, dragging its hind legs. Another, wet and trembling, couldn't hold back and fell from the staircase into the black abyss. A third, vainly looking around for something with lackluster eyes, strains to curl up and can't manage it.

It must be three o'clock now. It's dark, completely dark. Down below a woman is playing the piano. I'm positive it's a woman. I think it must seem to her that a tender friend lies at her feet. I think she's let down her hair. I open up Bartolomeo Taegio's dialogue "L'Umore" and read his thoughts in praise of and condemnation of wine.[13] On the friendship of wine and poetry. I go back to the first page, with its description of grape-harvesting day in the exquisite settlement of Robecco. The girls by the wine press praise the precious vines in song; the roads are full of peasants, carts, and tubs of grapes or wine. Other villagers step off the road with their baskets and satchels to free the vines of their fruits. Crowds of bandits move through the heady air, through songs and guitar-playing, making their way into the love-filled hearts of the village girls.

I recall a page from Longus's novel—"Autumn was already in full force, and the harvest time was nigh. Everyone was in the fields . . ."[14]

And the shade of Aphrodite flickered in the window.

I walk up to the window. Everything is so quiet! The light is so yellow, cast down on part of the street by the bulbs fixed to the tram poles! And that passerby is walking so sadly, shoulders hunched, along the pavement! Where is he going? Perhaps my heroes knew him. Perhaps he is one of my heroes, spared by some happy accident.

———

The sky is brightening. The rooftops are visible, with their chimneys and lightning-rods. Hooves clip-clop. On the wall behind me there's a map still left over from the time of the European War; it must have been about twelve or thirteen years ago that the whole family had studded it with Russian, French, Italian, and English flags. They were proud of the army's successes and lamented their retreats.

4. BALMCALFKIN AND THE UNKNOWN POET

AFTER the young ladies, their high heels clicking, disappeared into the stairwell, Balmcalfkin stood awhile looking at the place where they had just held out their graceful hands, and quickly walked away, stumbling as he went. Evidently, he was lost in thought.

"What do you think ..." Balmcalfkin stopped, distracted.

The bookseller smiled.

"You're always joking instead of just saying hello like a normal person. Have a seat, let's chat."

But Balmcalfkin started looking through the books hanging on the latticed fence of the park surrounding the Mariinsky Hospital.

"If you had money, you'd probably buy my whole library." And the street vendor started showing Balmcalfkin books.

And the books were truly marvelous: a recent French translation of Marcus Aurelius, bound in luxurious vellum and embossed in gold, almost kitschy; the *Zodiac of Life*, in a pocket-sized edition with dark-blue edging and a beautiful motif on the title page, carried one off into the late Renaissance.[15]

"Do you by any chance have Boethius's *De consolatione philosophiae*?" asked Balmcalfkin. "I'd have to take it on credit."

Booksellers were happy to give Balmcalfkin books on credit, since they could always sit and talk with him.

Boethius couldn't be found.

*

But how can this be reconciled with the unknown poet's conception of Bolshevism as immense, that the current situation resembles the first centuries of Christianity.

And Balmcalfkin walked the rest of the way there trying to unravel this knot.

A new religion always emerges on the periphery of the cultured world, he mused. *Christianity appeared on the periphery of the Greco-Roman world in poverty-stricken, woeful Judea, narrow of mind and crooked in spirit. Islam appeared among nomads, not in flourishing Yemen, where fountains gush, aromatic fruits tremble and fill the air with stupefaction, where women upon waking stretch sensuously and yawn lazily. Ugh, what filthy thoughts,* Balmcalfkin shook himself. *One might think I was daydreaming about women.*

He became lost in thought.

Even in my dreams, sometimes a woman's breast appears and breathes beside me. Black eyes, it seems, gaze into my soul, you embrace emptiness, stop suddenly and wait for something. And Balmcalfkin saw his room and the rose that Maria Petrovna Dalmatova had given him last Wednesday. It was not a centifolia rose of Campania, nor a Paestum rose.[16] *Her life is probably terrifying,* he thought of Maria Petrovna, *terrifying. We are people of culture, educated people—we will explain and understand everything. Yes, yes, first we'll explain, and then understand—the words think for us. You start to explain something to someone, you listen to the words you're saying—and you yourself come to understand a great deal.*

And he thought of the unknown poet. He had such great love for the unknown poet! The unknown poet might scribble down a few lines without even thinking, but it would come out clever, by damn, so clever. And there would be destruction in these words, and great passion, and a plaint for the sun setting for all time. The words themselves thought for the unknown poet. Oh, the brilliant things Balmcalfkin could do with the unknown poet's verse! What an abundance of meaning the unknown poet's metaphors revealed to him! To him it seemed that a republic was crumbling while a pure youth sang of the freedom of spirit, sang in secret, as if ashamed, but everyone listened and praised him for his obscure metaphors, the radiance emerging from his juxtaposition of words.

> You used to say: we won't go back to Hellas,
> Our ship will sink, the wind will cover its traces...[17]

The morning of that same day, the unknown poet thought that he had awakened in a house of ill repute: dressed up like hussars, and like Turkish and Polish girls, women were sitting on the floor playing cards; the piano player, his wig flapping, banged on the keys. Dragoons were walking around, spurs jingling. An uhlan lieutenant was sitting on the sofa writing his sister a letter in verse.

I am my father, thought the unknown poet and looked at the painting hanging on the wall—a buxom woman in a gorgeous skirt spangled with stars lay on a sofa with her eyes rolling back. *I*, the unknown poet crossed his arms behind his head, *am my father in the '90s, in some provincial city, because the Petersburg houses of ill repute are completely different: lions, marble staircases, doormen wearing gold braid, footmen in silk pantaloons, a fifteen-person orchestra, beautiful ladies in full ball dress.*

—Skree-kree-rah-rah-roo-roo—the orchestra played on.

It seemed to the unknown poet that he was his grandfather—enormous, imposing, sitting in an opera box; a silk playbill embroidered with fine lace lay on the railing; onstage, Louis XIII was saying something to Richelieu. The theater was built of wood, and all around it were little wooden houses and snow, snow... *Yeniseisk*, thought the unknown poet. *I am my grandfather, the mayor of Yeniseisk.*

In the twilight he sensed the approach of a troika. As if he were standing on the porch and hearing sleigh bells jingling, then the pounding of hooves, and then whickering, followed by girlish voices: "Is the ballroom ready, where are the footmen, why are there no lights?"

And he saw the footmen ceremoniously coming out of the house.

Dance music could be heard, ladies with long trains turned around—while outside it was a snowy night, a snowy night, untroubled, and he stood and looked out the window—down below was an avenue of statues, while far off, in the city, a blizzard was singing:

> Where you gone to, eyes, where you gone, bright eyes,
> Down the alleyways, down the lightless streets
> Flying to and fro, turning here and there,
> Choking in the end on a bloody swell.
> He's on that porch, the scoundrel,
> Like an apple tree
> In full bloom.
> Did he die by your side, no, he did not
> On that starry night.
> You were screaming, fighting to get free,
> Oh you poor soul.
> One of 'em yanked your hair,
> Th' other stuck that shank
> On account of that dreadful syphilis.[18]

"What the hell," shrieked the unknown poet. "She was not my wife, not my lover, and I don't even know whether she had syphilis."

Angry, he got up from the snow-white bed and went to the Hermitage to look at statues.

In the lower hall he felt himself lean down over his own self and sing:

> And his friends they been rotting awhile now
> In no cemetery, in no coffin box,
> One of 'em inside wandering,
> Through ruined walls a-flickering,
> Another down the river goes floundering,
> Floating under bridges and bloating up.
> And the third's in a room, he's behind bars,
> With the crazies he's cursing and swearing.

The unknown poet woke up. It was the first of May.

That's nice, he thought. *It's been four years since I broke with the night, with the illuminated and extinguished city, the glittering nighttime crowds and the prognostications.*

5. ASPHODELOV'S PHILOSOPHY

"Balmcalfkin's so odd," chattered the young ladies as they walked down Kirochnaya Street. "He's probably a virgin. We need to marry him off, or nothing good will come of him. You want me to offer you to him in marriage?" After some thought, Maria Petrovna Dalmatova started laughing. "He'll kiss your feet, work for you like an ox, and you'll spend all your time lying on the bed without any underwear on, leafing through novels."

"I want the kind of love where there's flowers dripping dew everywhere, where the world suddenly seems clear to me. Otherwise nothing makes any damn sense," sighed Natasha.

"Never you mind, we'll have a ball today—they'll read us some poems, wine and dine us, steal kisses," laughed Musya.

"But they're scoundrels," Natasha interrupted her laughter.

"Never mind," Musya snorted. "If anybody starts groping for real, I'll stick him with a pin where it hurts, he'll let go fast." She pulled out and brandished a broken hatpin, in all seriousness.

"I'm only going for your sake," declared Natasha: "are you sure it's not dangerous?"

"Nonsense. If anyone starts coming on too strong, punch him hard below the belt—he'll back off like a good boy."

They turned into an entryway. Candler opened the door for them.

"So, girls, you've come," he smiled, lighting a cigarette. "We'll have a fun little evening together."

Behind him appeared Asphodelov, freshly shaven, hands drenched in cologne, wearing a morning coat and gleaming pince-nez; he greeted the girls in an unhurried and distinguished fashion, inquired as to whether they had strolled in the Summer Garden today, had they written any new poems.

The four of them went into the living room.

A mummy-like man rose, tossed back his long hair and gave a bow at a distance.

"This is our friend Kokosha Fedora," Candler introduced him, "a poet, musician, artist, and world traveler. At present he's sculpting scenes of the revolution out of clay—he's a dreadful scoundrel."

The party in question smiled.

Asphodelov began cozying up to Musya, and Candler to Natasha. Kokosha kept joining one or the other couple and was visibly bored.

After supper Kokosha the universal artist sat down at the piano and began to improvise. In the neighboring room Asphodelov, having chosen a place with low light, dragged Musya onto the sofa. Langorous from the wine she'd drunk, Musya allowed him to glide his lips along her arm and kiss the back of her head, but then moved his hands aside and pushed his chin away.

Then Asphodelov tried to compel her using philosophy.

"What the hell do you need your virginity for," he whispered, pressing her close and gyrating the fleshy continuation of his spine, "or are you tempted by petit bourgeois moral virtues? No, no, I am offering you the fairy-tale life of *la bohème*, a truly aristocratic life."

And the fat man dropped his pince-nez.

"A girl is immature, green, a little sparrow," he continued his manipulations: "she smells like white bread; a woman, though—she is a flower, a sweet fragrance. Family is petit bourgeois, darning stockings, the kitchen." His hand darted in but was stopped. "We poets," Asphodelov heaved onto his other side, "are a spiritual aristocracy. Poetesses need experiences. How can you write poems without having known men?"

Meanwhile, across the room came Candler, dragging the giggling Natasha. She was utterly drunk, her head lolled to one side and she covered her mouth with her hand—she felt ill. He led her to the lavatory and began pacing excitedly back and forth by the door. He took her into the next room and dropped her on the bed.

Natasha buried her face in the pillow and fell asleep. Candler began to undress, whistling. He took off his shirt and began slowly unlacing his boots.

"Let her fall sound asleep."

He took off his boots and placed them neatly by the bed.

He used his hand to gag her, she struggled to throw him off but couldn't. Through his hand she sobbed and saw the lamplight.

He sat down on the edge of the bed to catch his breath. Natasha lifted her head, touched her breasts, looked at his back, then fell back onto the bed and started crying. He turned, joyfully patted her a few times and said:

"Sooner or later—what's the difference?"

"How are things?" he asked Asphodelov, returning to the living room.

Asphodelov was sitting there frowning. Musya started laughing. He led Asphodelov to the window.

"You're a fool," he said. "Where's that scoundrel Kokosha?"

"He left a long time ago, got sick of waiting."

"Your Kokosha's a fool, he could have gone into the bedroom now, while the girl's still sleeping. I told him he should wait."

"I'll go on in," said Asphodelov, his plump face smiling. He adjusted his pince-nez and went off.

Candler came over to Musya.

"Where's Natasha?" she asked.

But Candler kept a firm grip on her hands.

"She'll be right back."

Musya understood and became annoyed with her friend.

"Dummy," she thought and sat down.

Candler sat down and began cozying up to her.

"Where's Natasha?" she repeated. She got up to go find her.

Asphodelov came out smiling.

"Your Natasha is drunk as a lord. She'll be right out."

The sun was rising outside the windows. The girlfriends left without saying goodbye.

That morning Kovalyov sat in front of the window—here was Pierrot carrying Colombine, here's an old husband lying in lamplight while his young wife stands there—looking for fleas. Here's a girl, exposed, lying on an operating table; a gray-haired doctor leans over her, lost in thought.

So many memories . . . So many memories.

The postcard with Pierrot and Colombine was his favorite. The postcards with the flea-catching and the operating table were General Holubets's favorites.

But when Kovalyov was carting gravel onto the barge, Natasha walked past, returning from some revels, her nose hidden behind her raised collar; she didn't recognize Kovalyov, and Kovalyov was desperately glad that she hadn't recognized him; after all, he was no worker, it was just for now, for the time being, until he found a real job, that he was loading gravel. Natasha disappeared; Kovalyov lit a cigarette, sat on his cart and became lost in thought; he took out a crust of white bread with raisins and ate it with gusto, remembered Easter, the ringing of bells in the air, and sentimental love songs.

"That's all right, I'll break clear," he decided, "I'll be someone again. It's just hard to get into the union."

And he started thinking about the union the way he had once thought about the St. George's Cross.[19]

"No matter what, I have to get a foothold in civil engineering."

6. GENERAL HOLUBETS AND SUB-LIEUTENANT KOVALYOV

GENERAL Holubets, Natasha's father, was examining some sheet music and smoking a cheap cigar when Natasha, returning from the party, walked past him toward her bedroom. Her father felt like chatting on that spring morning. He got up, followed Natasha to her room and stopped by the door.

"The commandant was sitting at the window," General Holubets began his joke, "and he sees that a lieutenant of Regiment X is walking along without a saber. 'Ivan!' the commandant yells for his valet and points to the officer. A minute later the officer appears in his room, wearing a saber. The commandant sees the saber and gets confused. 'Excuse me, lieutenant,' he says, 'your face seemed unfamiliar to me. Have you been in our city long?' and, after a polite exchange, he lets the officer go. The lieutenant leaves, and the commandant sits back down at the window. A minute later he sees the same lieutenant walking along without a saber! 'Ivan!' yells the commandant. 'Call him in!' A minute later the officer comes in wearing his saber. The commandant gets even more confused and asks the officer to send his respects to the commander of the regiment. The officer goes out, the commandant sits back down at the window. A minute later he sees the same lieutenant walking along without a saber! 'Ivan!' yells the commandant. 'Bring him back!' A minute later the same lieutenant comes in again, wearing a saber. The commandant, utterly confused, invites the lieutenant to play cards that evening. The young officer goes out. The commandant sits down by the window. A minute later he sees the same lieutenant walking along without a saber! 'Liza, Elena Alexandrovna!' the commandant calls his wife and daughter and shows them the officer through the window. 'Is he wearing a saber?' 'No saber!' his wife and daughter answer in unison. 'But I'm telling you he has a saber! he has a saber!' yells the commandant in a pique."

General Holubets held the pause.

"Do you know where the lieutenant was getting his saber?" he asked Natasha. "It was the commandant's own saber!"

Ex-general Holubets walked away from the door into the dining room and sat down to read his music; his samovar and wife were nearby. He played the piano at the cinema, and she sewed voile dresses for the market. Beyond them, in her room, was their only daughter, a slender and giggly child, who studied at the university.

In 191—, when she had seen Mikhail Kovalyov off to war, Natasha had thought: he is a hero, a warrior.

And, back home, she cried: he'll be killed, he'll most likely be killed. She was fifteen; back then she couldn't have been called a giggly creature. True, even then she would smile regardless of whether it was appropriate, but this was the smile of a reserved person.

Mikhail Kovalyov, sublieutenant of the Pavlograd Hussar Regiment, her fiancé, went off to war back then like he was going to a parade. The fields and forests flew past him. He stood at the window, saw his St. George's Cross and the face of his fiancée. But a week after Mikhail arrived at his regiment the soldiers offered him the post of cook. "So these are my triumphs," he thought. Afterward he hid for a year in the woods outside Petersburg, then ended up on the Red front as an assistant to the cavalry inspector. He cursed the Reds whenever he could, but served them honestly. Later he was demobilized and found himself in Petersburg. But Natasha had lost interest in him. The years of hunger had transformed her; she had become a high-strung creature. One day she'd be studying in some theater studio, where she'd get groped all over, the next she'd be at the university, striding down the "Bois de Boulogne" (main hallway) and smoking a cigarette.

*

Mikhail Kovalyov saw Natasha rarely after the revolution. His utter lack of money and the impossibility of finding a position—he had no expertise—profoundly mortified him and brought him to despair. And yet he still thought that someday he would find a job and then he would marry Natasha.

Every year, on the first day of the Easter holiday, he would pull on his maroon hussar's trousers with their golden braid, his boots with their rose-knots, would drag his military jacket out of the depths of the closet. He took the golden monogrammed epaulets out from under the floorboards and got dressed quickly, quickly, stuck his spurs into his pocket and, in an overcoat with burned patches from the war against the Whites, flew over to Natasha's.

This was repeated year after year. He would dash up the stairs; her former excellency would be sitting in the living room reading a book. He would give Natasha the Easter greeting, eat a slice of *kulich* and a dish of buttery *paskha*.[20]

Then Natasha would sit down at the unsteady piano and sing something in a weak voice. She would open her mouth pitifully and look at Mikhail Kovalyov. She was sad, she didn't love him anymore. She found him tacky.

Sometimes Mikhail Kovalyov would stand up and ask Natasha to play "Oh, the Chrysanthemums Faded So Long Ago." He would stand next to her, open his mouth, and sing out of tune. Sometimes he would sing "All the Girls Love It So" or "My Pretty Girls, Pretty Girls, My Pretty Cabaret Girls, for You Love Is Pleasure After All."[21]

Oh, what a wonderful evening that was, he would think, walking home at night along the renamed and once again illuminated streets, among pointed Red Army hats and leather jackets, beneath the leaping street signs.

7. BALMCALFKIN'S BOOK

THE CREATION of thought requires a science of poetry, thought Balm-calfkin, lying in bed, the day after the reading—*and here, a completely unknown poet, through the juxtaposition of words, evokes a whole world for us; we analyze it, take it apart, translate it into the language of prose, remove its figurativeness, and the next generation, having already absorbed the fruits of our labors, will not see in his poems the sumptuous blossom-ing of the figuration of a new world. To them everything in his poems will seem unremarkable, poor; but for now they are accessible only to a few.*

Years will go by, the whole era will pass, everything around us will change, and people will laugh at the unknown poet, call him a barbar-ian, a madman, an idiot who tried to ruin our beautiful language. Schoolboys writing awful poems for schoolgirls, office clerks declaring their love to typists in between shuffling papers, trust directors and local committee representatives will say:

"Now that's what I call degeneration. The things idle people think up! Poems are supposed to convey thought, to follow in the footsteps of science. The radio's been invented—so write about the radio, the wireless telegraph's been invented—sing the praises of culture."

But for now even if the glory is brief—Balmcalfkin swung his legs over the side of the bed and sat up—*nevertheless glory awaits this unknown poet. Girls are already gluing their photographs onto his books, academics are greeting him with handshakes, university students are hanging his portrait above their boring books. And if he dies right now, at least forty people will walk behind his coffin and will speak of the struggle against the age and will depict him as a sly Odysseus, remain-ing on Circe's island (art), escaping from the sea (sociology).*

Balmcalfkin glanced out the window to see whether the unknown poet was coming and saw that indeed he was, tapping his walking stick, waving his hat and carrying a new manuscript.

I will now make merry in an unknown land, thought Balmcalfkin, and ran to open the door.

They kissed in greeting. Cursed the modern age. Spat with feeling at a group of young pioneers passing by.

"What a generation this is, lacking all humanist sentiment, soon to be genuine representatives of the Middle Ages: fanatics, barbarians, unenlightened by the light of the *studia humanitatis*."

"Yes, nastiness and beastliness all around—barbarization," nodded Balmcalfkin.

They sat.

"And there has always been nastiness and beastliness all around, loathsome tramping," Balmcalfkin continued, after some thought. "I'm imagining how those White Guard types must wreak havoc in their consulates abroad: before the new ambassador can move in, they tear down the wallpaper, spit all over the ceiling and rip up the parquet. They don't sit down by the fireplace to enjoy one last moment of melancholy, admire the walls hung with fine fabric; they don't stroll through the rooms or go out into the garden, if there even is a garden."

"Better not to philosophize," the unknown poet shrugged, "you and I have long since survived our own ruin—for me in artifice, you in literature—and no ruin can surprise us now. The man of culture lives out his spiritual life in many different countries, not just one, in many different times, not merely his own, and he can choose any ruin he wishes. He's not sad, just bored; when death comes to him at home, he'll just bellow: 'You again'—and it'll seem funny."

Balmcalfkin became sad, very sad. He walked over to the window.

What delightful, tanned children those pioneers are, he thought and smiled.

For some reason he felt a jolt of joy and freshness, as if a gust of sun-drenched air had burst into the room: *There it is, the youth of the world again*, he thought.

Meanwhile, Kostya Kissenkin came into the room.

"You write astonishing poems," he addressed the unknown poet: "truly baroque."

Kostya Kissenkin had a distinct way of moving, his whole body moved with elegance. He had come to Balmcalfkin's today to whisk away the unknown poet and have a talk with him about bad taste. He collected kitschy and pornographic things as exemplars of bad taste; often they, that is, Kostya Kissenkin and the unknown poet, would visit flea markets and pick out ashtrays: on one side the ashtray would be perfectly decent, while the flip side was entirely obscene; on the one side a lady would be walking with her admirer grinning after her, while on the other...

Kostya Kissenkin bought not only pornographic postcards, but also postcards that were decent and yet repulsive. A mustachioed, red-cheeked squire dining with a lady in a restaurant and pressing her foot under the table with his boot. A maiden with a rolled coiffure playing the harp. A naked nymph running with a mug of beer, chased by a man in Tyrolean costume.

When they left, Balmcalfkin sighed more freely. He looked around his room and found that he liked everything in it very much. He liked the ashtray with little flowers (it was there for his friends—Balmcalfkin did not smoke), and the vase with the Arab woman leaning on her pitcher, and the photographs—family scenes from childhood: here was six-year-old Balmcalfkin running after a butterfly with his little net, here was eight-year-old Balmcalfkin having dinner, here was ten-year-old Balmcalfkin dressed in knight's armor beneath a Christmas tree; here were photographs of his mother, his brothers, sisters, here were his friends, and, finally, a photograph of his Dream.

Balmcalfkin looked at the summer rocking chair and thought that it was no less comfortable than a wingback armchair. He decided to continue with his magnum opus and opened the trunk. The trunk was always covered with a green plush tablecloth and simulated—it was unclear what it simulated. He took out a notebook.

On the first page was painstakingly inscribed: "The Hierarchy of Meanings. Introduction to the Study of Poetic Works." In the lower corner of the second page (Balmcalfkin loved to be original) was a dedication: "To My Only One" ("Only One" was written with capital letters) and a photograph of his Dream. The third page had the Roman numeral I, in the middle of the fourth page one word stood out: "Foreword," on the fifth . . .

It was a solid start to the work. Further on, beneath the main text, were notes in French from all the major contemporary linguists, without Russian translation (the work was clearly intended for real scholars, not foolish students). The main text, it seemed, had also been written in a foreign language and just been given Russian endings. There were hints here of the possibility of new definitions of the concepts of the Romantic and of the classical; there was talk of poetic techniques for coloring the present with the past and the future; the absurd notion of meanings nesting in words was destroyed, and a definition was offered of the aesthetic as a phantasm, as the harmonization of nature and history.

And if a true artist, thought Balmcalfkin, *were to look into this book, he would not be able to tear himself away; the enchanting pathos of these pages would affect him: a work of art is always personal, personal as a matter of principle, a work of art cannot be seen as impersonal, the point is not in the name but rather in the way the personality is reflected in the work.*

Art is a state of rapture, it is an objective phase of existence. The aesthetic has no nature or history, it is a special sphere: not logical, not ethical, nor the sum of the two. No matter how much the artist reads, the leitmotif of this book would clamor in his ears: art is enraptured existence, fantasy is an objective phase of existence. And he would forgive Balmcalfkin his absurd language, and the French notes, and his room's décor, and the photograph of his Dream in a little hat, holding an umbrella, driving away in a carriage.

INTERMEZZO

FOR TWO days Kostya Kissenkin had been walking around the market in white trousers, a black jacket, and a felt hat. Tall and sturdily built, he leaned over the junk, fastidiously moving things aside with his stick, looking for pornography.

"What do you want?" asked the ladies who sold old scrap iron, sucking the edge of glasses with hot tea. "What are you digging for, throwing everything around?"

Kostya Kissenkin blushed and moved off. Across the way the unknown poet was standing by the market's antiques dealer, examining an ancient, mop-headed, witchlike Venus; she was leading a large-headed Cupid with one hand and holding a balalaika in the other. Venus's loins were draped with zigzag-patterned Mongolian fabric, her breasts were wrinkled and dangling, while the sides of her head were marked with her symbol (♀).

At that moment Candler walked up to him.

"You know, Kokosha Fedora sells stuff here at the market. The bastard put out a Red Army soldier dancing on an officer's chest, then he drew a bunch of little portraits of Lenin, stuck them in some medallions and started selling 'em to the Komsomol girls in their red kerchiefs.[22] Do you happen to know any university shebas? I love popping a girl's cork. Yesterday, while you were enjoying the parades,— I know, I know, you were sitting on a balcony somewhere spitting down at them—me and Natasha ..."

The former artillery officer made the pertinent gesture.

The unknown poet felt a sense of alarm. He remembered her as a little girl with pigtails, in a white dress, dancing at the children's balls in Pavlovsk.

"Ah, there you are, my friends," Balmcalfkin extended his hands to them, "you must be talking about literature, don't let me interrupt you, I wouldn't dream of it."

He bowed to them and went on.

Kostya Kissenkin finally found an appropriate match holder. Candler took off, peeking under ladies' hats.

Along the wall stood former fine ladies, offering things for sale: one—a monogrammed teaspoon, a second—a yellowed, useless boa, a third—two shot glasses in opalescent rainbow colors, a fourth—a rag doll of her own making, a fifth—an 1890s corset. That gray-haired old lady was selling her own hair, which had fallen out back in early youth and had been gathered into a braid; this relatively young one was selling the heavily used boots of her deceased husband.

8. THE UNKNOWN POET AND BALMCALFKIN AT THE WINDOW BY NIGHT

"YOU ARE committing a terribly vile act," the unknown poet once said to me. "You are destroying my life's work. My whole life I've been trying to show tragedy through my verse, to show that we were once radiant; but you're doing everything you can to vilify us in the eyes of posterity."

I looked at him.

"If you think that we've perished, you are sorely mistaken," the unknown poet continued, his eyes flashing. "We are an exceptional, periodically recurring state of being and we cannot perish. We are inevitable."

He sat down on a bench. I sat down next to him.

"You are a professional man of letters. There's nothing worse than a professional man of letters," he shifted away from me.

"A madman," I muttered. He turned his head.

"Sometimes contemporaries do not share the same consciousness; that does not give you the right to consider me mad."

I felt ashamed. Perhaps he really wasn't mad. We were silent.

Warily, he began listening to the rustling of the leaves.

Some Komsomol boys walked past us with their girlfriends.

No no, he's definitely mad!

"I am often absent," said the unknown poet, as if he were reading my thoughts. "But that is nothing more than dissolving into nature."

He got up and shook my hand.

"I am sincerely sorry that you live in the world that you depict."

Balmcalfkin was coming toward him.

Seriously, like well-mannered people, they greeted one another. They did not slap each other on the back.

They walked off down the alley. I walked past the mosque and got on the tram. *You're mad, you're still mad*, I thought.

I went into my building, put a fresh point on a pencil.

"No," I said, "I have to determine what they're doing now. They must be up to some noisome and shady business again."

I twisted the ends of my mustache, went out, put the key in my pocket, checked to see if I had a pencil and paper. It was a white night.

The columns stood out in pairs, or threesomes, or foursomes. A creature wearing a nurse's uniform glommed onto me.

"I am Tamara," she said.

"And where is your white satin coverlet?" I asked, "your coverlet of precious *stobi* fabric, of Indian corduroy, of Gilan silk, your violet-colored silk cushion, your tasseled golden veil?"[23]

She peered at me through her lorgnette.

"You reek of beer," she said. "But you must be a nice clean little fellow. Let's go to my place."

"All right," I answered, "next time. Right now I'm terribly busy. I don't have time right now."

"No problem," she answered, "we can do it here, come on over here."

Seeing that I wasn't stopping, she yelled:

"Or maybe you're really a man of letters, you're all dirt-poor, you bastards. I took one of your lot in, a Mr. Gadabout. He reads me poems about syphilis and compares himself to a prostitute. Calls me his fiancée."

"Leave me alone, dear creature," I said, "let me be. I am not a man of letters, I am just curious."

She kept following me and walked me nearly all the way to Victims of the Revolution Square.[24] There, she sat down on a bench and started to cry.

"Why on earth are you crying?" I asked her. "Are you sore about the ermine coat, or the other one, the fur from Karakum with pearls on the lapels, or the ring of Nystad turquoise, the Khorasan wool cloak? Or is it the fish-tooth chess pieces, the little amber caskets?"

"I wish I could take a bicycle ride. After all, I am one of Lieutenant Ladykin's fillies, I want to be surrounded by officers."

It was only now that I noticed she'd completely fallen apart.

"A drunk," I thought and quickened my pace.

It was already two o'clock in the morning when I came to the house where Balmcalfkin lived. The caretaker let me in. I went through to the half-wrecked side wing and stood facing Balmcalfkin's window. They were sitting at the table, reading something by the light of a kerosene lamp and arguing heatedly. Occasionally the unknown poet would get up and pace around the room. "What are they reading, what are they talking about?" I thought. "They're probably making fun of the modern age."

"I think," said the unknown poet, rising, "that ours is a heroic era."

"Most definitely heroic," affirmed Balmcalfkin.

"I think that the world is experiencing an upheaval akin to that of the first centuries of Christianity."

"I am convinced of it," answered Balmcalfkin.

"What a spectacle is being revealed to us!" noted the unknown poet.

"What an interesting time to be alive!" said Balmcalfkin in a rapturous whisper.

"But it's time for me to go," said the unknown poet, leaving the window. "I'll borrow your Dante."

"Of course," answered Balmcalfkin. The unknown poet came over, closed the book and put it in his pocket. He began making his farewells.

9. THE POET SEPTEMBER AND THE UNKNOWN POET

ONE DAY the unknown poet was reading poems in Kruzhalov's Corner.[25]

A drunken, bearded man in a calico peasant shirt circled around him, nearly weeping in rapture.

"My God," he kept repeating. "These poems are brilliant! All my life I have dreamed of poems like these!"

Young lady acquaintances gave the unknown poet friendly pats on the shoulder.

The man in the calico shirt smothered him in wine breath and shook his hand vigorously.

"For God's sake, come see me, my last name is September."[26]

The unknown poet pulled scraps of paper covered in scribbles out of his pocket, chose a free spot on one and wrote down the address.

"I've just come from Persia, come see me. I haven't heard true poems in such a long time," said the man in the calico shirt.

The next day the unknown poet set out to see September.

September lived in a different part of the city, in a so-called revenue house, that is, a tall building with an inner courtyard narrow as a well-shaft, with large, well-appointed apartments facing the street and small ones on the sides and back, mercilessly uniform, their layout repeated point for point from the bottom floors up.

The unknown poet rang. The door was opened by September, sober, in tall boots and a clean, belted shirt.

In the middle of the front room stood a table covered with a table-cloth, with the remains of a meal on it. Four Viennese chairs, warped by rain, stood around the table. A black overcoat gone rusty with age hung from a nail, along with a blouse belonging to the poet's wife. Half of the room was walled off by a wardrobe, behind which stood September's conjugal bed.

The unknown poet set aside his stick, adorned with an episcopal jewel,[27] set down his hat and looked at September with genuine affection. He already knew a great deal about him. He knew that seven years ago September had spent two years in a madhouse, and he knew the overwrought and dreadful environment in which September lived.

"Ever since yesterday I can't seem to calm down," said September. "Before the madhouse, in the madhouse, and in Persia I imagined poems like this, as if you had died more than once before, as if this were not your first time among us."

The unknown poet looked around the room.

"Read me some of your poems," he said.

"No, no, later. Here, this is my wife."

A thin woman came out from behind the wardrobe with a clean and lovely seven-year-old boy.

"This is my little bunny-rabbit, Edgar. This is a remarkable poet," he said to the child, indicating the unknown poet with a glance.

"Pushkin?" asked the little boy, wide-eyed.

September led the unknown poet into his room. The narrow bed (September's separate place of repose) was covered by a purple blanket with black horizontal stripes. The threadbare pillow served as a headboard. A manuscript covered with crossed-out lines languished in the middle of the bed. A glass stood on the windowsill and next to it an opened packet of cheap tobacco stood upright. A black table and chair stood by the wall. The room was pasted with wallpaper covered in gaudy roses.

September and the unknown poet sat down on the bed.

"Why did you come here!" Silent for a moment, the unknown poet looked out the window.

"Here is death. Why did you leave behind the shores where you were published, where your wife respected you because you had money? Where you wrote what you called Futurist poems. Here you won't write a single line."

"But your poems?" answered September.

"My poems," said the unknown poet thoughtfully, "are maybe not poems at all. Maybe that is why they have the effect they do. For me they are another way of saying something, a kind of special material that requires interpretation."

"I don't understand everything you are saying." September began walking around the room. "I only finished a four-year town school; after that I lost my mind. When I came out of the hospital I began writing Symbolist poems while knowing nothing about Symbolism. When I later came upon Poe's stories, entirely at random, I was stunned. I felt as if I had written that book; I only recently became a Futurist."

He stopped walking, lifted a corner of the blanket, pulled a wooden crate out from under the bed, opened it, took out a manuscript, and read:

> The world dissolved in trembling circles,
> There was a greenish glow within.
> A cliff, a ship, and a girl over the sea
> I saw, walking out the door.
>> The couples slowly walk along the Pryazhka,
>>> And their faces are disgusting. The flowers are disgusting too.
>> The high eyes of your soul can't tear away
>> Their lashes from my soul.

What an astonishing level of culture, thought the unknown poet while September was reading, *can be provoked by mental disorder.* He looked into September's eyes: *It's a shame he can't overcome his madness.*

"I wrote that poem," September once again began walking around the room, "before I was released from the infirmary. I understood it then, but now I don't understand it at all. For me now it is just a collection of words."

He bent down and took some other poems out of the crate. Straightening up, he began reading again.

Among the profusion of rhythmic chatter, overwrought images arose every once in a while, but for the most part it was weak stuff.

September sensed this, squatted down, and anxiously began digging in the depths of the trunk. He pulled out books of his poems that had been printed in Teheran, but there was nothing in them.

"The water's boiled," his wife, standing in the doorway, addressed her husband. "Pyotr Petrovich, invite your guest to have some tea."

"Just a moment, just a moment," and September in heedless, hopeless haste began reading his recent, Futurist poems.

The unknown poet, close to despair, sat on the bed.

Here is a man, he thought, *who had madness at his disposal, and he failed to tame it, to understand it, to compel it to serve humanity.*

The nighttime chill could already be felt from the window. September and the unknown poet went into the other room.

Pinkish round pretzels lay on a plate. September's wife was pouring tea. Small, dark-skinned, wrinkled, but lively, she spoke very very quickly, offered bread rings, spoke again. Finally the unknown poet began listening to her.

"Isn't it true," she continued, "that it was madness to come here, it's terrifying living here, while out by Baikal he has his parents, they're peasants, they have everything they need, we should have gone there and not here."

The kerosene lamp burned dully on the table. Having pushed his glass away, seven-year-old Edgar slept, his head on his arms.

"My little bunny," September said, leaning down and kissing his son.

Silence ensued.

"You'll ruin my son as well, we have to get away from here, away from here!"

Getting up, she commenced pacing around the room.

It was late at night when the unknown poet descended the stairs. Out on the empty street, listening to the dwindling echo of his steps, he rested an elbow on the stick with its large hierarchic amethyst, slackened his shoulders and fell into thought. He would like to be the leader of all the madmen, to be an Orpheus for madmen. For them he would plunder the east and the south and would dress the unhappy adventures they endured in a variety of robes, now falling away, now reappearing.

With hatred he lifted his stick and threatened the sleeping accountants, the dancing and singing artists of the stage. All of those who, so it seemed to him, did not experience this most terrifying agony.

"Help! Oh, help!" It seemed to him that a girl's voice was crying out from the first floor.

Understanding nothing, with a strength increased tenfold by despair, he ran, limping, up the building's staircase, leapt off it and threw himself into the window. His eyes stopped, his neck strained. One, two! He seized the back of someone's head and began punching; he was easily tossed off—he seized the throat; he was thrown off—he grabbed a heavy chair. And swung it.

Everything went quiet.

At his feet lay Candler. There was no girl in the room.

There you have it, thought the unknown poet, recovering his equilibrium. *The devil knows what just happened.*

The whole apartment sprang to life, doors were slamming, footsteps hurrying down the hallway.

The unknown poet wrinkled his forehead.

Someone ran to get the policeman on duty.

It was established that while Candler was sleeping, his acquaintance had broken into the room through the window and attempted to kill him.

What a strange life, thought the unknown poet. *Evidently, somewhere deep down inside me the sensations of childhood are still alive. At one time I thought of women as special beings, whom one must not offend, for whom one must sacrifice everything. Evidently, even now my brain has held on to some pale faces, loosed hair and clear voices. It must be that I subconsciously hated Candler, otherwise where could that hallucination have come from?*

Out of everyone, Candler was the most surprised by this event. He couldn't explain it for the life of him. He walked around, bandaged up, shrugging his shoulders.

10. SOME OF MY HEROES IN 1921–22

FOR SOME time now, after a two-year delay, everyone in the city—
I am talking about Petersburg, not Leningrad—had been infected
with Spenglerism.[28]

Spindly-legged youths, bird-headed young ladies, fathers of families only just rid of dropsy walked along the streets and alleys talking
about the decline of the West.

Some Ivan Ivanovich would run into some Anatoly Leonidovich,
they would shake each other's hands:

"Don't you know, the West is lost, it's decadence, my dear sir. That's
it for culture, I tell you, *phwut!*—civilization is coming…"

They would sigh.

Meetings were arranged.

People suffered.

Among those who started believing in the decline of the West was
the poet Triniton.

Returning home with the unknown poet, hiccupping from the
filling foodstuffs that had only recently appeared, he whispered
mournfully:

"We Westerners are lost, lost."

The unknown poet sang in response:

> I feel melancholy, as thick darkness settles
> In distant West, the land of holy wonders…[29]

He spoke of Konstantin Leontiev and giggled at his fellow poet.

After all, what is decline to an unknown poet? He couldn't care less, everything will recur, it's all a whirligig, my dear sir.

Lift up your footsies and gallop off, he felt like advising Triniton. He slapped him on the shoulder: "Enjoy the spectacle the world provides," he said, indicating a little dog shitting by the gate.

Triniton stopped—at that time there were still few dogs in the city.

"Anyway, it's still sad, my sweet—," he said, addressing the unknown poet affectionately. "You go on writing poetry, but who needs it. No readers, no listeners—it's sad."

"Write idylls," the unknown poet advised him: "You have an idyllic kind of talent: do your duty, the flower blooms, the grass grows, the bird sings, you are meant to write poems."

They were silent a while.

"The moon. Stars," Triniton yawned sweetly. "Let's walk this whole night through."

"Walk on," agreed the unknown poet.

On their worn-down heels, dressed in rags, the poets walked—to Intercession Square, to Peski, to the Garden of Laborers.[30]

"You are a man who loves and appreciates Petersburg," Triniton said, drinking in the stars above the Kazan Cathedral.

"That's no surprise," noted the unknown poet, examining his boots: "I have been here for four generations now."

"Four generations is more than enough to get a feel for a city," affirmed Triniton, taking out his handkerchief. "I'm from near Lake Ladoga," he continued.

"Write about Ladoga. Your childhood impressions are there, mine are here. As a child you loved fields full of cornflowers, marshes, forests, old wooden churches, while for me it's the Summer Garden with its sandy paths, its flower beds, its statues and outbuildings. You loved drinking tea peasant-style, from the saucer."

They were silent a while.

The unknown poet glanced over his shoulder.

"I saw parks before I saw fields, the armless Venus before any tanned country girls. How on earth could I develop a love for fields or villages? There's nowhere in me it could come from."

They sat down on rocks by the metal fence of the Yusupov Garden.

"Read me a poem," Triniton suggested to the unknown poet.

The unknown poet put down his stick.

"It's the damndest thing," Triniton said, moved. "Real Petersburg poetry. Look, do you see the moon there through the ruins?"

He stood up on tiptoe on top of a pile of gravel.

The unknown poet lit a cigarette.

"Don't look at the moon," he said, "it's an unsettling phenomenon." And, getting up in front of Triniton, he tried to block it.

In the year of Spenglerism, Misha Kittenkin first came to the city and was struck and fell in love with the power, pride, and disposition of the recently drowned Petersburg artist and poet Euphratesky, a tall, gray-haired old man who had been traveling with two valets.[31] The poet Euphratesky had been working on his biography since he was thirty-five. To this end, he summitted Ararat, Elbrus, the Himalayas—accompanied by an extravagant suite. His tent had been spotted by the oases of all the world's deserts. His foot had trod the floors of all the marvelous palaces, he had conversed with all the colored sovereigns.

Misha Kittenkin had never seen Euphratesky, but he was dazzled. Misha was a rosy, ginger, large-headed boy, neat and clean, with a tiny little mouth. "Astonishing!" he would often whisper, leaning over Euphratesky's books and drawings.

The wife of Alexander Petrovich Euphratesky wept when Euphratesky passed away and wrung her little hands.

Taking advantage of the situation, Euphratesky's friends began coming over to comfort her.

Candler was one of the comforters.

But the next day he was cursing:

"The silly woman, the goose—lying there like a piece of wood."

And he wandered throughout the whole smallish wooden house trumpeting:

"There you are with her, but she's sighing—oh, Alexander Petrovich!"

A year later, Misha Kittenkin, as an admirer of Euphratesky, made the acquaintance of Yekaterina Ivanovna.

One fine evening he brought over some wine and hors d'oeuvres; bowing his head, he spoke for a long time to Yekaterina Ivanovna about Alexander Petrovich—which gowns he had liked for her to wear, what Alexander Petrovich's hands were like, what exquisite gray hair he'd had, how enormous he had been, his manner of walking around the room, and how she had stood on tiptoe to kiss him.

Misha Kittenkin sat there, his tiny little carmine mouth half-open, gazing with his clear baby-blue eyes, and began stroking and squeezing Yekaterina Ivanovna's little hands, kissing Yekaterina Ivanovna's forehead. He went on asking:

"And what was Alexander Petrovich's nose like? And how long were his arms? And did our Alexander Petrovich wear starched collars or prefer softer ones? Did Alexander Petrovich perchance drum his fingers on glass surfaces?"

Yekaterina Ivanova answered all of his questions and began to cry. She took up a men's monogrammed handkerchief and raised it to her eyes.

"Might that be Alexander Petrovich's handkerchief?" asked Misha Kittenkin.

She sat silent for a long time, wiping away her tears with Euphratesky's handkerchief.

Then she handed the handkerchief over to Misha Kittenkin:

"Keep this in memory of Alexander Petrovich." And burst into tears again.

Misha Kittenkin carefully folded the handkerchief and quickly hid it away.

"Tell me, what did Alexander Petrovich say about art?" Misha Kittenkin asked, fondling the handkerchief in his pocket. "What was poetry for Alexander Petrovich?"

"He never spoke to me about poetry," Yekaterina Ivanovna said, opening her eyes and looking in the mirror. She leapt up and moved closer to the mirror.

"Here, look—isn't it true that I am graceful?" She began wringing her hands and tilting her head. "Alexander Petrovich always considered me graceful."

"And when did Alexander Petrovich begin to write poems, at what age?" Lighting a cigarette, Misha Kittenkin asked another question.

"Isn't it true that I look just like a little girl?" Yekaterina Ivanovna sat down in an armchair. "Alexander Petrovich always said that I look like a little girl."

"Yekaterina Ivanovna, which table should we set?" Misha Kittenkin asked angrily, getting up from his armchair.

"That one," Yekaterina Ivanovna said, indicating a small round table. "But I don't have anything."

"I brought some Bordeaux and..." Misha Kittenkin said with pride, "hors d'oeuvres and fruit."

"Oh, how delightful you are!" Yekaterina Ivanovna laughed out loud. "I just love wine and fruit!"

"Alexander Petrovich's friends have entirely abandoned me," she said, sighing, while Misha Kittenkin, standing on tiptoe, was taking wineglasses out of a cupboard.

"They have no concern for me at all, they know that I have no will, that I don't know how to look after myself, they ignore me entirely. They don't stop by, they don't talk about Alexander Petrovich. They don't pay attention to me. Let's be friends, let's go on talking about Alexander Petrovich," she added.

Misha Kittenkin had a drink and a bite to eat and began examining the objects around the room.

"Is this really the table that Alexander Petrovich wrote at?" he asked, indicating a small round table. "Why don't you dust?" he added.

"I don't know how to dust," answered Yekaterina Ivanovna. "When Alexander Petrovich was around, I didn't dust."

The next day Misha Kittenkin awoke in Alexander Petrovich's bed.

Next to him, her mouth open and arm sticking out, slept Yekaterina Ivanovna.

It's a shame she's so stupid, thought Misha Kittenkin. *She can't provide me with any valuable information about Alexander Petrovich. Well, no matter, I'll get my valuable information from Alexander Petrovich's friends. And from her I'll find out how Alexander Petrovich wrote.*

"Yekaterina Ivanovna, tell me, how did Alexander Petrovich write?"

Yekaterina Ivanovna woke up, threw her little arms wide, jabbed Misha Kittenkin with her little knee, turned over and fell back asleep.

For two weeks Misha Kittenkin visited Yekaterina Ivanovna, gathering various intimate details about Alexander Petrovich. Sometimes he would take Yekaterina Ivanovna to the cinema or the theater, and sometimes they just took walks around town.

Misha Kittenkin learned everything: how many moles had been on the body of Alexander Petrovich, how many calluses; he learned that in 191— a boil had popped up on Alexander Petrovich's back, that Alexander Petrovich loved coconuts, that during his marriage to Yekaterina Ivanovna Alexander Petrovich had had scores of lovers, but he had loved her very much.

And when he had found everything out and written everything down, Misha Kittenkin decided that Alexander Petrovich's lovers must be smarter than his wife and that they would be able to give him more information about the soul of Alexander Petrovich. He left Yekaterina Ivanovna. He was a squeaky-clean little boy, dressed to the nines; no speck of dirt ever got stuck under a single one of his little nails.

He learned that X, a university student, had been Alexander Petrovich's last lover, and met with her at a certain house where literary gatherings were held.

It was an astonishing house. Two young ladies—and they both wrote poetry. One with misty melancholy, the other with passion and authenticity. They had decided to divide the world in two: one would take its sadness, the other—its raptures.

There were also all sorts of young men and girls. A poetic circle had formed. It was also attended by poets of the previous epoch: thirty-five-year-old youths. Everyone read their poems, sitting in a circle, while some of them stood on the balcony, admiring the starry night sky and the chimneys. This is where Misha Kittenkin met with the student, X.

He also read poems here, sitting on a cushion from the couch, legs stretched out and eyes closed. The student X happened to be sitting next to him; she was fun, with nice long legs.

"What do you say, Eugenia Alexandrovna—let's go walk around the city after the reading, we can go to Thomon's Stock Exchange."[32]

"Only if the whole gang is coming too," answered Eugenia Alexandrovna in a whisper.

At two a.m. the gang was gathered.

The gang walked past the stallions raising their hooves above the Fontanka. Misha Kittenkin wooed Genia the whole way. He spoke of how astonishing and unusual a girl she was. When they made it to Thomon's Stock Exchange, Genia and Misha slipped away together, their heads bowed tenderly.

Misha Kittenkin flushed, sweet Genia turned rosy, and they got up from the steps.

"Tell me, sweet Genia," asked Misha Kittenkin, "did Alexander Petrovich love you very much?"

"He promised to love me for two months, but later he started avoiding our meetings."

"When was that?"

"February eleventh."

"Did Alexander Petrovich happen to speak with you about poetry?"

"He did," Genia answered, adjusting her skirt. "He used to say that every girl should write poetry. In France they all do."

"And what did Alexander Petrovich say about assonance?"

"He didn't like assonance, he used to say that it's only good for songs."

"Genia, sweet Genia, fix your skirt again, or people might notice."

The young people said their goodbyes. The city was gradually recuperating. Painted buildings were reappearing. The poet Triniton walked on, accompanying his pharmacy girl. This acquaintance with the pharmacy girl had been something out of the ordinary. One time, walking past the pharmacy, he had caught sight of a pretty little head behind the counter, gone in, and asked for a headache remedy; the pretty little head knew that it was Triniton. How could she not know! Triniton read his poems everywhere. He was terribly fond of reading poems.

She gave him his headache remedy, and Triniton began talking about the stars. He was just not of this world, Triniton; what else would he talk about but stars.

"Look," he said, pointing at the window, "how bright Ursa Major is."

"And what an enormous moon," answered the girl.

"And what fresh night air," said Triniton.

"Oh, do you know my poem 'La Dame aux camélias'?" asked Triniton.

"I don't."

"Would you like me to recite it to you?"

"Please do," answered the young lady. Triniton recited it.

What poetic poetry! The girl became dreamy.

Triniton had settled his elbows down on the counter. The young lady looked at her watch.

"My girlfriend is about to show up, I'm filling in for her today."

"I'll walk you home," said Triniton.

"All right," said the young lady, her eyes widening.

Half an hour later they were walking past Petrovsky Park.

"Let's have a snowball fight," suggested Triniton.

First she would run away, then he would. There were no other passersby. They sat down to rest, white from the snowballs.

Triniton looked around—no one was there. She looked around—no one was there. They went a little further off from the road.

The next day Triniton ran around the city telling everyone all about it. But over the next two weeks he kept walking the pharmacy girl home from work, appearing with her everywhere, while taking his friends aside to whisper in their ears:

"I'm sick of her. It's just perpendicular love. Like Don Juan, I am seeking true love."

The young people watched the departing pair and laughed at Triniton.

Misha Kittenkin was bidding farewell to Genia. They had agreed to meet the next day. Misha Kittenkin came up to the unknown poet.

"I'm working on Alexander Petrovich's biography. Can you give me any essential information?"

"Hm..." answered the unknown poet lazily. "Ask Triniton. He knows everything."

Misha Kittenkin ran to catch up with Triniton.

The next day Misha Kittenkin was sitting at Triniton's house. The room was half-dark. It smelled of raspberry jam. Gauze curtains hung on the windows. A touch-me-not grew green on the windowsill. The walls were hung with portraits of French poets, and engravings depicting Manon Lescaut, Ophelia, and the Prodigal Son were tacked up as well.

"Here is Alexander Petrovich's pen," Triniton said, holding out a penholder to Misha Kittenkin. "Here is his inkpot, and here is a handkerchief of Alexander Petrovich."

"I have one of Alexander Petrovich's handkerchiefs," answered Misha Kittenkin with pride.

"What, you collect poetic objects too?"

"These things are for the biography," answered Misha Kittenkin. "It's important to establish which handkerchiefs Alexander Petrovich carried in what year. See, you have a batiste one, while mine is canvas. Things are bound to their owners. A canvas handkerchief indicates one disposition of the soul, a batiste one indicates another."

"My handkerchief's from 1913."

"You see," noted Misha Kittenkin, "and mine's from 1916! So, Alexander Petrovich must have undergone some sort of internal drama or worsened economic circumstances. Through his handkerchiefs we can reestablish both the soul and the economic status of the owner."

"Well, I just collect poetic objects in general," said Triniton, getting out a little case. "Here is a lace from the boot of a well-known poetess (he named her). Here is a tie belonging to the poet Lebedinsky; here are autographs from Linsky and Petrov and here—from Alexander Petrovich."

Misha Kittenkin took Alexander Petrovich's autograph and began examining it.

"Where could I get one of Alexander Petrovich's autographs?"

"From Natalia Levantovskaya," answered Triniton.

"Ahh ..." thought Misha Kittenkin.

11. THE ISLAND

IT WAS still spring when Balmcalfkin moved to Peterhof and rented an unusual building.[33]

Standing at the entrance, he became lost in thought. Here he would receive friends, and together they would walk around the park like ancient philosophers, strolling here and there, explaining and elucidating, speaking on lofty subjects. Here he would be visited by his life's dream, an unusual and luminous being—Maria Petrovna Dalmatova. His philosopher would come too, his old teacher and an unusual poet, the spiritual descendant of the great Western poets; he would read his new poems to all of them here, in the bosom of nature. And other acquaintances would come. Balmcalfkin became lost in thought.

In the morning he awoke, threw open his window, and sang out like a bird. Down below sparrows were chirping and taking off, and a milkmaid was approaching.

So balmy, he thought and stretched out his arms toward the sun, gleaming through the tree branches. *It's quiet here, utterly quiet. I will work far from the city; here I can concentrate and not try to do too many things at once.*

He rested his elbows on the table.

"Ha ha ha," laughed the inhabitants of the neighboring dachas, pacified Soviet bureaucrats with their wives and kiddies, as they walked in the evenings down the paths from their country houses and plunged into the greenery of the park.

"Ha ha ha! A philosopher's moved in, and quite the lodgings he's chosen!"

"Ha ha ha, the ninny, he goes out picking flowers in the morning."

Balmcalfkin expected his friends to arrive any day now. He picked flowers every morning so that he could greet his friends with flowers.

Here he comes carrying an armful of bird cherry—Maria Petrovna loves bird cherry. Here he's turned a corner carrying a bouquet of lilacs. Yekaterina Ivanovna loves lilacs.

But why was there nothing to be seen of Natalia Ardalionovna? Where had she disappeared to?

"We are the last island of the Renaissance," said Balmcalfkin to the gathered company, "in the dogmatic sea that surrounds us on all sides; we, and we alone, are preserving the sparks of critical thought, respect for the sciences, respect for man; neither master nor slave exists for us. We are all within a tall tower, we can hear the raging waves beating against its granite sides."

The tower was as real as could be, left intact from a former merchant's dacha. The lower part of the house had been gradually carried off by the inhabitants of neighboring houses to feed their kitchen fires, but the top had survived, and it was cozy inside. A table stood covered with a green tablecloth. The gathered company sat around the table: a lady in a hat with ostrich feathers and an amethyst pendant, a little dog next to her, also sitting on a chair; a little old man examining his nails and undertaking a manicure right then and there; a youth in an army jacket with an antiquated student cap on his knees; the philosopher Andrei Ivanovich Andrievsky; three eternal maidens and four eternal youths.[34] In a corner Yekaterina Ivanovna was twisting her hair around a finger.

"My God, how few we are," Balmcalfkin shook his graying hair. "Let us ask our most respected Andrei Ivanovich to play for us," he said, turning to the tall philosopher, who was completely gray-haired, with a long bushy mustache.

The philosopher got up, walked to the case and took out a violin.

Balmcalfkin opened a window wide and moved away. The philosopher sat on the windowsill, stuck a corner of his handkerchief into his starched collar, tested the strings and began to play.

Down below bloomed late bunches of lilac. A violet color crept into the room. There, far off, the sea was glinting, illuminated by a moon that had been deposed, but was still charming to those present. Before the sea, the fountains sought to reach the height of the moon with their multicolored sprays, each of which ended in trembling little white birds.

The philosopher was playing an old-fashioned melody.

Down below, along the avenue of fountains, Kostya Kissenkin was strolling with a local Komsomol youth. The Komsomol youth had the eyes of a cherub. The Komsomol youth was playing the balalaika.

Kostya Kissenkin was drunk on love and the night.

The philosopher played on. He saw Marburg, the great Cohen and his trip through the capitals of western Europe: he remembered how he'd spent a year living at Jeanne d'Arc Square; he remembered how in Rome . . .[35] The violin sang more plaintively, ever more plaintively.

The philosopher, with his head of thick gray hair, his youthful face with its bushy mustache and spade beard, saw himself dressed splendidly, wearing a top hat, carrying a cane, strolling with his young wife.

My God, how she loved me, he thought, and wished that his dead wife would become young again.

"I can't do it," he said, "I can play no more," he set down his violin and turned away to face the violet night.

The whole group headed down to the park.

The philosopher walked for a while in silence.

"In my opinion," he said, breaking the silence, "a writer was meant to appear who would elegize us, our feelings."

"But that is Philostratus," the unknown poet, examining a just-plucked flower, stopped.

"Let it be as you say, we will call this unknown person who has appeared Philostratus."

"We will doubtless be vilified," continued the unknown poet, "but Philostratus must depict us as fair and radiant, not as devils of some sort."

"Well of course, that goes without saying," someone noted. "The victors always vilify the defeated and turn them—whether they are gods or men—into devils. That is how it has been for all time and how it will be with us too. They'll turn us into devils, they will, it goes without saying."

"And the transformation is already underway," someone noted.

"Will we really be pulling away from one another so soon?" Balmcalfkin whispered in horror, blinking wildly. "Will we really begin to see devils in one another?"

They were walking toward the Babigon Heights.[36]

The group laid down a traveling rug and everyone rolled up their coats into bolsters.

"What a divan!" exclaimed Balmcalfkin.

Up ahead, illuminated by a Mohammedan sickle, Belvedere rose like a dark mass; to the right lay Peterhof, and a Finnish village to the left.

When everyone had gotten comfortable, the unknown poet began:

> The strings were wailing like women.
> Do not now change us into black...

Leaning against a tree, Balmcalfkin wept, and in this night it seemed to everyone that they were terribly young and terribly beautiful, that they were all terribly good people.

And they rose—the *chers* with the *ma-chères*, and they danced on the flower-covered meadow, and the violin appeared in the philosopher's hands and sang out purely and sweetly. And everyone saw Philostratus in the flesh: a slender youth with wondrous eyes, shadowed by wings of lashes, in flowing robes and a laurel wreath—he sang, and beyond him olive groves rustled. And, swaying like a ghost, Rome arose.

"I plan to write a long poem," said the unknown poet (when the vision had faded). "A metaphysical plague is ravaging the city; the seigneurs select Greek names and retire to their castle. There, they spend their time studying the sciences, making music, creating poetry, paintings, and sculpture. But they know that they have been condemned, that the last storming of the castle is being prepared. The seigneurs know that the victory will not be theirs; they descend into the vault, stack up their effulgent images there for future generations and go out to certain destruction, to ridicule, to an inglorious death, since for them no other death could now exist."[37]

"Oh, isn't it true that I've become just awfully stupid," Yekaterina Ivanovna started flirting with Balmcalfkin. "I've become awfully stupid without Alexander Petrovich, and awfully unhappy."

"Listen," Balmcalfkin said, taking Yekaterina Ivanovna aside, "you aren't stupid in the slightest, it's just that life has turned out like this." *She's been thoroughly corrupted by Euphratesky, thoroughly corrupted,* he thought.

"But where is Mikhail Petrovich Kittenkin?" whispered Yekaterina Ivanovna: "Why doesn't he come to visit, to talk with me about Alexander Petrovich?"

Balmcalfkin was briefly silent.

"I don't know."

Yekaterina Ivanovna, lifting one foot, began to examine her slippers.

"These slippers of mine have gotten all tattered, you see," she said, her eyes widening. "And I haven't any blanket at home, I have to cover myself with my coat."

And she fell into thought.

"Do you happen to have any chocolates?"

"No," answered Balmcalfkin sadly.

"But Alexander Petrovich really is a great poet, isn't that right? Nowadays such poets are no more," she straightened up and said with pride. "He loved me more than anyone else on earth." And she smiled.

Musya came up to Balmcalfkin; she was wearing an old-fashioned straw hat with pale-blue ribbons and grazed his hand with slightly shimmering nails.

"Tell me," she said, "what does this mean:

In statues lurks the charm of wine
Intoxicating fruits of autumn . . ."

"Oh, my," Balmcalfkin shook his head, "these lines conceal an entire worldview, a whole sea of meanings that zigzag about, rising up like waves and then disappearing!"

"How happy I am with you," said Musya. "He told me"—she glanced at the unknown poet, who was conversing with an eternal youth—"that you all are the last, the only intact leaves of a sublime autumn. I didn't entirely understand, though I did finish university; but then, nowadays in universities they don't teach that sort of thing at all."

"That sort of thing is not taught, it is felt," noted Balmcalfkin.

"Let's go sit on that step," Musya gestured up with her chin.

They climbed a bit higher. They sat on a step between the caryatids of the Belvedere Portico.[38]

"How the nightingales sing!" said Musya. "Why do girls always get so excited about nightingales?"

"It's not just girls," answered Balmcalfkin, "I, too, have always been excited by nightingales."

He looked into Musya's eyes.

"But I'm afraid of women," he remarked pensively. "A terrifying elemental force."

"Why terrifying?" smiled Musya.

"Oh, what if she leads you along, leads you along and then drops you? This has happened to my friends, and when she drops you, there's no way to beg her to go on living together. How my friends once worshipped at the feet of their wives and carried their portraits in their wallets! But they always, always drop them."

Balmcalfkin felt hurt for his friends.

Musya took out her comb and began to comb Balmcalfkin's hair. Down below the young people sang:

Gaudeamus igitur . . .[39]

Balmcalfkin recalled the end of university, then dove into his childhood and, in it, met Elena Stavrogina. It seemed to him that there was something of Elena Stavrogina in Maria Petrovna Dalmatova, that she was like some sort of distorted image of Elena Stavrogina, distorted—but nevertheless cherished. He kissed her hand.

"My God," he said, "if you only knew…"

"What, what?" asked Musya.

"Nothing," quietly answered Balmcalfkin.

Down below they were singing:

On the Volga looms a cliff…[40]

In the morning Kostya Kissenkin and the unknown poet were riding the train back to Leningrad. The unknown poet felt unbearably sad. For nothing but absolute oblivion lay ahead. Kostya Kissenkin was entertaining him as best he could and talking about the Baroque.

"Isn't it the case," he said, "that you strive not for perfection and completeness, but for something that is always moving and becoming—not something limited and perceptible, but infinite and colossal?"

There was no one else in the train car, just the two of them. Kostya Kissenkin got up and began reciting sonnets by Goncourt.

The unknown poet gazed at Kostya Kissenkin with tenderness: so sarcastic and witty, he was faintly frivolous, read only foreign books, and admired the works of human hands with a certain condescension.

"We'll keep up the fight," he said, straightening.

"What's wrong?" asked Kostya Kissenkin.

"Nothing," smiled the unknown poet. "I'm mulling over a new baroque poem."

Fields of tall grass flashed past the windows. Kostya Kissenkin, who'd made his appearance, was already reading a sonnet by Camões and finding a tremendous resemblance between its disposition and that of the poem by Pushkin that begins:

For the shores of your distant fatherland . . .[41]

At the end of the train, alone in a car, Yekaterina Ivanovna sat tearing off daisy petals: loves me, loves me not, loves me, loves me not. But who it was who loved or didn't love her, she didn't know. Yet she felt that she should be loved and be taken care of.

And in the very last car rode the philosopher with the bushy mustache, thinking:

The world is nominal, not noumenal; reality is nominal, not noumenal.

Wha-wha—the wheels were turning.

Wha-wha . . .

And here's the train station.

Kostya Kissenkin carried a stick with a huge cat's-eye.

Kostya Kissenkin's eyes were blue, nearly the color of sapphires.

Kostya Kissenkin had long pink fingers.

"Where are we headed?" the unknown poet asked cheerfully. "We have absolutely nothing to do."

"Let's go listen to how the language of our native aspens is changing," smiled Kostya Kissenkin.

Kostya Kissenkin and the unknown poet spent the whole day together. They walked around the Summer Garden, along the Fontanka Embankment, the Catherine Canal, the Moyka and the Neva. They stood awhile before the Bronze Horseman and regretted that the city fathers had at some point cleaned off the green—the beautiful black-green patina. They had a smoke. Sat down on a bench. They talked about how the city had originated as an enormous palace.

They talked about books.

A summer evening. No official engagements. No university department. The midges circled and wove in the air. Balmcalfkin sat in a boat, rowing. By the shore the reeds were swaying, the Peterhof Palace could be seen up above, on the shore stood the unknown poet.

"You've arrived!" yelled Balmcalfkin and rowed to shore. "Finally, you've arrived. If you only knew how sad it is for me to live here, today I have been especially sad."

The boat reached the shore, the unknown poet got in, and Balmcalfkin, stoop-shouldered, graying, rowed away from shore. The unknown poet steered—the boat was racing toward the strand.

"It's come back to me," said Balmcalfkin, "how a few years ago I taught in a certain university town. I remember how on that very day, that very hour, we—the young students and I—set out for the opposite bank of the river and there, in a little grove, I delivered my lecture."

Twilight.

Finally, in darkness, they tied up the boat and set out to walk around the park.

A pink stripe of dawn had appeared in the east when, silent, they approached the tower.

The unknown poet listened to Balmcalfkin puttering around at great length on the second floor, in the sole room fit for habitation; taking off his boots and placing them by the bed, the spoon jangling in his glass.

He's drinking cold tea, he decided.

In the morning Kostya Kissenkin saw the unknown poet dozing on a white bench in the park by a huge spruce, straight as a mast. The friends greeted each other ecstatically and set out for the sea. Behind them grass was being mowed. Kostya Kissenkin squatted in the sea amid the waves, sturdy and pink. The unknown poet dozed on the rocks, on the shore, warmed by the morning sun.

"You know," Kostya Kissenkin appeared, "Andrei Ivanovich lives here now."

Shaking a foot and drying himself with a shaggy towel, he continued:

"I'm taking lessons from him on the methodology of art criticism."

The rocks and sand were scorching. Kostya Kissenkin tied up his round-toed boots. The unknown poet leapt cheerily from stone to stone, smoking.

The young men retreated from the cemetery and set out slantwise along the trail, through the still-unmowed woolly thyme, covered in little black bugs and greenish metallic beetles and snail slime, through fennel, red and white clover, and sorrel, to the road that led to New Peterhof, to its unrunning fountains (it was a weekday), to the statues with their flaking gilt, to the palace where an amputee was walking back and forth selling cigarettes, where a barefoot little urchin proffered caramels, and where, crossing his legs and leaning against a crate, a melancholic ice-cream vendor periodically dug around in his nose.

The young people went into the public cafeteria located near the palace and started eating sauerkraut soup. One of the soup plates was heavy, with a naval scene, while the other had a crest; the spoons were made of tin.

"What is the essence of Philostratus?" asked Kostya Kissenkin, lifting his spoon to his mouth.

But at that moment the philosopher Andrei Ivanovich came into the cafeteria, accompanied by a pharmacist and a lady researcher from the local institute.

Kostya Kissenkin and the unknown poet got up and greeted the new arrival. After dinner they all set out together for old Peterhof to celebrate the anniversary of the local institute. But on the way they decided they'd drop by to see Balmcalfkin.

Balmcalfkin at that time was taking a sun bath. He sat naked in a three-legged chair, wiggling his toes, smiling, drinking tea, and reading Chateaubriand's *The Genius of Christianity*.

Kostya Kissenkin was the first to come in. He staggered back, closed the door, asked those still coming up the stairs to wait a moment, opened the door again, and elegantly leapt into the room. Balmcalfkin blushed all over from the surprise.

The gathered company settled down by the tower, in the garden, with its broken fence and acacia bushes, with its remnants of garden beds, and was having a fine time. It had grown even bigger by now. A student of medium height sitting on a tree stump played the comb. Another, tiny student whistled along. The philosopher sat on a bench, recently installed and not yet painted; next to him sat the pharmacist, ceaselessly moving his lips; the lady researcher of the local institute sat neatly on the grass. At that moment Kostya Kissenkin and Balmcalfkin descended from the heights of the tower, hand in hand.

The pharmacist, finally, had just begun speaking; he was sorry that he'd been thwarted. He was enormously tall, in starched linens, and was not so much dressed in as addressing everyone with his suit. Right then, requesting that they not move, a young man quite taken with Freud photographed the whole group on a Kodak; he was even taking lessons in German here from Balmcalfkin, so that he could read Freud in the original.

"Gentlemen," said Balmcalfkin. "Perhaps instead of going to the anniversary party right now, we could go on sitting here awhile, because a pupil of mine is coming from the city in another hour."

While Balmcalfkin was helping prepare the labor school pupil for university admission, the unknown poet and Kostya Kissenkin went out for beer. Everyone took turns drinking from a cup that one of them happened to have, wiping off the brim with their handkerchiefs, as they slapped and waved away mosquitoes.

Manly strides were heard. A wrinkled Gypsy woman in tall blacked boots appeared on the road. When she saw the tower and the assembled company, she quickly ran over:

"Let me tell your fortune, tell your fortune! Your eyes are foreign eyes!" She walked among the lying, sitting, and standing figures.

"No, no, no need," they answered her. "We know our future already."

No one noticed how the pupil snuck out of the tower with Krayevich's physics under his arm.[42]

"La-la, la-la," sang Balmcalfkin, hiding his money and going downstairs.

The sun was already setting when the group approached the local institute. They were late, the scientific part of the program had ended, and music was wafting from the small assembly hall of the Leuchtenburg dukes' small palace. The glass doors leading into the park were thrown open, and pretty and not so pretty girls in carefully preserved delicate lace dresses were hanging around the entrance. Inside, people were dancing. Everything had a clean and innocent feel to it: the joyful faces of the young girls and young men; the piano player, maintaining the slow tempo; the professors sitting along the walls and conversing with one another in a dignified manner. The group walked single file into the assembly hall. The moon had long been dazzling. Kostya Kissenkin was dancing his heart out; the philosopher was walking carefully between the dancers and making conversation with the professors; Balmcalfkin sailed out of the doors into the park with the pharmacist. Moths flew all around, beating against the illuminated windows.

Darkness. The philosopher, pharmacist, and lady researcher moved like three silhouettes. The pharmacist watched to make sure that the philosopher didn't trip, that he didn't fall and hurt himself, that one of the last luminaries of philosophy did not go dim.

By the neat porch two silhouettes kissed a third.

"Good night, dear Andrei Ivanovich," they said.

In the morning students once again spread through the park gathering creepy-crawlies, beetles, and all kinds of plants; some of them sailed boats on the small ponds, catching algae in the water with their nets. It was hot, the sun beat down. It smelled of hay.

12. THE GOLDEN AGE

THROUGH the little southern town the naval squadrons strode with dashing flair, while the Red Army regiments scurried along, ragged and tired. The artillery and service corps dragged on. Vrangel had landed.[43]

He was only eleven miles away when, in the assembly hall of the two-story girls' preparatory school, next to the hospital and opposite the cathedral, a formal meeting was convened. At a long table covered with the usual green baize sat the Petersburgers. The first to leap up and give a speech was the newly appointed rector; after him spoke the deans, only just elected, and after them the just-elected professors and lecturers. After the third lecturer, Balmcalfkin rose.

"Citizens," he said, "you have honored us with the holy calling of professor and lecturer; to the north, due to hunger, epidemics, and moral suffering, Petersburg is dying. The library stacks have been abandoned, the museums are deserted. In the university students wander, gray as shadows; there are no longer any dogs or cats, crows are not flying, sparrows not chirping. There, people do not take off their outer clothing all winter long, they sit by their potbelly stoves like Eskimos. Dead horses lie in the streets with their legs pointing to the sky, and utterly transparent, hunger-swollen people cut them into pieces and, hiding a piece under their arms, steal back to their houses.

"Here, amid this southern landscape, in a gentle climate, surrounded by an abundance of the fruits of the earth, we will cultivate an intellectual garden, we will propagate the fruits of culture."

Balmcalfkin stopped, raised his face and wrung his hands.

"Here, in the south, culture will rise up as a many-tiered tower, the southern winds will fan it, innocent flowers will carpet its base, birds will fly in and out of the windows. In summer we will gather, crowds of us, and go out into the steppe to read enduring pages of philosophy and poetry. War and destruction should not confound you. I believe that you can sense the pathos that inspires us."

An elderly man, an expert in Sumerian-Akkadian scripts, couldn't help himself and began guffawing; another old man, whose interest in antiquity had more to do with its erotica than its grammatical formulae, snickered and covered his face with his hands; a biologist and notorious Don Juan wore an ironic look and adjusted the part in his hair. But the entire assembly hall applauded Balmcalfkin, and in the teachers' room afterward people pressed his hand and made conversation.

Following a brief meeting with his students, Balmcalfkin decided to teach a course on Novalis.

Balmcalfkin's first lecture was magnificent. He leaned over the podium, against a backdrop of rough boards, and periodically glanced at his notes.

"Colleagues," he said, "we will now plunge into the most exquisite stuff that has ever existed on this earth. We will leave behind strait-jacketed classicism to take in the captivating music of the human soul, to see with our own eyes the still dew-covered bouquet of youth, love, and death."

Balmcalfkin's voice, modulated like a nightingale's song; his tall, slender figure, without the slightest slump; his hands cupped behind his back; his inspired eyes—all of this swept his listeners off their feet, and when during the next lecture Balmcalfkin began to read out the original texts, translate them on the spot and provide commentary, citing God alone knows how many poets and in how many languages, many of the youths were utterly stunned, and the young ladies fell in love with Balmcalfkin. All the young students were seized by a physical yearning for youth, love, and death.

All winter long Balmcalfkin's lectures were overflowing. Spring came and weeds began to poke through the bricks of the city sidewalks;

the sun was warmer; Balmcalfkin was already wearing his summer suit and white canvas shoes.

When he walked down the street, young ladies with bouquets of flowers would follow him, talking about youth, love, and death. When he stopped by to visit the young students, he was greeted with respectful bows.

Balmcalfkin became the city's idol.

Some of the students took up studying Italian in order to read about the love of Petrarch and Laura in the original; others began reviewing Latin so as to read the correspondence of Abélard and Héloïse; still others attacked Greek grammar in order to read Plato's *Symposium*.

More and more impromptu lectures by Balmcalfkin were arranged.

A golden age, a golden age, he thought in agitation, and went on running around the city like an orchestra conductor.

One moment he would be reading about love and discussing *praegnans constructio* with someone; the next he would conduct an impromptu interpretation of Dante's *Inferno* and, reaching the middle of the fifth canto—Paolo and Francesca—would pace the room, overwhelmed; next he would provide commentary on Hector's parting from Andromache; after that he would give a lecture on Vyacheslav Ivanov.[44]

The university in the little town lasted for one year. Vrangel was driven off, and the university was given orders that it employ at least ten Marxists. At that time no Marxists were to be found; they were all busy at the front lines. So the university was closed. The classrooms housed in the granary were closed, the formal meetings and impromptu lectures in the assembly hall of the girls' preparatory school ceased. The needlessly exquisite climate and southern steppes invited Balmcalfkin to stay. Seizing his belongings, he returned to Petersburg.

13. AUTUMN

BALMCALFKIN spent the whole summer living in his tower, in the noble surroundings he found so congenial.

In late autumn, when scarlet leaves began to whirl in the air and rustle underfoot, he packed his books, his only treasured possessions, into his tarpaulin suitcase. He took one last stroll through the small but intricate, labyrinthine, English park, which was falling into disrepair. He moved on into the neighboring park, gazed sadly at Eve, her hand covering her forehead; black twigs could be seen between her hand and body (a prank played by local kids). He glanced at Adam—the continuation of Adam's spine was spattered with filth.

He sat down on a bench. On this very bench he had sat, just a few days ago, with Musya Dalmatova, but he had not spoken of love, but instead about how fine it is to live as a pair, how he no longer feared women. He recalled the golden words of Maria Petrovna's response:

"A woman should behave as a mother to her husband."

For Balmcalfkin did need a mother, who would love and caress him, kiss him on the forehead and call him her darling boy.

"My God, how beautiful this park is, how beautiful . . ." whispered Balmcalfkin, rising from the bench.

And although he was not a nobleman, he felt sorry for the noblemen, for the wrecked estates, for the cows with names like Ariadne, Diana or Amalchen, Gretchen; for all the many lady relatives and hangers-on, forever chilly in their gray, brown, or black kerchiefs, for the samovars, jams, albums, and games of solitaire laid out with trembling hands.

Can it really be, he thought, *that now all of that is gone, no one is moved by rose gardens somewhere in Kharkov province? Female adolescents who used to read only Pushkin, Gogol, and Lermontov and to dream of being saved by a Demon; is not the life of these former adolescents now dreadful, when the life they once knew, for which they were created, has ended? Are they not now surrounded by an unimaginably dreadful despair?*

14. AFTER THE TOWER

FOR BALMCALFKIN there began once again a time of studying in the city libraries, reading the letters and essays of the humanists' little helpers, humble soldiers in the army led by Petrarch and Boccaccio. He saw Petrarch wandering with Philippe de Cabassoles around the environs of Vaucluse, engaged in conversations on scientific and religious subjects, and spending the whole night reading; then Clement VI would appear, awarding prebends for Latin verses; or Henri Estienne, the famous publisher; or Étienne Dolet, who claimed that the Lord had put him on earth in order to wrestle the French language away from barbarism.

Next, with sorrow, he read reports of disputes. He felt that the extreme decline of the humanist sciences and the extreme scarcity of good books allowed for only empty chatter, and not a learned dispute.

Sometimes he leafed through new books. He was astonished by the style.

Today's writers, he thought, *are distinguished by an impossible style, by the utter absence of the spirit of criticism, by extreme ignorance and extraordinary audacity.*

Akim Akimovich began visiting Balmcalfkin. He would whisper information about his friends into his ear. One was living with his mama and working on occultism; another had developed a passion for little dogs; a third was a former drug addict, and his epiphanies were dubious to the highest degree. A fourth was busy bootlicking in other areas.

Balmcalfkin laughed.

"My friends are the elect, I will never believe slander. There is nothing higher than friendship."

But he began to take note that the young man so taken with the radio really did kiss his mama with a certain excess of passion. They would just be sitting there and suddenly tongue would meet tongue, and the tension of their tongues was so tremendous that they both, son and mother alike, would turn red from the effort. And he did notice that another one of his acquaintances was on quite familiar terms with disreputable people and that, upon meeting them, he would wiggle his rear. And a third was often unnaturally jumpy. But Balmcalfkin went on reassuring himself that this was all stuff and nonsense, and that friendship was higher than all else in the world! At this point a quotation from Cicero would be recited.

The unknown poet was waiting for Kostya Kissenkin in Catherine Square.

He stood a while.

Walked around the garden.

He noticed Misha Kittenkin sitting on one of the benches with the actress B. He was whispering something tenderly into her ear when he noticed the unknown poet and smiled unpleasantly with the corner of his mouth.

He's still collecting biographical information about Euphratesky, thought the unknown poet, turned his back to him and walked off toward the gate.

He bought a newspaper.

Sat down on a bench.

Read a bit.

Lowered the newspaper.

Then he remembered the philosopher with the bushy mustache and mentally bowed down before his tenacity; in times past this philosopher might well have expected to lead a magnificent department. Respectful young people would have been unable to tear themselves away from his books. But now there were no departments, or books, or respectful young people.

He yawned.

He thought lazily: *It is a heresy that the powerful pagan poets and philosophers disappeared with the victory of Christianity. They were met with no understanding, not even the most primitive kind of understanding, and they had to perish. What loneliness those last philosophers must have felt, what loneliness...*

He noticed Maria Petrovna Dalmatova on a bench.

He got up and went over to her.

"What are you doing here?" he asked.

"Reading your book," answered Musya, smiling.

"You'd do better to read Triniton. It's more appropriate for girls. What can you get out of this dry nonsense?"

I am losing the gift of speech, he thought, *utterly losing it.*

And he suddenly looked around sorrowfully, sorrowfully.

15. KINDRED SPIRITS

VERY DEEP into autumn, after Balmcalfkin had left his tower and moved back to the city, the unknown poet entered his room.

Balmcalfkin, as always when he was working, sat wearing a Chinese dressing gown; a peaked embroidered skullcap perched upon his head.

"I am studying Sanskrit," he said. "It is crucial that I obtain an understanding of Oriental wisdom; I will tell you in strictest confidence that I am writing a book called *The Hierarchy of Meanings*."

"Yes." Resting his chin on his stick, the unknown poet laughed. "The thing is that the modern age will ridicule you."

"What rubbish," exclaimed Balmcalfkin, irritated. "Me, ridiculed! Everyone loves and respects me!"

The unknown poet frowned and drummed his fingers against the glass.

"For the present day," he turned his head, "this is just entertainment. Take Triniton. One could argue about his greatness, but nevertheless, he is a true poet."

"I heard that Triniton collects poetic objects," noted Balmcalfkin, gazing at the back of the unknown poet's head.

"Well, it's because of his great love for poetry. To outsiders a great love often appears ridiculous."

"What about Mikhail Alexandrovich Kittenkin?" asked Balmcalfkin, thoughtfully.

Leaving Balmcalfkin, the unknown poet set out in response to an invitation received that morning.

Mad youths sat on unpainted iron beds. One flashed his pince-nez, another sang out his own poem in a birdlike voice. A third, keeping time with a foot, listened to his own pulse. In the middle sat their wife-in-common—a second-year student at the pedagogical institute. The room's bare wall reflected a window with a flowerpot.

The unknown poet entered.

"We want to talk with you about poetry. We consider you a kindred spirit," they said, breaking off their various activities.

"Dasha, get off that chair," said the man in the pince-nez. The pedagogical student turned and flopped down on a bed.

"Gompertsky," the man in the pince-nez proffered a hand, "thrown out of university for lack of academic excellence."

"Brokenko, agricultural specialist," sang out the second man in a birdlike voice.

"Runoff, future animal gelder," the third man introduced himself.

"Oriolova," the pedagogical student proffered her hand and scratched a finger across the unknown poet's palm.

"Dasha, rustle us up some tea," boomed the future medical assistant in an aside.

"I want to listen." Dasha started laughing, twisting her head to the side.

"What did I say!" The man in the pince-nez squealed hysterically, executed a pirouette, and gracefully swatted her on the derrière with the tip of his boot.

The pedagogical student skulked off.

Now I've done it, thought the unknown poet, turning to face the window. *This is no place to talk about the affinity of poetry and intoxication*, he thought, *they won't understand anything I say about the need to form the world anew through language, about descending into the hell of meaninglessness, the hell of wild sounds and shrieks, in order to find a new melody of the world. They won't understand that the poet, no matter what, must be Orpheus and descend into hell, albeit an artificial one, charm it and return with Eurydice—art; and that as Orpheus he is doomed to look back and see his dear shade disappear. How unreasonable are they who think that art is possible without this descent into hell.*

Methods of isolating oneself and descending into hell: alcohol, love, madness...

And instantaneously before his eyes dashed the lurid hotels where he, with a flock of half-witted vagabonds, slowly climbed up endless staircases lit by the dimmed light of nighttime. Every night the rocking of mattresses on which lay sailors, thieves, and former officers, and women's legs either under them or on top of them. Next came into focus the boarded-up, frightened streets surrounding the hotel. And he was running again, six years ago, fearing for his life, along the snowy veil of the Neva, for he was bound to observe hell, and he saw how cohorts of entirely white people were led out by night.

In the west the earthly sun still shines...[45]

a certain poetess will say afterward, but he knows for sure that the old sun will never again show its face, that you can't step in the same river twice, that a new circle begins on top of the two-thousand-year circle, that he is running ever deeper and deeper into the old, two-thousand-year circle. He dashes through the final age of humanism and dilettantism, the age of pastorals and Trianon,[46] the age of philosophy and criticism, and through the Italian gardens, amid fireworks and sweet Latin-Italian panegyrics, and comes running into the palace of Lorenzo the Magnificent. He is greeted there in the manner of an old friend who has been long absent.

"How is your work going up there?" they ask him. He is silent, goes pale, and disappears. And sees himself standing in torn boots, unkempt and insane, before a misty high tribunal.

The Last Judgment, he thinks.

"What did you do there on earth?" Dante says, rising. "Did you abuse widows and orphans?"

"I did not abuse anyone, but I created an author," he answered quietly. "I corrupted his soul and replaced it with laughter."

"Was it my laughter," said Gogol, rising, "laughter through tears?"[47]

"Not your laughter," answered the unknown poet still more quietly, lowering his eyes.

"Perhaps it was my laughter?" asked Juvenal, rising.

"Alas, it was not your laughter. I allowed this author to immerse us in the sea of life and to laugh at us."

And Horace shook his head and whispered something to Persius. And everyone became serious and terribly sorrowful.

"Were you all very miserable?"

"Very miserable," answered the unknown poet.

"And you allowed this author to laugh at you?"

"You have no place here among us, despite all of your art," said Dante, rising.

The unknown poet fell. The guards picked him up and threw him into the horrific city. How placidly he walked down the street! There was nothing left for him to do in the world. He sat down at a late-night café table. Balmcalfkin came up the staircase and approached him.

"There's no use in grieving," he said. "We are all of us unhappy in this world. After all, I also dreamed of carrying on the torch of renaissance, and look what happened."

The unknown poet was back in the room.

"You are striving for meaningless art. Art demands the opposite. It demands that we give meaning to the meaningless. Man is surrounded by meaninglessness on all sides. You wrote down a certain combination of words, a meaningless selection of words organized by a rhythmic scheme; you were meant to look deeply into this selection of words, to feel it deeply from within—perhaps it has allowed a new awareness of the world to slip in, a new form of what surrounds us, for every era has its own characteristic form or awareness of its surroundings."

"Give us a concrete example!" yelled those present.

It has to be simple, he thought, *simple.*

"The windows of dressers, the trees of parks...what does that mean?"

"Nothing," they yelled from their beds, "it's meaningless!"

"No," he said, fingering the slips of paper in his pocket. "Look carefully at the dresser."

"Dressers don't have windows," they yelled from their beds, "houses have windows!"

"Fine," smiled the unknown poet. "So, houses are dressers. But you agree that parks have trees, right?"

"Right," answered those present.

"So what we get is: dresser-houses have people living in them, the same way parks have trees growing."

"We don't understand!" yelled those present.

"Some kind of improvisation!"

"So that's what it means," said the unknown poet: "the windows of dressers, the trees of parks."

"Well, I'll be damned," hissed the men in beds when the unknown poet disappeared.

"Dasha, forget about the tea."

"But the poems that bastard writes," frowned the man in the pince-nez. "Beyonsensical and not beyonsensical at the same time. Go figure."[48]

Gompertsky went to the kitchen, sat on the windowsill and addressed Dasha:

"Make me an omelet." He began drumming his fingers on the table. "I'm a cultured man, a neurasthenic, you need to love me more than—" he pointed at the door. "I went to university, I am a refined type, whereas those guys—total ignorance. Oy, tra-la-la, tra-la-la . . ." he sang out.

"But for what it's worth, Dasha, we're your harem—you're our padishah." He went up to her.

"Ugh, buzz off," she pushed him away, "the omelet's burning."

16. AN EVENING OF OLD-FASHIONED MUSIC

AFTER he moved from the country back to the city, Balmcalfkin resumed offering free lessons in Egyptian, Greek, Latin, Italian, French, Spanish, and Portuguese. He had to succor the degenerating culture.

Thus, on this bright autumn day, in his room, against a backdrop of family photographs, he sat reading the Egyptian tale of the shipwreck survivor. He was decoding hieroglyphs and writing down words on individual slips of paper.

Sebaid—a commission
Mer—head of the city
Nefer—beautiful

And, gazing into space, he heard the illustrated birds singing, the painted boats speeding past, the palm trees swaying. And the exquisite image of Isis rose up, followed by that of the last empress.

Outside, in the courtyard below his windows, young pioneers were playing tag and blindman's bluff. Some were picking their noses like real-life children, and occasionally bursting into song:

We will build a brand-new world...[49]

or

We're off to the high seas...[50]

Meanwhile, on the canals and rivers that intersected the city, young Soviet ladies sat in boats, while behind them a suitor in a leather jacket would be playing the accordion, or the balalaika, or the guitar.

And at the sight of them the Petersburg madmen would be overtaken by such despondency that they would weep tearlessly, with shoulders hunched and fingers clenched.

The poet Triniton, meanwhile, returning to his hole-in-the-wall after what he had seen, lay down on his bed, turned to face the wall, and shuddered as if from the cold.

Yekaterina Ivanovna, meanwhile, in her unheated room, paced around holding a sheaf of papers. My God, how she had wished for a child from Alexander Petrovich. She remembered how Alexander Petrovich had accompanied her up the staircase, lined with mirrors and trees in planters, and had proposed to her, and she had led him into her pink, utterly pink bedroom. How he had read her poems deep into the night and how they had sat afterward in the bright dining room. She remembered that the tablecloth had been colorful and the napkins also colorful. And she remembered her father, a respected civil servant in one of the ministries. And her mother, tightly buttoned and stiff. And Grigory the footman in a new double-breasted livery jacket and white gloves.

Kovalyov too felt suddenly old in his soul at the sight of the boats, and looked around with horror and felt that time was racing, racing, but he had still not yet begun to live, and something inside him began screaming that he was no longer a sublieutenant, that he would never again mount a horse, never again ride around the circular riding track in the Summer Garden, never again salute, never again exchange bows with finely dressed young ladies.

Balmcalfkin had noted down a whole pile of words. He looked them up in his German-language book of Egyptian grammar, figured out the tenses.

Everything was ready, but the pupil hadn't shown up. One hour passed, another. Balmcalfkin walked over to the wall.

It's just before six o'clock. Maria Petrovna won't come for a while yet.

Today we will go to Konstantin Petrovich Kissenkin to listen to old-fashioned music, he thought with satisfaction.

The clock in the landlady's apartment chimed six o'clock, then six thirty.

In Troubadorova's room sat four suitors, drinking tea from saucers; none of the saucers matched. They were discussing the theory of relativity while by turns one and then the next would inconspicuously press his foot to Troubadorova's. Occasionally a spoon would fall, or a handkerchief would be picked up off the floor—and a hand would seize Eudochia Ivanovna's knee.

These were Troubadorova's pupils, and pupils, as is well known, love to chase after their teachers.

The clocks chimed seven o'clock.

Eudochia Ivanovna sat at the piano. Chibiryachkin, the widest and tallest of the four, sat next to her and began to clean his enormous fingernails with a match.

When will this riffraff clear out, he looked over his shoulder at his comrades, *damned hound dogs!*

Indeed, one of the hound dogs, a lanky twenty-eight-year-old with a red beard, was staring carnivorously at the back of Eudochia Ivanovna's head. Another one, short, wearing tall boots, slid his gaze along her thighs. The third, fat, with a shaved head, was sitting in an armchair.

Their hostess, playing a sensuous love song, was thinking:

"Oh dear, oh dear, how that virgin excites me!"

At eight o'clock Musya Dalmatova entered Balmcalfkin's room. Balmcalfkin took off his skullcap, wrapped his neck in a reddish down muffler, and buttoned his overcoat all the way up.

"I'm sensitive to the cold," he said. He put on a soft hat and took up his stick decorated with Japanese monkeys. Musya took his hand and they set out.

"Oh, if only you knew," said Balmcalfkin as they walked, "how lovely Classical Egyptian is! It's not that hard; you only have to know around six hundred symbols. But it is a shame that there is still no full dictionary of the Egyptian language anywhere on earth."

"What language family does Egyptian belong to?" asked Musya Dalmatova.

"Hamito-Semitic," answered Balmcalfkin.

"Where did the columns come from?" asked Musya.

"From their striving for eternity," answered Balmcalfkin after pausing to think. "My goodness, no," he caught himself: "the prototype of the columns was tree trunks."

When they stood before the house in which Kostya Kissenkin occupied a room, Musya said:

"I saw astonishing Egyptian jewelry in a museum once: rings made of lapis lazuli."

They went through to the courtyard, quite foul-smelling. The cats, upon seeing them, peeked out of the open trash pit, leapt out, and ran off one after the other. One cat, a ginger, ran across their path.

Balmcalfkin felt something unpleasant underfoot. Before entering he spent a long time wiping his foot on the fragrant daisies growing here and there in clumps.

They climbed up the stairs with their well-worn depressions. They stood a while. They knocked.

The door was opened by a lodger, a thirty-five-year-old red-haired girl with a cheap cigarette hanging out of her mouth, wearing a blue dress with roses and dreaming of the city nights of the nineteen-eights and tens. She would go on dreaming of them for her whole life, even as a gray-haired old lady.

"You've got visitors," she said, opening the door into Kostya Kissenkin's room.

Kostya Kissenkin and the unknown poet were sitting Turkish-style on the sofa, drinking Turkish coffee out of little cups. One wall had been decked out from top to bottom with kitsch of extraordinary vulgarity. There were all kinds of coin boxes in the shape of rude gestures, ashtrays and paperweights made to look like a hand groping breasts, all manner of little boxes with "moving bodies," little pictures in gold frames curtained in raspberry velvet just in case, and eighteenth-century books treating the corresponding subjects and situations, equipped with engravings.

The wall across from the sofa was decked out with the most fantastical and bizarre works of the Baroque—snuffboxes, clocks, engravings, works of Góngora and Marino[51] in red and green parchment and stamped Morocco leather bindings—while on a stunning straddle-legged table lay the sonnets of Shakespeare.

"All over Europe," Kostya Kissenkin continued their conversation, "there is growing interest in the Baroque, in this style wholly complete, as you said, in its incompleteness, extravagant and somewhat insane in and of itself."

And they leaned over Góngora's portrait.

"Every word in Góngora has multiple meanings," the poet lifted his head, "it is used by him on one level, and another, and a third. Every kernel in Góngora is Dante's epic in miniature. But what an incredibly desperate and tawdry artistry, attempting to hide its inner unrest; and those beloved cheeks and neck that were once, in the golden age, real, living flowers—roses and lilies. To understand Góngora one must be a person with the requisite inclination, with a properly Hellenic frame of mind; this has now become clear, but it was not understood until recently."

The unknown poet leaned back against the wall.

That was the moment Musya Dalmatova and Balmcalfkin walked into the room.

"How cozy," said Balmcalfkin, not noticing the crudities above the friends' heads. "And you're sitting like Turks and drinking Turkish coffee. But it's so smoky in here. If you don't mind I'll open the window." He went over. Opened the small top pane. "We wouldn't want Maria Petrovna to get a headache."

"Have you been waiting for us long?" he asked.

"We've been sitting here since yesterday evening reading Spanish, English, and Italian poets," answered Kostya Kissenkin, "and exchanging opinions."

"Has Aglaya Nikolayevna come?" asked Balmcalfkin.

"We're expecting her any minute now," answered Kostya Kissenkin.

There was a knock at the front door. Kostya Kissenkin leapt up toward the foyer. A moment later Aglaya Nikolayevna came in, gaunt and wriggling like a snake. Blue fox fur lay on her shoulders. A large emerald sparkled on her breast, but there was nothing on her ears. Kostya Kissenkin was wriggling along next to her, and a little dog was bouncing along on her other side.

"The evening of old-fashioned music will now take place," Balmcalfkin whispered into Maria Petrovna Dalmatova's ear.

Everyone moved into the neighboring room.

Already seated were deaf old ladies and little old men with sidewhiskers and goatees, bouncing young ladies, elderly young men lisping pretentiously as in the days of their youth. The walls were hung with portraits in round golden frames. The grand piano was open, its keys and strings trembling.

Aglaya Nikolayevna was bowing left and right.

Flowers were brought to her—roses, white. She took a sniff, bowed, smiled. The thin hands of the little old ladies and men clapped.

"She hasn't changed a whit in all these years," they whispered to one another, "our beloved Aglaya Nikolayevna."

"In 191— she was N's lover," whispered one elderly young man to another elderly young man.

"She has such a marvelous little dog," whispered one of the bouncing young ladies to another bouncing young lady.

Aglaya Nikolayevna sat down.

Once again, the hands were raised, again the keys were pressed, again pure music fluttered wildly like a butterfly.

Two young ladies presented lilies.

"Ah, Aglaya Nikolayevna," said Kostya Kissenkin, "today you have given us a real treat."

The dining room was suffused with light. On the walls, the few remaining plates from the imperial porcelain factory with their landscapes and portraits gleamed with gilt. Bottles of wine and decanters of vodka stood on the table; the little glasses sparkled. And all around was something pink, something red, something white, something pale blue. Nothing was missing.

But the little old men and the elderly young men had the sense that this was just a copy, that everything real had died, that this was a kind of recollection, always less vivid than actuality. They suddenly felt sorrowful, so sorrowful . . . Furthermore, they noted that in order to arrange this evening certain objects from the dining room had disappeared (had been sold).

"Bring me my purse," Musya Dalmatova whispered to Balmcalfkin, "it's in Konstantin Petrovich's room."

The moon illuminated Kostya Kissenkin's room. The wind lifted up the edge of the velvet that was covering certain illustrations. And then Balmcalfkin saw something that he was not meant to see.

He crushed the purse in his hands, opened his mouth and sat down.

But what is that? he thought. *What is that! A person with such subtle taste and then* . . . Above him the velvet was alternately covering and again revealing dozens of naked bodies, men's and women's, in all manner of positions.

He felt that something was not right in this house.

"Snakes," he screamed, "snakes!" and ran headlong out of the room.

And back at the table it seemed to him that there, leaning over, leaning back, laughing loudly, speaking, leaning in, lifting forks to their mouths with food of various colors, were snakes with little green hands and that only he and Maria Petrovna were alive.

He was particularly struck by the unknown poet. He noticed that the poet was utterly white, that his eyes were greenish, that he was no longer a young man at all.

"Eat, eat," Kostya Kissenkin's aunties ran around the table, "eat, eat."

And above their heads was not crystal, but drops of light—the chandeliers were crystal.

17. A JOURNEY WITH ASPHODELOV

THE REMAINING leaves on the black branches of the city trees burned crimson gold, and an unexpected warmth spread over the city, beneath a transparent blue sky. With this unexpected return of summer, it seems to me that my heroes imagine themselves part of a certain Philostratus, one who drifts down along with the last autumn leaves, falls along with the houses that line the embankment, is destroyed along with the people who once were.

"Many of us have visions of a beautiful youth," intoned the unknown poet.

"I've finally caught you. You are all deviants"—laughter was heard— "that's why you're being followed by a pretty little boy."

The unknown poet's drinking companion turned his head on his bullish neck, slapped his knee with a plump palm, smiled with all of his fat face and adjusted his pince-nez.

"Let's drink!" he yelled. "I love only women. I am not interested in boys, whether imaginary or real. But women have soft little cushion-hands . . . Me, I like to savor all of a woman, from the top of her head to the tip of her toes."

"I gather you're no longer writing poetry?" asked the unknown poet.

"I've gotten myself set up at a certain publishing house. I write edifying fairy tales for kids," answered the good-natured fat man, adjusting his pince-nez. "The idiots pay money for it. Plus I write little articles here and there for journals under a pseudonym," Asphodelov continued, savoring every word. "I praise prole-lit, write that its heyday will not only come but has already begun. They pay money for that too. I'm now intimately acquainted with all the proletarian literature, I'm considered an authoritative critic. Comrade," he grabbed a waiter by his apron, "another bottle."

The waiter listlessly shuffled off for the beer.

"What I'd really like to do now is take a fishing trip..." Asphodelov gazed fondly out the window.

They went out. The carriage driver cantered slowly down Trinity Street.

"Why don't you write criticism?" asked Asphodelov. "It's so easy."

"Out of stupidity," answered the unknown poet, "and laziness. I am lazy, ideologically lazy, and impractical on principle."

"Aristocratic manners," Asphodelov chuckled. "In our day you must be rid of aristocratic manners. And really, you're all such idiots!" he fumed. "You have absolutely no will to live. You're not willing to stand on the side of the modern age, you don't want to make any money."

The unknown poet placed his hands on his amethyst:

"You don't understand anything, my friend, you are a slithering animal."

"*I'm* slithering!" Asphodelov was irate. "You're the one drinking on my dime and blathering all kinds of rubbish! You're a cruel man, you should be ashamed, insulting me like that."

Asphodelov lifted his shoulders and began taking deep breaths.

"This is boring, I'm going to watch *Swan Lake*." The unknown poet got up, quickly bid Asphodelov farewell and made to jump out of the carriage.

"Where are you going?" asked Asphodelov.

"To the Academic Theater of Opera and Ballet," answered the unknown poet.

"Cabbie, to the Mariinsky!" the pork-barrel in pince-nez rose, sat down again, and embraced the unknown poet.

The driver headed down Rossi Street.

"I too was once devoted to poetry," lamented Asphodelov. "I love poetry perhaps more than anyone else on earth, but I have no talent." He squeezed the unknown poet to his chest. They were silent a while.

"You don't understand anything in my poetry, no one understands anything!" chuckled the unknown poet.

"What do you mean—something beyonsensical?" Asphodelov was surprised.

"There's different kinds of beyonsense," answered the unknown poet. "Sometime I'll take you to see the real beyonsense poets. You'll see how they tug new meaning out from under the dunce caps of words."[52]

"You're not talking about those green youths in tasseled brocade caps, the ones who had those strange last names?"

"Poetry is a particular kind of activity," answered the unknown poet. "It's a terrifying spectacle and also dangerous, when you take a few words, juxtapose them in an unusual way and sit down to observe them, first one night, then another, then a third, all the while thinking about these words you've juxtaposed. And you start to notice: a hand of sense reaches out from under one word and shakes the hand that has appeared out from under another word, and a third offers its hand in turn, and you are consumed entirely by the totally new world opening up beyond these words."

And the unknown poet kept on speaking for a long time. But the driver was already pulling up to the Academic Theater. The unknown poet leapt out of the carriage, and behind him the pork-barrel in pince-nez rose and paid the driver.

In the unknown poet's pocket were: a pile of unfinished poems, an unusual pencil in a velvet pouch, a coin with the head of Helios, some old book in parchment binding, a piece of yellowed Brussels lace.

In a box almost directly across from the stage sat Shacklekin with Natasha Holubets and some friends. The unknown poet put on his glasses and bowed solemnly, looked to the right: in the same row sat Kissenkin, a little further off—Kittenkin, and in the first row—Balmcalfkin and the philosopher with the bushy mustache.

Today our whole synclite has gathered, he thought, *it's labor-union day, we all got free tickets from our admirers and friends.*

*

Lazily the orchestra began playing, lazily the curtain rose, lazily the first act transpired.

During intermission Balmcalfkin thrice walked furiously past Konstantin Petrovich Kissenkin.

"Degenerate so-called lover of the arts!"

Kostya Kissenkin's small eyes illuminated his rosy cheeks, and his tiny pearly teeth laughed.

Kostya Kissenkin got up and went over to Balmcalfkin. Balmcalfkin, without looking, said hello and walked on.

In the foyer Balmcalfkin noticed the philosopher and the unknown poet, tranquilly conversing on the star in the parquet.

The unknown poet looked at Balmcalfkin, but Balmcalfkin walked past him as though he hadn't noticed.

18. BALMCALFKIN IMAGINES THAT HIS FRIENDS ARE CHASING AFTER HIM

ALREADY the trees retained not a single leaf. Already the moon was covering with false snow the limestone and asphalt sidewalks, and the sidewalks made of boards, of eight-sided and four-sided wooden blocks, of round elongated black-gray stones. Already its light was making ethereal the heavy two-hundred-year-old buildings with their columns, their porticos, their pediments and friezes. Already in the murk of evenings, beneath the yellow lights affixed to the shop signs, affectionate or arguing, priapic pairs, trios, and quartets glided past along the sidewalk. The winter theaters and variety show venues had long since opened, and the clubs, libraries, and schools were habitually and unhurriedly preparing for the anniversary;[53] the plump and thin owners of private shops had long since gotten used to displaying portraits of the leaders and decorating them as best they could; the festivities already had a popular and non-compulsory feel to them.

But my heroes were still attempting to sit things out in their tall tower of humanism, to contemplate and understand the age from there. True, they no longer felt like heroes; true, their sense of duty was gradually turning into habit. True, the unknown poet's divinations had long since run out, and Balmcalfkin now spoke about supporting culture ever more rarely and ineffectually. And the philosopher spoke ever more rarely of philosophy, and more and more of his youth. He didn't write books anymore; after all, they were not fated for publication.

Finally, real snow began falling in large white flakes.

*

The unknown poet was standing with Kostya Kissenkin in the court-yard of the Stroganov Palace, watching the dark-blue snow, listening to the buzzing of the trolley cables coming from the street.

"Oh, here you are, you snakes!" hissed Balmcalfkin viciously, appearing at the gate.

"What's wrong with him?" asked Kostya Kissenkin in astonishment. "What is he so angry about?"

Balmcalfkin leapt away from the gate and ran off, lanky, thin, at a gallop, bumping into the railings along the Moyka Embankment.

What's wrong with me? he thought. *What's wrong with me?*

And he felt with his back that his friends were running after him and prancing, and stamping their feet, and waving their hands around, making fun of him.

What's wrong with all of us? He felt tears coming and ran smack into Maria Petrovna Dalmatova. Maria Petrovna was walking in radiance, surrounded by snowy stars, to the Gostiny Dvor to shop for pretty shoes. Balmcalfkin calmed down and went with her to choose pretty shoes at Gostiny Dvor.

"Let's hurry," Musya picked up the pace, "it's nearly five o'clock, the shops will close soon."

Gostiny Dvor was brightly lit. Beneath the arcades Balmcalfkin followed Maria Petrovna from one shop to the next. He saw the tall Peterhof tower, saw himself awaiting his friends with flowers. How clear everything had been then, how delightful! How joyful we were!

Giddy-up, giddy-up.

"Oh, these shoes aren't right at all," moaned Maria Petrovna.

Giddy-up, giddy-up, from one shop to the next Balmcalfkin followed her, as if following his star.

He hung back for a second and saw: moving, swaying, the unknown poet was coming toward him.

"You'll see," the unknown poet said, lifting his head, "how the person creating us lives."

19. INTERWORD

I AWOKE in a room with a rotunda looking out onto the street. It's quiet here, though God knows what goes on in the evenings. Some philosophizing superintendent with a crimson nose will surface out of the darkness, or a wolflike dog will run past, dragging a person. Or two passersby, their collars lifted, will stop by the lamppost and, swaying, give each other a light. Or a loud shriek will light up the neighborhood. Or a man will fall asleep in the stairwell on his own vomit, like it's a carpet. But what a city it once was, so clean and festive! There were almost no people. The columns rose up like odes to the flocks of clouds; it smelled of grass and mint everywhere. In the courtyards goats plucked at grass, rabbits ran around, roosters sang.

20. THE APPEARANCE OF A FIGURE

LOOK, I've wrapped myself in the Chinese dressing gown. Here I am examining the collection of kitsch. Here I am holding the stick with the amethyst.

How time drags on! The bookstalls are still closed. Perhaps in the meantime it'd be better to get into coin collecting or read that tractatus on the link between intoxication and poetry.

No one suspects that this book emerged from the juxtaposition of words. This does not contradict the fact that something flashes before every artist in childhood. This is the fundamental antinomy (contradiction). The artist is given a kind of task outside of language, but then, throwing words around and juxtaposing them, he creates and subsequently comes to know his own soul. Thus, in my youth, by putting words together, I came to know the universe, and a whole world emerged for me in language and rose up from language. And it turned out that this world risen from language coincided astonishingly with actuality. But it's time, time . . .

It's already eleven o'clock. The bookstalls have opened, they've shipped in books from the regional libraries. Perhaps I will find a Dante, one of the first editions, or at least one of Bayle's encyclopedic dictionaries . . .[54]

"Welcome, welcome," chirped the bookseller. "There's been no sign of you for three days. We have books for you; if you will—here, up the ladder."

"And these striding Romans, reasoning Greeks, warbling Italians?

Do you have by any chance Philostratus's *The Life of Apollonius of Tyana*?"[55]

"Take your pick, take your pick."

"Not too expensive?"

"Cheap, very cheap."

"Where's archaeology?"

"Up the ladder to the right. Here, let me help you with it."

"You have such lovely editions."

"Of course, we aim to please the customer."

"Have you seen Balmcalfkin lately? Tall, nearly transparent, with a Japanese stick."

"Of course, of course, I know him. He hasn't come in a long time."

"What about the lady in the hat with feathers?"

"She was here yesterday after lunch."

"And the tall young man?"

"The one interested in drawings? He was here three days ago."

"And did a young man with blue eyes and a turned-up nose come asking for Euphratesky's books?"

Night. Down below lies white-blue snow, up above a starry blue sky.

I put bottles of wine out on the table.

Balmcalfkin arrived first and went to examine my books.

"We all love books," he said quietly. "Our philological education and interests are what distinguish us from the new people."

I invited my hero to be seated.

An hour later all of my heroes had gathered, and we sat down to table.

"You know," I turned to the unknown poet, "I followed you and Balmcalfkin one night."

"You are always following us spiritually," he broke in and looked at me.

"We are in Rome," he began. "Undoubtedly in Rome and in intoxication; I felt this, and words tell me this at night."

He lifted an Apulian rhyton.

"To Julia Domna!" he lowered his head and, standing, drank.[56]

Kissenkin rose elegantly:

"To refined art!"

Kittenkin leapt up:

"To a science of literature!"

Triniton teared up:

"To *la belle France*!"

Balmcalfkin lifted a Renaissance-era goblet. Everything went quiet.

"I drink to the ruin of the fifteenth century," he croaked, spread his fingers wide, and dropped the goblet.

I gave Piranesi engravings to all of my heroes.

Everyone sank into mourning. Yekaterina Ivanovna alone did not understand.

"Why are you all so gloomy?" she went around clamoring, "why are you so glum!"

The stove crackled, throwing sparks. My heroes and I sat around it in a semicircle on the carpet.

Kissenkin stood up.

"Let's start a collective novella," he suggested.

I got up and lit a candle.

"Go ahead," I said.

"From childhood I have been confounded," he began, sitting down in an armchair, "by kitsch. I am convinced that it has its own laws, its own style. One time I was told that a certain former privy councillor's wife was selling off the contents of her room. I hurried over. Imagine a former smoking room in a bureaucrat's house: a Turkish divan; a whole array of ashtrays shaped like shells, palms, and leaves, on tables high and low; little pouffe chairs; a writing desk left intact for some unclear reason. Walls decorated with pictures of actresses from lowbrow Parisian theaters. Giving a bow, I entered. On the divan, a charming creature was singing and playing the guitar. Its resplendent bluish skirts after the fashion of the previous century, embroidered with golden bees, its feet in blunt-nosed silk slippers! 'What an astonishing secret councillor's wife you are,' I said, bowing. 'Oh no,' it laughed, 'I am a young lad!' And with a glance it indicated that I should sit on the stool next to the divan. 'You're not cold?' it asked and, not waiting for my answer, wrapped me in a cashmere shawl.

"Lowering its head, it began examining a book with talking flowers: 'The time of lovely Nana, *la dame aux camélias*, has passed,' it broke the silence and adjusted its luxurious locks. 'You are trying,' it said, 'to restore that departed, frivolous, and carefree time.'"

The unknown poet sat down in the armchair:

"It was a girl though, after all. Sunk deep in the snowy Petersburg night, it had spent its early youth on the streets. It had loved silvery buildings, fast drivers, violin players in the cafés, and English military ditties."

The unknown poet smiled, got up from the armchair and walked over to the window.

Triniton sat down in the chair and continued:

"Looking at me, it spread its fan. It had been born not far from Kiev, on a modest estate."

Triniton ceded his spot and Kittenkin sat down in the chair with pomp:

"But in the evenings its mother had spoken of Paris, of the Champs-Élysées and cabriolets, and at sixteen it ran away to Petersburg with a ballet dancer. It loved Petersburg like a northern Paris."

Balmcalfkin shuddered and roused.

"Petersburg is the center of humanism," he interrupted the story from his seat.

"It's the center of Hellenism," broke in the unknown poet.

Kostya Kissenkin rolled over on the carpet.

"So interesting," Yekaterina Ivanovna clapped her hands, "what a fantastical story it's turning out to be!"

The philosopher took up his violin, sat in the armchair and, instead of continuing the story, was thoughtful for a moment. Then he got up and began playing a woozy café love song, keeping time with his foot.

Balmcalfkin, in horror, opened his already enormous eyes wide and reached out his hands to the philosopher beseechingly.

Don't, don't, the hands seemed to say.

And he suddenly ran out of the room and fell face first onto my bed.

But the philosopher, not noticing what had happened, was already playing a pure, beautiful melody, and his round face with its bushy mustache was profound and sorrowful.

I went over to the mirror. The candles were burning low. In the mirror I could see my heroes, sitting in a semicircle, and into the next room, where Balmcalfkin was standing by the window, sniffling and looking at us.

I lifted the blinds.

A dark morning was already dawning. The factory whistles could already be heard. And I see my heroes turning pale and disappearing, one after the other.

21. AGONIES

HAVING returned home, Balmcalfkin opened a carved wooden jewelry box, took out a fifteenth-century statuette and put it on a little trunk which evidently served as a pedestal.

"Deliver me from temptation, give me the strength to see the world as beautiful," he lowered his head, and when he lifted his face, it seemed to him that the statuette bore the face not of Elena Stavrogina, but of Maria Petrovna Dalmatova.

All night long Balmcalfkin remained deep in contemplation.

The canary was already singing in Troubadorova's room, Troubadorova herself, back home from some friendly revels, was already looking for some water to drink. Her slippers were already shuffling around the rooms, while Balmcalfkin was still intent on the image of that departing world where he had been youthful, utterly youthful.

By morning humanism had grown dim, and only the image of Maria Petrovna shone and continued to lead Balmcalfkin through the dark forest of life.

Evening found Balmcalfkin sitting by his desk and experiencing a certain agony. He had remembered that certain great individuals had practiced abstinence.

How can I, thought Balmcalfkin, *give in to temptation and take a wife? It may be that nature created me for something else entirely. I'll get married—and my memory will grow weak, my marvelous and obscure visions will disappear, gone too will be these lucid morning hours and peaceful nights. A woman will grow old by my side and I will notice that I too am growing old. Yes, it's a very difficult question.* Balmcalfkin began pacing around the room. *And perhaps I do not have the strength to take a wife, perhaps I am not a man. Perhaps my body is not fully mature. What then—I'd marry, and then horror . . .*

He became frightened; unthinking, he opened the door, but no one came in.

Balmcalfkin poured himself some cold tea and drank it down in one gulp.

And perhaps all of my masculine strength has shifted into my brain. What to do, what to do? He closed the door again. *I want to wed, but perhaps my body does not. But some people mature very late. Perhaps I too will mature at some point.*

Balmcalfkin began pacing even faster around the room.

Down below, in the collapsed basement, workers were making soap. Caustic steam seeped through the cracks in the floor. Outside, behind locked gates, the caretaker was sitting on a stool reading *Tarzan*, holding the book up close to his eyes.

And at this moment an exceptional twenty-three-year-old girl, Maria Petrovna Dalmatova, appeared in Balmcalfkin's room wearing a straw hat; it seemed she had picked flowers from the red floorboards and was offering them to Balmcalfkin. Balmcalfkin leaned over, lifted them to his nose, piously kissed them. Then she began dancing. Balmcalfkin heard extraordinary voices and saw that in her hands a tender stem was trembling and the bud swelling: a pale-blue flower was opening.

Oh, how corrupted is my brain. Balmcalfkin paced around the room.

At that moment the caretaker on duty finished reading *Tarzan*, paced a bit in front of the house, sat back down on his stool and dozed off . . .

Balmcalfkin appeared in the window.

What stars, he thought. *And under a starry sky like this I am imagining such filth. I am probably the vilest man in all the world.*

*

Balmcalfkin left the house. The windows of the houses were illuminated from within with a light sometimes harsh, sometimes sentimental, sometimes indifferent. Balmcalfkin walked along shivering in his autumn overcoat. This night he would test whether he was a man or not, and whether he could take a wife, could marry Maria Petrovna Dalmatova. Balmcalfkin went along, hurrying, from Lasalle Street to the October train station. Sometimes he would stop for a moment in the middle of the sidewalk, sometimes he would race ahead of the passersby and do something he had never done before—peek under ladies' hats.

He was looking for the most abominable woman possible, so that there could be no thought of love. He kept stopping, he was offered the services of youths, children almost, accompanied by lewd looks, vile little smiles, and exaggeratedly childish movements.

He felt rooted to the spot before them, while they, after exhausting their eloquence, lashed him with insults and hurried off into the distance. Sometimes Balmcalfkin would be overtaken by a creature on worn-down heels, with unrouged cheeks and an unimaginably yellowed ermine around its neck, and, attempting to retain its departed dignity, it would whisper:

"First gate on the right."

At long last he saw what he needed. Not far from Ligovka, a woman was coming out of a beer-hall—broad, heavy-boned, big-toothed.

"Do you believe in God?" Balmcalfkin addressed her.

"Of course I do!" The woman made the sign of the cross.

"Let's go, let's go." Balmcalfkin energetically dragged her down Nevsky.

"Not for less than three rubles!" she declared, sourly sizing up Balmcalfkin.

"It doesn't matter, it's of no importance," Balmcalfkin affirmed and kept dragging her further down Nevsky by the sleeve.

"Where are you dragging me? I live right nearby. And you're dragging me off to the devil knows where."

The woman stopped and jerked back her hand.

"Later, later, I'll come to you, but first you have to swear an oath."

"What, are you drunk or something? What kind of oath?"

Astonished, nearly frightened, she stared into Balmcalfkin's quivering face.

"Everything depends on this night," whispered Balmcalfkin, not listening. "All of my life to come depends on this night! I want to wed," Balmcalfkin moaned to himself. "To wed! The test is today, I am at a crossroads, a terrible crossroads. If I prove to be a man, then I will wed Maria Petrovna, if not, then I shall be a eunuch, a terrible eunuch of science!"

"What are you whispering for!" bellowed the woman. "How long are we going to keep on standing here in the open?"

"Let's go, let's go," Balmcalfkin began hurrying, "come on."

"You're what, taking me to the church?" The woman widened her yellow eyes.

But Balmcalfkin was already dragging her to the wall where an icon flickered.

"Swear that you aren't infected." He stopped before the icon. "Swear it!" he squealed.

"You low-down little devil!" Exasperated, the woman disappeared into the stairwell with her skirts swaying.

In her room with its muslin curtains Maria Petrovna sat at a small table, laying out cards to tell her fortune. Outside the window it was night, behind her on the wall was a photograph.

Around the chair she was sitting on stalked Cinderella the cat.

Maria Petrovna finished her fortune-telling and drifted off into a long-since shuttered singing studio back in the time of war communism. How she had dreamed of becoming a splendid singer! Here she is, standing by the piano singing, and here is her enraptured audience, the audience is breaking down the doors, the audience is making the walls expand, they are bringing Maria Petrovna chocolates, flowers, and expensive gifts. Maria Petrovna leaned on her elbows and, lost in thought, sank into the university she had recently graduated, with its arcades, its hallways, its many auditoriums, its professors and students. Had she dreamed of becoming an educated woman, of writing books about literature, of speaking in a circle of professors listening to her attentively?

The streets were already empty and only the policemen, neatly dressed, were whistling back and forth to one another, then walking around in pairs and conversing.

Maria Petrovna asked the cards: Who would she become? She saw Balmcalfkin, he was standing down below, pathetic, chilled, looking up at the illuminated window of the room where she was sitting and telling her fortune.

"He's in love, of course he's in love!" She began feeling warm and cozy.

Leaves rustling, bats flying around. She and Balmcalfkin walk toward the sea and sit down on a rock. Beneath the silvery moon, she gets up and sings, like a real singer having come from overseas on tour, and Balmcalfkin sits and looks at the sea, listening.

She glanced out the window: Was Balmcalfkin standing there? He was.

She saw what seemed like a bright morning. Balmcalfkin working; she standing, ironing his starched undergarments. Maria Petrovna glanced out the window: Was Balmcalfkin standing there? He was.

And it seemed to her that his eyes were plaintive.

But what to do about the wedding? Back at home, he sat in bed in the dead of night. The blanket lay on the floor, his graying hair stood on end. The wall flickered with moonlight. The whole room was permeated with it. *If I am an honest man, then I must marry Maria Petrovna Dalmatova. It's not right to string a girl along for a whole year.*

He got up in his nightshirt; the nightshirt was longer in front and shorter in the back. He got a candle out of the dresser, lit it, and waited for it to flare down. Finally, the candle gleamed bright as a star.

I have to distract myself, he thought. He wrapped himself in the blanket, sat at the table, and began comparing Pushkin with André Chénier.

Toujours ce souvenir m'attendrit et me touche.[57]

But despite his best intentions he got distracted from his comparison: quiet trees covered in yellow and reddish leaves quivered above his head. Maria Petrovna was sitting beneath them. In the distance the sea fluttered, and the wind sang.

Toward morning Balmcalfkin imagined the quietest of gardens. The sun inside churches, monks blowing their noses into their hands, blooming oleanders, the tender pink sea, church bells coughing like consumptives waking up, a grapevine still covered with dew, tea in a saucer, and the oinking of pigs wallowing on the other side of the fence. And it seemed to him that he believed in devils and in temptation. He wanted to leave this place, to sit down on a tall, magnificent mountain, to look out over the whole world and enjoy it. And it seemed to him that there he would undoubtedly be surrounded by demons, and he would turn away and refuse—*I don't want to go with you*, he would say, *I am not of your kind, I have struggled against you my whole life*. And the demons would get riled up and shout at him: "Too bad for you, eternal youth!" And Balmcalfkin also saw the unknown poet stand forth to lead the demons, and with him, on either side, wriggled Kostya Kissenkin and Misha Kittenkin.

"Disappear, damn you!" Leaping up, Balmcalfkin started stamping his feet: on the table were coffee and buttered bread, and his landlady stood by the bed.

"You were moaning in your sleep, but what a morning it is!"

Indeed, above the geranium that stood on the windowsill, the winter sky could be seen, blinding in its transparency.

"You're such a boy, just a boy," sighed the landlady after a short silence. "Even though you're going gray. Now, after I leave, you're sure to jump up again, get another book down from the shelf and start going into raptures."

And she scuttled out the door, rustling her dress like a snake does its tail.

22. MARRIAGE

BALMCALFKIN walked along the frozen sidewalk. He walked past the all-night tavern. Heard music.

The auletrides are probably playing there right now. He walked past the dicteriades, quite uninhibited, heavy-bodied women, hurling around typical phrases.[58] *The dialect of dens of vice*, he decided. *It would be interesting to investigate where this dialect comes from and how it emerged.*

He was carried off into eighteenth-century France, when argot was being created. All around him insults and curses whirled and fell.

Smothered in the scent of boots, Sappho-brand cigarettes, and wine, people were running along the steps in and out of the murky door. Off to the side a man was beating a skinny-legged dicteriad with his fists, trying to get her in the face, the chest, or some other sensitive spot. The dicteriad was fighting him off, yelling "Police, police!" But the policeman turned his back and went off to inspect his station.

A shrieking and whooping crowd gathered. There was too much beating, too much noise. Two cavalry policemen on trained horses showed up. They rode straight into the crowd and the horses began dancing as if they were in the circus, driving away the half-drunk revelers.

Balmcalfkin went into the building where Maria Petrovna Dalmatova was expecting him. The rooms had been tidied, the muslin curtains shone white. An old-fashioned icon gazed down with dark eyes. Balmcalfkin trembled, entering the room of a girl. His Musya was standing. For the first time he noticed that she had downy hair, a sharp little nose, small lips.

"I have come to propose . . . that you study Latin," he said.

"What for?" Musya was surprised and started laughing.

"That you might acquire a better sense of the city that we live in," answered Balmcalfkin.

"I know this city already, without Latin," answered Musya. "But I'm glad to see you. You are so, so delightful. Give me your hat and stick."

They sat down on the rather old sofa.

"Where is your friend?" she asked, to start the conversation.

"He's very busy," answered Balmcalfkin. "I haven't seen him in a while. Someone said that . . ."

"No, no, I was just asking," Musya broke in, "tell me what you've been working on instead."

"No, no, we shouldn't talk about me," answered Balmcalfkin. *How can I say it*, he thought. *How can I say the most important thing?*

"My mother will be back from church soon," said Musya. "We'll have tea with jam."

But how can you say the most important thing, thought Balmcalfkin, *to such an innocent and radiant creature?*

He went pale.

"Excuse me, I am in a terrible hurry," and, barely saying goodbye, he left.

What, did his stomach start hurting or something! Musya was angry. She felt bored. She walked over to the cage and, lost in thought, began poking the canary with a finger. He kept flitting from one perch to the next.

Rotten luck, thought Musya. *All my girlfriends have run off to the altar, but I'm left alone. It's so dull!*

She went over to the piano and began playing Scriabin's "Ecstasy." Her mother came in.

"Take the books off the table," she said.

"What books?" Musya turned her head, continuing to play. "Oh, Balmcalfkin must have forgotten them."

She walked over to the table and began flipping through the books. "*Vita Nuova*," she read out loud.

"That man is occupied with worthless nonsense," remarked her mama. A sheet of paper fell out of one of the books. Musya picked it up:

> My god is moldering but has preserved his youth.
> And above all I dread a buoyant bust and shoulders,
> A woman's thigh, the sob of female skin,
> That drank in agony the agony of passion.
> And so I wander now, like Origen,
> And watch the sunset, freezing and immense.
> It's not for me, Maria: the lock of wedlock;
> Your question, rising in the trembling black air...[59]

Balmcalfkin returned home in terrible agitation and only then realized he had forgotten the books.

"Oh God!" he nearly screamed. "Maria Petrovna has read it." He sat down on his bed and thrust his fingers into his graying hair.

At that moment the doorbell rang.

"It's me," called a voice.

The unknown poet walked into the room.

"Don't despair," said the unknown poet upon leaving. "Everything will work out. No one knows what girls are like."

Musya read the paper and became thoughtful. She quickly drank down a cup of tea. She said that she had a headache and got into bed.

How wonderful Balmcalfkin is! This means he really is a virgin. My God, how interesting! An extraordinary man right in our city. There's so many brutes, after all. How sad his life must be ... I will definitely marry him. We will live like brother and sister. Our life together will be extraordinary.

*

In the morning the unknown poet came into Musya's room.

"I've come for Balmcalfkin's books," he said. "Balmcalfkin feels horrible about having left so unexpectedly. Did you look through the books?" asked the unknown poet.

"No," answered the girl. "I never studied Italian."

"Balmcalfkin loves you very much and idealizes you terribly," noted the unknown poet, as if speaking to himself.

"I love Balmcalfkin too," noted the girl, also as if to herself.

"You would make a happy pair," said the unknown poet, as if into space, going over to the window.

Having seen that the girl was blushing, he bid her farewell and left, taking the books with him.

"They are selfless creatures," pronounced the unknown poet, coming into Balmcalfkin's room. "I said that you love her and are asking for her hand."

The choirboys were singing. Maria Petrovna and Balmcalfkin stood on a piece of pink satin. On their heads were light wreaths with imitation jewels. Maria Petrovna was in a white dress, Balmcalfkin in a black suit. Behind them were curious amputees, cigarette girls, and little old ladies from Mosselprom.[60] The marriage was conducted in secret.

After the wedding Balmcalfkin stood for a long time on the balcony, looking down on the city below, but he did not see the five-story and three-story buildings; he saw narrow walks lined with pruned acacias and, on a path, Philostratus. The tall youth walked along, his enormous eyes shaded by wings of lashes; fountains gulped down water; down below, arcs of moonlight quivered, while up above a palace spread its wings; and there, beyond the avenue of fountains, lay the sea, and alongside the youth, bending respectfully, walked he—Balmcalfkin.

23. THE NIGHTTIME WANDERINGS OF KOVALYOV

THAT WINTER Natasha began feeling better. It seemed to her that Shacklekin was bound to start loving her. She decided that it was time to quit fooling around and get married.

A month went by.

On a December evening, through soft snow, Shacklekin came. He was a technician.

"But my muscles, I've got real muscles," he said after tea. "I'm a real man, not like the feeble intelligentsia. My father was a doorman, but I've come up in the world. Now I can set you up properly, build you a golden cage, so to speak. You won't have to work; I've become a real person, so to speak, but I need a wife to take care of. All my comrades have the right kind of wives, higher beings."

"I'm not a virgin." Natasha modestly lowered her eyes.

"Now there's a shocker," answered Shacklekin. "Virgins have become obsolete these past few years. There's not a virgin in our whole city. I need to get my house on a good footing, with some vases, flowers, curtains. I make a good salary. And what would I need a virgin for? You, now, you've had a taste of learning, and you know how to dress nice. I need an educated wife so's not to look bad in front of my comrades. You'll set me up a salon. I'm a man with aspirations. We'll go travel abroad. I'll learn English. I bought an encyclopedia, got a French lady for my son. I've got two domestics, I'm not just anybody, I'm a technician."

*

Misha Kovalyov hadn't managed to achieve anything that year. Every once in a while he'd do day labor. On those days he'd get up at six in the morning, button up his burnt-out overcoat and head off to carry bricks, demolish ruined buildings, load gravel onto barges. Only toward the end of the year did he manage to secure a full-time position, get into the labor union, and become the cement foreman. He found himself thinking ever more often of marriage. He began to save money and decided he would ask for Natasha's hand on the first day of Easter.

The morning of that day, as always, he dragged his military jacket with its little pompoms out of the depths of the closet, got the golden epaulets with their zigzags and monograms out from under the floorboards, had a look at the jacket, shook his head, had a look at his jodhpurs and became even more thoughtful. They had become thoroughly moth-eaten. He got out a needle and thread and fixed up his treasures as best he could, got dressed, rinsed his hands in cheap cologne, shook his head as he observed his thinning hair, buttoned up the used civilian overcoat he'd bought for the occasion and, with a gesture of resignation, went out.

He even hired a coach, and as he rode along he thought: now as before he'd dash up the stairs, he'd be met, as always on that day, by Natasha at the door, he'd leap into the room, give the Easter greeting, "*Excuse me*," he'd say, throw off his overcoat and put on his spurs. Then they would again sing "Oh, the chrysanthemums have long since faded" together, then he would sing *Puppchen* by himself, then he would say that he had gotten a full-time job and offer her his hand and his heart.[61]

The driver stopped. Mikhail Kovalyov paid him and quickly ran up. He knocked for a long time. Finally, her former excellency opened the door. He went into the entryway, kissed her soft hand, wished her a happy Easter, said: "Forgive me, Eudochia Alexandrovna, I'll be right there." He put on his spurs, took off his coat and hung it up. He went into their room. The general's wife carefully locked the door behind him.

"What lunacy," yelled General Holubets and, instead of greeting Kovalyov, leapt up from his seat: "to be waltzing around in uniform seven years after the revolution. You'll be the ruin of us. How dare you appear in my presence in uniform!"

"Where's Natasha?" asked Kovalyov in embarrassment.

"Natasha got married," answered the market vendor.

But what about me? thought Misha Kovalyov. *What do I do now!* He stood there, kept standing.

"You had better leave," said the market vendor quietly. And she raised her handkerchief to her eyes. "Ivan Abramovich is upset."

She held out her hand.

Misha spent a long time fumbling around in the dim entryway, nearly forgot to take off his spurs, buttoned up his coat, raised his collar, put on his floppy summer hat.

"What now, what now?"

He thought of the room for two he'd been eyeing. He thought of how last week he'd been checking the prices for a little table, two bentwood chairs, a shabby sofa.

He leaned against the banister. His summer hat flew off his head. He went down a few steps, picked it up, left the building, stopped, looked up at the lit window on the top floor. He would never, never again go in there. No one would greet him sweetly, and he had no wife, and no uniform; he would never put it on again.

What a terrifying life, he thought.

All night long Kovalyov wandered in front of the dark mass of the women's preparatory school buildings. All the lights had gone out as the city forgot itself in deep slumber.

Through this deep somnolence cavaliers and their partners came walking up to Kovalyov. A junior officer twirled his mustache and danced the mazurka. How quickly he could drop onto one knee! How the young lady spun around him!

The masquerade lanterns shone—everyone was wearing half masks covering their eyes, all of the ladies had corsages. And paper stream-ers wound around the chandeliers and fell in a shock of color.

The empire fell so quickly, thought Kovalyov. *Our fathers have re-nounced us. I did not curse the last emperor as my father did, as did nearly all of the staff officers remaining in the city.*

"But will he love her as much as I do?" he leaned his head against the women's preparatory school.

"How unfortunate she is!" He was nearly weeping.

And he went on looking around the city for solace.

And kept returning again to the women's preparatory school, and stood there, mournfully twirling his hussar's mustache.

Natasha had taken charge. The table groaned under the weight of the appetizers. The crystal decanters held thirty-proof wine. The wine glasses, bought for a pretty penny from a certain ruined family, glinted. An enormous palm tree cast the shadow of its leaves onto Shacklekin, who was sitting in the middle. Around him sat Shacklekin's tipsy friends.

After supper a singer they knew from the Academic Theater sang for everyone. A long-haired poet read poems which spoke of the flowers of our life—children. Afterward he read about free love, after that there was a conversation about the latest news at the factory, about the latest embezzlements. After that N.N. got into a fight with M.N. and they long and obstinately beat each other about the face. And later they began crying and made up.

Toward morning the long-haired poet was telling Natasha about the need to fight against pornography.

"Just imagine," he said, expressing new and original thoughts, "soon, next thing you know, we'll get a new Verbitskaya.[62] And just where are the censors looking these days. We need to have harsh and merciless censorship. No letting pornographers off the hook."

"But you yourself write about free love," said Natasha, pensively twisting her ring with its little diamond.

The young poet began tracing circles with the tip of his yellow boot.

"Free love," said the young poet, incensed, "is not pornography. Women should be free, as men are. Pornography is the description of breasts and movements intended to provoke base instincts."

24. MOCK MOBILIZATION

A MOCK mobilization was scheduled, and many veterans thanked God that they were missing a leg or an arm, that they were blind in one eye, or that their fingers had been mutilated. Sitting in their cigarette booths, they looked out at the nervous faces of the city dwellers and thought that they, after all, had better chances of staying alive than these healthy people walking past.

And at night they returned home to their families and young wives, valuing life more than ever before.

The possibility of war, like swamp fires, flickered somewhere very close by, and to the lonely heroes of my novel a second war was as terrifying as a new death. Indeed, their spirit had taken shape at a dreadful time, and the smell of corpses, though not wafting all the way to the city, was nevertheless psychologically present in it. And although my heroes had no possessions at all, they would rather not set out a second time for the grave, albeit a psychological one.

25. BENEATH THE POPLARS

It was spring again. Time again for nighttime rendezvous by the Baroque, Neo-Roman, Neo-Grecian architectural islands (buildings). The plumped-up trees of the Summer Garden, the young saplings on Victims of the Revolution Square, the bushes in the little Catherine Square, all served as a reminder of the season for those distracted or consumed by the hubbub of life. Some young lady might run past, look at a sapling—"Oh, spring's here . . ."—and start feeling sad. Some other young lady might run past, look at the sapling—"Oh, spring's here!"—and grow cheerful. Or some amputee, a former lieutenant, recipient of a state pension, might sit a while on a bench and recall: "I used to play here in the sand," or: "I used to ride over there in a wagon." And sigh and, lost in thought, pull out a dusty handkerchief redolent of a whole series of odors—black bread, breaded cutlet, tobacco, soup—and blow his nose in desperation. When the handkerchief is put away—all the odors disappear from the air.

Or walking along a pathway might come a boy from the labor school, in a tender embrace with a girl from the labor school: they sit down together with the little old man, and the girl starts twittering, and the long-necked boy watches the back of her head like a rooster and starts cock-a-doodle-dooing. Or Misha Kittenkin, the well-known biographer, might appear once again and sit down on that very same bench by the small bush and pull at his newly sprouted goatee, open up his notebook, lower his little pale-blue eyes and begin to read through his list of Euphratesky's remaining acquaintances.

*

Over the last few years the unknown poet had grown used to the deserted city, to its lifeless streets, its clear blue sky. He didn't notice that his surroundings were changing. He'd devoted the last two years of his life to giving form to and coming to terms with, as it seemed to him, actuality in gigantic images; but unease had been gradually building up in his soul.

One day he sensed that he had been lied to—by both intoxication and the juxtaposition of words.

And on the banks of the Neva, against the backdrop of the city that was filling up again, he turned and dropped his sheets of paper.

The unknown poet hung his head, feeling that the city had never been the way he had imagined it, and he quietly opened his subconscious.

No, it's too soon, I might be wrong, and like a shadow he moved off down the street.

I have to lose my mind, ruminated the unknown poet, moving beneath the rustling lindens along the embankment of the Griboyedov Canal.

True, madness no longer holds the same enchantment, he stopped, bent down and picked up a leaf, *as it did in my early youth. I do not see in it a higher form of existence, but my whole life demands this, so I will calmly lose my mind.*

He moved on.

This requires destroying the will with the help of the will. You have to destroy the line separating the conscious and subconscious. To allow the subconscious in, to give it the opportunity to inundate the luminant consciousness.

He stopped, leaned his elbows on the stick with its large amethyst.

I will have to part forever from my own self, from my friends, the city, from all gatherings.

At that moment Kostya Kissenkin came running up to him.

"I've been looking for you," he said. "I was given dreadful news about you. I was told that you had lost your mind."

"That's not true," answered the unknown poet. "You can see, I'm entirely sound of mind, though I am working on it. But don't think that I'm busy making my biography; I don't have time for biographies, that's a trivial pursuit. I am keeping to the laws of nature; if I didn't want to, I wouldn't lose my mind. I want to—and so I must."

A terrifying night is beginning for me.

Leave me alone.

For a person standing before a gaping abyss must stand alone. No one should be present at the demise of his consciousness, every presence is degrading, at that time even friendship seems like enmity. I must be alone and speed off into my childhood. Let the big home of my childhood appear to me one last time, with its many rooms in various styles, let the lamp above my writing desk shine forth, let the city accept the mask and put it on over its horrible face. Let my mother play "The Virgin's Prayer" once again in the evenings; there is nothing horrible in that, after all, it merely shows the contrast between her girlish yearnings and the real situation. Let my father's study once again hold only classical literature, unbearable writers of belles lettres and popular science books—in the end, not everyone is obligated to love subtlety and to strain their brains all the time.

"But what will happen to humanism?" whispered Kostya Kissenkin, touching his pointy goatee. "If you go lose your mind, if Balmcalfkin gets married, if the philosopher starts doing office work, if Triniton starts writing about his pharmacy girl, and I quit studying the Baroque—we are the last humanists, we are obliged to carry on the torch. We have no concern for politics, we govern nothing, we have been dismissed from government, but we would still be busy with either the sciences or the arts under any regime, after all. No one can reproach us for having taken up art or science out of idleness. I am convinced that we were born for this and not for any other purpose. True, in the fifteenth and sixteenth centuries the humanists were in the employ of the state, but that time has passed."

And Kostya Kissenkin turned his enormous shoulders toward the canal.

The lindens swayed quietly. The young men crossed the Lions Bridge onto Podyacheskaya Street and began wandering around the city.

Eight years ago, thought the unknown poet, *I wandered just like this with Sergei K.*

"I have to go now," he said, "I'm off to bed." But as soon as Kostya Kissenkin disappeared, the unknown poet's face twisted.

"Oooh," he said, "how difficult it was for me to put on a calm face. He was talking about humanism, but I needed to be alone and to gather my thoughts. He was unrelenting, I had to relive yet again all of my life for one last time, down to its tiniest, most insignificant detail."

The unknown poet entered his building, opened the window:

"Hoppity-hop," he bounced, "what a stunning night."

"Hoppity-hop!—it's quite a distance to the nearest star."

> Fly to infinity,
> Dissolve into the earth,
> Scatter into stars,
> Melt into water.

"Keep away, keep away, I'm not here," and he leapt up.

> Fly like a flower into boundless night,
> O lofty lyre, that whirls the song.
> With this lyre I, like a flower of wax,
> Sit and sing over the departed crowd.

"The voice appears to be coming up from under the floorboards." He leaned down. "Smoke, smoke, gray-blue smoke. Is that you singing?" He leaned down over the smoke.

> I am Philostratus, you are part of me.
> The hour has come for our unity.

"Who's there?" He leapt back.

> Let the body walk and drink and eat,
> Still your soul is bound for me.

It seemed to him that he heard the sounds of a sistrum, saw something walking all in white, in a wreath, with a shadowed but lovely face.[63] Then he felt that his soul was being pulled out through his mouth; it was agonizing and sweet. He lifted one eyelid and slyly looked out at the opening city. The streets were flooded with people, the porticos gleamed, chariots raced past.

"So that's how it is!" He got up. "I seem to be waking up. I had some kind of terrible dream."

"Where are you going, where are you going, Apollonius!" he heard a voice saying.

"Stay here." Swaying, the unknown poet straightened up. "I'll be right back, I need to make some inquiries about a trip to Alexandria."

He left the building and, his slippers slapping, walked down the sidewalk.

Left and right he bowed to imaginary acquaintances.

"Oh, it's you," he addressed a passerby, taking him to be Sergei K. "How kind of you to have been resurrected!" he wanted to say but couldn't.

I no longer speak human language, thought the unknown poet. *I am part of the Phoenix when he burns on the pyre.*

He heard the music emanating from nature, plaintive as an autumn night. A lament emerged from the air; he heard a voice.

The unknown poet sat down on a bollard and covered his face with his hands.

He rose, straightened up, looked off into the distance.

In the morning the unknown poet was still sitting on the bollard, utterly white, his head sunk into his shoulders, his vacant eyes darting from side to side. Sparrows were chirping and tweeting, a cat was sneaking up, a window opened, and a naked man sat on the windowsill with his back to the sun. Then other windows opened, and canaries began singing. The splashing of water was heard, a hand appeared watering flowers, two hands appeared hanging out diapers, a man appeared and hurried off, another man appeared and also hurried off.

26.

THE UNKNOWN poet could be seen wearing a bathrobe, wandering around the garden, mumbling and scribbling and leaping up and down, and clapping his hands, and bumping into the trees. And it was evident that he was doing all of these things out of joy. Then he would straighten up and start pacing back and forth, his face shining. On the other side of the bars the watchman was sitting in his booth, talking with a policeman.

Snowdrops were blooming in the garden, and above the garden the sky was blue. The unknown poet was sitting on a bench and writing, and his hand kept gravitating upward. The lines of verse reached up further every day. Occasionally a sparrow would fly down to the bench to hop around and cast curious glances at the unknown poet; the pencil dashed across the paper. Then the unknown poet would walk into his ward and go to sleep; when he woke up, he would snatch up his pencil like a maniac and continue writing. Then the doctor would come, check his pulse, make him sit down, knock on his knees. With each passing day the unknown poet's legs would jump ever more weakly beneath the blows of the doctor's mallet. With each passing day the doctor's face became ever more smug, with each passing day the unknown poet wrote less and less. Finally the time came that the unknown poet wrote no more.

27. INTERWORD

ACTUALLY, the idea of the tower was present in all of my heroes. It wasn't a feature specific to Balmcalfkin. They would all have loved to shut themselves up in the Peterhof tower.

The unknown poet would have occupied himself with verbal fortune-telling there. Kostya Kissenkin couldn't have resisted the tower as obvious kitsch.

As I write, odious time flies. My heroes live in great dissipation, scattered across the face of Petersburg. They no longer meet, no longer convene. And although spring is already here, Balmcalfkin is not wandering enraptured around the park, not picking flowers, not awaiting his friends . . . His friends will not come to him. He will not rise early in the morning, will not read one book today, another tomorrow.

They will not talk here in the sleeping park, which wants to bewitch them into thinking they are the representatives of high culture.

28. BALMCALFKIN AND MARIA PETROVNA

BALMCALFKIN read his folios, which had once so powerfully excited humanity. But my God, books have always excited humanity! And how are new books any better than old ones? They too will one day become old. And one day people will laugh at them too. And old books contain sun and spiritual subtlety, and ridiculous eccentricities, and ignorance, and monstrous debauchery; for old books have everything in them. But Balmcalfkin saw only sun and spiritual refinement in them, the debauchery and ignorance grew somehow obscure for him and became an incidental phenomenon, an intrinsic part of the universe. For him creation had one face, and the Renaissance shone for him with only one of its sides. For him the Renaissance was entirely luminous.

Here sits Balmcalfkin, while flies buzz around him, landing on his neck and on the pages of the book. By his feet Maria Petrovna is sitting on a little bench, peeling potatoes. But are not potatoes an American plant, and did not Virgil drive the flies out of Naples?

"Maria Petrovna," says Balmcalfkin, "do you know the marvelous legend about the Phoenix of Latin poetry—about Virgil and the flies?"

Two years passed.

Balmcalfkin was already thirty-seven years old. He was now fully bald and suffered from arteriosclerosis, but he still loved reading Ronsard, and, when he would return home from working at Regdip to have his dinner, he would sit surrounded by Petrarch and the

Petrarchists and La Pléiade, and tender and wise Poliziano would be standing right next to him.[64]

Maria Petrovna would sit on Balmcalfkin's lap and kiss his neck and, rotating his head, kiss the back of it and occasionally give joyful little shrieks.

Yes, Balmcalfkin philosophized, *Maria Petrovna is, of course, no Laura, but then I am no Petrarch.*

In his quiet apartment—the apartment had two rooms—it smelled of monkeys—the water-closet was not far off—and pickled cabbage—Maria Petrovna was the responsible party. By the windows stood two-year-old grapevines, stunted and transparent. Above the spouses' heads glowed an electric lightbulb.

Balmcalfkin no longer had any thoughts about the Renaissance. Immersed in familial comforts or what seemed like comfort to him, and in physical love encountered late in life, he persisted in a sort of hibernation, which deepened with every touch from Maria Petrovna. It was not that he did not notice Maria Petrovna's flaws, but he loved her, in the way an old widow loves the portrait of her husband that depicts the time when the departed one was her fiancé. Kissing Maria Petrovna, he felt that in her there lived an exquisite dream of an impossible brotherly love, and that were she to start talking about this love, it would sound stupid.

He had long since let go of all his hopes, denied them as a delusion of unbalanced youth. "Those were all infantile dreams," he would occasionally say in passing to Maria Petrovna.

These days he carried a clean handkerchief in his pocket and a carefully laundered collar around his neck, and the elegantly dressed Shacklekin stopped by to see him often, to talk about the new way of life, about how factories were being built, about how the villages now had not only electricity but radios too, about how a life was unfolding more picturesque than the Eiffel Tower, that a grain elevator was being built in the south, the second in the world, after the one in New York, that thousands of people were puttering along—engineers, workers, sailors, mining and construction foremen, stevedores, cooperative members, cabbies, watchmen, mechanics.

GOAT SONG · 127

"All right then," Balmcalfkin would say, "the villages may be brightly illuminated by electricity, the cows may be mooing on exemplary collective farms, the agricultural machinery may be working away in the meadows, life may be unfolding more picturesquely than the Eiffel Tower—still, something is missing in this new life."

Maria Petrovna would pour tea into cheap but pretty little cups decorated with muscular figures. Bidding them farewell, bowing his head, Shacklekin would tenderly kiss Maria Petrovna's hand and invite Balmcalfkin and Maria Petrovna to come and spend an evening with them.

Balmcalfkin's heart no longer beat with quiet music, for in the depths of his soul he no longer believed in the coming peace and silence, the imminent partnership of nations.

Hand in hand with Maria Petrovna, Balmcalfkin was walking down 25 October Avenue to the Shacklekins'.

They walked along, a bald man and a small woman, while all around them were government shops. If one raised one's eyes, the buildings had been painted. Even sidewalks could be felt underfoot.

Shacklekin greeted the couple affectionately.

"Well, how are you?" he addressed Balmcalfkin. "How are your lectures going? Are things better now, financially speaking? I was sorry to see such a man going to waste."

"Yes, he's entirely taken up with them," Maria Petrovna answered for Balmcalfkin. "He's grateful to you, he's been studying social uprisings from Egypt through the present day."

"Do you remember," Shacklekin ambled around the room, "how, a few years ago, I randomly found myself at one of your lectures? I understood then that you were an exceptional person. Though you were lecturing about God knows what kind of nonsense."

"I wasn't lecturing about nonsense," Balmcalfkin defended himself. "It just all came out sounding like nonsense."

*

Spring had still not come. Water gushed and sprayed out from under the soil whenever one of the early vacationers or people spending their two weeks at resorts or sanatoria set out into the fields. The trees stood revoltingly bare, and in front of them roosters fought, dogs barked at passersby, and children, fingers stuck in their mouths, contemplated the power lines.

Balmcalfkin felt melancholy. Walking home, he thought about how those fingers could be interpreted in a Freudian sense; he thought about how this revolting concept had been created so recently.

If he happened to be reading a philosophical poem, suddenly a single phrase would arrest his attention, and even his favorite poem by Vladimir Solovyov:

> No more speeches or questions between you and me.
> I am coming your way like the stream to the sea[65]

took on the most revolting meaning for him.

He felt that he was a pig wallowing in filth. Pursing his lips, he stood lost in thought.

A milkmaid was coming back from the city, making a din with her empty milk canisters.

Yes, she dilutes it with water, he thought and pursed his lips even tighter.

The milkmaid glanced over at the gaunt man with pursed lips and walked past him.

The sky darkened again, the small light space was covered over, and a fine rain began falling.

Balmcalfkin didn't care, he just put on his hat and closed his eyes. *I have to go.*

"You're here," Maria Petrovna greeted Balmcalfkin. "What were you doing wandering around in the rain? That's not very clever. You've gotten a notice: a second edition of your book is being put out."

"The biography!" exclaimed Balmcalfkin. "They're publishing all sorts of rot. The worse you write, the greater the joy they receive it with."

"What are you going on about? Don't write if you don't want to, no one's forcing you," said Maria Petrovna angrily.

"The age, this repulsive age has broken me," said Balmcalfkin and suddenly teared up.

"You'd think I live with an old woman," Maria Petrovna leapt up: "Endless hysterics!"

Balmcalfkin was walking around the garden; the apple-tree, gnawed down by the goats, stood to the right, a lilac bush with miniature leaves to the left. He walked around the garden in his galoshes, his pince-nez, his felt hat.

"No one wears pince-nez anymore!" Maria Petrovna yelled from the window, just to get his goat. "People wear glasses now!"

"As if I care!" Balmcalfkin yelled up. "I am a man of the old world, I will wear my pince-nez, I have nothing in common with this new filth."

"Why are you still walking around in the rain!" came down from above.

"I want to walk and I'll go on walking!" came up from below.

29. KOSTYA KISSENKIN

THE OBVODNY Canal was suffused by a particularly foreboding quiet and a particularly impoverished, picturesque quality. Though it was intersected by two large avenues and many bridges lay across it, one of them even a railroad bridge, and though it was abutted by two rail stations, it nevertheless looked nothing like the granite-clad canals of the city's center. Wild fennel and elderberry and pestilent leaves climbed out of the water itself and traced a crooked line up to the wooden barriers. There were iron privies on little legs left over from czarist times, but they were gradually being replaced by little heated buildings—made for the same purpose but cozier, surrounded by small trees. The writing on the walls was, as always, obscene and insulting, and in time-honored tradition, the walls of this sort of place were covered in subversive political literature and caricatures.

Certain young men would take notebooks out of their pockets here, observe the walls attentively, and, chortling quietly, note down these "popular sayings" in their books.

One clear spring day a young man could be seen walking with seven fox terriers along the wall along the Obvodny Canal. By his cat's-eye stick, his gait, the disintegrating cupid in his buttonhole, by the way his face shone—any one of my heroes would have recognized Kostya Kissenkin.

"My darling chickies," Kostya Kissenkin stopped, "you go run around, and I'll go copy down some inscriptions." He bent over, slapped Caterina Sforza on her doggy shoulder, shook Marie Antoinette's paw, smushed the ears of Queen Victoria, ordered everyone to behave themselves modestly; disappeared into the outhouse.[66]

While he stood with his pencil copying down graffiti, the dogs ran around, frolicked, sniffed at the corners of buildings; some, their muzzles twisting, chewed last year's grass.

Kostya Kissenkin came back out, called his dogs, tucked his notebook away and headed on to the next outhouse.

On Sundays he usually made the rounds and added to his book.

Back at home, in his out-of-the-way apartment on the outskirts of town, he lit a lamp; the dogs were leaping around him, licking his hands, jumping up and down, licking each others' necks and his as well, and Victoria took a great leap and licked him on the lips. He lifted Victoria up and kissed her belly. He was almost in love with these little dogs, to him they seemed to be gentle and fragile creatures, he guarded their virginity sternly and did not allow a single hound dog anywhere near them. In vain did his pups sob in the springtime, in vain did they writhe around on the floor, whine, and climb onto various objects—he was unyielding.

He would pick up the one who whined the most and walk around the room shushing and singing lullabies to her, as to a small child.

This evening, after returning from their walk, his fox terriers were whining and convulsing, gnashing their jaws pitifully; only Victoria was calm, that is, terrifyingly calm.

In vain Kostya Kissenkin, tucking his notebook into his desk, offered them lumps of snow-white sugar; they whined and gazed at him wretchedly.

Then he began shouting at them.

As if beaten, they calmed down.

Drifting off alongside them, he began thinking about his novel.

That red-headed lady thinks that he's in love with her.

In the morning he reread the "popular wisdom," as he called it. He fed his temporarily calmed pups and set out for work.

There, beneath porcelain chandeliers festooned with tiny crystal bouquets with metal droplets, with buttons and chainlets, he walked around smiling; setting up for display, assessing, and pricing objects designated for auction. There, he sat on furniture with straight, curved, and other kinds of backs, and conversed with other young men who listened to him attentively; squeezing a moistened sponge, he pasted price tags on the statuettes presented to him.

Sometimes he grew bored. Then he would ask one or another of the young men who worshipped his expertise and good cheer to strike up some music.

"Ach, mein lieber Augustchen, Augustchen, Augustchen," or a Viennese waltz, or "The Hills of Manchuria," or "Clair de Lune."

Kostya Kissenkin would listen attentively.

The room to the right comprised five drawing rooms in groups, while the room to the left contained three bedrooms.

While Kostya Kissenkin, sitting in an impossible pose on an armchair, surrounded by young men, examined and elucidated various objects, a man walked in carrying a yellow briefcase, wearing yellow boots and spotted socks—a market expert. After that a round man rolled in with a guitar under his arm; after that two young ladies rushed in and started running from one object to another; next came the director in a shantung suit.

On Monday, the eighteenth of April, Konstantin Petrovich Kissenkin came home late at night from a research scholars' party.

Smiling beatifically, Kostya Kissenkin undressed, lay down on his extremely threadbare couch, turned to the wall and grew quiet. He saw the fifteen newly opened rooms that looked out onto the Neva. They were all crammed with collections. This was vulgar kitsch that he himself had donated.

The suites were crowded with foreign scholars and travelers and local professors and researchers.

He was exchanging bows with everyone and giving explanations.

Kostya Kissenkin's nose whistled in his sleep.

Misty splotches: green, red, violet. A banquet *manifests*.

Kostya Kissenkin is sitting, gray-haired, surrounded by his admirers, who are delivering speeches and reading him telegrams.

Now the custodian of the Hermitage rises:

"Dear colleagues, we salute Konstantin Petrovich *sub luce aeterna*.[67] It is not so easy to discover a new direction within art. For this, one needs genius"—and, tenting two fingers on the table and holding a brief silence, he continued: "Beginning at nearly the tenderest age, when other children are busy running around or hopping ecstatically on train platforms, Konstantin Petrovich Kissenkin was already experiencing the agitation of a true scholar. In vain was he invited to go for strolls, in vain was he commanded to go for a spin in a carriage—he was studying books on art history. At age seven, when napkins were still being tied under his chin, he already knew all of the paintings in the Hermitage and, from reproductions, those in the Louvre and Dresden. By age ten he had already spent time in Europe's most important museums and had attended auctions like an adult.

"And when everything had been thoroughly learned, only then did he commence his life's work.

"On behalf of the workers of the Hermitage, please allow us, Konstantin Petrovich, to salute and thank you for this newly discovered direction of art and for the pieces you have donated to our repository."

Next rises the unknown poet, who has already achieved fame all over Europe. His gray hair falls to his shoulders. Gold drachmas embossed with the head of Helios sparkle at his cuffs.

"Our generation was not barren," he says, acknowledging the applause, "and at an unimaginably difficult time we banded together and continued our work. Neither distractions, nor mockery, nor the absence of monetary resources could make us abandon our calling. In Konstantin Petrovich I salute my dear comrade in arms and beloved friend. The blossoming we now see underway would not have been possible if our generation had faltered in its day."

Everyone rises and applauds the gray-haired friends.

The renowned public figure Balmcalfkin rises with his wine glass—a withered old man with beautiful eyes. His head is encircled by a halo of gray hair, tears of rapture flow down his cheeks.

"I remember like it was yesterday, dear Konstantin Petrovich, the clear autumn day when we all gathered at the tower, in that old dilapidated dacha..."

*

Sorrow seized hold of Kostya Kissenkin. He woke up. Sat up with his elbows on the pillow. He gazed out . . . flakes of snow were falling, looking like Christmas.

It's early, he thought. *Winter.*

This country is terribly poor, he thought, getting up after all. *All she has right now is the bare necessities, she can't afford the slightest bit of intellectual luxury. Let's say that everyone actually approves of my book. But who would be capable of publishing an enormous volume geared toward a small readership?*

How many years had he spent in libraries, examining pornographic booklets and reproductions, how often had he visited museum departments closed to the public and studied figures in marble, ivory, wax, and wood . . . How many paintings, engravings, sketches, sculptures thronged in his imagination . . .

Renaissance pornographic theater (antiquity substrate), eighteenth-century pornographic theater (national ethos substrate). Still, he did have predecessors in this field, and there were relevant studies in the West, but in the field of vulgar kitsch studies there was no one. He was a trailblazer here. This was a more difficult enterprise, entailing greater responsibility. Here one was required to begin with the basics, with the most primitive collecting of material.

That blue morning, as in times past, Kostya Kissenkin saw the whole world with its forests, boundless despite all the felled timber; with its oceans of deserts, despite the railroads; with its towering cities of ferro-concrete and of paper; with its brick settlements and settlements of wood. Past him filed the races, the tribes, the few surviving clans. *While it's easy to discern vulgar kitsch when standing in the middle of a room*, thought Kostya Kissenkin, *to discern elements of vulgar kitsch in Western European art, how much harder it is with Chinese and Japanese art, and nearly impossible in such an under-studied area as Negro art, despite the enormous interest that has emerged in recent years. But if we look at the art that has been returned to us by archaeology, such as Egyptian, Sumero-Akkadian, Babylonian, Assyrian, Cretan, and other arts, then the question becomes even more complicated and problematic.*

In the brightening day Kostya Kissenkin's hands drooped; his back curved and he experienced genuine agony. He had suddenly remembered that everything had changed.

His friend, the unknown poet, had gone into hiding, hadn't been seen anywhere, had perhaps left the city.

Balmcalfkin had, according to rumor, married and acquired a new circle of friends.

He, Konstantin Petrovich, was now a researcher, but that was a labor of love.

Konstantin Petrovich set out for his institute, which was located on the embankment. He greeted the doorkeeper Elena Stepanovna, who was sitting in an armchair next to the fireplace.

"How's your health, Elena Stepanovna?" he asked.

"I'm freezing," she answered, "freezing."

He went up the stairs and into the foyer; there the porter shook his hand and affectionately led him over to the wall newspaper.[68]

"They've torn you to shreds."

And indeed, on the wall amid a group of professors and research-ers he saw himself sitting and demonstrating, with a scientific air, urinals. He went up to the library. Looking up from a book, he began examining the people there.

Without him noticing, for Kostya Kissenkin the whole world had turned into vulgar kitsch; he already experienced greater aesthetic stirrings from depictions of Carmen on candy wrappers or boxes than from paintings of the Venetian school; more from little dogs on clocks that periodically stuck out their tongues than from Fausts in literature.

Theater, too, had become valuable, significant, and interesting for him when it showed elements of vulgar kitsch. Some woman with bared breasts wearing a dress from his mother's heyday, dancing and scattering flowers on prancing cupids against a background of Doric columns, was now seriously appealing to him, not as a joke. Out-of-the-way cinemas with jagged, hastily montaged films excited him and exhilarated him with the crassness of their composition. Little review articles written by visiting provincials, which abounded in bad taste, illiteracy, and cheap swagger, made him laugh until he cried, to the point of the purest and most elevated rapture. He went to every meeting and carefully noted the vulgarity in everything. He received ecstatic letters from young men infected, as he was, with a passion for the vulgar. Sometimes it seemed to him that he had discovered the philosopher's stone, which could make life interesting, stirring, and full of rapture. Indeed, the world for him had become vivid in the extreme, attractive in the extreme. His acquaintances suddenly yielded a whole abyss of curious little features that were newly attractive to him, because he could discover hidden vulgarity (unsuspected by them) in their discourse.

And at this point he began to receive letters from the provinces. Provincial youth, who had through mysterious pathways gotten word of his activities, awakened; out in their backwaters they began to collect vulgar kitsch as a cure for boredom.

Philostratus was aging along with Balmcalfkin—now for Balmcalfkin he had become a rather desiccated clean-shaven little old man with rings bouncing on his fingers, the compiler of a court novel.

This feeblish and despised shade followed Balmcalfkin for some time thereafter, but finally it too disappeared.

30. BLACK SPRING

IN KARPOVKA, in a two-story building, a former single-family townhouse that looked like a gray crate with holes, adorned with a gable and a crest with the crown knocked off, the philosopher lived as before. Besides him, the building housed some Chinese people who had come from Shandong province and who made the paper fans that mid-level artisans would put as decorations on the wall where the mirror stood.

Andrei Ivanovich felt clearly that he was illuminating problems of philosophy and methodology for the wrong audience, not the one for whom they should be solved, that this was, all told, some kind of outrageous diversion. What use was the methodology of literature to his constant companion, the pharmacist? Why did he read his tractatuses to these constantly moving and practical people? Nevertheless, the philosopher began preparing his lecture. Certain theses had long since been sketched out, they needed to be developed.

He looked down on the evening city, on the crowds moving along with different movements, sprawling gaits, pipes in their mouths.

The tolling of bells carried over from somewhere nearby.

This is where I worked with specialized philosophical journals, and there were nearly enough of them. This is where my work, at one time quite famous, was published, this is where I defended it to earn the rank of professor.

The philosopher walked around the large room papered in expensive but faded wallpaper.

He saw the sitting room as it had once looked.

Heard philosophical and literary-philosophical conversations.

Now he was riding a train. Opposite him sat Pyotr Konstantinov-ich Kissenkin.[69] He recalled first meeting his wife on an estate outside Moscow, where he was staying with one of his friends.

Once again, he felt that light and breezy stroll amid tall golden fields.

She was walking alongside him in a long dress, wearing a straw hat, under a light parasol, laughing joyfully.

Collapsing her parasol, she took off running down the road and, looking back, invited him to catch her; and he, catching her, held her hands for a long time as she stood there without saying a word.

After this incident they had the feeling that they were close to one another and dear.

The philosopher walked around, banged into a chair, a rickety chair with a gilt back—a chair from his wife's bedroom.

Outside the door someone was scratching.

A four-year-old barefoot tot came in and began striding in step with the philosopher, singing a little tune and clapping her hands.

"I'm russkie, I'm russkie."

On the other side of the wall, in the neighboring room, a guitar began to sigh.

The sweeper woman passed by the door, one-eyed, with a twisted mouth.

He stopped. The child stopped too. He looked down. Next to him was a teeny-tiny lass—the daughter of his Chinese neighbor and the sweeper woman.

"Sweetie, go away," he said, "uncle needs to be alone now."

But the child just sucked on her finger and wouldn't leave. He escorted the girl out and locked the door. He sat down in his leather chair—the chair from his study—undid the small package lying on the table, sliced some cheese and made sandwiches.

I won't go, he thought, *I won't go, what do they need my lectures for anyway!*

Crumbs fell onto the napkin tucked into his collar, but an hour later he went out anyway. On the embankment he ran into the pharmacist.

"I'm going your way!" declared the pharmacist joyfully. The building on Shpalernaya was brightly lit.

The elevator was working.

The building was in the modernist style. An endless number of round-bellied little balconies, placed asymmetrically, had been tacked on here, there, and everywhere.

The rows of windows, each of which was peculiar in some unique way, were illuminated. The tiled depictions of women with flowing hair against a gold background had been restored.

He squeezed the metal handle of a door with fluted glass panes, on which lilies were illuminated from within.

Through the main foyer he went up to the first floor, to the spacious chambers occupied by the family of the traveling engineer N.

The pharmacist followed him.

After the lecture a discussion was supposed to begin.

"Here, Andrei Ivanovich, please allow me to pass you the jam," said the engineer's pretty young wife.

A comedian from a nearby theater ate cookies disdainfully.

"So, sweetie, did you have a good time?" the engineer asked after the philosopher's departure.

The Chinese man, having piled up some money or, perhaps, called by urgent events, left for his homeland.

That very evening the sweeper woman shacked up with a different Chinese man.

Two months later she died from a botched abortion.

The "russkie" settled into a corner of the philosopher's room, rather like a cat. Sometimes he would buy her milk.

He'd let her out into the courtyard and see how she ran around the tree.

This was not an act of charity. He simply knew that she had nowhere to go.

He even bought her a toy one time and watched her romping about with it.

Gradually something resembling a bed appeared in the corner, and a calico dress and little dress shoes on the child.

That spring Yekaterina Ivanovna felt deeply sad. When Euphratesky was still alive, she hadn't needed a child. She felt that she herself was a little girl next to this large, traveling man.

By night she was seized ever more frequently by a horror of poverty and the street. Sometimes she would get up, walk over to the window wearing only her nightshirt and, flinging her eyes open wide as windows, look down. Across the street a nightclub roared and shone, as disgusting scenes played out by the entrance.

There was Misha Kittenkin, Yekaterina Ivanovna would sometimes recall in the evenings, *but he too has disappeared; I could talk about Alexander Petrovich with him*. She got out a portrait of Alexander Petrovich.

Misha Kittenkin asked me to give him one of Euphratesky's manuscripts, she would remember. *But I don't have anything left, Alexander Petrovich's friends took everything. I suppose I have this album of landscapes*.

In the afternoon the organ-grinder with his trembling, morose, disheveled green parrot began playing in the courtyard, eking out happiness as before. From the courtyard dully wafted the feeling of returning home from the countryside or from abroad; the black spring resembled autumn.

"Wouldn't it be fine to go to the ballet," she rose in a classical pose. She did a pirouette.

"Though ballet is now obsolete, after all."

"Mikhail Petrovich has been saying that it's obsolete for ages."

She stopped, sat down on her bed and started crying.

"Everything that I love is long since obsolete . . ."

"No one understands me…"

"Did even Alexander Petrovich understand me, he was so clever, so clever!"

"Maybe he always despised me a little?"

"Men always do look down on me, after all."

She lifted her face, wet with tears, and, like a fully adult person, fixed her gaze into space.

Someone knocked at the door and delivered a letter.

Dear Yekaterina Ivanovna, I managed to procure a pension for you. Please excuse me for not having written to you earlier. It was very difficult until the last.

The letter was from a prerevolutionary friend of Alexander Petrovich's from Moscow.

It was so unexpected that Yekaterina Ivanovna was suddenly seized by the feeling that she had grown old. She went up to the mirror.

Little wrinkles were running around her eyes and around her mouth. Her hair was thin. She felt the urge to be young and pretty again.

She put on a hat and a light-colored jacket, looked in the mirror one more time and put some lipstick on her pale and feeble lips.

She set out for Euphratesky's mansion.

Yekaterina Ivanovna climbed up the marble staircase, fitted out with all manner of Oriental gargoyles, which had still not been removed.

The building now housed the Educenter.

Classes were in session, and girls in red kerchiefs were running up and down the staircase, calling other girls and youths to the meeting. Young men in greatcoats were walking through all the rooms. They would sit down on benches to listen to the lectures.

The drawing room where Euphratesky used to have conversations had been transformed into a meeting hall and decorated with posters.

Opening the door to Euphratesky's bedroom, Yekaterina Ivanovna saw Balmcalfkin. Leaning over the lectern, he was assiduously giving a short history of world literature.

She sat down on the back bench and began to examine him.

He's really let himself go, she thought.

A sparrow flew in the small ventilation window, sat on the window frame for a moment, then began flying around the room. The students, boys and girls, got up from their benches and set about chasing the sparrow. Balmcalfkin stood at his lectern and waited. With her rather heavy gait Yekaterina Ivanovna came up to him.

"Yekaterina Ivanovna!" Balmcalfkin was astonished. "What a surprise to see you!"

"I didn't know you were lecturing here." Yekaterina Ivanovna fluttered her eyelashes.

"Nothing surprising about that..."

The sparrow was driven out, and the lecture resumed.

Yekaterina Ivanovna, alone, made her way home from the Educenter. The wind tore at her skirt. After sitting a while in a little square under springtime snowflakes, she went home.

Dear Mikhail Petrovich, she wrote to Misha Kittenkin, *my dear, dear friend, won't you agree to come and see me, to have a chat. I found an album of Alexander Petrovich's for you. We can talk about his poems. I do hope that you will be so kind as to come by.*

31. THE UNKNOWN POET

THESE days the unknown poet was driven to fury by his earlier poems. They seemed like feckless tomfoolery to him. The music he had heard when he wrote them had long since gone silent for him. He had turned away from his audience, which had loved him so passionately and forgiven him his numberless failings.

Bald, overcome by spleen, he returned to his mother, whom he had once abandoned for the sake of great art.

She stroked his bald birdlike head, took him by the chin, counted the wrinkles around his eyes, asked whether he was still drinking a lot, still spending sleepless nights with his friends.

The unknown poet paced around the room. The wide two-story building had been built in the 1820s by a French émigré, and had been marked for demolition before the war. Now, sitting in its courtyard, a postman took his rest, along with his snub-nosed family; sewing kept afloat the variously-nosed and variously-haired family of a former gentleman-in-waiting, whose manservant was an artist's model; coming down the staircase, laughing and leaping, was a woman who caroused with sailors in cinemas and along the embankments; and a little old man—the former owner of the Bauer wine shop, now working at the Concordia wine shop—on Wednesdays and Sundays hosted other vint-playing little old men, accountants, and former counts.

All of this information had previously passed the unknown poet by, even though he had been renting his light-filled oblong room from this vint-playing little old man for a long time. The co-op employee had a spouse with cute rouged cheeks and an older sister, an eighty-year-old *distinguée*. The little old man had at one time been the Spanish consul.

The apartment that belonged to Spanish consul Heinrich Maria Bauer had once been cozy.[70] The drawing room was gaslit, the dining room was heavy and oaken, decorated with papier-mâché birds on little stands, with lithographs in ebony frames, with stuffed birds mounted on the walls, with a round oak table with a single bulbous leg and eight supplemental legs; it had been pleasant to spend time there. The Spanish consul felt himself to be an official figure: the drawing room was fitted out with mahogany furniture, the study had couches and portraits of monarchs: the German emperor, the Russian autocrat, the Spanish king. Also electrotype images of Luther and the apostles. An enormous German-language folio lay on a velvet-covered table: Goethe's *Faust*, with color illustrations. In the uncommonly clean kitchen stood Gretchens, Johannchens, Amalchens, with round bellies and all manner of handles, every possible kind of spout. The Spanish consul did not speak Spanish. In the evenings he would set out for the German club, Schuster-Klub. There, in a special room called "the German room," he would drink beer from a mug, as everyone else drank beer from mugs; there were no decorations on the walls other than an enormous full-length portrait of Wilhelm II in a heavy golden frame.

The unknown poet sat with the vint-playing old man's family on Wednesdays and Sundays and observed the game. The poet now felt himself to be only Agathonov.[71]

The Hungarian count played with dignity, occasionally smoothing his sideburns with a gentle movement. There was a certain inexpressible gentleness to all his movements. His jacket, sewn in the first year of the revolution, fitted him magnificently. The count spoke magnificent French. Beside him sat his spouse, dressed entirely in black, who spoke only French and resembled a marquise in her tall snow-white wig. Further along sat a former border guard with a dashing mustache and obviously military bearing, then an accountant with a fabulous income. No one ever spoke about the modern age here.

The conversation was always either about the court, or the guards and the army, or the court celebrations in Peterhof on the occasion of the French president's visit, or the cunning dodges of black marketeers.

The balding young man drank tea with the old people. The conversation constantly circled back to the end of the nineteenth century and the beginning of the twentieth. The little old man, lisping, having told a joke, began to fall asleep, lulled by reminiscences, and even to snore a bit. The eighty-year-old *distinguée* looked at her watch.

Everyone got up from the table.

Silence ensued.

Scrubbed with coffee-grounds and sand, the Johannchens, Wilhelmchens, Gretchens in the kitchen shone—crockery on the shelves.

In the morning the former unknown poet stuck his head out the window and called to the Tatar man who had been wandering around the courtyard, his face raised and yelling.

"Listen, friend," he said, when the Tatar had appeared in his room with an empty sack under his arm, "I've got all kinds of junk piled up in here—take a vase, an ashtray, books, here's a handful of old coins."

The Tatar strode morosely around the squalid room, where the bed was never made, where books lay all over the floor, where coins from the time of Vasily the Blind lay on a plate alongside a flattened piece of soap, and the windowpanes were so cloudy that they barely let in a dusty gleam.[72]

With an experienced hand, the Tatar went up to the bed and groped the blanket, went over to the table, knocked, looked to see if the nightstand had been eaten away by worms.

"No good," he said. "How 'bout coat? Trousers? I buy coat or trousers."

"You must be joking, I sold you all that stuff ages ago!" the former unknown poet said angrily.

"Why you say untruth, what's in closet?" The Tatar walked up and threw open the wardrobe doors.

"What you need for? Later you buy new ones!" He started examining the trousers.

"How about that rug in the corner," the room's owner agreed.

"You sell bed?" asked the Tatar.

After pacing around his room a while that evening, the former poet set out for a most notable building.

He climbed up the staircase. Hunched over, he paid the fee.

Opposite the bald young rosy-cheeked croupier sat Asphodelov, who was in the midst of losing the advance he'd received that morning from his publisher.

"Oh, Agathonov," said Asphodelov, reaching over to shake his hand. "Where have you been?"

"I'm busy."

"But what's been keeping you busy?" Asphodelov was astonished.

"Let's not talk about it," the balding young man said evasively. "I came here to have some fun, not to talk about business."

Asphodelov looked at him. *He's all wound up*, he thought.

"Life is beautiful," Asphodelov began philosophizing. "One must take from life everything that she gives. Look at these gorgeous palms," and with a fluid motion Asphodelov indicated the scraggly houseplants. "Listen, music!"

He walked up to the glass doors with Agathonov. A chansonnette was carrying over from within.

"Have a look at these faces, panting with the thrill of chance, look how their eyes are burning, how the players are scraping the cloth with their nails."

But the former poet saw none of this. He saw how the croupier pulled out ten percent from every round into a slot in the table for the needs of the people's education, while hiding every tip in the pocket of his vest, saying *merci*. That they were all bald, well-fed, dressed in the latest fashions, that the embezzlers and bribe-takers crowded around the tables losing money to the needs of the people's education; appropriating funds from one government office, they were willingly handing them over to another one.

Here there were no ladies with heavy earrings, no creatures with frisky haunches, here the passion for the game did not commingle with lust; true, some of the players would get excited, they still, against all odds, hoped to win.

"You're a romantic," the former unknown poet turned back to face Asphodelov. "You're an obnoxious overgrown child, can you really not sense the enormous grayness of the world? I come here because I have nothing to do, because after I failed to go mad I feel like nothing, a goose egg."

"So you tried to go mad? What a romantic you are!" Asphodelov taunted the former poet.

"Of course I didn't try," the young man backpedaled. "That was just a turn of phrase. Do you really take me for a fool?"

"Come now," said Asphodelov. "No one respects you as much as I do, and no one loves your writings as well. A person needs a dream, you provide that dream—what more could one ask for?"

"I never gave anyone any dreams," answered Agathonov.

Already the new arrivals had sat for several hours in the club restaurant. Already a dozen beers and several more glasses of ghastly cognac had been tossed back, and they'd moved on to red wine. A Gypsy girls' choir appeared onstage to sing their old songs, and a Gypsy man with a guitar walked around and, stamping his feet, accompanied them, and two Gypsy girls in their bright colorful dresses, wearing red slippers, broke away from the crowd, and the fluttering began.

"Nonsense, what nonsense," muttered Agathonov and went back to the gambling room, sat down at a free spot.

The two Circes came up behind him.

Feeling someone's elbows on his shoulders, Agathonov turned his head.

"Don't bother me," he pushed them away, "please!"

The girls, sticking up their noses, backed away.

Agathonov had an unpleasant feeling: *I used to feel so differently toward them.*

Two players flew over to the croupier, who'd just gotten up, and began apologizing and begging for chips on credit. The croupier was walking away from them, refusing; they followed on his heels. Asphodelov and Agathonov were leaving. The two Circes were following them, then the Circes fell back.

"Exquisite," Asphodelov was saying, "exquisite..."

"Listen here," Agathonov interrupted Asphodelov, "can I stay the night at your place?"

A porcelain chandelier glowed in Asphodelov's study.

An enormous, Alexander II-era writing desk adorned with sphinx-shaped candelabra stood opposite the door. On it, pyramids of recently published books, booklets and pamphlets towered halfway to the ceiling, all with their pages carefully cut and equipped with paper bookmarks. In the mahogany bookcases, recently delivered, stood Goethe in German and Pushkin in the Brockhaus edition. The Golicke and Vilborg illustrated editions of *Eugene Onegin* and *Woe from Wit* lay on tables nearby.[73]

"You'll have to excuse me," said Asphodelov, "my wife is sleeping."

He set out a bottle of vodka and pickles.

Deep into the night Agathonov declaimed his poems.

"This is so stupid," he interrupted himself. "I never heard a thing."

At three in the morning he rose:

"What idiocy it is to think of wine as a path to comprehension."

He saw himself wandering:

"What am I to the city and what is the city to me?"

"Morning!" He walked over the window. Sat down on the couch and opened his mouth wide.

Rays of slightly warm sun illuminated his noticeable bald patch and the thinning hair around his temples. Agathonov lay on the sofa. One foot in a purple sock was sticking out from under the blanket.

The rays moved down and illuminated his shoulders, then the glass next to the empty bottle flared up gently.

Agathonov woke up—someone touched his shoulder.

"I'm sorry, my dear," said Asphodelov. "I've been brought a new marquetry cabinet."

The shelf was standing behind Asphodelov; two porters were smoking cheap tobacco.

That evening Agathonov read in the company of a largely unfamiliar family.

As always in such situations, tea had been prepared, along with various sandwiches, cookies, candies and jam, but, as was almost always the case, there was no wine.

Agathonov, as almost always, was late and showed up after they'd given up on him.

Sitting at the tea table, he began reading poems.

> In polychromatic twilight
> . . . .
> I feel it always, the connection,
> With the star shining up above
> And for the last time, it may be.
>
> But no, but no, the words have lied,
> For she perished long ago.
> I disbelieve it like a lover
> I wait: she shall arise again.
>
> Friend, step back, for one more moment . . .
> Let me behold her golden brow,
> Her delicately foaming shoulders,
> Her chin adorned with lace.
>
> Psyche won't rise into the air
> But nonetheless I feel her now
> I see, I see—she clambers out
> And makes a seat upon her broom.

We fly above the former city
Above the swan-like Neva river,
Above the thinning Summer Garden,
The factory with a tall smokestack.[74]

"Tell me," said a girl, turning to him, "do your poems have any meaning or no meaning at all?"

"None," answered Agathonov.

"I hold," said the co-op operator, "that it's not worth it, writing meaningless poems."

After tea the young men and ladies sat down in a corner and began telling each other jokes. A girl with hair bleached by peroxide was the first to begin:

"A certain stupid young man loved to ride horseback. We were staying at our dacha then, at Lakhta. He lived in the city and would go riding in the show ring and around the islands.[75] Once, coming onto the veranda where we were having tea, instead of saying hello he declared, beaming: 'All of the fillies I've ridden have gotten pregnant.' We exploded laughing and ran off to tell everyone about the stupid thing he'd said, but our father saved the day. 'So,' he asked him, 'do you think the foals will look like you?'"

"One time there was this incident in the bathhouse," the journalist, touching the leg of the girl sitting next to him, began his tale. "One of the bathers poured a tub of cold water onto the fellow sitting next to me; the latter ran at him, fists raised. 'Excuse me,' said the pourer, 'I thought you were Rabinovich.' The fellow who got poured on started cursing. 'Whaddya know,' shrugged the pourer, 'Rabinovich has a real advocate here.'"

"During the imperialist war," Kovalyov raised his voice, lighting up a cigarette bummed from the journalist, "a certain sublieutenant, who was on a special mission, needed a smoke. The officers were standing out in the fresh air, in the presence of the newly arrived army commander. The sublieutenant slipped off and lit up, hiding the cigarette in the sleeve of his overcoat. 'Sublieutenant, who gave you permission to smoke! This is outrageous! Discipline is falling!'

yelled the army commander. 'I'm sorry, your excellency,' blurted out the sublieutenant, touching the peak of his cap and not knowing how to answer. 'I thought that out here in the fresh air...' 'You forget, sublieutenant,' roared the general: 'whenever I'm around, there is no fresh air!'" Having finished his joke, Kovalyov smiled, pleased with his witticism.

In the middle of the room a game of cat and mouse was underway. Young ladies, older ladies and men were running around.

On his way out, Agathonov ran into Kostya Kissenkin. They were so emotionally overcome by this meeting that they began walking each other home. They noticed neither the nighttime chill, nor the fact that the streets had emptied. Three times now Kostya Kissenkin had walked Agathonov to the gates of his building, three times now Agathonov had walked Kostya Kissenkin to the gates of Kostya Kissenkin's building, and finally Agathonov found himself in Kostya Kissenkin's room.

They sat down on the enormous sofa. But his auntie didn't bring them tea on a tray, rich bread cut in slices; toward two in the morning Konstantin Petrovich's father, a little old man, did not crack open the door and peer into the room, and did not advise them to go to sleep, reminding them that Konstantin Petrovich would have to teach English the next morning to some old ladies; and Kostya Kissenkin and the unknown poet did not smile joyfully in response and did not go on delighting in the metaphysical poets.

Still, excited by the unexpected meeting, they began talking. The moon once again did not seem like the moon to them, but a dirigible, and the room was not a room but a gondola that whisked them off above the endless space of world literature and all the different arts. Konstantin Petrovich in his forgetfulness was already reaching for the bookshelf to get down Fracastoro's epic poem about syphilis to compare it to Barthélemy's poem about syphilis—a public-relations poem from the mid-nineteenth century, which said it hadn't really been Napoleon's fault that the French were now short in stature, it was the syphilis that had been absorbed and transformed by the nation.[76] But his hand hung in midair, because in the window there appeared a stick belonging to an Irish poet recently arrived in Russia[77] and the shoulder of the German student Miller, and then a couple of faces pressed up against the window—one fitted out with a poetic English beard, the other clean-shaven and smiling in a tall collar, a real baby face. Next, climbing onto the friends' shoulders, a woman's pre-Raphaelite visage peered into the room.

A few minutes later a procession set out from the gates onto the street.

At their head walked the creature with the exquisite face. It was dressed in a sheepskin coat, suede to the thighs and wool below; on the creature's feet shone astonishing little patent-leather shoes, and a little hat twinkled on its head.

The creature was followed by the Irish poet, wearing a floor-length Ukrainian leather coat.

Behind him came Agathonov in his autumn overcoat.

Behind him came the German student in a summer coat.

Bringing up the rear of the procession was Kostya Kissenkin in a raccoon-fur coat. At an intersection, surrounding the creature in the sheepskin coat, the emergent company began conferring over possible methods of conveyance.

"*Das ist ganz einfach*," remarked the German. "We'll take an automobile."

He quickly ran to the intersection and began bargaining.

They sped off to a bar.

"I am so fond of you," said the Irish poet. "Everything is strange here, I am staying, a poet can really live here! There are questions of worldwide significance here. Here you can walk around wearing whatever you like and no one pays a whit of attention. Back home the papers say everything has been destroyed over here, there's hunger, grass growing in the streets. To poetry!" He clinked glasses with Agathonov.

"You have Tolstoy, Gorky," affirmed the German. The conversation had essentially ceased to be held in one language and was happening in all languages at once: the Greek *chi* would suddenly flare up, then instead of "gymnasium"—*palestra*, or for some reason *urbs* or *Akte* would ring out;[78] Italian sounds would flow in, or something French would be produced through the nose. A withered gray-haired beggar woman was singing at the bar door.

Now, sitting at a bar table facing the bottles, Agathonov recalled the day when he had first embarked on his experiment, that is, he couldn't remember the exact day, but it seemed to him that it had been a sunny autumn day, after the summer holidays; that he and his friend Andrei had been standing on the staircase of their school, bathed in sunlight by the enormous window not far from the teachers' room; that instructors wearing regulation suit jackets with gleaming buttons had been walking past down below; that the superintendents, Spitsyn and the baron, had been standing in the hallways; that in the teachers' room the form masters had been conversing with the instructors; that the director had stood above them on the staircase, while all the way down below in the entryway, among countless coat hangers, had sat Andrei Nikolayevich, the doorman.

The former poet drank and drank in vain. Even intoxicated he felt his nullity, not a single great idea struck him, no pale rose petals came together to form a wreath, no pedestal appeared beneath his feet. No longer did he approach wine with purity, with self-respect, with the awareness that he was doing something great, or the presentiment that he was about to reveal something beautiful, that the world would be stunned. Now wine revealed to him his own creative impotence, his own internal loathsomeness and spiritual desolation, and everything was savage and terrifying within him, and everything around him was savage and terrifying, and although he hated wine, he was drawn to wine.

The former poet walked back home. He chose the narrowest, darkest little streets, the poorest. He wanted to once again feel himself in 1917, 1920. He was ready to turn once again to any poisonous substance at all in order to provoke a vision. The thirst for intoxication grew inside of him. He couldn't hold back, got onto a tram and took it to Pushkin Street. But it had changed over the intervening years. Flocks of vagrants no longer wandered the sidewalks. The agreed-upon whistle did not ring out upon his arrival. There was no Lida standing in a doorway, smoking a cheap cigarette. He remembered: this was the spot she'd taken his stick and his ring to wear for a while and returned them two hours later. This was where she'd stood cursing her girlfriends, and he'd implored her not to curse, since only cabbies cursed. In this green building he'd stood by the window while she sat on a filthy bed, mindlessly shaking her head. She'd leapt up and tried to throw herself out the window. Here, at the intersection, he'd met her for the last time, she was being taken off to a concentration camp, and he stood as if paralyzed.[79] He knew every nook and cranny here, but there was not a single familiar face.

It was late in the night when violet eyes blazed out from a stairwell.

"Lida," screamed Agathonov, beaming, and ran off. The face that turned to him was decidedly youthful.

"Lida," he screamed in despair, "we are still terribly young!" And ran after her, stumbling.

And suddenly one figure stopped; the sound of a slap rang out, repeated by the echo of the locked gates; and then quick strides could be heard, also echoing; a man remained standing in place, holding a stick decorated with an amethyst. And there were stars in the sky, pale blue, yellow, red, but the buildings did not strain upwards and did not fall, and snow did not fall in thick flakes, and no cards lay forgotten in the doorway.

32. MISHA KITTENKIN

MISHA Kittenkin raised the chair with the patient. The electric machine started tooting, and, attached to a rubber tube, the needle with its serrated bulge began spinning; electric light illuminated the ceiling and gently fell downward; the patient's face was piercingly illuminated by a small adjustable lamp. Half an hour later the root had been cleaned and it was possible to put on a crown.

Misha Kittenkin took out a tiny bottle, scooped up some liquid with a little steel instrument, then from two other bottles shook out two little mounds onto a thick matte glass.

He was preparing a paste, and suddenly rhymes came to him.

But the quick-drying paste did not allow him to concentrate on them; it demanded his attention.

Mikhail Petrovich stuffed the patient's tooth with a protective agent, filled the golden crown with paste and with a deft movement mounted it on the barely visible walls of the tooth.

He began holding it there with two fingers and looking out the window.

Now he was free for some time.

Kittenkin had been seeking a topic for quite a while. *There's no external inspiration*, he sighed. "Just a moment," he said and took out his hand. He looked into the mouth. The crown was glittering like highlands of pure gold.

Misha Kittenkin cheered up and lowered the chair with the patient.

Ecstatic, Misha Kittenkin walked over to the window.

That's just what I needed: golden highlands, that's a piece for a poem.

"Next," he half opened the door. A housewife walked in and started moaning and groaning.

"Which tooth is bothering you?"

"The front one, sonny," came echoing out of the depths of the chair.

"It's rotten," Misha Kittenkin boomed out suddenly. "I'll have to remove it. Why didn't you come earlier?"

"Didn't have any money, it's just yesterday my nephew came back from China."

"From China?" Misha Kittenkin was astonished.

Misha Kittenkin was washing his hands. Without closing his mouth, a young man with a silver filling had just left. Misha Kittenkin got a flyer out of his pocket:

Today at 8 p.m. at the Academy of Sciences, a lecture by Professor Schmidt: "On the Islands of Liu-Kiu."

"Who the hell would expect such a striking combination?" Misha Kittenkin was astonished. "This is just what I've been looking for. Like nightingales singing and cats meowing. Now if you could put that into a poem…"

He wiped down his instruments, placed them in a glass cabinet on a glass shelf and went home to change his clothes.

He put on his only pink silk long underwear and polka-dot socks, knocked on his young chest, walked over to the mirror.

"I am a gentleman," he looked himself over, "I am invited, I am wanted, I must go."

He reread Yekaterina Ivanovna's letter.

"Well, yes. I know women," he smiled condescendingly.

Along the way a spring downpour let loose. Mikhail Petrovich was forced to duck into the first doorway he could find. There he met Triniton.

Triniton, beaming, was rereading a sopping-wet note.

Misha Kittenkin slapped him on the shoulder.

"I'm pursued by women," Triniton addressed Misha Kittenkin. "I'm a hot item."

"It must be a consequence of the war," Misha Kittenkin explained. "We men are a hot item these days."

Taking each other by the arm, they leaned against the wall.

"Indeed, there are but few of us men these days." Triniton felt moved. "Such a shame, so many wonderful men killed!"

"You know, Alexander Petrovich considered women to be creatures of a lower order." Triniton's head popped out onto the street.

"Why, of course I knew that!" Misha Kittenkin leapt out onto the street. "Thanks be to God, I've studied Alexander Petrovich's life down to the smallest detail."

Triniton's head went back into hiding.

Kittenkin stuck his hand out into the rain.

Triniton's head popped back out onto the street.

And suddenly, with no transition, the young men began praising each other's poetry. Though Triniton's praise was beyond all measure, and Misha Kittenkin's was measured.

"Africa breathes in your poetry," said Triniton.

"Well, your poems are beautiful too," Kittenkin answered condescendingly. "They're nice," he continued, as if pondering.

The rain, though light, continued to fall. Misha Kittenkin walked into the entryway once again. But despite the fact that Triniton's head and Misha Kittenkin's figure had not stood long in the rain, they were noticed by a member of the rights-advocacy association standing in a neighboring doorway, a man who had at one time memorized Pitiscus and still wrote mythological poems.[80] He adjusted his collar and tie, tucked his stick under his arm and ran over to the doorway where the real poets were taking shelter. He walked up to them obsequiously.

"Oh," he said, "how long it has been since we last met! I've been occupied with completely pointless affairs. Today I defended my superintendent. Let's read some poems while it's still raining."

All three of them began taking turns reading poems.

Triniton howled in ecstasy.

Mikhail Petrovich read in the voice of Alexander Petrovich.

The public defender gestured like an orator.

The rain stopped. The sun peeked out. The poets set out for the nearest beer-hall. There they struck up a vehement discussion.

"If I'm not mistaken, you were reading your older work?" the member of the rights-advocacy board pointed out to Triniton.

"I don't read my new poems to anyone," Triniton took offense. "The modern age would not understand my new poems. I now write poetry just for myself. One set of poems for myself and my descendants, real, romantic poems, while the others are for my contemporaries."

"I see," noted Misha Kittenkin with pride, "that only I am writing new poems and reading them to whoever wishes to hear."

He gazed with satisfaction on the balding heads of his friends. Then he said that he was in a hurry, excused himself, paid for the beer, and left.

Triniton took the advocate by the arm and they got onto a tram, determined to continue their discussion in more romantic surroundings.

Snowdrops and coltsfoot were already blooming on the islands.

"Yes," Triniton said, walking along the path beside the sea. "In your poems one senses the uneven quality typical of youth."

"Excuse me," the lawyer interrupted him. "I am not at all young, you and I started our literary careers at the same time."

"I didn't mean it like that," Triniton corrected himself. "I meant to say that your technique is minor."

"I don't agree with that either," objected the lawyer. But just then Triniton caught sight of some young ladies sitting on a green park bench. The young ladies were nudging each other's shoulders and giggling softly.

"Splendid girls," the lawyer stopped short.

"I was thinking the same thing myself," Triniton turned in their direction. They sat down on either side of the girls. The lawyer took off a black glove and dusted off his boot. Triniton asked:

"What do you think of Meyerhold's theater?"[81]

Edging closer and closer, the balding young men moved in on the young ladies. The girls trilled with laughter.

Triniton, as if accidentally, kissed his neighbor's shoulder.

The lawyer, seemingly casually, stuck his boot underneath one of the young ladies' slippers.

Already, swinging his legs and getting a joke ready, the advocate was walking along; already Triniton was walking bent over; in pairs the young people walked off along the grass. On the island's spit Balmcalfkin and Maria Petrovna came into view; they were walking in slow and dignified fashion.

Balmcalfkin sat down on a bench. Maria Petrovna approached the sea and began singing the aria from *Ruslan and Liudmilla*.[82]

Balmcalfkin sat lost in thought and counting sparrows.

"Maria Petrovna," he addressed her when she had finished singing, "where did you put the sandwiches?"

33. MATERIALS

MISHA Kittenkin had been thinking on and off for a long time about sending the materials he'd gathered to the Quiet Haven, but today, coming back from visiting Yekaterina Ivanovna, he finally made his decision.[83]

Deep into the night, he stacked his cards in chronological order and tied them together with twine. On the reverse side the cards had pictures of peasant huts and accordion players and girls and fragments of geographical maps. The front sides of the cards were lined and filled with Euphratesky's handwriting, which Mikhail Petrovich had mastered.

When everything had been bound together, some duplicates were left over. Mikhail Petrovich moved the lamp closer. With the packages as background he read again:

1908 May 15. Wednesday. 3 o'clock p.m. Alexander Petrovich had dinner at the European Hotel. At 5 p.m. Alexander Petrovich left the European Hotel and set out for Gostiny Dvor with Eugenia Semyonovna Sleptsova (a ballerina). He bought her kid gloves and a sapphire ring.

Now (1925, 5 January, 6 p.m.) Sleptsova is a well-preserved brunette. She has small breasts, shoulders wider than her hips, muscular legs, like all ballet dancers. Based on the intelligence I've gathered, in her prime she was astonishing. From her account I was able to conclude that A.P. was distinguished by uncommon virility. From her account I was also able to conclude that from Gostiny Dvor A.P. went to her place.

1912 April 12, Friday. Between 8 and 10 p.m. A.P. gave a lecture in his mansion. I was unable to ascertain the exact topic of the lecture—it was either about Leconte de Lisle or Abbat Delille.[84] After the lecture a footman came up to Gunther and reported that A.P. requested her presence in his office, regarding her poems about India.

I was able to determine that the small mahogany table was laid, that they drank champagne, and that A.P. recounted how he had traveled around India.

P.S. Gunther is a blond of diminutive stature. Now (1926, February 15), she has prematurely aged. She no longer writes poems. She remembers A.P. with gratitude as her first teacher. She says that he was a fascinating man.

1917. Winter. In the evening, before his departure (destination unknown), time unknown. Involvement with the manicurist Alexandra Leontyevna Chicklina. Chicklina says that she doesn't remember any details. A foolish, uneducated nature. She says that A.P. was just like all other men.

At this point Mikhail Petrovich looked at his watch.

"What a springlike morning. Who could believe that I am drawing forth the life of Alexander Petrovich from oblivion."

In the morning, before leaving for the clinic, still not fully dressed, Mikhail Petrovich sat down. He began creating a poem about India in Euphratesky's handwriting. It featured irreproachable Parnassian rhyme, exotic words (Liu-Kiu), wildly sparkling geographical names, jungles, golden hills reflecting the sun, a spring festival in Varanasi, and the leopards and Knights Templar of Asia. And hunger, and plague.

The poem was metallic.

The voice was metallic.

Not a single assonance, no metaphysics, no symbols.

It contained everything, everything except Mikhail Petrovich.

If Alexander Petrovich had, in his day, written this poem, some would find the poem wonderful, would think that it revealed the pull of exotic lands on the cultured person, away from everyday grayness, from factories and works, libraries, to a mysterious, colorful life; others would think that a pioneer spirit lived within Alexander Petrovich, that in the olden days he would have been a great traveler and, who knows, perhaps even a second Columbus. Still others would have said that the poem revealed clearly, at last, Alexander Petrovich's total estrangement from the Russian literary tradition and that this was, essentially, a French and not a Russian poem, that it lay far beyond the bounds of Russian poetry.

When he had finished the poem, Misha Kittenkin fixed his eyes on Euphratesky's portrait.

Euphratesky had been painted against the background of a palace amid cactuses.

"Tough old bird," he thought.

Mikhail Petrovich remembered that it was time to go, that people were waiting for him, that there might be quite an assembly of patients, that he would once again have to thrust his fingers into open mouths and to palpate gums.

Mikhail Petrovich took his stick, the spring lock clicked shut behind him.

A girl was coming up the stairs; she stopped on the landing and read the metal plate: "Dentist Mikhail Petrovich Kittenkin. Hours 3–6 p.m." She rang the bell.

A spring evening. Not the slightest breeze. Smoke rose from the chimneys toward the heavenly reddish fleecy clouds and dispersed, unnoticed.

Down below Mikhail Petrovich left his private clinic and, stopping for a moment, admired the sky.

He felt like taking a stroll.

Then he remembered that he had agreed to meet with Yekaterina

Ivanovna today. He got on the tram; at Theater Square he got out and headed for New Holland.

Reaching the furthest point of the embankment, he sat down on a bench and gazed at a little corner of the sea.

Out there the Mining Institute building was visible.

Today he had chosen this meeting spot.

The young dentist often dreamed here about far-off seas, endless oceans. For six years now a ship had been appearing to him, an enormous European ship. And on it he would see himself, departing.

But now, with the materials collected and sent off, when he felt himself to be an ordinary dentist, he realized that he would not be departing for anywhere, that he would never follow the path of Alexander Petrovich, that only in the zoo would he encounter anything exotic: a mangy lion, pacing back and forth behind its bars.

Or in the circus, where toothless beasts did things they would never do in their homelands.

The dream of travel had burned low and gone out.

Yesterday he had received a bronze medal from the Quiet Haven. And that was his entire recompense for six years of toil. And his poems, would anyone publish them? Everyone would just laugh. True, he was a member of the Poets' Union, but what kind of poets were they. As soon as you started reading your poems, they'd say—that's not you, it's Alexander Petrovich.

But he would marry Yekaterina Ivanovna. Yes, she was stupid, but Alexander Petrovich had, after all, married her in his day—thus he too, Mikhail Petrovich, must marry her.

Yekaterina Ivanovna had been standing for a few minutes already, gazing at the back of Misha Kittenkin's youthful head. He was holding his hat on his knees, then she came running over, covered his eyes with her hands, and sat down next to him.

"What are you dreaming about here, Mikhail Petrovich?" she asked, taking her hands away. "I got your letter. I am willing."

Misha Kittenkin gazed at the sea.

"I have loved you for a long time," continued Yekaterina Ivanovna, "but it's only been two months since you started showing up again."

"Dear Yekaterina Ivanovna," as if waking up, Misha Kittenkin rose. "You are willing?" he asked gallantly. "Now begin my days as a Philistine!" he sighed. "But you are the link to my past, to the romantic period of my life."

Yekaterina Ivanovna sat next to Misha Kittenkin, fiddling with her purse. Inside the purse were a batiste handkerchief, a pocket mirror and powder in a little cardboard box, and a tiny lip pencil. She took out the mirror and brought the pencil to her carelessly painted lips.

She's past thirty. Misha Kittenkin turned toward her.

"I thought you were stupid," he said, smiling. "But over the past few years I have known so many women."

"I have a childlike quality," Yekaterina Ivanovna's little face started laughing. "And men are attracted by the childlike. I am not at all stupid, I am glad you've realized that."

Misha Kittenkin, leaning down, kissed her on the forehead.

"So, then," asked Misha Kittenkin, "it's decided?"

"It's decided," answered Yekaterina Ivanovna.

An hour later in a different part of the city they were climbing up the marble staircase of the Quiet Haven.

"Here," Misha Kittenkin turned, "is where they are keeping the materials I gathered about the life of Alexander Petrovich, my notes and diaries."

A thin little old man up above, having caught sight of them coming up the stairs, began descending.

"Oh, what a tremendous service you've done us all!" Having greeted Yekaterina Ivanovna, he began effusively shaking Mikhail Petrovich's hand. "Your materials about the life of Alexander Petrovich are astonishing, though they have a certain strangeness to them, but that doesn't matter—such is youth. What a shame it is that there was no such young man as you during the time of our sun.[85] How interesting it would have been—day after day, hour after hour, to trace the life of a genius."

Enraptured, the old man gazed at the portrait.

The old man was called. He disappeared in the chambers.

The meeting had not yet begun. And Mikhail Petrovich and Yekaterina Ivanovna stopped in the room where the great writer's library was kept.

It was quiet on the square in front of the building. To the right it smelled like fresh young buds, while to the left plaster busts of emperors, shipped in from the surrounding institutions, continued their slow decomposition.

From the Neva, like a person, the wind blew. People were strolling there. They were strolling around by the university, past Thomon's Stock Exchange building, past the Ethnographic Museum, past the Admiralty, blocked off by buildings, and past the horseman erected by Catherine the Great.

Yekaterina Ivanovna and Misha Kittenkin walked over to the window.

"How glad I am, now we will talk about Alexander Petrovich forever," Yekaterina Ivanovna roused, leaning her elbows on the back of the armchair. "Don't you think this toilette suits me?" And she sniffed a little bouquet of violets.

The bearded researchers of the Quiet Haven were bustling about. Like ants, they protected the Quiet Haven, expanded it, wiped off the dust, showed it with dignity to visitors, held in reverence those who patronized or aided the Quiet Haven in any way. Here hymns of praise were raised to that pinnacle of poetry, unattainable in subsequent eras.

Behind Agathonov trailed pairs of lovers, going in various directions, and they smiled, and came back, and stood awhile above the Neva, and walked again, and came back again. They smiled at the sun, burning out on the water, and at the last sparrows, skipping along the walkway, pecking at oats and victoriously raising them high.

Agathonov, lacking all sense of himself, sat down on a granite bench, took out a sheet of paper and pencil, and began to put together, as he once had, the first words to come into his head. A first line resulted. He pored over it, making sense of it, then began removing sound clashes, then normalizing the syntax and adding a second line. Once again, like little boxes, words began to open up for him. He went into each little box, which all turned out to be bottomless, and stepped out into space, and found himself in a temple sitting on a three-legged stool, simultaneously uttering, and noting down, and arranging his notes into a poetic line.

Proud as a demon, he stepped back onto the embankment. He set out for the Summer Garden.

I am gifted in knowledge, he thought once again. *I have ties to Rome. I know the future.*

Proudly, and even slightly insolently, he strode down the main walkway of the Summer Garden. The statues looked out at him from every side. To him they appeared to be pink with green eyes and slightly dyed hair.

The flowers on the banks of the pond, the granite vases, the Engineers' Castle—all attracted his attention for an instant, but he turned back and noticed the philosopher on a bench, sitting with a half-Chinese child. The little girl was wearing a light-colored half-length coat and a straw hat. On her legs were little socks with colored cuffs. The philosopher was wearing an inexpensive coat and an inexpensive felt hat. The little girl was sucking on a chocolate bar. The philosopher was reading a book.

Agathonov walked slowly past. He was afraid that someone might hinder him, that something might interrupt the state he was in.

Where there had once been gardens and boulevards, he could still sense them.

He walked the whole day through.

The white night that ensued, trembling, resembled the evaporation of the ether and intoxicated him more and more. Figures, fairly distinct, moved along the sidewalks. Every once in a while automobiles with creatures in fancy dress came tearing past. Then everything died away. In some of the jewelry store windows the clocks were keeping perfect time. The fact that it was perfect time was announced on boastful signs.

He went into the hotel, clutching his sheet of paper like an entrance permit:

> Wartime and famine, like a dream,
> Left but a bad taste in the mouth.
> We bore that lofty chime across.
> It was a weak trial, after all.
>
> His loving and devoted friends
> Gaze at the motions of his mouth,
> The blue hollows of flaccid cheeks,
> The stupefaction of his eyes.
>
> The crowds teem along the streets,
> Another generation pulses,
> They laugh at our prideful stride,
> Disdain the heartbeat of our souls.

34. TRINITON

TRINITON walked along and felt tears welling up. He really loved Petersburg. For him this city had at one time been Sirin, the Bird of Paradise;[86] the city had called him with its lights.

Earlier Triniton had felt Petersburg to be a fairy-tale city, a Russian city. What wasn't Russian about the Dormition Cathedral in Moscow, even if it had been built by a foreigner? Or St. Sophia in Kiev? In Petersburg, Russian Manon Lescauts, *dames aux camélias*, stepped out to admire the Neva, its floating pearls.

Here were Perrault's fairy tales and the Bohemian life with guitars and balalaikas. Here were masquerades with lights like rubies. Yes, these days Triniton still danced at balls, he still read his old poems at dawn to girls and ladies with bobbed hair, he still, prancing up close to the mirror and doing a little spin, smiled in self-satisfied fashion; but without anyone noticing, not even himself, the Sirin Bird had died inside him.

Walking to Yekaterina Ivanovna's place, Triniton thought: *I just have such a wild and reckless nature, and I do pity her, but I can't marry her—it doesn't befit a poet to wed. To sit with a girl by the stove, read your poems a bit, and then, the next morning, to be on your way, then meet up in the evening at a concert, a ball, do a little fox-trotting, read her your poems on the sofa. To enthrall. And, back home, to sleep off the whole day. That is the life of a poet.* And, walking up to a pharmacy mirror and doing a little spin, Triniton smiled in a self-satisfied fashion.

*

Electric chandeliers were burning bright under the ceilings with clouds and cupids. A jazz band played. People were fox-trotting in the small space; the morning would bring visits to publishers, the search for reviews, the search for money, standing in line at the cash register. And, guiding a girl over to the fireplace, he would try reading her his poems, while in a semicircle around them journalists, editors, and prose writers were having supper, and he was looking at the girl he'd pulled out of the dance.

"Shall I read you my poems?" he asked.

"Forget about it," said the young lady. "I've known all your poems for ages now."

"What a fine little knee you have," Triniton was enchanted.

"Don't look!" The young lady laughed. "Looks like you're balding," she giggled uproariously.

"Yes, the devil be hanged, I'm balding," laughed Triniton.

How, in fact, did it, in fact, happen, that he had changed from being a young man to being bald?

But is it not typical of a poet to become bald and sigh over himself and make an effort to enthrall, with his long-dead dreams, some young lady with lips like cherries, with drops of sweat on her brow after the foxtrot?

Although the young lady had been making fun of Triniton at the ball, outside she agreed to go home with him all the same. Not because he was a poet, and not because she'd been dumped by somebody else, but because, why not?

She had hair like a torch, cherry lips, and charming blue eyes. Her scrawny figure was draped in a short dress with a brocade bust, and on her pinky finger a peridot emptied out like green glass.

Triniton did not treat young ladies to wine, and he didn't get them drunk. He would take them to his room, get out a little jewel case and begin showing them all sorts of poetic objects. This was what happened with this one too, but it really was cozy in his room. Outside the window was a white night, quiet, very quiet. On the walls were pictures of the Kremlin and Manon Lescaut, and an engraving of the prodigal son. And sitting on the bed, Triniton kissed the young

lady, and his boots stood by the chair, next to the young lady's dancing shoes.

And the dawn would light up their heads together on the pillow
with mouths open, quietly snoring in opposite directions and holding
hands. And perhaps she will dream of family life, and he—of fields,
a small stream, and himself as a gymnasium student.

That night the former poet, who now felt himself to be only Agathonov, looked for a long time out the hotel window onto the spacious
avenue, the white Petersburg night. He sat down at the table, drank
some beer, put down a sheet of paper, and began reading his last poem:

> In our youth fair Florence shone for us,
> Revealed on our streets gentle Philostratus,
> We called him forth without charms or philters
> Not on the city's outskirts, choked with trash.
> With poetry as sweet-voiced as the morning
> He was called forth on the elusive street.

And when he had read it out loud, he saw clearly that the poem
was bad, that his youthful blossoming had ended, that his talent had
come to an end along with his dreams. He sucked for a while, for
some unknown reason, on the barrel of the revolver, went over to a
corner of the room, and shot himself in the temple.

Triniton was sleeping in bed with the young lady when Misha Kittenkin, dropping everything, ran over and began frantically knocking. Triniton, hastily pulling on his trousers, came out into the foyer.

"Oh, what a shocking incident! Last night in the Hotel Bristol
the last lyric poet shot himself."

And Triniton suddenly burst into tears.

"We will all meet the same fate. I'm the last lyric poet too, after
all."

Forgetting the young lady, he set out with Misha Kittenkin to the hotel.

They kissed the dead man on the forehead and burst into tears, and Triniton, blowing his nose, surreptitiously pulled off the dead man's tie and shoved it into his pocket, while Misha Kittenkin slid off the pale-blue enamel cufflinks and hid them in his cigarette case. Having hidden the things away, the two of them exchanged glances and felt somewhat satisfied and reassured.

And then Triniton remembered his young lady and ran home and began apologizing.

"What kind of respect is this," the young lady was incensed, "leaving a woman alone?"

But when she found out and saw Triniton weeping and examining the tie, she too burst into tears.

Sunday. Morning.

"I have an exotic profession," Misha Kittenkin was saying, walking alongside Yekaterina Ivanovna through the noisy park.[87] "I have to deal with gold and silver and even silver compounds all the time. You're standing there and you see, lower down, a ring on a finger—an emerald of some sort—and you envision some country where everything is dripping with emeralds—a belly dance comes to mind. Or a young man with a turquoise on his little finger comes in, you're choosing teeth of the right color for him, but inside you're thinking about Persia, about sweltering movements. I am creating the exotic here through my dream. Isn't it true that I am a strong man, Yekaterina Ivanovna?"

"But why did you choose this profession?"

"I didn't choose it, it chose me," Misha Kittenkin shook his head.

"At first I thought that it was all just fiddle-faddle, a temporary gig to make money, some evening courses, but then I turned out a dentist."

"My brother's a cobbler, you see, but what kind of cobbler can he be when he's a guardsman?"

And slowly, slowly Misha Kittenkin and Yekaterina Ivanovna went on walking through the park.

The paths of the park in Pavlovsk were quiet and deserted. At one time Misha Kittenkin had ridden around here on a tall tricycle.

"We were, of course, the oppressors," he said and felt that he'd succumbed to propaganda.

And slowly, slowly they walked on.

It was noon.

In the regenerated city center, Triniton was sighing about the great love of Don Juan, gazing at the springtime that had come to the courtyard. Children were leaping about, cheered by the spring.

He saw little ventilation windows being opened and damp children's heads with weak little hairs sticking out and then hiding again. Door handles quivered and children began appearing on unsteady legs.

Afternoon.

Above the canal, opposite the Educenter, Kostya Kissenkin was walking through the auction hall and reading a book of dreams. Two or three figures were unhurriedly walking back and forth and examining the objects on display.

Leaves were rustling outside the window. The whitish sky was gradually darkening.

Kostya Kissenkin glanced at his watch—it was time to close up.

The latecomers were going down the stairs.

He went down.

Said something to the doorkeeper.

Riding the tram, he thought about how life was beautiful, how, overall, his work was not hard, how, overall, it was even interesting to buy porcelain and paintings for cheap and then to display them in the auction hall, how a little teacup bought randomly and resold made it possible for him to live.

He went into a house and examined the things inside. The lady of the house, who had at one time appropriated the porcelain of the vanished owners, was getting married and moving away, selling everything off.

Well, no reason to be timid with this one, thought Kostya Kissenkin and bought a few knickknacks for a song.

He felt a hankering to examine his purchase; he had a sharp eye, he knew that he had bought highly regarded objects. In a nearby cemetery, he laid out the little teacups and figurines on a bench, and squatted down.

"My dear *saxe*," he muttered.[88]

Birds were warbling on the trees.

He packed up. Set about reading his dream-book.

How queer—he let the book fall to his knees and lifted his eyes to the birds—*the sweet little bourgeois sing warmly.*

After that he began walking around and examining the tombstones and reading epitaphs.

Standing before one of them he began prancing and guffawing.

> Your love to me was without measure,
> This gave me, as your spouse, great pleasure.

He took out his notebook and wrote it down.

Evening.

Kovalyov was going with his young wife to the operetta. Yesterday he'd run into Natasha. Natasha was going abroad for two months.

Yes, he thought, *she's really made it.*

In the evenings, Misha Kittenkin painted—after all, in his day Alexander Petrovich had also painted. Misha Kittenkin tried hard to choose the same paints, to paint in the same tones, when possible even with the same brushes. They'd been in Yekaterina Ivanovna's dresser. In addition, he managed to secure imported paints from former amateur artists, the children of wealthy families. In the evenings he would sit holding a brush at his easel, and when he tired of painting he would read the books that Euphratesky had loved to read. All of life for him was in Euphratesky's image.

A splendid evening.

The sun was setting.

Maria Petrovna in a peasant hut was boiling milk on a primus stove.

Grasshoppers were chirring. The lake was gleaming.

"Say what you will, country living is very fine in the summer."

Balmcalfkin, broad-chested, with unbuttoned collar, was sitting in front of the hut in his slippers, and with his stick, its handle decorated with monkeys, he was tracing figures in the sand.

35. INTERWORD

I TOOK my novel and went to Peterhof to reread it, to muse over it, to wander, to feel myself in the company of my heroes.

From the train station I walked to the tower that I'd taken note of and described. The tower was no more.

Inside of me, under the influence of the unfaded flowers and grasses, once again awoke that enormous bird which was felt, consciously or unconsciously, by my heroes. I see my heroes standing around me in the air, I walk accompanied by a crowd to New Peterhof, I sit down by the sea and, while my heroes levitate above the sea, shot through with sun, I begin to leaf through my manuscript and converse with them.

36.

BACK IN winter on a certain day, at a certain time, there was a meeting of the housing cooperative society in a railway worker's apartment; at a certain time, the neighborhood instructor appeared.

Balmcalfkin, experiencing a presentiment of disaster, didn't want to go. But the genteel tenants of the building wheedled him so relentlessly that he decided to sacrifice himself, to go and to agree to everything.

For a long time before the day of the meeting the population of the building was whispering conspiratorially in the apartments and gateways. Balmcalfkin had to be elected president; he was a cultured person, he was no thief.

The meeting dragged on deep into the night. Hour upon hour Balmcalfkin refused, seized by a despairing melancholy. At long last the portfolios were distributed. The president's portfolio was handed to Balmcalfkin, after which they moved on to proposals. Everyone proposed that a red corner be set up in the building and began arguing over which apartment it should be set up in.[89] Should they allocate the room next to the caretaker's, or set it up in one of the communal apartments. They couldn't argue their way to a conclusion so entered it into the report as a proposal. The instructor, a former navy man, was constantly expounding and clarifying and was very pleased. He was pleased that people were listening to him and putting their trust in him, and the building's tenants were pleased that they were being listened to and that they inspired trust. The instructor left in the best possible mood, and the tenants parted ways in the best possible mood. They went down the staircase. Out in front walked a waiter, the new secretary of the administration; he was followed by members of the new revisionary committee—a doorman at a certain foreign firm, an accountant, and a doctor. Behind them came a crowd, and behind the crowd came Maria Petrovna and Balmcalfkin, adjusting his pince-nez. Out in the courtyard everyone began exchanging farewells: some kissed the ladies' hands, others pressed them, still others hurried off, tipping their hats. All around them cats yowled, and above them a small moon illuminated the wide courtyard.

Back in the last days of June, sitting in the little garden that he had set up with Maria Petrovna, Balmcalfkin felt that all of world history was nothing other than his own history. The little garden was exquisite. It took up a small amount of space in the courtyard by the red brick wall and had been created single-handedly by the two of them. Last year in the spring some trees near the zoo had been pruned, and when she saw this Maria Petrovna had remembered that if recently pruned branches are planted, they will put down roots.

Together she and Balmcalfkin had taken two of the just-discarded branches (Balmcalfkin was already president of the building management). The branches took. The two of them cobbled together a small fence out of wooden slats, painted it green with oil paint, stamped down tiny paths, loosened up the earth, and laid down turf. For the turf they made a special trip out of town. They put in a little table and a bench, planted forget-me-nots, pansies, flowering tobacco, poppies, and even a lilac bush. Balmcalfkin kept one key to the garden, while the other stayed with the building superintendent or caretaker, so that the tenants, whenever they wished, could sit in the garden. But the quiet tenants of that building, respecting the labor of others or, perhaps, scorning such a tiny garden, which looked more like a terrarium, never entered it.

Maria Petrovna went down every morning with her watering can and watered the flowers; Balmcalfkin would sit there of an evening, hatless; sometimes they even had dinner there. Balmcalfkin would sit at the little table, covered with a white tablecloth, and Maria Petrovna would rush down the staircase from upstairs with a steaming bowl, and the children playing in the courtyard would look at them with curiosity. Now Balmcalfkin had grown utterly content and would stroll around the garden, if one can put it that way—strictly speaking, he could barely turn around inside it.

One day, sitting in the garden, Balmcalfkin suddenly felt that the culture he had long defended was not his, that he did not belong to that culture, that he did not belong to the world of luminous spirits among whom he had ranked himself until now, that nothing had been given him to accomplish in this world, that he would pass by like a shadow and would leave nothing behind to be remembered by, or would leave only the most unsavory trace. That any office clerk had the same sense of the world that he did, just with different variations, that there was no abyss separating him from an accountant, that all of them spoke in a general way about a culture to which they did not belong. And at a concert with a visiting conductor something blurred down Balmcalfkin's cheeks, but it was not the music making him cry. He wished he could stay a youth forever and look at the world in wonder.

And when it seemed to him that there was no difference between him and a griping Philistine, then he became repulsive to himself and felt sick to his stomach, and he got irritated with Maria Petrovna for no reason and even sometimes broke plates.

Maria Petrovna took terribly good care of Balmcalfkin. She made sure that he only made useful acquaintances.

"We only seek out useful acquaintances," she would say occasionally. "Unuseful ones are of no use to us. Isn't that right?"

And Balmcalfkin, after a short pause, would usually answer, moving his lips:

"Yes, unuseful things are of no use, of course."

And although he almost entirely did not believe in life after death, Scipio's dream was captivating to him;[90] the music sang and swelled and fell in cascades, and although he felt that his love for renaissance was ridiculous and unfounded, there was no way he could part from it, break with the breadth of the horizon.

A bald man races to the bookstore as if chasing the water of life.

"Isn't that right, Maria Petrovna, we can't live without Cicero," he would say, warming his feet by the tiled stove. And the fire crackled, crackled.

It was a winter day. The frosty sun, a crimson sphere, hung above the city. The frost pinched desperately at the passersby. But the heart was seized by an astounding joy.

Balmcalfkin was sitting by the woodstove and reading one of his favorite books, but the reading was hard going. He was listening to what was happening inside him. It was unpleasant and painful. He was beginning to realize that it was not at all the historical Philostratus, the romantic court poet of the age of Julia Domna (and also not the other one, composer of erotic letters to hetaerae and youths, and not the third one either), whom he loved.[91] His heart became clear and light. And he was no longer horrified that office clerks shared his sense of the world, that there was no abyss separating him from an accountant.

When Maria Petrovna went out visiting, Balmcalfkin worried terribly: What if she were to fall under a tram? Or what if she for some reason left the party early and robbers fell upon her? After all, she had a weak heart, a very weak heart.

Not only in the evenings, but in the daytime as well, Balmcalfkin worried. He would stand at the window, stand and wait. Sometimes he would even get his old binoculars down from the tall black bureau and look down to the street, he would even paw through the crowd with his eyes to see whether Maria Petrovna was coming behind them. He was anxious all the time. He would see Maria Petrovna hurrying along, with a bundle of some kind under her arm.

And then steps could already be heard on the stairs, pitter-patter, and she had a newspaper in her hands, a bad newspaper, of course, with foul language, but nowadays there are bad newspapers everywhere you look on this earth. And Balmcalfkin would begin reading the paper, and he would become terribly sad that in Mexico, when a general was hanged, a military orchestra had played, and other generals and the people ate ice cream. And not only because a general had been hanged, but because the hanging had been accompanied by music, public festivities and the eating of ice cream. Or he might read that Aviakhim was organizing an anti-fly campaign, and be struck by the poverty of human affairs.[92] Or that tomorrow a three-day exhibition and canary-singing contest would commence, or that one or another provincial cooperative had been delivered voile for the winter season instead of regular textiles. Balmcalfkin might be on the verge of forgetting that his whole life was a confusion of turmoil, anxiety and ambivalence, of plunging into the eternal question of the correspondence between great and small, but dinner was already ready, a modest dinner, and the soup was already being brought to the table in its tureen, and Maria Petrovna was already fussing around, and setting down the soup spoon, and drying off the plates. She sat down and asked: "Is it good?" and blew on her spoon and smiled.

"I fried up the bread crusts," she said, "look at the color of the broth!"

Today their dinner was magnificent. For the main course they had duck with lingonberry jam, and for dessert—baked apples. After dinner Maria Petrovna got up and said:

"Just look what I got for you! I'm walking around the market and see—by this old lady, next to some paintings, there's a little book, well, I thought, probably *La Dame aux camélias* or a French prayer book. But all the same I stopped and picked it up, and what do you know—*Arcadia* ..."

"Giacomo Sannazzaro!" exclaimed Balmcalfkin.

His wife nodded and brought out the book. Balmcalfkin looked at it and read:

IL PASTOR FIDO

"But this isn't *Arcadia* at all," he exclaimed, "why did you want to trick me?"[93]

Maria Petrovna became embarrassed and blushed.

"That one I bought for myself, there's a French translation to go with it, I want to start working on Italian again. For you I did buy *Arcadia*."

But Balmcalfkin wouldn't let go of Battista Guarini, he was admiring the heart pierced by two arrows, he noted the inscription on the ribbon: RVRIS NON CUPIDA VENVS.[94] After that he set about examining the two figures in long robes, who seemed to be emerging from caves. A fat-cheeked Eros, a little goat, a kid, lambs, a little angel—he found it all enchanting. He began reading the dedication. *V* instead of *U* and, on the contrary, *U* instead of *V*; *S*, *P* and *C* where they would now be absent, the small number of contractions, the rag paper itself, which had over time acquired the smell of old wine, the split parchment binding—it all carried Balmcalfkin away into his favorite epoch.

Of course, this was not at all fifteenth century and not quite sixteenth—the book had been published in Paris in 1610—but of course Italian had still been held in high regard in France at that time. And Balmcalfkin began reading the translation of the pastoral, famous in its time, done by an anonymous student of Italian.

"Give it to me, I want to study it," Maria Petrovna broke the silence. "It's my book. For you I bought *Arcadia*."

Maria Petrovna took out another little book, with gold-edged pages, in a black binding—this was new binding, from the 1880s—but inside it, Venice was smiling; true, this was not the astonishing script of the Aldine Press or even poor Manutius the Younger, who only had one disciple and a magnificent library, but still...[95]

The couple sat at the table drinking tea. And Maria Petrovna struggled to once again take up her studies.

Balmcalfkin was sitting in his garden-study. Perhaps the sky was too clear, or Maria Petrovna had let the goats out of the woodshed to walk around the courtyard, or it was some other phenomenon, or some conversation that he'd had with Maria Petrovna before her appearance in the courtyard—for whatever reason, Balmcalfkin was sitting in his garden-study, his book on his knees, unable to concentrate. It was hard to say whether Balmcalfkin was thinking at that moment. If someone had asked him, then he would not have answered right away, but would have tried to recollect what he had in fact been thinking about, and with bitterness would have to acknowledge that he had not been thinking about anything at all. One association was followed by another: first the sun reminded him of a watermelon, then the flowers on Maria Petrovna's blouse reminded him of a steamship, then the billy goat, butting the brick wall, called forth in him an indistinct notion of a god indulgently dwelling on earth amid the human race. And from time to time Balmcalfkin got up from the bench, leaned his elbows against the fence, wrinkled his nose and moved his lips:

"I have some kind of presentiment."

And, with an awareness of his own worth, he looked pointedly at the people walking past the little garden. And Maria Petrovna, her arms around the billy goat, ran with it across the courtyard to the place where Balmcalfkin was sitting, and Balmcalfkin, retreating somewhat from his lofty concerns and from becoming one with nature, consumed by the cosmos, came out of the garden and, exchanging a few words with Maria Petrovna, walked out the gate onto the street.

After being in this kind of state Balmcalfkin felt the sweetest allure of the world. It seemed to him that the sun was shining more brightly, indeed that everything in the world was brighter, that he himself was an exalted person, worthy in all respects. At such moments he would be seized by compassion for all living things and would forgive everyone their shortcomings. His limitless love for Maria Petrovna blazed forth and he would say:

"Maria Petrovna, how about we go look for toys!"

Then he would walk grandly down the street with Maria Petrovna, they would walk up to the windows of toy stores and, stopping, Maria Petrovna would press her nose to the glass, and they would go into the shop.

"What age are you looking for?" the shop owner would ask.

"We need decorative toys," Balmcalfkin would answer.

And, leaning over the counter, Maria Petrovna and Balmcalfkin would begin selecting toys.

"Do you perhaps have a wooden bird?" Maria Petrovna might ask. "Or a wooden lion with a stylized mane?"

"And why don't I see any nesting dolls here?" Balmcalfkin might interrupt.

And bringing their toys home, the couple would jointly admire them.

But more and more often Balmcalfkin, sitting in his little garden, would notice that Maria Petrovna was aging, that her face no longer had the same pure color, that she didn't feel like walking at all, that she would say:

"You go take a stroll by yourself, have a breath of fresh air, and I'll make you some dinner in the meantime. Would you like me to make you crayfish soup?"

And then Balmcalfkin would draw Maria Petrovna close and, pressing his nose to hers, look into her eyes, and Maria Petrovna, still young, so young, was walking through the park like Diana, just like Diana.

In his brighter moments Balmcalfkin no longer blamed the war or the revolution for his barrenness and that of his era. And then the autumn leaves would rustle for him as they once had in the brightest of springs, in the most relentless summer. And out from behind the trees mesmerizing little faces with little horns and hooves would peek out at him, and nymphs with eyes of wakeless depth would rise above the water like steam, and he would hear their speech inside of himself, mesmerizing and astonishing; and he would say to himself that, look, creatures from another world come to visit him and he is not at all lonesome, that a great epoch of humanity is departing along with him.

In these tender moments Balmcalfkin would reread his letter to the unknown poet:

My dear friend, you are a paganist. This is a deeply negative trait, you do not accept Christian charity, while in fact one can unite Christianity with faith in the beautiful gods and sense the special silence of the world. After all, say what you will, but you love the sun, the warm morning sun, you love morning birdsong, and it is not mere decoration, mere decoration is not all that attracts you to pagan religion, not the multitude of deities, not the materialization of the forces of nature, but that specific holiness, that arcane knowledge that is generated by contact with nature. You love the agony of this feeling, but is it not better to love its dawn? You love dying, but is it not better to love life? Do you remember our conversations in the park in Peterhof, in the Monplaisir Garden, amid trees already shedding their leaves, observed by that barefooted girl guarding the garden and cracking pine nuts? I have heard rumors that you have denied your own self. Dear friend, come to your senses, you are very ill right now, return to paganism, but to a serene and lucid paganism, without poisonous substances, without chuckles and without scorn. After all, the nymphs and satyrs who appeared to us did not appear to other people. Dear friend, why do you malign yourself so? Maria Petrovna and I often talk of you here, here in the hall with the Botticelli collection, we often think of you—you too loved his paintings. You always aspired toward Rome, but Florence, after all, is closer to us and dearer. You are experiencing a dreadful trial, which I already underwent; remember your own words about our transformation into devils. Now I accept the world in all its grievous beauty. It was not our dream but we ourselves who were a lie. We were already unworthy of that which was revealed to us. I see our weaknesses, but they do not frighten me. I know that we are weak, insanely weak, that we are depraved, that we are covetous, but also that we loved the spiritual sun, and who knows, perhaps we love it even now.

37. THE DEATH OF MARIA PETROVNA

MARIA Petrovna exited the door of an enormous building, which was illuminated inside by chandeliers, oil lamps, and candles, and which outside resembled either a pepper grinder or an inkstand,[96] buttoned up her jacket, took out a squashed Chinese lantern, straightened it out, stood between the columns and, sheltering the flame from the wind, placed a candle inside the lantern.

Part of the crowd was headed for 25 October Avenue, part headed off down Mayor Avenue. Some people, including Maria Petrovna and Balmcalfkin, went off down Galernaya Street to Lieutenant Schmidt Bridge.[97] The streets, dried out by the frost, reflected the starry sky, bells rang out from the inkstand's roof, the trembling lights of all the candles illuminated faces, hands, streets, alleys, and side streets, and Maria Petrovna, who had lost her sense of religion, felt that she was participating in a carnival parade. No longer a Christian, she still loved church for the rituals, like an archaic theater, a stylized performance. In keeping with this, she preferred Tikhon's church to the living church.[98] She thought that a sublime spectacle required a special language and a certain amount of incomprehensibility, while the living church, failing to understand this, strove to simplify things as much as possible, thereby destroying the psychic framework and bringing high drama down to the level of everyday life. There should be an element of the irrational in art. So thought Maria Petrovna, as she walked along Lieutenant Schmidt Bridge with her husband, holding a lantern, like someone taking part in a lofty theatrical drama.

Balmcalfkin was also carrying a lit candle in a paper cone made of yesterday's evening edition of the *Red Newspaper*. Drifting into daydreams, he was carried away to his childhood. He saw himself in a washroom colored with oil paint, the icon of St. Panteleimon with its raspberry-colored many-faceted lamp. Protecting his candle's little flame, Balmcalfkin turned onto the First Line of Vasilievsky Island, but Maria Petrovna, gazing into her lantern and taking someone else's back for her husband's, turned in the opposite direction. And suddenly she felt that she had to scream. Inside her something was pulling and rocking, it was hot all around her, her eyelids wouldn't open and, holding back the urge to vomit, she heard voices:

"Run to the medical locker, tell the ship's master we had a man overboard."

And further off another voice:

"I was just come on deck up the gangplank when I hear a yell, right, I look—a man overboard, I dove in, there's a sou'wester on, rain lashing too, and that water, holy Moses, it was cold. At long last I made it out, pretty heavy load I had, she might not have weighed much, but she was big enough, and shaking like a leaf."

"So we're sitting there, like, plenty bored, thinking how to toss back a few or more. Seryozhka's floundering about down there, I look and think—got to drag 'im out. Then I see he's dragging some broad by the hair, tugging in a whale of a fishy! Now there's a meal, I think, an Easter feast; she threw back a glass of vodka, started sputtering, pinked up, whaddya know, like gettin' holy baptism, the river Jordan."

Maria Petrovna lifted her heavy head and looked around. Two men, a bathhouse, the other people in the doorways, in striped jerseys; a porthole up above was drawing in air, some other man was going to refuel the lantern on deck.

"See now, she's opened up her peepers, unfasten the porthole, heave her out to get some air."

They wrapped up Maria Petrovna warmly. The sailors wanted to accompany her, but she set out on her own. And as she walked off she heard:

"We've got the hot water all ready, some nice tea brewed in the galley, gave the girl a nice cuppa, she'll get over it, woes aplenty in this life, she'll croak an' cough a bit, then bounce right back."

Balmcalfkin was meanwhile running, now along the street, now back to their building. Maria Petrovna was nowhere to be seen. He'd already run fifteen or so times to St. Isaac's, stood many times at one end or the other of Lieutenant Schmidt Bridge, sometimes stopping at the two sphinxes, looking out at the black strip of water between the shore and the ice. A presentiment clenched his heart.

"My God, where is she? Where?" his soul wept.

And he ran on, hurrying through the snow, and when the day was fully breaking, he ran for the twentieth time up the stairs to their doorway and saw: Maria Petrovna with a bandage on her head, sitting on the top step and shaking with fever. She was not holding her colorful lantern and her face was terribly pale, and her hat sat on her head at a strange angle.

"My sweet one," he shrieked, "what happened to you?" Seizing his wife by the shoulders, he led her into the apartment.

Maria Petrovna burst into loud sobs.

The thermometer held under her arm, Maria Petrovna lay on the bed. Balmcalfkin, in deep and sorrowful concentration, was pacing around the room. His unshaven face was trembling.

How quickly family happiness can be lost, he thought, *just any trifle, a random accident, can destroy it.*

It grieved him that this young life was departing so purposelessly.

"Maria Petrovna," he sat down on the chair and took Maria Petrovna's hand.

"My treasure," Maria Petrovna opened her eyes, "my dear treasure, I am leaving you."

And the strangest thing about it was—she really did leave.

This was accompanied by strange phenomena. She asked that Balmcalfkin carry her around the room. He brought her over to every object and she, holding onto his neck with one hand, used the other to touch the objects: little knives for cutting open the pages of books, the books themselves, the backs of chairs, the flowers by the window, the curtain, the ashtray with little flowers; then she demanded that he turn her, she couldn't get enough air. Balmcalfkin, pale, fulfilled her demands, turned her and turned around himself. Opposite them two receivers attached to the balcony were broadcasting the radio-newspaper. What happened after that Balmcalfkin could never remember, because he had noticed that Maria Petrovna was quieting down. He carefully put her into bed and sat down next to her and started looking at the little medicine bottles, the lampshade, her illuminated face. He noticed that dust had settled on the bottles and began wiping them down. He'd pasted paper around the lampshade, leaving only a narrow slit so that the lamplight would fall to the side. He kissed Maria Petrovna on the forehead and sat down on the windowsill. He began looking at his little garden in the courtyard, covered in snowflakes. Dozing, Balmcalfkin was horrified by how everyone talked about decay, while no one talked about renaissance. When it was night he rose from the chair and sat again on the windowsill. *The universe, that lively garden where Dante and Beatrice wander, isn't a wife a sort of guiding light for a man, don't we open up to our wives a certain image that appeared to us in childhood, one that is astonishingly harmonious?* Balmcalfkin went on musing that the life of such spouses would be impossible. On tiptoe, enormous and mournful, he went into the next room and began reading his manuscript. And he began to be tortured by the non-correspondence between his own figure and the ideal image, his thinness tortured him—in his view, it prevented him from heroism.

What would happen, he thought, *if I had muscles, if I had the face of an ascetic, if I wore fetters?* Bathed in moonlight, "Balmcalfkin" cast his eyes heavenwards, and an even greater melancholy overwhelmed him. *What would happen*, he thought, *if my last name was not Balmcalfkin, but something completely different. The two syllables 'balmcalf' are obviously an onomatopoeia, the word "kin" could be sort of ominous, like "king," but that's prevented by the consonantal "lf" sound, while if I had a syllabic "f," then it'd be Balmcalofkin, which would be terribly doleful. Lord*, Balmcalfkin straightened up, letting his book drop. *No one else was thinking about the Renaissance, it was just me. Wherefore this agony!* And he fell back into reality again.

He remembered that that night had been quiet to an extreme, that, looking for Maria Petrovna, he had found himself by the sphinxes, that the breathtaking monsters had reminded him of other nights—Egyptian ones, even then.[99] Setting his book aside, he went into the next room, but Maria Petrovna was not in her bed. He looked around. She had gotten up on her own and was feeling her way around the room, sitting down on everything that could be sat on. She sat on the chairs, and the table, and the windowsill, and the trunk covered with a plush green tablecloth.

"Maria Petrovna," Balmcalfkin rushed over to her. "Don't leave me."

Maria Petrovna burst into tears and had a coughing fit in his arms. Balmcalfkin could feel her wheezing ever more softly and then he felt that he was carrying a heavy and still slightly warm body. Unable to hold out, he tried to sit down on a chair, but the chair couldn't take this triple weight and he (Balmcalfkin) sat down on the floor.

A pink flush was already playing on the cheeks of what had been Maria Petrovna, while the arms flopped weakly, the fixed eyes gazed at the ceiling, and the lower jaw hung open and the white face of Balmcalfkin looked out the window. Like sublieutenant Kovalyov, he felt that the world truly was horrible and that he was alone, utterly alone in it.

When late that night, as usual, the doctor came, he found a rosy corpse in a white dress on the bed and Balmcalfkin holding his hat and suitcase.

As Balmcalfkin walked along in predawn melancholy, a pigeon smiled at him; the white bird with reddish spots turned its neck and looked at him with one round eye.

"Oh, my dove," Balmcalfkin stopped, "my dear dove," and he set out after the pigeon, and the pigeon, stepping purposefully, walked along the sidewalk, and Balmcalfkin followed it:

Now you've come back here again, birds of peace. But I am different now, an utterly different person. The one who dreamed he'd light up the city with love is gone, a different man stands among you now, dear birds.

And the pigeons, assuming that he would now start to feed them, flew down from the cornices, and gathered in little flocks, and conversed with one another.

And the Kazan Cathedral, bathed in sunlight, and the small square with lone figures, slightly chilled, and the benches still damp from the dew called to Balmcalfkin to stretch out, his hands beneath his head, to take a nap amid the ambulating birds. And the sky, the impossibly sweet Petersburg sky, pale, powder blue, feeble, closed in like a cupola above Balmcalfkin, who could not forget that he was bald and utterly alone.

A large moon illuminated the House of the Arts, which no longer existed. An employee with the face of the last emperor was getting ready to lock up. Balmcalfkin and Maria Petrovna went down the back stairs to the exit and came out into the empty regenerating city.

God damn—how long ago that all was!

Light stood above the spit-covered buildings, while Balmcalfkin and Maria Petrovna walked along together. And in the predawn languor the heart clenched, and the cold wind tore and pinched and whistled.

The author is looking out the window. His ears are ringing, and singing, and howling, and singing again, and ringing again and, shifting into an unintelligible whisper, the Goat Song falls silent.

The author is still young. If people will listen to him, he will tell another Petersburg fairy tale.

And so, until tomorrow night, my friend.

1926–1928; 1929

ADDITIONAL CHAPTERS
From Earlier Drafts of Goat Song

FOREWORD

written by the real author on the banks of the Neva

THE WORK of art opens up like a circus tent—where the creator and the spectator enter. Everything in this tent is connected with the creator and the spectator. It is impossible to understand anything without knowledge of them both: If you know the spectator, then you will only understand part of the tent, if you only know the creator, then you probably won't understand anything. Furthermore, reader, remember that the people depicted in this book are not represented in and of themselves, that is, in all their fullness, which is anyway impossible, but rather from the point of view of a contemporary.

The author in the following forewords and in the book is the same kind of actor as the rest, so if you can, do not correlate him with the really existing author; restrict yourself to what is given in the book and do not stray beyond its limits.

But if your mind is built in such a way that you correlate every literary work with life, like most people, rather than with other literary works, then correlate it with the era, the class, whatever you want, just not with the real author—show that you have good manners.

20. THE APPEARANCE OF A FIGURE

Look, I've wrapped myself in the Chinese dressing gown. Here I am examining the collection of kitsch. Here I am holding the stick with the amethyst.

How time drags on! The bookstalls are still closed. Perhaps in the meantime it'd be better to get into coin-collecting or read that tractatus on the link between intoxication and poetry.

Tomorrow I'll invite my heroes to dinner. I'll ply them with wine that I buried in '17 in the courtyard beneath the big linden tree.

And again I fall asleep, and the unknown poet appears to me in a dream, pointing to his book that I'm holding.

"No one suspects that this book emerged from the juxtaposition of words. This does not contradict the fact that something flashes before every artist in childhood. This is the fundamental antinomy (contradiction). The artist is given a kind of task outside of language, but then, throwing words around and juxtaposing them, he creates and subsequently comes to know his own soul. Thus in my youth, by juxtaposing words, I came to know the universe, and a whole world emerged for me in language and rose up from language. And it turned out that this world risen from language coincided astonishingly with reality. But it's time, time…"

And I wake up. It's already eleven o'clock. The bookstalls have opened, they've shipped in books from the regional libraries. Perhaps I will find a Dante, one of the first editions, or at least one of Bayle's encyclopedic dictionaries…[1]

Night. Down below lies white-blue snow, up above a starry-blue sky.

Here's my shovel. I have to prepare everything for the arrival of my transforming heroes. My courtyard is quiet and bright. Devoid of leaves, the linden remembers how we sat beneath it many, many years ago, white, yellow, pink, and spoke of the end of the century. We had all of our teeth then, our hair wasn't falling out and our posture was erect.

The place is two paces from the linden trunk, facing my lit window. Here. The moon is behind clouds, snow is falling in large flakes, I will have to dig in the dark.

That's all right...

Did I remember where it was?

Once again, two paces from the linden toward my window.

One, two.

It's here, of course it's here! Deeper?

Finally!

Have to fill in the dirt and pack it down. The snow will cover everything.

With the crate and my shovel, I went up the stairs like a somnambulist, turned my head and looked out on the darkness: is there anyone in the courtyard?

No one was there.

I put bottles of wine out on the table. Neatened up the room for the arrival of my friends.

The unknown poet arrived first, limping, with brooding brow, the lower part of his face nearly atrophied, and went to look at my books.

"We all love books," he said quietly. "Our philological education and interests are what distinguish us from the new people."

I invited my hero to be seated.

"I hold," he began, "that the greater threat to the remnants of humanism comes not from here, but from the new continent. The former European colonies are threatening Europe. It's curious that at first America appeared, in contrast to Europe, like a primitive land, then like a land of freedom, then like a land of action."

An hour later all of my heroes had gathered, and we sat down to table.

The stove crackled, throwing sparks. My heroes and I sat around it in a semicircle on the carpet.

Apples rose up on a broken dish.

Nearly everyone had empty cigarette packs and mountains of butts in front of them. Neither I nor my heroes knew whether night was ongoing or morning had come.

Kissenkin stood up.

"Let's start a collective novella," he suggested.

35. INTERWORD OF THE ESTABLISHED AUTHOR

I FINISHED writing my novel, lifted my sharp-edged head with its eyes half-covered in yellow membranes, looked at my hands, deformed from birth: there are three fingers on my right hand, four on my left.

Then I took my novel and went to Peterhof to reread it, to contemplate and wander, to feel as though my heroes were with me.

From the Old Peterhof station I walked to the tower, which I had sought out and described. There was no more tower.

Inside me, under the influence of the nonfaded flowers and grass, once again awoke that enormous bird which consciously or unconsciously had been felt by my heroes. I see my heroes standing around me in the air, I walk accompanied by this crowd to New Peterhof, sit down by the sea, and, while my heroes are standing in the air above the sea, shot through with sun, I begin to leaf through the manuscript and converse with them.

When I am back in the city, I want to fall to pieces, disappear, and, halting by the woodstove, I begin to toss in the sheets of manuscript paper and burn them.

It's hot.

I slowly undress, walk over to the table naked, open the window, look out at the passersby and the city and begin to write. I write and observe the gait of the building superintendent, and how the NEP-lady walks, and how the girl university student hurries along. I'm amused by the fact that I'm sitting here naked at the window and that on my desk there's a pinkie-sized laurel and a spray of myrtle. And between them is a blistered inkpot and books, all sorts of conquering of Mexico and Peru, all sorts of grammars.

I am kind, I muse. *I am high-minded in the Balmcalkinian sense. I have the utterly refined taste of Kostya Kissenkin, the conception of the unknown poet, Triniton's soft-headedness. I am made of the dough of my heroes*...and right there at the desk I set to making cocoa on the primus/camp-stove—I have a sweet tooth.

In my two-room apartment I walk around naked all day (Attic recollections) or wearing only a shirt. I wear monastic slippers, made of velvet with gold stitching.

When I've made the cocoa and drunk my fill, I dust the books again and, dusting them, read them as I go, today one, tomorrow another. Ten lines from one now, and a few minutes later—a few lines from another. Now something political in French, then some poem in Italian, then an excerpt from some travelogue in Spanish, finally, an aphorism or fragment in Latin—that's what I call dashing from one culture to another.

I figure that across all of Europe there is no shortage of eccentrics like this. I am for the most part satisfied with the new life, I live in a heroic country, at a heroic time, I follow events in China with great curiosity.

If China joins forces with India and the USSR, the old world is really done for, really!

Sometimes I look at my monstrous fingers and laugh contentedly: "I really am such a freak!"

My hands are always damp, my breath smells like raspberries. I wear a smock, long unfashionable trousers, on my finger is a ring with turquoise, I love this ring as vulgar kitsch. Sometimes I wear a fashionable suit, yellow shoes and a wristwatch.

I also love gingerbreads frosted with sugar people wearing short little skirts, intimations of classical ballet; on my writing desk I always keep one of these gingerbreads with a ballerina next to the blistered inkpot and a naked woman representing Venus; at her feet is a plate with the remains of Tanagra statuettes. This is also where a bottle of cognac dozes along with a leaning package of colorful mint gingerbreads shaped like fish, lambs, rings, horsies, which I eat with my cognac.

My naked figure, sitting on a chair by the desk, drinking cognac and washing it down with mint gingerbreads, is utterly ridiculous. I take an optimistic view of life. I suppose that writing is something like a physiological process, a sort of purging of the organism. I don't like what I write because I can see clearly that I write pretentiously, with the metaphors and poetic coquettishness that a real writer would never allow himself.

The fact that my work is almost never published doesn't bother me in the slightest. I wouldn't have been published in times past either.

For instance, take England—I'm warming up to the topic now—they don't publish real writers there either, at best two or three friends will publish 200 copies of an elegant little book with all sorts of hinting references to little known texts, and no one will read it anyway. Everyone is busy doing foxtrots and reading ephemeral novels.

I could live well enough on the compensation received from various professions if it weren't for my curiosity. I love walking around, going to theaters and spectacles, clubs, listening to music at concerts, driving around the suburbs, foxtrotting, sitting a girl down on the couch to read her my excerpts—not because I think that my excerpts are so marvelous but because I think that there are no better works to be had in the city, and because I think that the girl won't understand any of what's in them, and I enjoy not being understood—and then going off with her somewhere, joining her and another girl and reading them my excerpts together.

Every evening before bed, when I'm at home, I read or reread some pastoral novel in Old French translation, for sometimes it seems to me, especially in the evenings, that I think more in French than in Russian, although I don't speak any languages besides Russian; sometimes I display such spiritual refinement, draw out such a subtle philosophical thought that I myself am astonished / have trouble believing it.

"Did I really write that or was it someone else?" And I suddenly lift my hand to my lips and kiss it. My precious hand. I praise myself to the skies. "Who do I take after, no one in my family was talented."

FIRST AFTERWORD

THE AUTHOR tried to save Balmcalfkin the whole time, but he was unable to save Balmcalfkin. After his apostasy Balmcalfkin lived not at all in poverty. The place he occupied in life was not at all minor, he was never seized by self-doubt, he never thought that he did not belong to high culture; instead of himself he considered his dream to be a lie.

Balmcalfkin did not become a poor club worker at all; he became a respected but stupid bureaucrat. And he didn't lay out a little garden in his courtyard, on the contrary—he yelled at other bureaucrats and was terribly long-winded and proud of the position he'd achieved. He acquired four pairs of trousers and demanded that there be roast chicken for his dinner every day.

But it is time to lower the curtain. The play has ended. Onstage it's dimly lit and quiet. Where is the love that was promised, the heroism? Where is the art that was promised?

And the sorrowful three-fingered author comes out onstage with his heroes and takes a bow.

"Look, Mikey, look at the freaks," says a spectator: "well, well, what a scallawag, feeding us this filth."

"Good lord, it's so awful, are all people really like that? You know, Ivan Matveyevich, there's something Balmcalfkinish about you."

"Oh, I'm gonna settle things with him tomorrow. I'm gonna sit him on a landmine. I'm gonna ..."

The author waves a hand—and the typesetters start to set out the book. "Thank you, thank you." The author exchanges kisses with his actors.

He takes off his gloves and starts removing his makeup. The actors and actresses stretch, straighten out and start scraping off their makeup right onstage.

And the author and his actors take off for a cheap bar/tavern. They have a ball there. Surrounded by bottles and emptied glasses, the author tell his actors about his plan for a new play, and they argue and get heated and toast high art, fearing neither infamy, crime nor spiritual death.

The typesetters have already set half of *Goat Song* and the author with his real friends walks out of the bar into a gorgeous spring night in Petersburg, a night that flings souls up above the Neva, above the palaces, above the suburbs filled with centaurs, a night that whispers like a garden, that sings like youth, and that flies like an arrow already gone whistling past them.

1927

SECOND AFTERWORD

I LIE IN my bed in the room that gives out onto the street like a rotunda. On the couch, the floor and the chairs lie sheets of paper, like autumn leaves around the base of a tree, but these sheets do not resemble the wide yellow leaves of the oak, the patterned maple leaves, the rounded leaves of the linden; the truth is, they didn't fall, the connection between me and the sheets has not been broken, they're still on the branches, some have curled up into tubes, others have broken or stuck together.

I look carefully at the sheets: they're not sheets at all, they're the lids of cigarette packets, half-sheets of paper torn out of notebooks, book covers; they're all covered in my handwriting. I can see they have increased in volume, become transparent, dissolve in the air, and the room I am lying in is no more.

The sun keeps getting lower, and the evening shadows are settling in already, and the greenery now seems darker than it did in the morning, and I recall another day, when at midday it became as dark as it is now and, running all the way to the Belvedere, picking flowers along the way, we saw a ray of sun suddenly gleam, illuminating the pediment of a tree, and then it lit up the whole field and, rising, touched the leaves with gold. And, following the periodically appearing butterflies, we set off across the gleaming grass toward the tower. At that time I was not Balmcalfkin, the unknown poet, the philosopher, Kostya Kissenkin, Misha Kittenkin; at that time I was one person, whole and undivided. At that time I had not yet disintegrated into different people, and at that time I felt a terrifying light inside myself and, in fact, it was not we but I alone who walked all those roads; later an unexpected fragmentation occurred.

And it is again a white night, as it was during the most exquisite days of my life, and again I want to see only the quiet buildings of the capital city, only the incomparable pale-blue Neva, to sense the suburbs filled with centaurs, and to stand on the bridges, surrounded by stars.

But have I stepped out of my book once and for all, have I been liberated from my heroes, have I driven then into a world other than the one I inhabit, what will happen to me if I really drive them away, perhaps a void will appear, an enormous nothingness, and other beings will throw themselves into this void, beings no less sorrowful, and settle there?

1927

THE WORKS AND DAYS OF
WHISTLIN

1. SILENCE

HIS WIFE, having taken off her dress and grabbed a shaggy bath towel, was bathing as she did every evening in the kitchen. She splashed around and, holding one nostril closed, blew out the other one. Cupping her hands under the faucet, she lowered her head, rubbed her face with wet palms, stuck fingers into her pale ears, soaped up her neck, part of her back, then traced one arm along the other to the shoulder.

Out the window could be seen: a little house with illuminated square windows which they called the cottage, surrounded by snow-covered trees and recently painted white; two walls of the conservatory and part of the sand-colored Academic Theater building, with its long windows that shone in the evenings; beyond all that and a little to the right, a bridge and the straight street where the Milk Union was, and a pharmacy, cutting a fine figure, and the Pryazhka muddying into the Griboyedov Canal, not far from the sea. A large building with a garden gave out onto the Pryazhka.[1]

Whistlin gazed out the window at this part of the city, where the theater met the Milk Union and the pharmacy.

The canal flowed behind the building Whistlin lived in. In the spring, mud dredgers appeared on the canal, in the summer it was boats, in the fall—young drowned ladies.

Beyond the canal were streets with taverns, where drunk women with battered faces peered out from corners, their throats hacking hoarsely.

Whistlin had the urge to don once again his student's cap with its sky-blue band and his galoshes, and to head out into the nighttime city, where he'd find the Admiralty with its spire, the General Staff building, the arch, St. Catherine's Church, the City Duma, the Public Library building. He wished for youth.

Out the window everything had long since disappeared, and it was quiet in the apartment. Only the clock, which had survived all manner of moves but lost its ability to chime, went on ticking in the dining room.

Whistlin had a dream:

A man is hurrying down the street. Whistlin recognizes himself in the man. The walls of the buildings are half-transparent, some buildings are missing, others lie in ruins, and behind the transparent walls sit quiet people. Look, they're *still* drinking tea, sitting at a table covered in oilcloth, and the head of the family—a simple crafts-man—has pushed back his chair from the table. He studies his own face, lengthened by the samovar, and plucks at a guitar, while the children, kneeling against the chair and resting their heads on their little fists, gaze for hours at the lamp, the hearth, a corner of the floor. This is their rest after a hard day's work.

Meanwhile, behind another transparent wall sits an office worker, smoking a pipe and lending his face an American expression. For hours he watches the curling smoke, a half-sleepy fly crawling across the windowsill or, just opposite, in the window across the courtyard, a man devouring a newspaper to see if he can find another fascinating murder.

And meanwhile, across the street, all the widows have gathered to chatter about the intimate details of their interrupted married lives.

Whistlin sees that he, Whistlin, is chasing after everyone even in the daytime now, pursuing them as if they were rare wild animals. One moment he peers down into a basement like a hunter into a wolf's den, to see if someone might be there; the next he sits for a spell in a city park and chats with a citizen reading the paper; here he flags down a child on the street and, giving him candies, asks about his parents; the next moment he quietly drops by a corner store, has a look around and talks a bit of politics with the seller; or, pretending to be a compassionate person, he gives a coin to a beggar and delights in his blather; or, claiming to be a handwriting expert, he makes his way around to visit all of the city's famous men.

In the morning, with a glance at the clock, Whistlin had forgotten all of that. Trying not to wake his wife, he sat down half-dressed to do some editing. He corrected a few things, fixed a few more, hurried off to the writers' club. There, people wearing hats and caps were already sitting and exchanging rumors and the latest goings-on. A lady editor, rosy-cheeked and round, sat smoking and reading at her battered desk, sighing from time to time and peering out from behind the manuscript. She was interested in all these conversations, which were sometimes funny, but the din of footsteps and cackling laughter made it hard to work. Whistlin said hello to the lady editor and the others present. She gave him her hand and sank back into her reading.

The writers sat a while, chatting for four hours or so, waiting for someone else to come, watching to see who'd get up first. Having sat like everyone else, and having had his fill, like everyone else, of conversation, Whistlin disappeared into the elevator and found himself out on 25 October Avenue. It was already fairly late, and the writers and journalists were strolling extravagantly back and forth between the publishing house and the House of Print. Warmed by the spring-time sun, they were discussing how Kruglov wrote like Chesterton, how fine it is to visit the Crimea, how great it'd be to pitch the kind of book they reprint every year. They went down to the Moscow Stock Corporation, ate fried pirozhki, read the evening *Red News*, looked to see if there was anything written about them in current events, bought the Moscow journals and checked there too to see if anyone had written about them. When they found something, they laughed. What nonsense! Occasionally a student newsboy would run over to them and ask what they were working on. Then the writers would lie.

It was hard work sitting in the editorial office for four hours at a stretch, sometimes even five. By five o'clock the writers all got head-aches. Back at home they would eat dinner and, exhausted, lie down for a little nap. Toward evening, having determined that the day was over and that there was no point in trying to get anything done today, they would go with their wives to have a cup of tea with friends.

In the evening, Whistlin lay down on his bed and thought about what he ought to read: perhaps something about Old Russian household goods, which might come in handy for his new story? Or perhaps he ought to learn some brevity and precision from Mérimée? Or take up a volume of the Collection de l'histoire par le bibelot, since trifling details are astonishingly instructive and help catch the era off guard.[2]

But Whistlin did not bother putting on his slippers, which he'd made out of beaver-fur during the time of universal scarcity and hunger. He did not get out from under the blanket, did not climb up on a chair, did not quickly find the books. Instead, he turned to his wife and began telling her about the news he'd heard in the editorial office.

"Lenochka," he said, lighting up.

Lenochka lowered Panayeva's notebooks to the blanket and, settling back on an elbow, looked at her husband.[3]

"Count Ekesparre," Whistlin drawled listlessly, "used to call his Gypsy lover 'Dulcinea.'[4] He divided his dominion into satrapies and made a satrap head of each satrapy. He would give his soldiers the Genghis Khan ration—three rams per month—while the officers got two rams."

"Really?" asked Lenochka.

"He dreamed of forming a pan-Mongolian empire with German as the official language, and of setting his colored hordes against the West."

"Now there's a topic for you. You could write an interesting short story."

"I still haven't told you," Whistlin said, brightening, "that he declared himself the Buddha, corresponded with Chinese generals, and even found an aspirant to the imperial throne, some sort of Anglified Chinese prince living in America, who would blush when people called him a Chinaman."

Whistlin stretched out under the blanket and smoked, gazing at the ceiling; then he turned and began gazing at the wall.

"Ah, it's a shame, Lenochka," he said, "that I have never been to Mongolia. Monasteries are the breath of that country. You can't make breath out of German fairy tales. Perhaps I should tag along on Kozlov's expedition, make it an assignment from the evening *Red News*"[5]—and at this point he closed his eyes and was about to fall asleep when somewhere off to the side a thought popped up about hunting and hunters.

He felt an urge to write. He grabbed a book and started reading. Whistlin did not write in a systematic manner; it was not the case that an image of the world suddenly appeared before him, or that everything suddenly became clear, and that was not when he wrote anyway. On the contrary, all of his works emerged from messy scribblings in the margins of books, stolen metaphors, skillfully rewritten pages, overheard conversations, inverted rumors.

Whistlin lay in bed and read, i.e., wrote, since for him this was one and the same thing. He would mark off a paragraph with red pencil, then use a black one to insert it, in reworked form, into his own manuscript; he didn't worry about the meaning of the whole or the coherence of it all. Coherence and meaning would appear later.

WHISTLIN READ:

In the vineyards of the Alazani valley amidst the great number of gardens that enclose it, there stands the city of Telav, which at one time was the capital of the Kingdom of Kakheti.[6]

WHISTLIN WROTE:

Chavchavadze sat in a Kakheti cellar and sang songs of the vineyards of the Alazani valley, of the city of Telav, which at one time had been the capital city of the Kingdom of Kakheti. Chavchavadze was no fool and loved his homeland. (His grandfather had been a captain of cavalry in the Russian army, but no, no, one must return to one's own people.) Chavchavadze looked with disgust at the merchant sitting nearby, singing a Shamil' song and playing the guitar. "Profiteer," muttered Chavchavadze, "cursed brood, flunky." The merchant looked at him mournfully: "Don't be cruel. I am a good man."

Having written this excerpt, Whistlin laid the page aside. *"Chavcha-vadze,"* he repeated, *"Prince Chavchavadze. What does engineer Chavchavadze think of Moscow? Fine,"* he decided and continued reading about the death of King Irakli and the sorrow of his wife Daria.

On the low couches sat the dignitaries' wives, wrapped from head to toe in long white mantles, as, beating their chests, they loudly mourned the passing of the king. Across from the women to the right of the throne sat the officers of state, in order of rank, in silence, with grieving faces. Higher than all the rest sat the high-ranking ministers, behind them the masters of ceremony with broken staffs. From the window of the room the king's favorite steed could be seen, standing by the palace gates, saddled on the wrong side. Beside the horse an official sat on the ground, his head uncovered.

Perfect, thought Whistlin. *Chavchavadze is the Georgian ambas-sador under Paul I, Count Ekesparre is a descendant of the Teutonic knights. But perhaps not the Teutons... Have to check...*

The distant expanses of a future work began to appear to Whistlin. *A Pole*, he thought. *There should be a Pole, too. And I should invent an illegitimate son, one of the Bonapartes, who commanded a Russian regiment in the 1880s.*

The loving eyes of Poland gazing intently at France, Henry III absconded, Bonaparte on the island of St. Helena. Napoleon III, the failed uprising. Now France and Poland are once more two cultured and knightly sisters, thought Przesmycki, walking past Notre Dame de Paris—and the third knight is looking at us: Georgia.

Having written this, Whistlin sat down on his bed: *We'll take Paris too.* He looked down at the floor. *I'll have to go see the booksell-ers tomorrow.* And Whistlin, curling up in his blanket, began snoring.

In the morning, after visiting the editorial office, he set out for Volodarsky Avenue and made the rounds of the bookstalls with his briefcase, like a lady at Gostiny Dvor with her little clutch.

The shop owners and assistants asked about his new novel, talked about how eager they were to read it, that here's a curious little book and perhaps he'd recommend this book here to one of his acquaintances.

The book bacchanal had ended, and rare books had once again become rare.[7] The booksellers' trade, in other words, was in a bad way. Libraries were no longer selling them books for 1 ruble 20 kopecks a pood.

Whistlin dug around looking for Polish émigré books, books on Georgia, on the Ostsee region. The booksellers, retreating to a corner, drank vodka, chatted with the regulars, looked out at the street from afar.

Contented, Whistlin went back home. He had found:

1) *Recueil de diverses pièces, servants è l'histoire de Henry III roy de France et la Pologne. A Cologne, chez Pierre de Marteau, MDCLXII* (A collection of various plays on the history of Henry III, King of France and Poland. Cologne, Pierre de Marteau, 1762). This book had a crossed-out *ex libris* with the crest of D. A. Benckendorff; the crest bore the motto: *Avec Honneur* (With honor.).[8]

2) *The Russian Baltic Sea Region*, issue 1, publ. Yu. Samarin. Prague. 1868.

3) *Essai critique sur l'histoire de la Livonie...par C.C.D.B. MDCCXVIII* (Critical Essay on the History of Livonia...1718).

And many more in soft pigskin and calfskin binding.

Whistlin did not like electricity, so candles were already lit in his apartment. Lenochka was sitting at the table, reading:

...I lay down on the luxurious bed and slept very soundly for about four hours, but when I awoke, I saw a flute lying at the window; I took it up and began playing an aria in honor of the beautiful woman in the portrait, not knowing that this flute had been made through magical guile; for the very moment I began playing all of the fountains gushed forth their water with a great noise, and all the different birds that were in the garden, each according to its nature, sang forth trumpet-voiced songs, which caused many of the trees to drop their fruits straightaway. I was seized by a great terror following all this strangeness, and immediately ceased to play, fearing that this great noise would cause someone to come to my quarters and put me to death for my boldness. And since by this time the day was already declining toward evening, I judged it better not to leave this exquisite place, but remained in the pavilion to sleep and stayed the next day there until noon, but seeing that not a soul was to be seen in the garden...[9]

Whistlin had bought this tattered and filthy book at the Lenten market along with other junk, a few years ago, when he had been interested in various literary styles.[10]

Lenochka sat by candlelight. This novel bored her. After all, it was far less interesting than Walter Pater. She was hungry but was waiting for Whistlin, so that they could dine together. She walked over to the middle window to see if he was coming.

She returned and settled down to finish her book, but remembered that she hadn't dusted yet today. She went into the next room, set up the brown ladder and began to wipe down Whistlin's books. *How long it's been since my Andrei wrote poems*, she thought, got down Whistlin's notebooks, and stood still on the ladder, still holding her rag.

She leafed through Whistlin's notebooks, which contained poems that had once been considered incomprehensible, and then too comprehensible. She found a lock of her own hair in them, and dried flowers. The poems were washed out, faded with time, but for her they still shone.

Lenochka ran her rag over the spines of the books. There were now so many books, but, my God, what books: unpublished diaries of unknown functionaries, "daybooks" of lustful students; the correspondence between some husband, evidently a railway employee, and

his wife; skinny brochures published by graphomaniacs; philosophical books written on the spur of the moment by actors; the long-
format leather-bound albums of ecstatic adolescents; a Saint Petersburg
calendar for the Year of Our Lord 1754. There were inscriptions: "6.
Let blood from the foot; 19. It snowed; 28. Straw bought." There were
books about cosmetics—from *Gli ornamenti della donna*, by Giovanni
Marinello (1562), to the most modern. Cookbooks, books of home
cures, books dedicated to dances and card games long since obsolete,
and shelves of classics, and volumes and stacks of books arranged and
propped up every which way.

Sitting down on the ladder, Lenochka began reading the poems.
She read and thought back to when and where Andrei had written
each one, what Andrei had been wearing then, and she too. But then
the doorbell rang and Lenochka, putting away the ladder and tossing
her dusty rag, opened the door.

Whistlin, reading the paper, used his red pencil to circle phrases that
Lenochka should cut out and glue onto pieces of paper.

The soup was getting cold.

"You can read later on!" said Lenochka. "Tell me a story."

"What do you want to hear?" replied Whistlin, as he continued
reading.

"You could at least tell me what the weather's like today," Lenochka
tried to start a conversation. "Have the buds come out, and where are
we going this summer?"

"To Toxovo, I suppose," muttered Whistlin lazily, getting up. "The
air is so fine there."

He went into the other room to have a rest. He'd drunk some
wine with dinner, and this made him unable to read and write. Lying
on the couch, he examined Lenochka, watching her walk around the
room and dig through the books.

"Lenochka, read me some clippings," he said.

Lenochka got out the sheets of paper covered in newspaper clippings and, sitting down closer to the candles, began reading.[11]

———

November 1914

According to wounded Germans, the morale among the soldiers is quite low. The officers keep talking to them about victories, but the soldiers no longer believe these tales.

———

"OSMAN"

A model of perfection!...
Smoking this is pure elation,
A cigarette that's extra fin—
Gives you pleasure en plein.
Glory to Shaposhnikov goods,
Criez, messieurs, bravo, extra good!!!

UNCLE MICKEY

The American Millionaires' Ball

...most of the ladies appeared at the ball either in simple peasant dresses or in costumes inspired by popular children's fairy tales. By doing so they wished to emphasize their critical attitude toward the militant S_U_F_F_R_A_G_E_T_T_E_S.

Invasion Of The Fleas

An unheard-of quantity of fleas has descended upon the city. Houses, hotels, theaters, cinemas all complain that masses of fleas have moved in. Poor cleaning practices in the summer promote the rapid spread of fleas. Entire buildings are turning to the Workers' Wellness Bureau with requests to be cleared of fleas. Decontamination is carried out using gases and is quite inexpensive. Certain hotels have requested that they be rid of bedbugs. This work is also being carried out as quickly as possible.

IMPASSIONED SPEECHES AGAINST GERMAN DOMINATION...

"Lenochka, how many times have I asked you to gather all of the clippings and reglue them in chronological order. I really don't think that should be so hard! And how many times have I asked you to write the date and the name of the newspaper on every clipping, even the most insignificant ones. This would make things so much easier, after all."

Lenochka, flipping through the clippings, looked up at her hero.

"All right, all right," she assured him, "I'll be sure to put the dates."

"The month *and* the day, *and* the name of the paper," Whistlin reiterated.

But overall he was pleased by the reading. It had shaken his imagination awake.

Lenochka took up a wooden darning egg and socks and began

mending. The candles in their alabaster vine-leaf candlesticks crackled lightly. Whistlin felt bored.

"Lenochka," he said, "read me some novellas."

Novellas was what he called the other newspaper clippings.

Lenochka got up from the armchair, got down the morocco-bound ..lume and began leafing through it.

"About the tailor," Whistlin requested.

This was novella number thirty-three.

NOVELLA THIRTY-THREE

THE "EXPERIMENTAL" NOVELIST

Before you write anything, you yourself must experience the phenomenon described here.

This principle is propounded by... Dmitri Slotkin, a tailor. For about two years now he's been writing a "novel of modern life," with all its horrors.

Two months ago Slotkin needed to finish a chapter of his novel in which the protagonist attempted suicide by poison.

With this aim in mind, Slotkin wished to experience himself the sufferings ordinarily experienced by suicides.

He acquired some poison, took it, and then lost consciousness. Slotkin was brought from his apartment to the Mary Magdalene Hospital. He spent about two months there.

Having recovered, Slotkin continued his "novel."

Now his protagonist needed to experience the sensations of suicide by drowning.

Today at two in the morning Slotkin threw himself into the Little Neva from the Tuchkov Bridge.

The drowning man was noticed in time by a river policeman and the bridge guard. They rowed out to Slotkin and dragged him out of the water.

The "experimental novelist," unconscious, was brought to the very same Mary Magdalene Hospital. This morning he was revived.

That's not all. Now he needs to experience what it's like to throw oneself under a train: "Only then will all the phenomena in my novel be both real and sensational."

The novelist-tailor is in critical condition.

"Should I keep reading?" asked Lenochka.

Whistlin nodded and closed his eyes.

NOVELLA THIRTY-FOUR

A STRANGE STORY

As everyone knows, strange stories sometimes occur in the courtroom. So strange that one wants to laugh until one's stomach hurts, and sometimes cry. For instance, one of the latest issues of the Leningrad journal *Court in Session* relates the following humorous case from the Aktyubinsk regional court.

The district attorney's office received a petition from a certain citizen claiming that a man had raped a cow.

At the prosecutor's suggestion, the case officer commenced to investigate this astonishing crime.

The investigation was underway. The case grew and mushroomed. The "Rapist" was informed of the accusation and, finally, the case came under the jurisdiction of the regional court on a criminal indictment.

But our criminal code contains no article under which such a crime could be tried, and the Aktyubinsk court found itself at a loss.

What could be done? How could this case be closed?

The regional court found a most witty way out of this dead-end situation. In order to initiate proceedings on a rape case, you need testimony from the victim—so states the law.

And do you know what the regional court did? It closed the case, "in light of the absence of testimony from the rape victim"…

Lenochka continued:

NOVELLA THIRTY-FIVE
THE TATTOOED MAN

According to articles 846, 847, 848 and 851 of the Statute of Criminal Procedure, and by a ruling of 3 December 1910 by the Ashkhabad regional court, Ivan Grigoriev Bodrov, of peasant background, from the village of Chernyshevo in the Nikolo-Kitskaya district, is wanted under articles 1.13 and 1 of the penal code.

Distinctive features of the suspect: 29 y. o., full-grown, medium height, medium build, well-proportioned, gray eyes, the following tattoos: 1) on the chest between the nipples a crucifix with the cross emblazoned "I.N.R.I.," to either side tattooed flowers: by the right nipple, something from the lily family, by the left nipple, an indeterminate species; 2) below the crucifix to the right and left on the ribcage—two-headed eagles, on the right half of the ribcage—a copy of the Russian state coat of arms, with the letter *N.* in the center of the sheaf of wheat, on the left half of the ribcage—a two-headed eagle, not resembling a coat of arms . . . 3) on the abdomen above the navel and slightly to the right is a lion with a mane and raised tail. The lion stands on an arrow, which is pointing to the right; 4) to the right of the lion and at the same height is St. George the Victorious on a steed, defeating the dragon; 5) to the left of the lion and at the same height is a woman (an Amazon) sitting on a horse. The horse's head is turned toward the lion; 6) on the front part of the left arm slightly above the elbow is a woman lifting her hem; 7) on the front part of the same arm, below the elbow, are unidentified flowers and below them, a lily; . . . 10) nearly on the elbow itself, slightly lower down, is a butterfly, its head turned toward the above-described flowers; 11) on the right arm slightly above the elbow is a woman who has pulled up her skirt and exposed one leg to the thigh; 12) below the elbow on the inside part of the arm is a heart pierced by an arrow, an anchor, and a cross; 13) directly below the anchor, heart, and cross is a naked woman standing on someone's head and raising a sword with her left arm; 14) to the right of the naked woman with the sword is another woman, half-naked and more generously proportioned, her right arm bent behind her head; 15) to the right of the latter there is another woman, half-naked, holding an opened fan behind her head; 16) to the left of the woman with the sword is a siren with a sword; 17) on the front of the right leg, above the knee, is a woman with curly hair, wearing a necklace, legless; her torso ends in an obscure drawing;

Lenochka blushed.
Whistlin took the book and read the rest by himself:

. . . .
. . . .
. . . .

Anyone who has any information regarding the whereabouts of the suspect is under legal obligation to indicate his location to the court. Any establishments in whose authority the suspect's property may be found are under obligation to turn it over immediately to official custody.

Whistlin felt that soon he would be able to get down to work. The novella about the tailor had pricked him as an obscure insult. The second he had ignored. The third had struck him as worthy of attention. It was food for thought. He handed the book back to Lenochka, no longer listening as his wife went on reading. He pictured to himself the thirty-fifth novella.

"The damnedest thing," he muttered.

His wife broke off what she was reading and looked at him.

"Andrei, darling," she said, "you've had too much to drink again. Do you feel ill?" She came over to the bed.

"A sheet of paper, on the double," said Whistlin. "Give me a pencil," he added.

He took the paper and began drawing a naked man on it.

Whistlin began with feet, large and muscular ones, standing on a wooden floor; drawing an upward line, he sketched a robust torso and hands with shovel-like nails, and crowned the whole thing with a nice little head with a small but dashing handlebar mustache.

"Do you have any watercolors?" he asked.

"I think I can find them," answered Lenochka and, after a short search, brought them in.

Whistlin painted the entire image an even pink and, taking up the thirty-fifth novella, started in on the most important part.

Having selected a slim little brush and wet it with saliva, all the while looking over at the novella, he began to apply symbols in various colors. On the chest between the nipples he placed the silver crucifix, on the sides, a white lily; below the crucifix he drew a coat of arms and an eagle; on the abdomen above the navel he sketched a luscious lion with a mane and lifted tail. He made the skirts calico, gave the woman with the fan a circus-like manner, made the dog lascivious, the snake funny and green, and he wrote the motto "God Save Me" in gold letters above the private parts...

He covered the background with black paint.

Sitting up in bed and spitting out the fly that had flown into his mouth, Whistlin began looking for a little book up above him on the shelf—then down below in the nightstand. He lit several candles in bronze Empire candelabras. He took a shaving mirror out of the nightstand.

"Lenochka, put the kettle on," he said.

While Lenochka was putting on the kettle, Whistlin smoked, thoughtfully examining his drawing, which was propped between the candles and the mirror. The black background let barely any light through, and the pink man was emerging from a corridor. Whistlin dressed the new arrival in the uniform of a noncommissioned officer. The national coat of arms, the women, the animals—they all disappeared and became the spiritual, internal qualities and strivings of one more occasionally appearing character. Afterward, putting aside the drawing, he began to shave and to think about where he ought to go and whose acquaintance he ought to make.

*

Whistlin entered the House of Print. A literary evening was under-way.[12] A young lady writer was reading her work. After seven years of truly excellent literary efforts that had endeared her work and herself to the best part of society, she had pulled a stunt that was so unacceptable and cynical that everyone just lowered their eyes and experienced an unpleasant sense of spiritual emptiness. First a man had come out leading a toy horse, then some youth had gone cart-wheeling past, then the same youth, wearing only underpants, had ridden around the auditorium on a child's green tricycle—and fol-lowing him, Marya Stepanovna had appeared.

"Shame on you, Marya Stepanovna!" came shouts from the front rows. "What are you doing to us?"

Not knowing why exactly she was up on stage, Marya Stepanovna read her poems in an even voice, as though nothing had happened.

Whistlin was sitting in the next room in an armchair, leaning back against the flowered backrest with black caryatids, and listening to the voices.

A voice in a gray cap was talking about how Abel and Cain could be treated in an ironic mode.

A voice in blue explained that it was writing a book of deaths that would be dedicated to Pushkin, Lermontov, and Yesenin, among others.

A voice in spectacles boomed out that literary criticism was getting mixed up with administrative measures.

Someone drinking tea in a third room shrieked: "Take it, please."

Someone sitting and holding a hat quipped: "A dead man doesn't elbow anyone."

During the intermission Whistlin made his way through the bustling crowd to the auditorium.

The audience was grumbling about the show.

"So, you're not angry with me?" Whistlin asked Wallowkin, who was on his way out.

"Of course, I understand, it's art—but must it be a guillotine?" Wallowkin wrung his hands.

They pushed their way into the cafeteria and sat down at a table by the fireplace. Whistlin examined the angles of the glass he'd raised into the air.

"Let's drink," he toasted, "to your future public appearances, to your performance. What talent nature has lavished upon you!"

A little later on, more litterateurs joined them at their table, and an informal and merry company quickly took shape. Jokes were interspersed with beer, freshly written poems with the scathing remarks of reviewers, and conversations about recently published books with uproarious sketches of their authors.

Meanwhile Wallowkin alternated between cheering up and resuming his melancholy.

He cast his eyes around the cafeteria.

He had thought he would be greeted with open arms but, as if on purpose, no one was paying him any attention at all.

"Oh yes, everyone knows that. In Moscow people who read poetry"—glancing over shiftily in the Muscovite's direction, a man at a neighboring table burst into nervous laughter—"he'll come out on stage, big barrel chest, striped stockings peeking out, he'll stick out his arm and start lauding himself: 'Shakespeare and I . . .' Or he'll just start listing objects in funny voices and think it's poetry. Over in Moscow you all live like little canaries, there's no room to breathe; here, we've got plenty of space." The man speaking was now addressing the Muscovite directly. But he was interrupted by a different young man—an advertising agent:

"Our literary men breathe fresh air, they live out in Tsarskoe Selo, to be closer to Pushkin's *penates*![13] We do serious work here, not like your Moscow moochers."

"Quit it, there's no reason to fight." The local trade union secretary tried to smooth things over. "Moscow has her fine points, and Leningrad isn't devoid of charm, either. We do work, it's true, here in the quiet, while they get all excited, but it's not clear yet which is better—calm or excitement."

Cuckoo, who was sitting at a different table, wanted to move where the piano was playing. He was drawn to a girl with an enormous mouth;

with a blackhead-covered, mournful nose; with hair that began nearly at her brows and that had seriously thinned following multiple abortions. She was banging on the keys with pseudo-finesse and singing:

Farewell, my friend, farewell ...[14]

To Cuckoo the room seemed quiet, and the girl desirable. But since spring had not yet commenced, the girl did not attract him quite strongly enough. He really did admire the line of her shoulders, extremely sloping shoulders, and how she jiggled her hands in the air, then produced patterns on the keys with her fingers.

Although Cuckoo was known to everyone, until now Whistlin had ignored him. Right then, on the hunt for material, Whistlin felt it was essential to meet Cuckoo.

Whistlin drained his glass and followed Cuckoo over to where the piano was playing and the girl was singing. Whistlin was surrounded by a crowd of laughing young people.

"Introduce me to Cuckoo," he said. "I need him for my new protagonist."

Some of the young people broke away and ran off.

Ivan Ivanovich Cuckoo suffered from a peculiar passion for writing letters. He was a stout forty-year-old man, magnificently well-preserved. His face, adorned with muttonchops, his brow, crowned with chestnut-colored hair, his soulful voice—they all evoked, at first, deep respect in all who made his acquaintance. "Such an intelligent face," they would say, "such muttonchops, such thoughtful eyes. Ivan Ivanovich is doubtless a person of significance." Ivan Ivanovich felt this. He made sure to take the most meticulous care of his muttonchops. He strove to keep his eyes ever shining with inspiration, to keep his face smiling affectionately, to be sure that everyone sensed that he was always thinking about something lofty and sublime. He shaved with majesty, smoked alluringly, pronounced even meaningless trifles with flair: "I could eat a steak today."

He would sometimes stop short before a mirror on the street: *I truly do resemble a great man.* And even the vocational-school students would ogle him and say: "Hm, who do we have here?"

Ivan Ivanovich had nothing of his own—no mind, no heart, no imagination. Everything in him was but a temporary guest. Whatever everyone approved of, he approved of as well. He only read books that everyone respected. He would not read any other books, as a matter of principle. He wished to be a bright mind and a worthy soul. He was always doing what other people were doing. When people got caught up in questions of religion, so did he. When everyone was swept away by Freudianism, so was he. The sole original feature of his character was his passion for letters. Ivan Ivanovich loved writing letters and wrote them with frisson. They all began the same way: "I am an honest man and thus am obliged to inform you that you are a contemptible soul," or: "You have taken the liberty of spreading repulsive rumors about a respectable man, you scoundrel," or: "You refused to come, at my invitation, to a household I personally recommended to show your drawings. I must inform you that your drawings are repulsive and that I was only indulging you by showing an interest in them." His friends shrugged their shoulders when they received letters like these. "Oh, Ivan Ivanovich," they would say to one another when they met on the street. "We'd better go visit him and reassure him. After all, this is all nerves. And if we abandon him, he'll be left entirely alone, and who knows what will become of him." But before they were able to agree on a time to visit him, Ivan Ivanovich, looking haggard and hanging his head, would come to them himself and apologize.

The acquaintance was made beneath the light of chandeliers.

They—Whistlin and Cuckoo—met each other halfway. They expressed astonishment that, for some reason, they had been strangers so long. Cuckoo said that he had been following Whistlin's work since his youth and had long since wished to make the author's acquaintance, in order to doff his cap in respect. Whistlin said that he had heard all kinds of wonderful and interesting things about Cuckoo and that it was a shame that Cuckoo didn't write anything, and that if Cuckoo were to take up the pen, a very interesting tale would doubtless result.

Ivan Ivanovich felt his soul begin to flutter. It seemed to Ivan Ivanovich that he had found a kindred soul, and Cuckoo began to sing like a swan, to pose like a beautiful woman for Whistlin. *Just look what a mind I have,* he seemed to say to Whistlin, *what marvelous erudition. Oh, my friend, my dear friend—how I suffer! I barely have anyone to talk to. After all, I am surrounded by unreal people! Ivan Dmitrievich is, of course, a good man, but his knowledge of biology is nil. Dmitri Ivanovich isn't bad at philosophy, but he's a terrible person. Konstantin Terentyevich is quite knowledgeable, but he never says anything. Terenty Konstantinovich is chatty but hardly well-read.* "Have you read this book?" he asked, taking out a book he'd just received. "It upended my whole worldview."

They left the House of Print together. Cuckoo was enchanted. Whistlin was glad. They agreed to strike up a friendship.

Cuckoo lived in an enormous building, nearly its own city, which had all its own amenities—its own pharmacy, shops, nursery, bathhouse—on Ligovsky Avenue. Ivan Ivanovich Cuckoo was the object of his friends' tender affections. They considered him a failed genius. They were amazed by his erudition; they attributed his flitting around to the scatterbrained nature of genius. "If Ivan Ivanovich were to gather up his knowledge and focus it on one point, he would turn the world upside down," they would say when parting from Ivan Ivanovich Cuckoo. And they pitied him terribly.

Spring came, and Ivan Ivanovich Cuckoo decided to go out for a ride. He got on a train. Disembarked in Tsarskoe Selo and took a bus to the Catherine Palace, which had been turned into a museum.[15]

Ivan Ivanovich got out at the lycée and stopped by the entrance. Ivan Ivanovich stood sideways, in profile, since he found that his figure was that much more impressive from this angle. He gazed at the street and pretended to read. From time to time he leafed through his book, watching to see whether any of his acquaintances were around. Meanwhile a crowd was gathering around the lycée. Some were running up to the Pushkin monument and gazing intently, trying to remember, then returning to their posts and sharing their impressions.

"Of course, it's a striking resemblance."

"Not at all, it's not the right nose."

"But did you notice his forehead?"

"And he looks like he's wearing a frock coat."

"What do you think—what kind of a hat is he wearing?"

Carrying Delvig's poems, Ivan Ivanovich Cuckoo set out.[16] The crowd followed him at a distance. He strolled past the monument.

"What if he's wearing makeup?" a young lady whispered.

"Now there's a thought! Maybe they're going to shoot a film in the park."

"Hush, or everyone will come along."

The crowd melted away, only the young people continuing to follow Cuckoo. He walked on past the palace, turned to the left past the outbuildings, strolled across the Chinese bridge, again turned left on the gravel path and passed over the little bridge onto a small island. Cuckoo loved great men with a strange and tender love. He could spend hours standing before a portrait of any great man. His soul yearned for greatness and for some great, unusual feat. He passionately loved the biographies of great men and was delighted when aspects of his own biography coincided with those of a great man. Having walked around the island a bit, Ivan Ivanovich returned to the lycée, approached the Pushkin monument with solemnity and great feeling, sat down on a bench and began gazing at the bronze youth . . . Meanwhile the young people were still standing on the Chinese bridge, waiting for the filming to begin. They kept running outside the gate, looking right and left for an automobile fitted out with a movie camera, a cameraman, directors, and other actors. But no clouds of dust on the road materialized, and lunchtime was at hand.

Somewhat disappointed, the young people drifted off to their respective dachas, discussing what it all meant.

Meanwhile, Whistlin was hurrying toward the lycée.

*

Morning. Office workers were still hurrying through the park on their way to work, and Whistlin was already sitting on a bench waiting for Cuckoo.

It was cold, it was gray, it was unpleasant. Whistlin got up from the bench and took a turn around the park.

The busts looked black against the frost-clad trees.

A cart came through beneath the Admiralty gates.

Sailors were marching along the sidewalk behind the iron fence.

Wooden carriages were moving along toward the Bridge of the Republic.[17]

The Palace of the Arts, freshly painted in its historical colors, seemed to be lifting off from the square.[18]

An angel on a column, and below it a dashing quadriga, and below that two stories and an archway, out of which an automobile had just come flying.

Up above, a small airplane was flying back toward the Peter and Paul Fortress.

Finally, Cuckoo got off the tram, wearing a summer hat.

Whistlin went to greet him.

Shook his hand.

Today they were going to the Hermitage. Whistlin wanted to seek out depictions of the hunt.

Cuckoo wanted to walk through the galleries, to show himself off and look at the other people.

"If you can believe it," Cuckoo was saying, "as a child I was extremely distressed by the fact that I didn't have a nose like Gogol's, that I didn't limp like Byron, that I didn't suffer from jaundice like Juvenal."

2. TOXOVO

THE TRAIN was climbing slowly. Cuckoo and Whistlin got off at the station, bought cigarettes and took off bouncing in a cabriolet. The cottage had been rented ahead of time. The room that Whistlin and Cuckoo moved into had windows looking out onto the road. Besides the one room and a log-framed entryway, there were no other rooms in the cottage. It had been built especially for vacationers, in a hurry. The walls had been pasted over with the cheapest wallpaper possible; bunks and a small table had been knocked together with pine boards.

The renters adorned the walls with the books they'd brought. Cuckoo turned his corner into an office for working. He tacked a sheet of dark-blue blotting paper to the table, placed candlesticks and a stack of clean writing paper on the table, and got out goose quills, giving one to Whistlin and keeping one for himself. Sitting side by side, they would work in friendly concord like the Goncourt brothers, he would think up plots and Whistlin...[19] Of course, it was time, high time, for him, Cuckoo, to get down to work.

One evening a campfire was burning a few versts from Toxovo, at the base of one of the hills. The vacationers lay about in a half circle, tossing in pine branches and talking politics.

May beetles were flying around the young pine seedlings.

Lower down, the greenery fell away steeply in a wall of sand.

Whistlin, the deaf washerwoman Trina Rublis, Cuckoo, and Nadia the city girl sat among the vacationers.

Trina Rublis was a woman with a riotous and opulent past. She had until recently possessed great beauty. But about two years ago she had let herself go, gone flabby. Her ash-blond hair no longer provoked similes, and her once pink cheeks were now yellow and puffy.

It was unclear what this creature might be thinking this evening, living as she did in a world deprived of sound. Perhaps her imagination was calling to life the dashing officer of the Savage Division who had hurriedly wed her in Tsarskoe Selo during the Yudenich offensive on Petrograd, using his murdered comrade's passport, and who had then disappeared without a trace, perhaps through no fault of his own.[20]

Cuckoo sat solemnly at the feet of the girl, gazing over the fire at the ripples on the lake.

Whistlin squeezed the washerwoman's hand and, certain that no one could hear him and knowing that she wouldn't hear him, told her stories, ridiculing the deaf former beauty. She watched his lips and wondered at what point she ought to laugh.

"Here I've gotten Cuckoo together with this girl," Whistlin continued, stroking the deaf woman's hand. "Later I'll transplant them to another world, one more real and eternal than this momentary life. They will live in it and, when they're already in the grave, they'll only just have started to experience their prime and will go on changing ad infinitum. Art is extracting people from one world and drawing them into a different sphere.

"There are few true fishers of souls in this world. There is nothing more terrifying than a true fisherman. They are quiet, these true fishermen, they are polite, because politeness is the only thing that links them to the outside world. Naturally, they have neither horns nor hooves. Naturally, they pretend to love life, but they only really love art. Please understand," continued Whistlin, knowing that the deaf woman would understand nothing, "art is no celebration, art is not labor. It is the struggle to populate that other world, to ensure that it too is densely populated, that it contains diversity, that life there, too, is full; literature can be compared to life after death. Literature in actual fact *is* life after death."

The campfire was dying down. The vacationers dispersed to gather kindling.

Cuckoo was dozing solemnly at Nadia's feet.

Whistlin got up, walked over to the sleepers, sat down beside them, and began carefully examining the lake, the line of the lonesome crooked birch tree by the escarpment, the vacationers returning with their kindling, the sleeping young people.

"Imagine," he continued, politely leaning in, "a sort of poetic shade that leads living people to the grave. A sort of Virgil among the vacationers, who unobtrusively leads them into hell, while the vacationers, just imagine, go on picking their noses and, clutching bouquets, follow him in single file, assuming they're just going for a stroll. Imagine that they see hell beyond one of these hills, just a kind of low depression, grayish, terribly gloomy, and they see themselves there naked, utterly naked, not even a single fig leaf, but still holding bouquets. And imagine then that their Virgil, also naked, makes them dance to the sound of his pipes."

In the evening twilight Whistlin's voice grew stronger.

Trina was surprised, wondering who had gotten Whistlin so worked up; she looked from side to side.

Before long, they had come down one hill and climbed up another; they came down from that one too and climbed a third, all the while walking with lakes on either side.

The deaf-mute signed that she loved the grass and how the sun warmed her back.

Turning her face to Whistlin, she touched her own back.

Whistlin thought that Trina felt cold. He took off his jacket and threw it over her shoulders. She smiled, and then took off running, looking back all the while. Whistlin ran after her.

They reached the lakeside.

"I want to swim," signed the deaf woman.

Turning away, Whistlin walked off and sat with his back to the lake. Trina Rublis went off into the bushes and undressed. She left on just a chemise. The chemise was supported by two pink ribbons, a rose was embroidered on the breast. The deaf woman hung her stockings on a bush.

Wearing only her chemise, Trina Rublis ran into the lake. In the water she began to make a racket. Whistlin understood that she wanted him to turn around. Unwillingly, he walked toward the water. At some distance from the shore the deaf woman's head could be seen, wrapped in a cloth. Then the deaf woman swam toward shore; barely covered by the water, she lay by the shore.

Whistlin entered the water in his undershirt. Taking each other by the hand, they swam off.

By the campfire the others had not noticed their absence or pretended not to.

The deaf-mute woman sat closer to Whistlin and stared hard into the fire.

And either under the influence of the night and freshness coming on, or for some other reason, Teddy—a reciter of poems and an orator—suggested leaping through the fire, but his suggestion was rejected. Then the cultural educator suggested they play tag.

It was a Sunday, and since it was a sunny day, the distant railway station, built in a Gothic style, saw scores of people setting off on excursions, preceded by musicians. Trumpets glittered in the sunshine. Workers hurried after their flower-laden wives, plucking bits of grass or leaves from bushes and chewing on them.

Other excursions were made up of adolescents in red kerchiefs, or young men in shorts carrying sandals. A third variety consisted of university students who had for some reason found themselves stuck in the city. All the processions were fitted out with posters and group leaders wearing armbands.

On days like this the "Russian Switzerland" tavern came to life.

The tables got noisy. People were clinking beer glasses, embracing, eating ice cream, chortling, running from one table to another, eating sausage omelets, buttermilk, pickles, tugging hard candies out of their pockets or purses and sucking on them. Here and there came sounds like *doo-doo-doody-doo*.

Even the hills above the lake came alive after two in the afternoon;

the orchestra was located at the very top of the hill, beneath two or three pine trees. Crowds in multicolored bathing costumes swam and then, lying on their stomachs, tanned. And once again, *doo-doo-doody-doo* could be heard here and there and carried beyond the hills.

The Toxovo heights were transformed into living human mountains, and the wind-rippled posters seemed like noble flags and standards, and they shone in the sun with their white, yellow, black and gold letters.

Dried-up Tanya and dried-up Petey went out. Petey locked the door and ran his hand over the lock.

"Here we are out in the great outdoors again. It's been ten years since we were here at the dacha. Did you grab the magazines and newspapers? It's lovely, reading while you lie in the shade of a tree."

"You're the same as ever," said Tanya, putting on fingerless gloves and opening a long summer parasol with lace trim and a bone handle, joyfully giving herself over to reverie.

They set out right through the field toward the lake. Tanya was wearing a short plaid skirt that allowed young people to laugh at her crooked legs, and a crepe-de-chine blouse with a triangular cutout, decorated with a rather bedraggled pale-blue ribbon.

"The sun is so warm," said Tanya.

"Yes," affirmed Petey.

"Look—flowers," Tanya leaned down.

"Buttercups," added Petey. "Tanya, you look so delightfully young!"

"Here I go!" And Tanya set off down the path, leaning down to pick flowers and plait a wreath. Petey sat down on a stump and opened the paper. Petey's face was covered in wrinkles. His back was hunched, his eyes myopic.

Tanya sang a sentimental love song and, plaiting her wreath, walked slowly down into the valley.

Her withered little hands were rather quickly picking clover, daisies, bluebells. Her desiccated little legs stepped through the grass almost confidently.

"It's very nice here, Tanya," she heard a wavering voice from above. And silence again.

Only the rustling of newspaper from above.

Down below butterflies fluttered noiselessly. Gray hairs worked their way out from under her pale-blue cap. Yet Tanya was laughing. Oh, youth, youth! She laid down her handkerchief, sat down on it, took off her cap and, putting on the flower wreath, listened to the grass as it hummed and sang and murmured.

In the mornings, by old habit, Tanya rubbed Petey down. What a lot of bother husbands are! The thin little old man would stand there in the tub, and she would rub him down.

At one time Petey had played the flute in the Academic Theater. He had played with feeling, and Tanya—Tatyana Nikandrovna—had sat there with her girlfriend and listened.

Now, up above, Petey let the newspaper drop to the grass, took his flute out of its case, and played.

Whistlin, strolling around above the lakeshore and observing the holiday crowds, heard the sound of the flute.

The couple had a little dog. She was a substitute child for them. A splendid little nine-year-old fox terrier, who had aged so quickly and imperceptibly. True, she still wore a pink ribbon round her neck, and she still ran muzzle-down along the road, but the couple no longer called her Traviata—just "little old lady." The little old lady sat with her pink bow next to the little old man spitting into his flute, and down below lay another little old lady with a pale-blue bow, her hair bobbed, wearing a flower crown and chewing on a green leaf, gazing at the sky.

But now the fox terrier ran off and settled down next to the little old lady and gazed into the grass, apparently dozing off.

Whistlin walked along, pushing the bushes apart with his stick.

The deaf-mute woman walked along mincingly, her head cocked.

The old man played with increasing gusto.

Whistlin gazed down from the hilltop for a long time and listened to the flute. Then he descended.

"Allow me to introduce myself," he said. "Andrei Whistlin."

"Pleased to meet you." Taken by surprise and flustered, the old man lowered his flute.

Whistlin sat down next to the old man. The deaf-mute woman stood some distance away.

"You play magnificently," began Whistlin. "I love music. I have long wished to make your acquaintance."

The old man blushed.

"Many an evening I've heard you play…"

Strolling around the lake, Whistlin and Cuckoo met Nadia, who was walking accompanied by the Calveskin siblings. Nadia was walking slowly, toying with a twig; the brother and sister walked to either side. This was twenty-year-old Pasha, who considered himself an old man and said smart things as a matter of principle; seventeen-year-old Violet, a know-it-all. Pasha was focused and grim, since he believed himself cursed by bad heredity and felt that he had been corrupted from infancy. Violet was exuberant, talking about Anatole France. The siblings were both friends with Nadia and hated each other.

Catching sight of Whistlin and Cuckoo, the Calveskins bowed and headed over to say hello.

"Andrei Nikolayevich," said Violet, "just wait 'til you hear my new joke!" And she set out to the right with Whistlin.

Cuckoo, Nadia, and Pasha followed them. Pasha considered Whistlin a man of formidable talent. So he watched enviously as Whistlin talked with Violet. Pasha was terribly pleased when Whistlin, still walking, glanced back over his shoulder and addressed him; the youth immediately ran over and commenced walking on his other side. The siblings were ambitious.

Cuckoo and Nadia hung back.

"Maybe we should play a game of skittles?" Whistlin suggested to the siblings, when their dachas had appeared in the distance.

It was too awkward for Pasha to refuse, though he considered this a pointless and despicable way to spend time. Violet delightedly assented and ran off to fetch the sticks and pins. Whistlin took his stick and began to sketch out the configurations in the dirt. But then above them, on the hill, Cuckoo and Nadia came into sight. Whistlin went to meet them.

"We're going to play skittles," he said. "Perhaps you'd like to join us?"

But Cuckoo declined.

"An extraordinary man, that Whistlin," said Cuckoo, walking down toward the lake, holding Nadia by the elbow. "There is such vivacity in him, such good cheer, such wit. He evidently loves it here in Toxovo. But I don't like it at all. The nature here evokes no spiritual agitation. And I would prefer to live where everything is sublime. How fine it is to be among great men, to converse with great men."

Nadia raised her eyes. "Wait, Ivan Ivanovich. Look how fine it is here."

Her eyes really were exquisite, half-green and half-hazel.

There were fleecy clouds in the sky that evening, and the lake was full of both azure and fleece.

Cuckoo laid his coat down over a stump. Nadia sat down. Cuckoo sat lower down.

"Nadia," he said tenderly, "this evening has got me terribly excited. Wasn't it on just such an evening that Prince Andrei caught sight of Natasha at the ball and remembered her? Do you love Natasha?"[21]

Nadia was smoking dreamily, watching the smoke rings float apart in the air.

"Why do you smoke, Nadia?" Cuckoo asked. "It doesn't suit your image at all. You ought to be utterly unselfconscious and filled with great *joie de vivre*. Quit smoking, Nadia." Genuine suffering could be heard in Cuckoo's voice.

Nadia tossed her cigarette. It fell onto the dry turf and went on smoldering and letting off smoke.

"But I'm planning to be a film actress," said the girl after a pause.

"Nadia, that's impossible," stammered Cuckoo.

"Why is it impossible, Ivan Ivanovich?"

"If you have any faith in me, don't go down that road. Trust my life experience. You must be Natasha!"

Up above Whistlin appeared with the siblings. Whistlin sat down with Violet under a tree. Pasha began to read the writer his poems.

"Great," said Whistlin. "Very talented."

Pasha beamed.

"So I should keep writing?" he asked.

"Of course you should!" affirmed Whistlin, and looked down. "It's time," he thought. "Would you be so kind," he said, turning to Violet: "Go and ask Ivan Ivanovich what time it is."

Violet took off at top speed.

Ivan Ivanovich was admiring the lake when Violet appeared and, smiling, broke his reverie with her question:

"What time is it?"

Cuckoo took out his watch.

"Ten," he answered authoritatively. "Where is Whistlin?"

"He's waiting up top."

Violet walked up to Nadia.

"Bored yet?" she asked quietly.

Soon they were walking as a threesome—Whistlin, Nadia, Cuckoo. The Calveskins brought up the rear.

"Don't you think," asked Pasha grimly, "that Whistlin was playing skittles with us on purpose so that Cuckoo could have a chance to flirt with Nadia?"

"Cut it out, won't you," answered Violet. "Why so suspicious? Whistlin just likes young people."

It was a Sunday again. Cabriolets were parked by the Lutheran church. The church was full of young women looking like paper roses, and guys with yellow hair. The organ was playing. Light fell through stained glass windows. Nadia and Cuckoo stood on the upper level. Whistlin and Trina Rublis were behind them. Nadia and Cuckoo gazed down at the baptism, sometimes casting a glance toward the aisle and seeing a bride, groom, and witnesses preparing to set off for the altar as soon as the baptism was over.

The groom was nervous and kept shifting his weight from one foot to the other. The bride was red as a lobster.

"What material for us, Andrei Nikolayevich," Cuckoo, tossing back his head, whispered into Whistlin's ear. "Nail it down, I beg you, nail this down!" And Cuckoo resumed watching.

The back of Nadia's pale blond head was exciting him, and he imagined his own wedding. Cuckoo's face expressed pride. He saw himself standing next to Natasha—that is, Nadia. Nadia wore a white dress and bridal veil; she held a candle with a white ribbon, and the echoing arches of the cathedral . . .

Taking out his handkerchief, Cuckoo solemnly wiped his face.

The deaf-mute woman recalled Riga—the beautiful city of Riga— and her hopes, and her stroll with the student Toporov, home for vacation, to a little wood.

But Cuckoo was hindering her recollections. He coughed and puffed out his chest. Now he was gazing down scornfully. The happy couple was on the move. Everyone in the church began to stir. Everyone's heads turned to the aisle. Whistlin was also watching.

The organ played. Then the pastor spoke. Then the organ played again.

Through the stained glass, leaves could be seen fluttering on trees. The sun shone on the leaves.

"Lovely," said Cuckoo. "But for my own wedding I would want more grandeur."

When Nadia, Cuckoo, Whistlin, and the deaf-mute woman left the church, the cabriolets flew off.

"Let's go in and have a beer," Cuckoo suggested and, merging with the crowd, they went into the tavern garden. All of the tables and benches were occupied. Laughter, the heavy smell of beer, streams of smoke, flushed faces, songs, the sounds of balalaikas, guitars, and mandolins.

"It's a real Auerbachs Keller *en plein air*," Cuckoo said to Whistlin. "The only thing missing is Faust and Mephistopheles."[22]

"Oh, Ivan Ivanovich," Whistlin answered. "Always these literary references. You need to relate to life more simply, more immediately."

Finally one of the tables became free. The four friends sat down and ordered beer. At that moment the siblings elbowed their way through to them.

"Can we join you?" they asked and squeezed in somehow at the end of the bench.

"I can hold my liquor," said Violet after the fifth glass, "but you, Pasha, really can't, even though you're a man."

"I can hold my liquor too," Pasha answered. "I'm just restraining myself."

"I just remembered a very interesting joke."

"I'm not interested in your jokes."

"And I'm not interested in your poems!"

"Stop fighting," Nadia implored them.

At a neighboring table a lively conversation was underway:

"But you're wrong about the Germans, brother. When I was a German prisoner of war..."

"She's a sweet broad, really not bad. I'm gonna make a pass."

"Where ya think you're going, flabbypants. Sit tight!"

To the left:

"No, no, Mitya, look at that bum. Masha, Masha, c'mere."

On the right under the pines:

"Yes, Petey, culture's a hell of a word. Ivan Trofimovich told me people burned at the stake for it."

"Right, and you're gonna build culture. Have another drink, dummy."

"Mitya, I saw the light just recently, now I go to church. But don't tell nobody, for real, nobody."

A voice from the crowd still waiting for free tables:

"Volodya, Volodya honey! go sleep in the trash heap."

A drunk man, staggering, yelled:

"Come on over, I'll whack ya!"

A group came into view on the other side of the fence: some guys were leading a young miss by the hands, little boys jumping up and down around them. The girl's dress was rumpled and her hair undone. She was crying scalding tears and yelling:

"Ay, miserable me, ay, such misery. Ay, let me put on my scarf!" She was trying to pull away. The guys, laughing, twisted her arms. She tried to throw herself down on the ground but, caught beneath the armpits by the snickering fellows, merely drooped.

"She was sleeping with a man in the bushes," the guys explained to the crowd. "We're taking her in to the police."

"No, no, you're not Natasha—you're Gretchen," tipsy Cuckoo whispered. "And I am Faust, and Whistlin is Mephistopheles, and the deaf-mute woman is Marthe!"

"Stop talking nonsense," Whistlin snapped.

With a heavy tread, an elderly worker approached the friends' table.

He stopped, swaying.

"You people are educated, maybe you can answer, why..."

Cuckoo elbowed Whistlin in agitation.

In a whisper:

"The scene outside the city gates"—ecstatically—"and now he'll call me a doctor!"

The worker, peering intently into Cuckoo's face, pondered:

"Citizen, if I may be so bold, are you by any chance a doctor?"

Cuckoo laughed smugly.

Cuckoo, Nadia, Whistlin and the deaf-mute woman, Pasha and Violet, having agreed to take a festive stroll, set out for a distant lake. They'd packed blankets, cushions, canned meat, cigarettes, and a little cognac.

The sun was only just illuminating the tops of the hills when they left. It had rained the day before, and now a whitish fog was scurrying down the hills toward the lakes, but the sky was blue, and sparrows chirped and ascended to the damp leaves covered in gleaming droplets, rocked upon the bushes, then descended to the road snaking off into the distance. The ditches to either side of the road, which were drying out and turning yellower by the hour, were full of water.

Violet earned a good salary; she was wearing yellow boots, an imported coat she'd snapped up at the right moment, and a yellow schoolbag with shoulder straps. She'd bought the cognac, a round of Dutch cheese, a can of fresh caviar, and a few cans of fruit in syrup and fruit candies. She was walking out in front with a green sack slung over her shoulder.

Pasha hadn't bought anything, but he was Nadia's protégé. She had loaded him down with a packet of her favorite cookies, little jam pies, a blanket, a little pillow, a towel, soap, a mug and toothbrush. The deaf-mute woman was carrying cheese danishes and meat patties.

Cuckoo was very grand: he had made a special trip to the city in advance of this stroll and had brought back gaiters. He had purchased a gray kepi and donned a mackintosh. An elegant little suitcase in hand, he walked along in high spirits. In the suitcase, rubbing shoulders with Pushkin, lay veal, roast beef, knives, forks, stackable cups and a bottle of French wine.

Whistlin wasn't lagging either. He was carrying a collapsible tent, a mirror, and a camera.

Whistlin was pretending to court the deaf-mute woman. He was curious to see what kind of rumors would ensue.

He leaned down and offered her flowers plucked by the ditch.

Nadia turned around in astonishment.

Cuckoo, wishing to keep pace with Whistlin, also plucked some flowers and, gathering them into a bouquet, offered them to Nadia.

Pasha ran off deep into the field and brought back bunches of cornflowers.

"Can you whistle?" Whistlin asked Violet. "Whistle something."

Violet began whistling away virtuosically.

"March in step," Whistlin suggested. "Let's all march in step together."

Cuckoo, smiling, changed step.

Nadia asked how this was done.

Cuckoo showed her.

And so they marched to the nearest village. Violet whistled a foxtrot.

They approached the village. Milkmaids and children watched curiously to see where they were going in such military formation. And feeling these curious glances, the procession smiled.

"Keep pace," said Whistlin. "Louder, Violet. Even louder."

"Should we perhaps have a bite to eat?" Cuckoo asked suddenly.

"I could eat a horse," Violet said, turning her head.

"What about you, Nadia?"

"I'd love to."

"Let's go to that pine, it's shady and cool and completely dry."

"Give me my case," Nadia asked.

Pasha handed it over.

Violet threw down her green sack and began digging through it.

Cuckoo opened his suitcase and began taking out knives, forks and cups.

"Just think, only a few years ago," Cuckoo said, "there were wolves on the outskirts of Petersburg."

"Really?" asked Nadia.

"We all thought we were done for then, but here we are now, drinking and eating, and everything is as it was before."

"You think so?" Whistlin asked and smiled.

"Yesterday I read a new biography of Napoleon and regretted that I'm not short."

Violet was opening the bottle. In vain Ivan Ivanovich kept trying to take the corkscrew away from her. Nadia sliced the roast beef and veal. She had been unanimously elected hostess.

Nadia was truly having a wonderful time.

When everyone was sated, Cuckoo took out Turgenev's correspondence with Dostoyevsky and began reading, but the travelers were drowsy from eating and began falling asleep where they sat.

Nadia had a vision of a room with two windows. It was so, so bright—it was sunny outside. By one of the windows sat a girl, and a man was leaning over her, tall, emaciated, with a repulsive face, bald on top with long straight hair. The eyes on the gray face were especially repulsive. They were somehow penetrating. He was wearing a dirty brown sixteenth-century costume, as in a historical film. She knew that he was the master of her fate and that he would do with her, with Nadia, whatever he wanted, and she was terribly frightened of him.

She began running through endless rooms. The house was enormous, like a labyrinth. Only that man lived in it. She ran down a hallway, again through bright rooms, through a drawing room with stucco walls, sometimes seeing him at the end of the hallway. He was laughing malevolently and she was running again, knowing that he saw her the whole time and would find her. Finally, she ran into a room like a kitchen and knew that there was a door here that led outside. She looked at the wall and immediately realized why the man always knew where she was: there was a map of the house on the wall and her whole route was displayed there by a thin copper wire that laid itself down wherever she walked, showing all the while where she, Nadia, was going. Only a small free end of the wire was left, and Nadia saw herself bend it back so that it stuck up. Now she knew that the wire wouldn't show anything anymore.

She ran outside. All the buildings were still under construction. They were still just tall empty boxes, six stories and higher, with enormous, two-story-high openings for windows. Dirt, lime, and rubble were piled up on the street.

Among these buildings one was finished, but it was far off. A light was visible, and she decided to run there.

Among the unfinished buildings, down through the foundations, she went along, stumbling, further and further. Up ahead it was totally dark, like a mineshaft, and sharp iron rods stuck out like stubble. She was lost! The buildings pressed in on her, she was afraid they would collapse any minute, and then she saw a light.

A very young man was walking toward her, and behind him light could be seen, forming a path. He had a very kind face. She ran to him and told him how she had just escaped the labyrinth. When she told him she had bent back the end of the wire, the young man's face became exultant. He took her by the hands and, stepping very lightly, led her to the light. Then he carried her over to the big house and said: "We will live here. I know a particular room, and although the labyrinth is nearby, he won't ever think of looking for you so close to home."

People were running and bustling all around, but no one paid them any attention. And they were walking down the dark hallways where the light was barely visible, as in paintings by the Dutch masters . . .

Nadia woke up with a jolt and looked around. Cuckoo was sitting beneath a large pine, leafing through a book. Whistlin, leaning against a tree, stood watching her. She found this discomfiting.

Pasha lay with knees bent and it seemed to him that he was flying into an abyss, that in the abyss his big toe began swelling, that he had an abscess, that it turned into an eye. This was disgusting and he woke up. Rubbing his eyes with his fists, he reached for his foot. Yawned.

"I had a stupid dream," said Pasha, "that an eye grew on my foot. They say you're a dream expert, Ivan Ivanovich."

"Oh, you can interpret dreams?" Nadia brightened.

Now here's a conversation topic, thought Cuckoo and answered authoritatively:

"In ancient times people attached tremendous significance to dreams. There was even an entire branch of science, if one can call it science—oneirocriticism. The ancient world never doubted that it was divine power that engendered dreams in the soul." Pleased with his knowledge, Cuckoo looked at everyone to see whether they were all listening and how attentively. "Seen from this point of view," he continued, "dreams are a portent; but if you take into account the time of day when you have the dream, and the fact that we enjoyed a heavy meal beforehand, then your dream, Nadia, is not entirely tenable."

And Cuckoo victoriously surveyed his listeners and, in order to inspire still greater respect toward himself on Nadia's part, he decided to bring in Apuleius.

"According to Apuleius, a hearty meal can result in dark and cataclysmic dreams," he pronounced with grandiloquence. "What is more, oneirocritics assert that alcohol vapors, even in the morning, hinder visions of the truth in dreams. But I myself don't believe this at all, Nadia, though I do not even know your dream." Cuckoo wrung his hands.

"Won't you tell us what you dreamed? It's really very interesting, and I can remember the dreams of great men, and in these reminiscences we can while away the time 'til sunset. I'll tell you about the dreams of great men ... Only now do I see how beautiful it is here, hills all around ..."

And forgetting that Nadia had not yet recounted her dream, Cuckoo, lost in thought, began:

"First and foremost we must recall ..."

Violet and Pasha came closer and stopped. But Nadia felt sad, and she listened inattentively. She was not interested in the dreams of great men. Although her dream had had an entirely happy ending, it still seemed to her that everything around her had gone dark, even somehow chilly. And indeed, during their after-luncheon rest the sky had become overcast, all covered in storm clouds.

Rumbling began far off in the distance.

They all dashed to gather their things and carry them to the pine tree. Whistlin, helped by the siblings, set up the tent. Now everyone crammed into it and brought their supplies over from the pine.

"Humph, where's the rain," joked Ivan Ivanovich.

"Just wait, Ivan Ivanovich," Violet interrupted. "I write the 'Nature Corner' column for *The Red Gazette*. I'm a weather expert."

It was dark in the tent. Whistlin lit up.

"Andrei Nikolayevich, don't smoke," Nadia said with hostility. "It's stuffy in here."

Whistlin tossed his cigarette.

"Pasha, don't you dare—go outside," Nadia ordered.

"Nadia," said Cuckoo. "Now is the best possible time. It's dark, a storm is raging. We all promise to listen to you most attentively."

The storm passed.

Alone, clutching the pine trunk, Pasha smoked. He was pondering Nadia's kiss. Was it a brotherly kiss, or not brotherly? No, it was definitely just brotherly. Too light, too airy. *She doesn't love me*, he thought, *and can't ever come to love me. To be loved one has to be talkative—plus I have no future. I'll finish the institute and start teach-*

ing geography, he broke out laughing. *So it shall be, but I won't work in newspapers. Violet can make all the money she wants. But Nadia loves the theater, sweets, the cinema . . .*

"Are you daydreaming?" asked Nadia, coming up behind him along the path. "That's nice. I'll sit down and you can lay your head on my lap and go on dreaming. I'll imagine that I'm the lead actress in a film, a woman who's led a life of pleasure, and you're an unhappy young man in love with me. I'll stroke your head."

Pasha obediently lay down on the grass and laid his head on the hem of Nadia's dress.

"I do love," he said quietly. "I really do love you."

"Perfect," Nadia interrupted him. "A bit more suffering. Right, right. Oh, my darling!" She lowered her gaze and pressed a hand to her heart. "I believe that you're suffering! How terribly sad that we met so belatedly, when I already love another! He may be worthless, he may be corrupt, but he has a heart." She sighed deeply. "There's nothing to be done. You are pure, you are subtle, you just . . ."

"Nadia!" moaned Pasha.

"Kiss my hands and cry, get up, and go over to the escarpment. I'll approach you," Nadia said, trying to keep her mouth closed.

Pasha obediently got up, kissed her hand, and walked slowly toward the escarpment.

Nadia sat and watched, then ran off and yelled, trying to run gracefully:

"Arnold, Arnold!"

"You're so sweet, Pasha," she said. "Let me kiss you."

The pine branches rustled, fruits showed red on the rosehip bushes. The former anarchist Ivanov was getting up. He was of medium height, pale-faced, long-maned. He walked leaning on a stick. Dropped onto a bench by the front gate.

At one of the dachas not far from the lake, Zoya Znobishina came out onto the veranda, yawned, crossed her arms behind her neck and, lifting her face, stuck her elbows forward and yawned again. She sat down in a rocking chair and began examining her hands. Then she turned her head to the right toward the garden, yawning again. With great interest she watched a cat creeping stealthily toward a pigeon. She walked across the veranda and down into the garden; she thought that the sun was very hot and it was time to get dressed.

At the next dacha over, on the hill, a bunch of mamas were pointedly discussing their playing children. Naturally, their children would all be engineers, they were already now showing unusual capabilities. One was tooting like a steam engine right here and now. Another was daydreaming about a submarine.

Zoya Znobishina came back out onto the veranda. She drew her shawl tighter and then let it drop again. Chewed her lips. Now everything was so dull! She walked along, chewing her lips, making zigzags along the path. Ivanov got up and bowed.

"You're bored?" asked Zoya and sat down next to him. "Tough life," Zoya informed him.

"Yep, this is no life—a busted tin can." Squeezing her knees together and lifting them up, Zoya looked at Ivanov. "I like people like Whistlin. He's a cheerful guy."

"A hollow man."

"You're jealous," Zoya decided.

"You're always going on about Whistlin."

"Wait! Just you wait, I'll introduce you to him, and he'll describe you. He'll take a good look at you and then describe you. You'll make good material for him. He likes the ones who are a little bit dead."

"I'm not dead, Zoya."

"Don't blow smoke, you're definitely a little dead. How dull," she said, chewing her lips.

Zoya's birthday had come...

She made no effort to hide her age. Pink and rosy, with recently dyed hair, she was waiting for her guests.

Among these were Pavlusha Dropoff, a thespian; Allochka Bazykina, or Birdie, as she was called to her face and behind her back;

Vanya Galchenko—a cultured young man; Senya Ipatov—a failed singer. They were all very interesting people. At least, that was their opinion of one another.

Early that morning Pete the ice-cream seller had been directed to drive up with his cart at five o'clock, so that there would be ice cream immediately after dinner. From early morning Zoya and her maid had been cleaning raspberries. Ivanov helped them. From early morning delivery people had been coming by: one brought farmer's cheese and sour cream, another mushrooms, another fish.

Vanya Galchenko—the cultured young man—was the first to show up. He brought a nineteenth-century whimsy bought at a flea market. The whimsy was in the form of a vessel, to all appearances of Pompeiian design.

"Oh, I can't, I can't," Zoya waved her hands around. "You see, I'm cleaning raspberries."

"That's all right," answered Vanya and took her bare elbow into his hands and kissed it. "Happy birthday." And he put the package onto the chiffonier.

"Go sit in the garden for now, I'll be done soon."

Vanya went down into the garden and sat on a bench. His face was unremarkable. With a smallish forehead, Vanya had the look of a slightly rumpled and underslept person. His eyelashes were very short. He was wearing a faded dark-blue suit, and his tie stuck out in a hump from under his vest. Vanya could play a little piano, sing slightly, dance a bit; after having read Kurbatov, he loved Petersburg and its environs.[23] For lack of anything better to do between 1914 and 1924, he had visited museums. Now he had a job in a government office somewhere.

Having sat a while and gotten bored, Vanya stepped outside the gate and onto the road and, turning his face toward the Gothic railway station, began waiting for the other guests.

Dust kicked up on the road, and the head of a horse appeared. The horse clambered up the hill and delivered a carriage with Pavlusha Dropoff and Birdie.

Vanya Galchenko ran over and helped Birdie climb out and said hello.

"Well, how are things? What's new?" he asked, not really hoping to hear anything new.

Discussing the weather and the train and how dusty it was in the city, Vanya walked the guests to the veranda. He went back out onto the road and once again strolled along the ditch, having donned a large scarf with knotted ends instead of a hat.

The guests for the afternoon were almost all gathered . . . They were sitting on the benches and on wooden chairs brought out from inside, playing forfeits, when suddenly Psychofsky appeared—that collector of filth, as he himself liked to quip.

"Now you see"—by hand and word he greeted Zoya, who had just come out onto the veranda—"I didn't forget that today is your birthday. I may not have been invited, but I did come." He was a rather heavyset older man, yellow-faced with slightly curly gray hair, extremely unkempt. His trousers had scalloped edges and his vest was covered in greasy stains.

Having said her greetings, Zoya left again to busy herself with the preparations.

All along, the guests had been tossing a handkerchief back and forth and saying words, periodically getting down on their knees, trying not to get their clothes dirty. Vanya Galchenko's navy-blue visored cap, which lay on its own chair, was gradually getting fuller. Inside it, little pencils, penknives, brooches, rings, and a little notebook gleamed in the sunshine.

Dasha, the maid, sticking her head out the veranda doors, gazed joyfully at the visitors who'd come to have some fun. She was plump, rosy, barefoot, cheerful, and loved Zoya's guests, who were always so polite and considerate. Just now she watched as Pavlusha Dropoff, portly and resistant, was blindfolded and made to sit on a stool; bald Senya Ipatov held the cap full of personal items and Birdie, standing on tiptoes and choking with laughter, took out a pencil in a silver holder and asked in her piping voice what had to be done for this forfeit. Pavlusha Dropoff thought for a minute and said in a sepulchral tone: "Spin around on one leg." And the bedraggled maid watched as, on the spot where a metallic pink sphere stood next to a flowerbed, Vanya Galchenko lifted one leg, his arms crossed on his chest, and began to spin.

"More, more," everyone yelled and clapped. And he spun faster and faster. Birdie took the little notebook from the cap and asked again: "Now what should be done for this forfeit?" and laughed provokingly.

Pavlusha Dropoff thought again and, raising his arm as high as he could, proclaimed: "Feed the pigeons!"

Stretching out her neck, Dasha saw the chairs get lined up in single file, the guests sit down and quickly turn their heads, and she saw Cuckoo kiss Nadia.

After lunch the evening crowd began to gather, that is, the vacationers. It was getting cooler and Zoya handed out warm things to the guests. The ladies got wraps, little jackets, and scarves. She draped Dropoff in a raspberry-colored velvet blouse that was destined to be altered (and offered for that reason).

The talent show commenced.

Dropoff declaimed:

> The devil swings the swing
> With his shaggy hand . . .[24]

He declaimed loudly and brilliantly, and his navy-blue suit stood out pleasantly against the greenery.

Pasha, stammering, read his poems.

Birdie performed a chansonette about a clown.

Psychofsky, resting a foot on one of the fence railings, chatted with Whistlin.

"You see, I'm an interesting type for you. Make me one of your characters. I once punched an Austrian prince, and women flock to me. This here is just a gathering of vermin. Don't know why you're bothering with them"—he looked at the guests. "Now me, I'm another story. What? Are you listening? If you like I can tell you foul anecdotes about each and every one of them? Okay? And don't forget about me! Stick me in no matter what. Take out your notebook and start writing."

Whistlin, smiling, took out his neat little book.

"I am a doctor of philosophy. You don't believe me? You can describe me with all my drivel and foul anecdotes. Yes, I'm ambitious. Tell me, are you talented? Perhaps ingenious? You'll describe me well. I want everyone to point fingers at me. You can leave my last name as is—Psychofsky. It has a proud sound."[25]

"Do women really flock to you?" Whistlin asked, smiling.

"I'll tell you all about it. You know—lakes, Switzerland, and all that jazz. I was a student, I tormented her against an alpine backdrop, tormented and then dropped her."

"You couldn't do it?" Whistlin asked.

"I like tormenting women."

"You know, that's old hat, no good for my novel."

Whistlin, putting down his notebook, fiddled with the pencil that was attached with a silver chain to his pocket.

"Let's try something different with you," he said. "You're a quiet, uncomplicated man who loves the little things in life. You're not drawn to universal questions because you know that you're not up to grappling with them. Your curiosity is more womanish than creative. You took philosophy out of curiosity and studied botany out of curiosity..."

"Right, you know, I entered university just to pick holes in it. I learned philosophy without having the slightest faith in it and got my doctorate just so that I could mock it."

"There is something otherworldly about you," Whistlin joked.

"My life is going to waste, an artistically constructed life!" Psychofsky burst out dolefully. "I can't write about my own self. If I could, I wouldn't have turned to you."

"This is all just romanticism," Whistlin said, tucking away his pencil. "Tell me something more interesting."

"What goddamn romanticism?" Psychofsky brought his face closer to Whistlin's, spraying spittle. "A man has spent his whole life wanting to pick holes in everything but he can't, he hates absolutely everyone but can't manage to disgrace them! He sees that everyone scorns him but can't subject them to the glare of truth. If I had your talent, I'd bring them all down, under my heel! Can't you see what a tragedy this is!"

"It's an incident, my dear Vladimir, but not a tragedy."

They heard:

The diamonds in those stone caves can't be counted ...[26]

Psychofsky was silent, as was Whistlin.

It was getting dark.

The brightly lit windows of the house showed silhouettes embracing one another and slowly walking.

Whistlin's interlocutor broke the silence. "Do you really find me no more interesting than these people?"

"Nonsense. Everyone is interesting to me, each in his own way."

"I'm not asking about that, I don't mean just for you, but overall."

Zoya appeared on the porch, and then in the garden. Seeing the white figure approaching, Whistlin uttered quickly:

"Give me your address," and wrote it down in the darkness.

Zoya appeared before the suddenly silent men. "What are you doing standing out here?" She addressed Psychofsky. "Don't you dance?"

Psychofsky bowed.

"I do, I do."

Entering the house, they ran into Nadia at the door and—following her, moving in rhythm with the music—Cuckoo.

"Where are you going?"

"We're all danced out. We're going out into the garden for some fresh air," Nadia answered, breathing heavily.

"Fine, but come back soon, y'hear."

Nadia and Cuckoo sat down on a bench.

"The moon," said Cuckoo. "So sentimental. But in our sober age we have no need for romance ... And yet, Nadia, such is the baseness of human nature—the moon has an effect on me. Makes you think back, reminisce."

He moved a branch aside and continued:

"Various legends, the lore of ancient times. Nadia, right now I feel like speaking to musical accompaniment—about pernicious doubles, evil knights, an exquisite townswoman! I would like to have lived in those distant times. I see myself in a Gothic castle, at the requisite time of night..."

In a clarifying whisper:

"Midnight. And my double. He is tall, ashen, and pale, and he motions to me. The bridge lowers all by itself, its chains rattling. We step out into a black field, and there my double throws down the gauntlet, and we duel, and I suffer so—for there in my tall castle remains my young wife in our lonely, abandoned bed. It is you, Nadia!"

"That's a fantastic film," Nadia answered. "Too bad the music stopped!"

"Oh, Nadia, Nadia," Cuckoo said, "be wax in my hands. What a person I shall make of you!...We will live in such serenity; better yet, we will travel. We will visit noteworthy countries, see ancient monuments, and, by all means, I will win renown, though I am awfully lazy..."

Nadia shook her head. "I won't quit the cinema."

"Would you really not quit, even for me?" Cuckoo asked, trying to sound jocular.

"Look, there's Pasha."

Pasha was indeed standing on the illuminated porch and trying to catch sight of Nadia in the darkness of the garden.

Cuckoo and Nadia froze.

"What an unpleasant man," Cuckoo said quietly.

But Pasha, having stood awhile, hesitatingly turned back.

The revelers, weaving slightly, were noisily taking their leave.

Whistlin stepped out of the gate with Ivanov:

"I was told that you're an extremely unpleasant person."

"Idle gossip," Whistlin answered, taking Ivanov by the arm.

"Being a writer," Whistlin said, "is not particularly pleasant. One must not reveal too much, but also not show too little."

"First and foremost, one must avoid causing others sorrow," Ivanov noted.

"Of course," Whistlin answered. "What a quiet night this is! What a marvelous person Ivan Ivanovich Cuckoo is! Such marvelous strivings! An extraordinary fixation on great men! Have you known him long?" he asked Ivanov.

"Oh, five years or so."

"Do tell me, how do you explain the fact that he ..."

Whistlin and Ivanov returned to the dacha early in the morning.

Zoya was still sleeping amid the chaos of objects, bits of paper, mountains of cigarette butts, gifts.

She was lolling around in her bed and sighing.

"Well, what did you think?" she asked Ivanov at lunchtime. "Did you like Whistlin?"

"A charming man."

"All right, now just wait."

Cuckoo became more convinced with each passing day that Nadia was Natasha, and new qualities appeared within him: the willpower and spiritual tenacity and the manifold capabilities that accompany newly emerging love. He seemed to grow younger. His eyes took on the gleam of youth, his limbs became supple. He felt life bubbling up inside him. He began to emanate genuine charm.

What is more, autumn was already coming on with its golden foliage, the time when the vacationers begin to disperse and silence falls, along with rain outside the windows.

And a song swelled in Ivan Ivanovich's soul, just as if he were genuinely in love.

Nadia gazed at Ivan Ivanovich and couldn't look away. She was drawn to him. She blushed when they met, her eyes gazed at him trustfully.

Finally, Nadia left.

Cuckoo left too.

3. CUCKOO AND COCKADOODLE

THE TRAIN was crawling at a snail's pace toward Leningrad. The vacationers' coaches rattled. Trina Rublis was reading a book; her fingers, made crimson by the setting sun, turned the pinkened pages. She was caught up in the plot and skipping the descriptions. She was going to have a man again. She was calm.

Whistlin stood by the window, feeling anxious.

Not far from the monument they hired a carriage. In another hour the Hotel Angleterre came into view.

Whistlin helped her with her coat, dimmed the light, and sat down at the table. The deaf-mute woman began changing the bedding. She took off the blanket and sheets, then made it up again. She fluffed up the pillows. She was bored. This was hardly the joy of domesticity.

Whistlin was working. He wrote, read, and acted quite at ease. He transposed living people and, pitying them slightly, strove to intoxicate his readers with rhythms, the music of vowels, and intonation.

He frankly had nothing to write about. He just took people and transposed them. But since he had talent, and since he saw no fundamental difference between the living and the dead, and since he had his own world of ideas, everything came out in a strange and original light. Music in art, courtesy in life—these were Whistlin's shields. This is why Whistlin went pale when he committed a *faux pas*.

The deaf-mute woman slept, having given up on Whistlin. The electric lamp was still on, despite the sunrise. Pages were covered in minute uneven handwriting, the notebook was frequently consulted, its contents checked anxiously, hurriedly. The hands of the man working shook like those of a drunk. He turned around to see if she'd woken up, if she was going to bother him. But the deaf-mute woman slept on, and a virginal expression had returned to her face. And this virginal expression distracted Whistlin from the world that was taking shape before him. He put aside his pencil and walked over on tiptoe, took off his clothes, sat down at the head of the bed and gently stroked the deaf-mute woman's head, looked at her open mouth, listened to her even breathing. He felt safe. She would never listen in on his thoughts or tell anyone the specific details of his art. He could talk to her about anything at all. This was the ideal listener. Let the rumors circulate, let people say of him what they will, but he would not, of course, deign to live with her. He didn't need her for that. But then he thought about the fact that he ought not to spurn her, that her profile—her past, present and future—might, perhaps, come in handy for one of his chapters, and he began calling to mind everything he'd heard about her and, sitting back down, lost in thought, began to transpose her too into literature. This was accompanied by painful phenomena: his heart raced, his hands shook, cold sweats exhausted his whole body, he felt intense mental strain. By morning Whistlin sat by the window like a doll. He felt like screaming from ennui. He felt the painful, utter devastation of his brain.

In the afternoon they drank coffee together and parted ways.

The deaf-mute woman smiled crookedly. But Whistlin, heading off to the publisher's, bought a newspaper, read it, and stewed. He had nothing but contempt for a publication that tore him to pieces. He knew that today the reviewer, meeting him on the stairs at the publisher's, would take him aside and start apologizing.

"You know how it is. Demands of the day. I really like your books. But you know very well, Andrei Nikolayevich, it was my duty to tear you to pieces."

And indeed, as Whistlin was making his way upstairs, the reviewer ran up to him.

"Do you have any idea whom you're dealing with here!" Whistlin was shaking. "I will make an utter laughingstock out of you! You think you're just small fry to me ..."

Back home, Whistlin spent the whole evening trying to take revenge on the reviewer, but he just couldn't do it. The man was of no literary interest to him. He decided to go right away, without wasting any time, to a talk at the Geography Society, so that he might run into Pasha.

"Nadia really is a fine girl, isn't she?" Whistlin asked during the break. "Cuckoo seems to be in love with her."

"He'll deceive her," Pasha said, turning red. "A man endowed with such knowledge is a terrifying thing. I was at a ball at the cinema institute yesterday, Cuckoo danced with her all night. He wouldn't let me get close, kept strutting around her like a rooster."

"You know what, Pasha? Let's ditch the talk and go have a beer."

"Thank you, Andrei Nikolayevich. I could really use a drink."

"And cheer up, Pasha. She'll come back to you."

"If I had money, I'd be a real boozer, Andrei Nikolayevich!"

"Don't let your talent go to waste," Whistlin replied. "Believe me, my dear Pasha, this is all fiddle-faddle. Look after yourself for the sake of literature. Did you write a story about your life, as I recommended? It would distract you from your unhappy passion, and in the meantime Nadia would come back to you."

Pasha took out a notebook.

"This is my confession. But please, Andrei Nikolayevich—promise you won't show it to anyone."

"I'll read this carefully later on," said Whistlin, tucking the manuscript into his pocket. "Didn't Cuckoo dance splendidly? Yes, yes ... and she was radiant? And then Cuckoo ... did he leave to accompany her home? Didn't they take a carriage, and didn't Cuckoo give the doorman a generous tip? And you desperately wanted a drink ..."

"Nadia didn't once ask me to dance all evening, Andrei Nikolayevich! And anyway, why weren't you there, Andrei Nikolayevich?"

"I forgot to go," Whistlin answered. "You know what, Pasha—I got paid today. Let's go for a ride out to the islands.[27] That'll be a nice diversion for you."

"I could go for a bite of something zesty, Andrei Nikolayevich."

"Yes," Whistlin said, "pickled herring and ice cream. Really, anything zesty and cold helps with grief!" And Whistlin, regretting that he hadn't been at the cinema institute, decided to take Pasha for a jaunt just as Cuckoo had taken Nadia for a jaunt after the cinema institute. "Would you like flowers, Pasha?" Whistlin asked.

Pasha looked at him in astonishment. They were walking past the Bolshoi Drama Theater, past the Apraksin Market, past Gostiny Dvor.

Whistlin bought Pasha flowers.

A carriage drove through the deserted islands. Inside were Whistlin and Pasha.

"Is this all right?" Whistlin asked.

"Very nice."

"What does this greenery make you think of, Pasha?"

Pasha sadly recited:

> I love the lustrous withering of nature,
> The forests dressed in crimson and in gold . . .[28]

Sounds more like what Cuckoo would answer than Nadia, Whistlin thought.

"Which orchestra was playing at the cinema institute?" And Whistlin spent the whole way there recreating the evening at the cinema institute and making conversation with Pasha the way that, in his opinion, Cuckoo must have talked with Nadia. Then, sitting back, he took out his notebook and began writing:

Cockadoodle and Verochka stepped out of the Bolshoi Drama Theater.

"Verochka," Cockadoodle said, "let's head to the islands, where Blok used to go."

"Will we take an automobile?" Verochka asked.

"If you like," Cockadoodle answered. "But I'd prefer a carriage."

"No, no, let's go in an automobile!"

"In that case, let's go over to Gostiny Dvor. Do you like flowers?" Cockadoodle asked and, crossing the street with Verochka, bought three roses.

They walked past the empty arcades of Gostiny Dvor, past

the guards dozing behind taut ropes, and came out onto 25 October Avenue.

"Do you like this street, Verochka?" Cockadoodle asked. "Just think how many times it's been worked over in literature. How lovely!" he added.

Verochka walked along with eyes wide and flowers clutched to her breast. She thought that her dream was coming true, a beautiful life was beginning. But she was a little sorry that the action was not taking place in Berlin, where the asphalt was so shiny it reflected the automobiles and the people. Cockadoodle hailed a taxicab, helped Verochka in, and off they went to the islands.

Cockadoodle kept looking out to either side . . .

But Pasha stirred.

"What are you writing, Andrei Nikolayevich?"

"Just a moment, Pasha." And Whistlin hurried to finish his sketch:

Cockadoodle walked Verochka to the gate. Dawn was illumining the upper stories of the buildings. He looked out at the Alexander Garden and sighed:

> I love the lustrous withering of nature,
> The forests dressed in crimson and in gold . . .

After reciting these lines, Cockadoodle kissed Verochka's hand and walked away whistling. He was pleased that he, like Blok, had restrained himself and had delivered Verochka home safe and sound.

Back at home, after a rest, Whistlin began reading. He read slowly, as if strolling amid charming surroundings. He loved to take his time thinking about each phrase, sitting a while, and smoking. He would reread the places he found most interesting in old and new translations. The night was over before he knew it; he began thinking about the new day, what he would do, where he would go. He watched the tram running along, the people hurrying, the yellow piles of sand, and wrote to his friend, asking him to place at his disposal candy wrappers, notes, the diaries of his relatives and friends, and promising to return everything perfectly intact.

Afterward he decided to sleep a bit. While he was getting into bed, it seemed to him that he knew like the back of his hand not only all of Ivan Ivanovich's words and deeds, but also his secret innermost intentions; that now he could begin his systematic creative work. He thought about how under no circumstances should he do away with Cuckoo's stoutness, that Ivan Ivanovich's muttonchops were indispensable, that his passion for Tsarskoe Selo ought to remain, that one cannot invent anything better than what exists in real life; that perhaps when all this was already written, a few things could be changed, that right now a last name ought to be selected along the same lines. Not Cuckoo, but Cockadoodle, a last name thought up quickly during his nighttime stroll.

Ivan Ivanovich appeared on paper. His self-satisfied figure winked here and there from the pages: here it was luxuriating on a couch that had belonged to Dostoyevsky, there it was in the Pushkin House reading books from Pushkin's library, here it was striding around Yasnaya Polyana.[29] The house where Cuckoo lived was also borrowed, though Whistlin did move it to a different part of the city; and Cuckoo's manner of speaking was put on display.

Whistlin treated himself with a similar lack of ceremony. He would take some object from his own writing table, or some fact from his own biography, and attach it to someone else. And then everyone around would gasp: "Look how he's taking himself to task," and rumors would spread like wildfire, each one more outlandish than the next. And Whistlin would fan the flames.

He took his half-finished likeness of Cockadoodle, rolled up into a tube, to a society of relatively young gossips of both sexes.

The society was waiting for his arrival, getting ready to be consumed by excitement, to delight in the correlation of invention and reality, to be shaken up, acquire some food for thought and imagination.

"Oh, that Whistlin," they said. "Now there's someone who writes interestingly. So who's that Kamadasheva—probably Anna Petrovna Ramadasheva!"

The collective of gossips considered its members true connoisseurs of literature. They'd get their claws into some writer and ask him to indulge them.

The writer, assuming that he was reading to people simply from the soul, would comply. And the gossip's eyes would gleam, he would become positively radiant. And he'd slap the writer playfully on the back: "I figured it out: Kamadasheva, of course, is Ramadasheva, and the structure of your work resembles that of Pavel Nikolayevich." And the stunned writer would sit there. *Well, I've got egg on my face*, he'd think. *Why on earth did I read to them?*

The gossips of the city fell into different circles. But the gossips of each circle knew all the other gossips. When the rumor began to spread that Whistlin was planning to read at Nadezhda Semyonovna's, they all began to wait for invitations. A few gossips of both sexes even dropped in on Nadezhda Semyonovna ahead of time to find out whether they could bring their acquaintances from other circles.

So, when Whistlin arrived, he found the riotous assembly in full swing. On the couches, the matching hassocks, the chairs, the carpet, the windowsills sat the mature, the young, and the elderly alike. They were waiting for him and conversing animatedly.

Whistlin kissed all the female gossips' hands and shook all the male gossips' hands, then made himself comfortable at the table. Nadezhda Semyonovna, as the hostess, sat down close beside him so as not to miss a single word, and everyone began listening attentively.

From time to time there were eruptions of giggling, whispering back and forth. People recognized some acquaintances, didn't recognize others. Then they would whisper to one another: "Who's that?"— and their faces would start looking worried. And finally, the right guess would hit them like lightning, and they would take up their whispering again. Crowding around Whistlin, they gushed over his achievement.

"No, no," Whistlin repeated in such a way that everyone heard: "*Yes, yes.*"

Everyone came to the table and began drinking tea, the samovar puffed away, the cookies crunched, and this was when Whistlin started gathering new gossip.

"Oh, do you know what happened? Aleksei Ivanovich has been rejuvenated. He married a little young thing. Now there's a character for you!"

"That, let me tell you, is real material, to die for. And the way he got married. He went all the way out to Tsarskoe Selo, to get closer to the spirit of Pushkin, and the wedding took place out there in the St. Sophia Cathedral."

That's for Cockadoodle, thought Whistlin, *that's just what Cockadoodle needs.*

"And then you have Nikandrov—he's been looking his whole life for a girl straight out of Turgenev. And now at forty he's finally found her. Got married. Now he's living in bliss too!"

Whistlin left, and the rumor took off around the city: Cockadoodle was none other than Cuckoo!*

When he got home, Whistlin took his fresh impressions and began expanding one of the chapters:

> Cockadoodle gradually became convinced that Verochka was a girl straight out of Turgenev, that there was something Liza-like about her.[30] He felt his love growing ever stronger. His heart went pitter-pat. Her mother let Verochka go out with Cockadoodle, and together they would visit Pushkin House, and the Literary Necropolis, and even went out to the village

---

*By doing this, Whistlin infringed upon that which can be called *Intimität des Mensches* (the intimate part of a person), publicly displayed Cuckoo naked, as well as depicting him in circumstances that could indirectly bring Cuckoo down in the world. Meanwhile Whistlin had long since forgotten about his conversation with the deaf-mute woman, which had been provoked by temporary irritation.

of Mikhailovskoe.[31] Their romance took its course slowly. Cockadoodle often listened to Verochka playing the piano. Sitting there in an armchair, he sometimes felt himself to be, to some extent, Lavretsky. And Verochka played Chopin ever more sweetly and gently, and the room grew ever darker, and finally, the electric candles sputtered to life.[32]

Cuckoo really was falling ever more deeply in love with Nadia. For lack of time he met with Whistlin ever more rarely, and still didn't know that Whistlin had already lived his whole life for him. Cuckoo rode around the suburbs with Nadia. He too visited the village of Mikhailovskoe, only he kept comparing Nadia to Natasha, not Liza; but he believed that she would remain Natasha forever and never become an ordinary woman.

The rumor went round and round. People spied on Cuckoo. Watched him walk down paths already written for him. Finally the rumor reached Cuckoo himself, and he was ecstatic—he had finally made it into literature.

And he told Nadia about it as if it were the most significant thing ever to happen in his life.

"Nadia," he said solemnly, taking her hand, "I am transported. Our friend Whistlin has immortalized me! He has written a novel about me. According to rumor, it is excellent. They say there hasn't been a novel like this since the time of the Symbolists. And stylistically it's exceptional, and it spans the entirety of the age."

"But weren't you planning to write something together?"

"I'm lazy, Nadia, nothing came of it."

Nadia gazed at Ivan Ivanovich. She admired him, considered him a very clever person.

"All right, then, Ivan Ivanovich," she said fondly. "I am so, so glad that you're pleased. Andrei Nikolayevich often told me that he loved you very much, that you are an exceptionally interesting man."

"I feel almost as though it's my birthday. Let's go for a stroll along the Neva, Nadia. We'll buy a cake and celebrate this event. My sweet Nadia," Cuckoo continued, "soon, very soon we will celebrate our wedding. Only your girlfriends and my friends will be there. But don't tell anyone yet. We'll send out cards—so-and-so and so-and-so request your presence at the St. Sophia Cathedral in Tsarskoe Selo..."

A letter to Whistlin from Lenochka in Staraya Russa:

My sunshine! How's your new novel coming along? Does it take up a lot of your time? Don't wear yourself out. Get enough sleep and eat well.

How are your Pole, your Count, and your Georgian? Did you get the materials you needed? I read in the papers that your novel will come out soon.

You asked me to write what I remember about Liza in *A Nest of Gentlefolk*. Goodness, you sure are lazy, my golden boy. Just joking, sweetie! I understand that you need to know what people generally remember about her. I brought it up after lunch. Here are the responses, in character:

Older lady, emaciated, 48 y.o., pointy-nosed:
Liza loved to be alone. To read Holy Writ. She really loved nature, birds. And daydreaming. She didn't have any friends. As a child she was greatly influenced by her nanny. She considered it a sin that she fell for Lavretsky, a married man, she felt like she was to blame.

Teacher in training, 26 y.o.
Daughter of a landowner. A very vague impression. A garden. She leaves for a monastery because she fell for Lavretsky. Her nanny read the lives of saints instead of fairy tales. Woke her up early and took her to churches.

Local critic:
Can't remember a single thing. I read it such a long time ago that nothing's left.

Local Don Juan:

I remember Lavretsky standing on the staircase. The sun is shining through Liza's hair. I remember her taking a walk with an old man. I remember the postcards. Him sitting and her standing with a fishing pole.

That's all I was able to gather for you for today, my dear. Just picture the boredom here. People only talk about their illnesses and how much their husbands earn. Many kisses.

Sitting against a background of books long unopened, Whistlin began writing the next chapter. He was working well, breathing freely. Whistlin loved flowers, and there were violets on the table in a big cut glass vase.*

Whistlin found himself writing today as he had never written before. The whole city rose up before him, and in this imaginary city his various characters moved, sang, conversed, got married. Whistlin felt himself in a void or, rather, a theater, in a dimly lit box, playing the role of a young, elegant, romantically inclined spectator. At that moment he loved his characters to an extreme degree. They seemed radiant to him. And the rhythm he felt within himself and the insatiable desire for harmony were reflected in both the selection and the order of the words being laid down on the page.

A knock came, and the enchantment fell away. *Now, who's that?* Whistlin thought in irritation. *There's really no reason to answer. People are always disturbing you.* And he listened carefully.

The knock repeated. "God knows," Whistlin whispered, "they won't even let a person work. I won't be able to write anymore anyway."

---

*Whistlin wrote in the past tense, sometimes in the past perfect, as if what he was describing had ended long ago; as if instead of thrilling reality he was taking up an event long since completed. He wrote about his era as another writer might write about distant times with which his readers were not well acquainted. He generalized the events of everyday life rather than individualizing them. Without suspecting as much, he described contemporaneity using a historical approach, one extraordinarily offensive to his contemporaries.

And, closing his folder, he opened the door. On the threshold stood Cuckoo.

"Forgive me, Andrei Nikolayevich," Cuckoo pronounced, "for barging in on you so unexpectedly. But you know how it is—business. Pre-wedding fever."

"By all means, by all means," Whistlin answered and helped Cuckoo with his coat.

"Well, what news here?" Cuckoo asked. "How's the writing coming along? I heard your novel is coming out magnificently."

Whistlin fidgeted with the manuscript.

"Still a long way to go," he answered.

"Could you possibly just—a few excerpts? They say I'm already in there."

"Good heavens, come now, Ivan Ivanovich," Whistlin answered.

"But they said it was me," said Cuckoo, stout and dignified, and now growing agitated in his dismay. "No, Andrei Nikolayevich, it's just not possible," he said, after a moment's silence. "For old time's sake, read it to me."

Whistlin felt it would be cowardly to refuse. He sat down in his gaudy armchair, took up the manuscript and began to read his novel. As the reading went on Cuckoo's face took on an ever more enraptured and astonished expression.

"What prose!" He shook his head. "What depth! Andrei Nikolayevich, I would never have thought you'd lavish so much talent on this."

Whistlin went on reading. And now Cockadoodle came onto the scene, and Cuckoo went pale. He fell back into the chair and, mouth open, listened all the way to the end.

"Andrei Nikolayevich, but this is . . ."

After the reading Ivan Ivanovich, colorless, went outside. He thought about how now, he stood utterly naked and defenseless against a world that laughed at him. Fear lay on the face of Ivan Ivanovich and a vacant, apologetic smile played around his mouth. Crestfallen and tormented by his image, he was afraid of running into someone he knew. It seemed to him that everyone could already clearly see his utter insignificance, that no one would bow to him, that they would turn away and walk on, chatting with deliberate cheerfulness with their companion, wife, or girlfriend. Tears appeared in Ivan Ivanovich's eyes. Consumed by an internal lament for himself, he leaned against the wall and watched Whistlin go off somewhere.

That evening Cuckoo did not, as he usually did, leave his enormous building and did not pick Nadia up for a stroll and a pleasant evening; he shut himself up in his room. He didn't know what to do with himself. He felt like killing Whistlin, who had taken away his life, and, nearly crying, he saw himself punching Whistlin first on one cheek, then the other, knocking all his teeth out, gouging out his eyes, and dragging his body through the streets. Then he remembered that this was out of the question, that he, Cuckoo, was a well-bred person; he burst into tears and decided to write a letter. But he remembered that Cockadoodle had already written the letter for him, and suddenly the thought of Nadia slashed through his heart. He imagined her reading Whistlin's novel, saw her get caught up in the rhythm and begin smiling at her fiancé's foibles, saw her begin to laugh at him, scorn him.

And in the next room, a voice began singing the nanny's aria from *Eugene Onegin*. Cuckoo banged on the wall with his fists and everything fell silent. A terrifying silence ensued, then steps and a resounding voice: "Don't interrupt people practicing." Imposing and fat, Cuckoo sat at his table and thought about how another man had lived his life for him, had lived it pathetically and contemptibly, and that now he, Cuckoo, had nothing to do; that now he himself was no longer interested in Nadia; that he himself no longer loved her and could not marry her, that it would be a repetition, an unbearable traversal of one and the same life, that even if Whistlin tore up his manuscript right now, nevertheless he, Cuckoo, already knew his life; that his self-respect was irrevocably destroyed, that life had lost all its appeal for him.

All the same, Cuckoo went to see Whistlin the next morning. He had decided to at least hide himself from his acquaintances, and he tearfully begged Whistlin to tear up the manuscript.

"So what then, you'll have me get down on my knees and beg?" Cuckoo cried. "If you are an honorable man, you are duty bound to tear up the manuscript. To so mock a man respected by all. If we lived in another time you'd never be able to hide from my seconds! But now, God knows what," he whispered, covering his face with his hands, and Whistlin felt that what stood before him was no longer a man, but something like a corpse.

"I beg you, Andrei Nikolayevich, give it to me, I will destroy your manuscript..."

"Ivan Ivanovich," Whistlin replied, "it isn't, after all, *you* that I rendered into literature, not your soul. The soul can't be portrayed, after all. It's true that I borrowed certain details..."

But Cuckoo would not let Whistlin finish. He threw himself at the writing table and tried to grab the sheets of paper. Whistlin, fearing the demise of his world, and wishing to distract Cuckoo, asked:

"How is Miss Nadia?" A crazed face with clenched fists walked over to Whistlin.

"You're no human, you're a subhuman. You are a serpent! You know better than I do how things are with Nadezhda Nikolayevna."

Fists clenched, Cuckoo strode around the room.

The air was getting close. Whistlin threw open the window and noticed that the courtyard was full of people already home from work, chatting. *I'm late*, he thought, *I'll have to take it to the typist tomorrow.* Cuckoo wouldn't leave. Cuckoo was thinking things over, sitting in the armchair.

Whistlin reflected awhile, thinking that some of the episodes that had so upset Cuckoo could, by all means, be changed, that people had pestered him in the past as well, but never... there had never been such pain.*

---

*Whistlin knew that not all of his characters would become Gramonts, that they might not be thrilled at all to see their reflections, as the marshal's brother had been thrilled to see himself depicted in Molière's *Le Mariage forcé*. And yet he had not expected that Cuckoo would have such a strange response.[33]

"I have to go." Whistlin smiled crookedly and stood waiting while Cuckoo put on his coat.

They went out together. Whistlin was carrying the manuscript. Cuckoo kept peering at the manuscript, saying nothing. He was struggling with the desire to snatch it and run off. Without saying a word to one another, they parted ways at the intersection.

Cuckoo did not visit, did not write. The days grew agonizing for Nadia. She would go into the house-city, but never found Ivan Ivanovich at home. Joyous and imposing, he did not reach out his hands in greeting. His bass voice did not resound. Sometimes from the courtyard she would see a light in his window, run up the stairs and ring the bell in vain.

Ivan Ivanovich had descended into a genuine hell. The image of Cockadoodle stood before him in all of its absurdity and stupidity. True, he, Ivan Ivanovich, no longer rode around the city's suburbs. True, he had shaved off his muttonchops and changed his suit, and moved to a different part of the city, but there Ivan Ivanovich experienced the most terrible thing of all—that he had essentially become a subhuman, that everything inside him had been purloined, that within him and around him there remained only filth, spite, suspicion, and a lack of trust in himself.

He had changed physically. He had become thinner, his lips pursed; his face had taken on a spiteful, fastidious expression.

Having become a subhuman, Ivan Ivanovich began to seek a different fate.

Deciding that Whistlin had mainly been mocking his respect for great men, Cuckoo began scorning great men. Now he told his old acquaintances that one should not sit with self-satisfaction on Dostoyevsky's couches, and that there was really no reason to hang on to Dostoyevsky's couches at all, or Pushkinian relics and so on, that all that stuff should be burned for sowing harmful thoughts and provoking harmful desires.

He took Whistlin's mockery of swaggering love for mockery of love in general, and began to say that love did not exist, only the contact of epidermises.

Afraid of running into people he knew, he decided to decamp to another city.*

*Having committed spiritual murder, Whistlin was untroubled. *This occurred in accordance with specific laws*, he thought. *Cuckoo was not a real person. I committed an unethical act in using him for my novel. In any case, I shouldn't have read it to him before finishing the final draft, where I elevate him to the level of a type. He believed in me, in my friendship. My act was unethical, but Cuckoo came to my apartment unexpectedly, and I had no other option. It was involuntary manslaughter, after all.*

4. A SOVIET CAGLIOSTRO

PSYCHOFSKY lived on the Bolshaya Neva Embankment in a small wooden house, whence he traveled across all Russia. The house was quiet and astoundingly transparent. Out front lay a quiet garden, and the quiet and unfrequented embankment.

At some distance away stood a small co-op store with dusty windows, and a teahouse.

No one knew that this was where the Soviet Cagliostro lived.

Flowers in little yellow pots lined the windows. The self-proclaimed doctor of philosophy was strolling around the garden and plotting out his latest venture—a hypnosis session in Volkhov.

Everyone knows Volkhov, where the houses stand as if on chicken legs, where the local club director arranges dance parties for his wife's birthday.

Where magicians stop by once every other year, while no real actor had ever set foot in Volkhov.

The good-natured cynic strolled around the garden, plotting. In his daughter's room the electric lightbulb glowed beneath a pink bouquet-covered lampshade. The father walked over to the window and peered in. *Sweet child*, he thought, *she's going to bed. She doesn't know how hard her father works to earn his bread.*

The Soviet Cagliostro was sad this evening.[34]

A sole passerby was hurrying down the embankment.

The passerby lit a match to read a piece of paper he had taken out of his pocket.

Psychofsky recognized Whistlin and stepped out of the gate.

"Have you come to see me?" he asked.

"No, not you," Whistlin answered. "I'll stop by tomorrow. Today I'm hurrying to a different house."

"You'll never come." Psychofsky flicked his hand dismissively.

"My, it does smell bad here," Whistlin said, coming in the next day and casting his eyes around the room. "Do you never take off your outside clothes or remove your boots? You sleep here on this couch? This is quite a blanket you have! Hoo, this day has worn me out, my esteemed Vladimir Evgenevich!"

Whistlin picked up a photograph from the table.

"This must be you as a child?"

"Make yourself right at home, have a look around."

"Might you let me take a look at your correspondence? Letters written to you, from you—it's all very interesting. May I open this?" Whistlin asked, approaching the wardrobe.

"So, a tailcoat, very moth-eaten . . . and there must a top hat somewhere you've hung on to? And where is your family photo album?" Whistlin asked.

The host went away and brought back an album with a lacquered cover. The guest flipped through it, examining the photographs, daydreamed. Psychofsky stood by the table, resting his head on his fists.

"Introduce me to your family," Whistlin said.

"No, that is totally impossible . . ." Vladimir Evgenevich flushed pink.

His fourteen-year-old daughter came running into the room. "Papa, papa, the countess is asking for you."

"Just a moment, Masha." Psychofsky became flustered and made a dive for the door.

Whistlin approached the adolescent. "Let's get acquainted."

Masha curtsied.

"You must study at the labor school?" Whistlin asked, letting go her hand.

"No, papa doesn't let me."

Whistlin looked at her scrawny, well-dressed little figure. Psychofsky came running back in.

"Masha, get out of here, go!"

The daughter gave Whistlin a coquettish look.

"Go on, what did I say?"

Masha left. But a minute later she came running in again.

"Papa, the prince is here."

"I'm terribly sorry, you'll have to excuse me." And taking Masha by the hand, Psychofsky once again made a dive for the door. The drapes closed. Whistlin smoked and waited. He cast a glance over the spines of the dusty, mildewed books and started reading the titles.

"How come you keep getting visits from these titled types?"

"It's just a coincidence," Psychofsky answered, embarrassed.

"Fine. So, what do you intend to regale me with?"

"Are you interested in who's sleeping with whom?"

"To be honest, not very."

"So what are you interested in?"

"Your observations of the past few years. Your feelings and thoughts. Tell me, why were you trying to find fault with science?

"I thought it was original."

"You must have written poems in your youth?"

"About gonorrhea."

"Amusing!"

"Very amusing."

"Papa, papa, mama's calling for you," came a voice from behind the door.

"Coming, little one."

Whistlin walked over to the bookshelf. He opened Blok to the spot marked by a bookmark:

I'll dream no more of tenderness or fame,
It all has passed me by, my youth's no more![35]

Whistlin suppressed his guffaws. He walked over to the window. Down below Psychofsky was coming back from the co-op with a loaf of bread.

Psychofsky's room contained a full library of occultism, Masonry, and sorcery. But Whistlin understood that Psychofsky did not believe in occultism or Masonry or magic.

Everyone likes to leaf through things. Young ladies and women like to daydream over fashion magazines, the engineer likes to be stirred by the invention of a foreign motor, the old man likes to shed a few tears over photographs of his dead children.

Psychofsky, shaking his head, would leaf through pictures of mandrakes resembling old wise men; talismans with the Sun, Moon, and Mars; geomantic trees; a diagram of Sefirot, pictures of demons; of a stocky Azazel leading a goat; the Mephistopheles-like Haborym flying on a snake; the winged and slightly bony Astaroth, with his enormous eyes.[36]

In his youth Psychofsky had wanted to be a tempter. Between 1908 and 1912 he even wore a white robe and a black velvet hat with a red feather. His family considered this a rich man's whim.

In his youth he'd spent pleasant nights reading tracts on the true method for making pacts with spirits. Visionary nights.

Among ordinary laypeople he passed as a mystic. In his youth Psychofsky had enjoyed this greatly. And even now he liked it when people looked at him fearfully. There were rumors that he was the hierophant of some secret order, that he had advanced through all the ranks and stopped at the top. He told people that he was a Thessalian Greek by origin, and, as is known, Thessaly has always been famous for its sorcery.

Indeed, in one of the small rooms of his house hung portraits from the times of Catherine and Alexander, portraits of Greek women and men wearing wigs and caftans; a mother-of-pearl crucifix stood beneath a glass bell taken from a clock; and there was a family album from the 1830s with watercolors, poems, and vignettes, as well as a Greek Bible with the family names Rallis, Hari, and Maraslis.

Having looked over the apartment, Whistlin became fond of the Soviet Cagliostro. *How sad his life is!* he thought. *What use is his fame as the Soviet Cagliostro when he himself knows that he's an impostor, that he is neither Greek nor a soothsayer, but just Vladimir Evgenevich Psychofsky. Even the pope in Rome could send him his blessing every year. But he doesn't believe in the Roman pope.*

Sitting in the bedroom beneath the old-fashioned portraits, the host and his guest smoked, drank some vodka, and washed it down with tomatoes.

Psychofsky talked about his noble order. Whistlin, dragging on his cigarette with pleasure, smoked and let the smoke out of his nostrils. Whistlin saw the night of Psychofsky, because in the life of every man there is a great night of doubt, which is followed by victory or defeat. A night that can last months or years.

And now, to the sound of Psychofsky's ranting, Whistlin was trying to reconstruct this night. Back then Psychofsky had been young, and the leaves had rustled differently, and the birds had sung in a different way. He had believed that he would succeed at whisking the shining veil off the world, that he was something like the devil. He rode a black stallion out in front of a cavalcade. The young people were sucking candies, whipping their horses and joking cheerfully.

Whistlin felt his heart sink.*

Psychofsky noticed Whistlin go pale and thought he had made a powerful impression on his guest.

"Psychofsky-Rallis-Hari-Maraslis!" Whistlin broke the silence

---

*Whistlin's works and days are not to be diminished. His life consisted not merely in eavesdropping on conversations and hunting people down, but also in an extraordinary degree of infection by them, in a certain spiritual engagement in their lives. Thus when his characters died, something died in Whistlin too; when they surrendered, Whistlin too experienced a certain amount of surrender. Furthermore, however strange it seems at first, Whistlin believed in the magical depth of words.

mockingly. "Tell me how you made your pact with the devil! You are a very interesting person, I am very glad to take you for my novel."

The master of the quiet apartment felt hugely encouraged. Delightful, solemn and enchanting music surrounded him and bit by bit grew ever louder, such that its harmonious sounds seemed to fill the entire room and pour out the window into the small front garden, reaching the walls of the neighboring building. Music like this can be heard by brides and grooms if they are very young and very much in love.

Psychofsky got up from the armchair and squared his shoulders.

"In order to make a pact with one of the major spirits, I set out, cutting myself a stick of wild hazel with a new, unused knife and, drawing a triangle in a remote place, set out two candles, stood in the triangle and pronounced the grand appeal: 'Emperor Lucifer, lord of all rebellious spirits, be thou well-disposed toward my call...'"

Whistlin smiled.

"Vladimir Evgenevich, I'm not asking you about that pact, I'm asking about the internal pact."

"What do you mean?" asked Psychofsky.

"About the moment when you felt you had lost your will, and realized that you were lost, that you are an impostor."

The music stopped. A man was sitting across from Psychofsky, drinking vodka and making fun of him. Everything was suddenly repugnant to Psychofsky, and he appeared uninteresting even to himself. But a moment later he roused.

"What do you mean, I'm an impostor?" he asked. "So you don't believe that I'm a doctor of philosophy?" The host's face grew angry and hostile.

"Oh no," the guest answered politely, "I meant something completely different. You call yourself a mystic. But perhaps you're not a mystic at all. You say, 'I am an idealist,' but perhaps you're not an idealist at all."

Vladimir Evgenevich furrowed his brow.

"Or perhaps, assuring each and every person you meet, albeit with a smirk, that you're a mystic, you think that you'll actually become one for real? I'm asking for the novel," the guest continued, smiling. "Don't be angry. After all, I have to test you. I'm always just joking around, you know."

Psychofsky's face brightened and his eyes began to gleam.

Whistlin watched this man who was talking about the gymnosophists, the priests of Isis, the Eleusinian Mysteries, the school of Pythagoras, while, to all appearances, knowing quite little about all these things. In any case less than one could know.

"Is everything all right?" asked the host. "Do you like it here at my place?"

"Very much," answered Whistlin. "Sitting here is like sitting with an ascetic." And Whistlin's voice became dreamy.

Psychofsky was meanwhile trying to speak in a way that made absolutely clear to Whistlin that he belonged to a powerful secret society.

Whistlin's host was for the most part a nice person. He called May Adarmapagon, June Khardat, July Therma, August Mederme, and his home Eleusis.[37] He sometimes signed his last name out in number code:

15, 18, 4, 10, 5, 12, 19, 10, 5, 8, 7, 7.

And closed with a flourish.

Of course, it came out rather long, and instead of "Psycho" it came out "Psicha";[38] but in his more secret papers he wrote using special hieroglyphs and called himself Mephistopheles.

What the guest and his host spoke of that evening, the reader need not know; but on the threshold they kissed fervently, and the guest disappeared into the nighttime darkness, while the host, enraptured, watched him go for a long time, and then lit a candle and went upstairs.

And it was evident that Psychofsky did not sleep all night, that his shadow was pacing back and forth across the room, that he was thinking something over. Then he sat down at the desk and covered a piece of paper with numbers.

Whistlin meanwhile walked through the fog and thought about what would happen if they both believed in the existence of evil powers.

At the appointed time, in the evening, as late as possible, the novitiate Whistlin was admitted to a dimly lit room. The voice of Psychofsky was coming out from behind a curtain. A naked sword lay on a table in the middle of the room; a large cut glass lantern illuminated the whole scene with a faint light.

From behind the curtain, Psychofsky's voice asked Whistlin:

"Do you persist in your desire to be initiated?"

After an affirmative answer from Whistlin, Psychofsky's voice sent the new initiate to think things over in a room that was completely dark.

Having been called once again, Whistlin saw Psychofsky standing by the table holding the sword. Questions followed upon questions. Finally there came:

"Your desire is just. In the name of the serene order which grants me my authority and power, and in the name of all of its members, I pledge to you our protection, justice, and aid."

At this point Psychofsky lifted the sword—Whistlin noted that it was not very old—and pressed its point to Whistlin's chest, continuing with exaggerated feeling:

"But if you prove to be a traitor, if you become an oath breaker, then know…"

Then, placing the sword on the table, Psychofsky began to recite a prayer that Whistlin repeated after him. Next, Whistlin pronounced the oath.

"Congratulations," said Psychofsky.

And they went downstairs and headed for the teahouse.

*

Taking him by the hand, Psychofsky smoothly brought Whistlin into his circle. They were all women, no longer very young. Whistlin's nostrils were unpleasantly tickled by the scent of perfume. His eyes were unpleasantly assaulted by affected, languorous movements. Some of them were smoking scented cigarettes, others were discussing sublime matters: whether tables can or cannot fly.

Brought in by Psychofsky, and unknown to these unknown women, Whistlin bowed all around and stood still. The hostess walked up to Whistlin and said:

"You are a friend of Psychofsky's, so you are our friend as well."

Whistlin smiled courteously.

"Allow me to introduce you." And, taking the initiate by the hands, Psychofsky went from lady to lady introducing Whistlin.

They reminded Whistlin of animals. One was like a goat, another like a horse, a third like a dog. He felt an overwhelming antipathy, but his face expressed respectful affection.

"You are a man of letters, Andrei Nikolayevich? We love all the arts unspeakably! Vladimir Evgenevich was just telling us about you!"

All Whistlin had to do was bow.

And, to prevent a silence, to give the guest a break, the hostess approached Psychofsky and asked him to carry out his promise and play each guest her leitmotif.

Psychofsky assented.

Whistlin examined the hostess. In her he read egoism, consummate and courteous, the sort typical in people with Mercury in the Ascendant, as Psychofsky would say (able as he was to make his vices serve his interests). She was courageous and canny.

Psychofsky played her a corresponding piece of music.

There's no doubt, thought Whistlin, *Psychofsky has a gift for improvisation, a phenomenal memory, knows the Old Masters, is able to perform marvelous themes in unexpected counterpoint and astonish people.*

One by one, Psychofsky played all the ladies their leitmotifs. The ladies listened, immobilized by pleasure. Psychofsky threw Whistlin a victorious glance.

"I was playing for you," he said in a whisper. "Just for you!"

Whistlin squeezed his elbow...

"We are avatars of Orpheus today. You are the word and I am music," Psychofsky beamed.

"Yes!" Whistlin affirmed in mock rapture.

In the company of ladies, Psychofsky felt himself to be *un homme fatal*.

"Our silence told you more than our applause would have," the hostess said, coming up to the men standing by the piano.

A general conversation started up about music and souls.

The conversation shifted to Psychofsky's recent trip to Italy. Psychofsky took out a statuette of three-faced Hecate and began showing it to everyone.

"She has quite the nose," he said, "look—it's rounded and who knows if it's the real thing. I bought her in Naples and now she's with me wherever I go." He hid the statuette back in his pocket. "Closer to my heart," he said and gave Whistlin a sweet look.

"Shall I tell you about Isis?" he asked.

He sat down a bit closer to the ladies sitting in their half circle.

"Please do, how fascinating!"

"Isis is a hermetic deity. Long hair falls in waves upon her divine neck. On her head is a disk that shines like a mirror or stands between two intertwining snakes."

Psychofsky demonstrated how the snakes writhed.

"She holds a sistrum in her right hand. A golden vessel hangs from the left. The breath of this goddess is sweeter than all the perfumes of Araby.

"I experienced all of this."

Psychofsky tried to lend his eyes an air of mystery. He immobilized them. He rose from the armchair, his arms raised in a ritual gesture.

"She is nature, the mother of all things, lady sovereign of the elements, origin of the ages, the empress of souls." Psychofsky went pale. "In the unearthly silence of darkest night, you move us and inanimate objects alike. I realize that fate has had her fill of my long and terrible sufferings.

"And now you quietly approach me, O transparent vision, in your changing dress. Here I see the full moon and the stars, and flowers, and fruits!"

Psychofsky fell silent.

And suddenly in the corner of the room a woman's squeaky voice could be heard:

"I am touched by your entreaties, Psychofsky. I am the Ur-mother of all in nature, the lady sovereign of the elements..."

Everyone's heads turned. It was Whistlin who had spoken... But Psychofsky collected himself.

"You drove away the vision," he said.

The night flew by without anyone's noticing. Psychofsky determined the colors of the ladies' souls. Maria Dmitrievna turned out to have a pale-blue soul, Nadezhda Ivanovna's was pink, Ekaterina Borisovna's was pink shading into purple, and their hostess had a silver one with black spots.

"So that's how we spend our time," said Psychofsky while taking leave of Whistlin on the embankment, in the sun's morning rays. "What did you think, was it all right?"

"Magnificent!" Whistlin answered. "Absolutely fantastic!"

Meanwhile Applekin the salesclerk, whom Psychofsky called Cato, was putting together his portrait at Psychofsky's instigation.[39]

He wrote the names of his grandparents and parents, what they did, who his enemies were, what his friends were like, what kind of income he had, and rooted around in his own soul.

Elated, this new Cato began reading Plutarch's Cato, which had been entrusted to him by the false hierophant. Questions rose up on every page for Applekin, and he filled the margins of the book with question marks.

He lived on the sixth floor, and the city spread out below his feet. The sunsets and sunrises illuminated his room. He began rising earlier and going to bed later, he read, and with each rising and setting felt himself more and more intelligent.

Whistlin met Cato at Psychofsky's. The hierophant, seated below the old-fashioned portraits, was explaining the number alphabet to his disciple.

Whistlin sat in another chair with a collection of astonishing and notable stories, copying out the pages he needed on a sheet of paper...

La nuict de ce iour venu?, le sorcier meine son compagnon par certaines montagnes & vallées, qu'il n'aoit oncques veues, & luy sembla qu'en peu de temps ils aouyent fait beau coup de chemin. Puis entrant en vn champ tout enuironne de montagnes, il vid grand nombre d'hommes & de femmes qui s'amassoyent la, & vindrent tous a luy, menans grand feste...[40]

Whistlin began musing. What would happen with all these women and men when they read his book? At present they flocked to him in joy and celebration, but later, perhaps, a looming roar of voices, insulted pride, betrayed friendship, dreams ridiculed, would rush in.

Applekin wrote:

12, 11, 10, 9, 8, 7, 6,
A, B, C, D, E, F, G.

Whistlin sat by the window like a shadow.

Psychofsky looked after his health carefully. Jars, glasses, cups of buttermilk speckled with flies stood all over, and tomatoes had been left to ripen on the cracked windowsill.

"Your heart must be pure," Psychofsky was telling Applekin, "and your spirit must be flaming with divine fire. The step you are taking is the most important one of your entire life. By promoting you to cavalier, we expect of you noble and great deeds worthy of this title."

And Applekin felt that he had partaken of a mystery, and when he left, the whole world appeared to him in a new light. The city was lit up differently somehow. People appeared in a new light, he felt that he needed to work toward perfecting himself and toward enlightening others.

Whistlin guessed what was going on with Applekin; he felt sorry to puncture his dream, to plunge him again into a pointless existence, to convey Psychofsky's figure to his consciousness. He knew that Applekin was sure to read his book, a book by Psychofsky's closest friend.

"Well, there's nothing to be done about it. Psychofsky is essential to my novel," Whistlin decided and, settling in more cozily in Psychofsky's room, in Psychofsky's armchair, he began to transpose Psychofsky into his book.

Their host was dusting his relics. He was talking about Applekin, making plans. The Neva was freezing, soon the Red Army soldiers would be skiing on it. Soon a skating rink would be set up and in the fenced-in space young people would dance to the sounds of a waltz.

Whistlin looked at Psychofsky. *The poor guy*, he thought. *He's really asking for it.*

"Chum," he said, "could you heat up some tea, it's gotten a bit chilly?"

"Should I fire up the woodstove?" asked the host.

"Now that would be really fine," answered the guest. "We are really having the most marvelous time. What does it matter that it's snowing outside? We'll sit here in warmth and comfort."

Psychofsky went outside and brought in wood.

Whistlin had written down everything he needed to.

"Now we ought to have ourselves a little game of cards," he said. He walked up to the woodstove and, rubbing his hands good-naturedly by the blazing flames, thought awhile, then continued: "You must have cards? Let's set up the card table and ask your wife and daughter in, we'll play a game of whist."

Whistlin played whist until midnight and kept losing. He liked to do a small kindness. He saw Mrs. Psychofsky's cheeks redden and read her thoughts about how she'd be able to buy burgundy, her husband's favorite, for tomorrow's dinner; that they would certainly also have to invite this kind Andrei Nikolayevich, whose friendship had so enlivened her husband.

Psychofsky wielded the chalk adroitly, reddening as well.

They took turns shuffling the deck; the cards were well-thumbed, greasy, gold-edged. They were marked even though they weren't meant to be.

Whistlin kept losing. He was content. At least he could do something to repay his hosts for their hospitality.

Snow fell outside the window in magnificent flakes. Magnificent portraits hung above the card players' heads. Masha and Whistlin sat with their backs to the black window. Masha was flirting with Whistlin. Whistlin cracked jokes and told her Gypsy tales.

Masha was vexed, blushed, and said that she was not a child.

Poor Psychofsky, Whistlin thought, stepping out the door of the hospitable home.

Too bad it's already too late to visit Applekin. He looked at his watch. *I suppose I could just walk around the city.* Raising his collar, Whistlin set out.

Applekin had a girlfriend. Her name was Antonina. Antonina worked at a candy factory and wore a red kerchief.

Applekin started corresponding cryptographically with his girlfriend, writing that he loved her and was ready to marry her. He wrote her about all this using numbers. They had no one to hide their love from. He and she were both alone.

The young man began telling her stories in the evenings, as they strolled along the wavering embankment or in the factory garden, suffused with the odor of sweet essences. He decided to introduce her to the enlightened and amiable people who lived over in that freestanding little house. He thought that Whistlin lived with Psychofsky.

"They're so learned, Ninochka," he would say. "It's even kinda scary. You stop by and they're sitting there with some kind of drawing, looking at circles and rectangles. The older one's explaining something to the younger one, and he's listening and diligently writing everything down."

Moan, my guitar,
The songs of fields and freedom . . .
And that's where we'll forget our sorrow . . .
My cherry-bang, my cherry . . .[41]

"Here come your guys." Antonina smiled. "My, they're making a lot of noise."

One after another the heads of Psychofsky and Whistlin appeared in the window overlooking the garden.

"What's this performance?" Whistlin was asking. "Good times at your place, Vladimir Evgenevich."

"Oh, we do this every Saturday."

"Would you play us some Mozart, say? or whatever you want. Something old-fashioned."

The window slammed shut.

Applekin stood with Antonina opposite the illuminated window. They saw the corner of the room with the old-fashioned portraits. Vanya whispered:

"So cozy in there. Look at the shelves, the flowerpots. Shhh!"

The music fell silent.

Psychofsky and Whistlin came down off the porch and set out along the garden path.

"Now then, my dear Andrei Nikolayevich, it seems that you still have doubts about the antiquity of our order. Believe me . . ."

At the time of the new moon an academic gathering took place in the two-windowed room that Psychofsky called the chapel. The old-fashioned portraits and a Masonic armchair bought at the Alexander market had been brought in. The beds had been taken out.

Psychofsky sat in the president's seat wearing boots with spurs and a ribbon across his chest, reading and interpreting passages from the Bible, Seneca, Epictetus, Marcus Aurelius, and Confucius. To his right sat Whistlin, to his left were Applekin and a former cavalry officer, and opposite was the prince/ice-cream man. When he had finished interpreting, Psychofsky began asking his pupils one by one about the books they had read since the last gathering, about their observations or the discoveries they'd made, about the labors and efforts they'd contributed toward expanding the order, about what sort of people they'd encountered and in what way they might be suitable for the order.

Applekin watched Psychofsky intently, trying to grasp everything.

The cavalry officer was evidently getting ready to object. He was squirming impatiently in his chair.

Whistlin was bored and rather uncomfortable. It was increasingly ridiculous and unpleasant to him that he was deceiving everyone.

In order to distract himself, he began laying out matches on the table, built a tower, and then burned it down. Everyone looked at him in consternation. *Yes, they genuinely believe Psychofsky, they assume that the mighty order really does exist. And for all I know, Psychofsky will send a note to the pope and, you never know, he'll receive money from America after all. And the order will blossom, and everyone will believe that it really did always exist.*

"Brothers, let's talk about refining our spiritual capacities. Let us focus our efforts on that. We shall develop the strength of our thoughts. I am convinced that we will soon be able to move objects from a distance. I shall soon make a trip to the East and shall there solicit blessings for you, the newly admitted brothers. They will pray for us there, and your souls shall be radiant and at peace.

"Who wishes to ask a question? I will try to bring you answers from the East."

The gathering lingered well past midnight.

One evening Whistlin was sitting with Psychofsky talking about the Knights Templar. A man came in with eyes bulging from their sockets—evidently, he suffered from Graves' disease.

"Baron Medem," Psychofsky introduced the new arrival and, taking the baron aside, gave him his last ruble.

The baron bowed and disappeared.

"Back in the eighteenth century, being a count, after all, he used to receive me in his castle," Psychofsky said pointedly. "It's too bad you weren't there."

Whistlin smiled.

"Wait," said Psychofsky, "I'm remembering, you were there. You wore an azure kirtle made of some exquisite material. I remember you gave me a ring with a cut stone."

"And you gave me this," Whistlin answered, and took from his pocket a ring with a heart, sword, and cross.

"That's right," exclaimed Psychofsky. "How could I have failed to recognize you?"

"Allow me to call you count. You are Count Phoenix, after all. And we are now in Petersburg," said Whistlin.

"Naturally, baron." Psychofsky took Whistlin by the arm. "We must drink to this occasion."

And they bowed deeply to one another.

Count Phoenix disappeared behind the portiere. The buffet creaked, and vodka appeared.

"Olya, Olya!" Psychofsky yelled, "bring a tablecloth."

"Andrei Nikolayevich has turned out not to be Andrei Nikolayevich at all. He's that friend of mine. Remember? I told you about him."

"Oh!" his wife answered.

Psychofsky bustled about. The eighteenth-century silver pepper grinder could not be found.

"Run over to the co-op," he told his wife. "Today we will sup by candlelight."

Psychofsky and Whistlin had read the same books. The two friends' memories coincided. The candles in their antique candlesticks illuminated the table, set with antique tableware, with tongues of flame. A mound of fruit from the LSPO co-op presided on a silver plate.[42] Finger grapes shone green. The vodka was put aside and red wine appeared. Count Phoenix recalled how he had been received by Catherine the Great, and said that he was still angry at his wife. The host was putting on a con, and so he suddenly glanced at Whistlin— to see whether he was perhaps also putting on a con. But Whistlin was genuinely pleased. He loved improvised evenings. He had lucked out tonight.

"Tell me, count," he asked, placing grapes in his mouth, "why did you choose to be incarnated as Psychofsky?"

In the morning, as he hadn't had any tours in a long while, Psychofsky was making beads out of a paste he'd invented and stringing them into necklaces, while speculating about earrings and brooches.

His wife was doing the same thing, as was his daughter.

The paste was kept in tin cans that had once held fruit drops and tea. Red, blue, white, orange, black, and green lumps sat on the table. His wife would tear off a small green blob and turn it into a long sausage by rubbing it between her palms. His daughter would slice the sausage into evenly-sized pieces, and Psychofsky would turn the pieces into beads. Thus even their quiet little house was affected by Fordism.[43] In the evening Psychofsky would string the beads onto a thread and cover them with copal varnish, and two or three days later sell them to his acquaintants and at Gostiny Dvor as the latest novelty from Paris. His daughter was bored by the bead work. She wanted her father to take her to a secret ball, where people wore colorful costumes. She wanted to see her father win at cards in secret gambling dens, and then give away the money to the needy. But in the meantime, instead of splendid balls, her father took her every once in a while to the cinema or the summer gardens, where she would guess what he had in his pocket using a system of questions, or to his magic shows, after which he was supposed to expose his methods and tell everyone from onstage that it was just sleight of hand, and show how it was done.

Whistlin decided to take a break from Psychofsky, collect new material, take on some other characters. *Let Psychofsky rise for a while, like bread dough.*

5. COLLECTING LAST NAMES

WHISTLIN walked past the low white wall of the monastery, past the level-two labor school, past the obstetrics center, entered a gate, went around a church, went around a little wing with small high windows curtained with gauze, and entered another gate.

He leaned down over the tombstones, lifted his eyes to angels with crosses, stuck his nose to the glass panels of crypts, and took it all in. Relatives of the dead people walked ahead of him to sit on the graves, which were speckled with colored eggs and breadcrumbs. By the monument to the writer Klimov he noted an elderly dwarf holding a bouquet. The little old man, putting aside the bouquet, was piously watering the grave and sticking his fingers into the soil, tying up the flowers. Touched, Whistlin stopped. Then he moved on, peeking into the crypts. In one crypt he saw two good-for-nothings playing cards, sitting on peeling iron chairs. The crypt was locked from the outside.

An old man sat on the grave of a Japanese man. Seeing that Whistlin was watching him intently, the old man explained:

"You see, no one comes to see him. I have nothing else to do, so I come. I feel sorry for him."

Some drunkards were lying around picturesquely on a smallish plot. The least drunk one went off and brought back a priest. The least drunk one went around to everyone and took off their hats. The priest quickly began to officiate, glancing over his shoulder. When he was finished, the half-drunk one paid his fee, went back to all the people putting their hats back on, and, addressing the grave, pronounced contentedly:

"Well, Ivan Andreyevich, we did a nice job commemorating you, drank to your memory, and gave you a proper funeral service. Now you ought to be happy."

Whistlin, having written all this down, wanted to keep moving. But not far from a tombstone shaped like a propeller he had noticed a well-known columnist chatting with the priest. The columnist's face was feigning faith, hope, and love, calling the priest "father" —but, when he got the chance, he winked at Whistlin. Whistlin smiled.

When the priest, deeply moved, had left, thinking that not all of the decent young people had died out yet, Whistlin walked over to the columnist.

"On the hunt?" he asked. "The hunt is a great thing."

"Yes, I want to do what I can to elucidate modernity."

"Do you happen to have any material related to . . ." and Whistlin leaned over to the columnist's ear.

"I do, I do!" The man's face brightened. Joyfully lighting up a cigarette, the columnist pitched the match into the distance. "But don't use it yourself. I'm hanging on to it for an adventure story."

"I'll change it. I need it as a detail, for overall atmosphere."

"Listen!" And the columnist's eyes gleamed. He looked around and, noticing an old lady, began whispering into Whistlin's ear.

"How about letting me have the priest and you?" asked Whistlin, when they were finally saying goodbye. "I'll take the cemetery, and the flowers, and the two of you."

The columnist's forehead wrinkled.

"Andrei Nikolayevich," he said. "I would have never expected such a dirty trick from you. I trusted you entirely. You have betrayed my trust."

Whistlin took pleasure in the birds singing, the railway bed, the children playing tag behind fences.

Pasha, pencil in hand, finally found him. They sat down and Pasha began suggesting last names found at the cemetery for Whistlin to choose from.

Whistlin recalled Pasha's manuscript. "Your little story's not bad," he said. "Have you heard anything about Cuckoo?"

"I haven't heard anything," Pasha answered.

"Here, give this note to Violet."

6. EXPERIMENTING ON VIOLET

VIOLET walked bold as brass into Whistlin's apartment.

She believed she knew everything and had the right to talk about everything, and the right to decide about everything, and, planting her foot, to assert that she was right.

Violet had been told that Whistlin had an interesting setup at home, that he lived by candlelight, that he kept splendid gems and cameos in a special oak cabinet, that he had extraordinarily rare objects hanging all over the walls of his room.

She went in the front door and out into the courtyard and climbed up the back stairs.

She tugged at the doorbell pull, and the bell jangled loudly.

Whistlin had been waiting for her and quickly threw open the door.

Violet entered the dim anteroom.

A candle flame was reflected in the mirror. The cheap wallpaper caused Violet to shiver scornfully.

Whistlin helped his guest with her coat, led her through the utterly dark dining room into the bedroom.

Violet immediately began pacing the room and stating her opinion about each object.

After examining a grand array of truly interesting seventeenth-century treatises, she informed him that these must be Racine and Corneille and that she did not much care for Corneille and Racine.

After glancing at sixteenth-century Italian booklets, she noted that in our day there was no reason to dally with a Horace or a Catullus.

Whistlin sat in his armchair and listened attentively.

He asked her opinion of the plate hanging over there on the wall.

Violet strode over, took down the pale-blue plate with little white muscular men on it—half rams, half mermen—and arrogantly declared that she knew her way around this sort of thing and that it was doubtless a Danish wedding plate.[44]

Pleased with herself, but displeased by Whistlin's general setup and his things, she sat down on a Venetian chair that she assumed to be a poor imitation of the Moorish style.

"Would you like to hear a chapter from my novel?" asked Whistlin. Violet nodded.

"Yesterday I was thinking about one of my female characters," Whistlin continued. "I took Maturin's *Melmoth the Wanderer*, Balzac's *The Wild Ass's Skin*, and Hoffman's 'The Golden Pot,' and threw a chapter together. Listen."

"This is an outrage!" Violet exclaimed. "It's only in our uncultured country that people can write like this. Even I could do that! And to be perfectly honest, I don't like your prose, you've overlooked the modern world. You might say that I don't understand your novels, but if I don't understand them, then who would? What kind of a reader are you expecting?"

Leaving Whistlin's place, Violet felt that she had done an excellent job upholding her dignity, that she had made it quite clear to Whistlin whom he was dealing with.

7. SORTING BOOKS

WHISTLIN had caught a chill in his unheated apartment. His nose was inflamed and red. He had a slight fever. Whistlin decided to stoke up the woodstove, sit at home for a while, and put his abandoned library in order. But sorting books by section, as everyone knows, is hard work, since any division is artificial. And Whistlin began to ponder what sections he ought to divide his books into, so they would be easier to use when he needed them.

He divided the books according to nutritional content. He took on the memoirs first. He allotted them three shelves. But then, memoirs could include works by certain great writers: Dante, Petrarch, Gogol, Dostoyevsky—after all, they were all ultimately memoirs, so to speak, memoirs of spiritual experience. But works by the founders of religions, travelers, also belonged here . . . and isn't all physics, geography, history, philosophy viewed in historical context one enormous memoir of humanity! Whistlin didn't feel like dividing his books on false premises. For a writer everything is equally nourishing. Isn't time the only principle? But putting a 1573 publication with some from 1778 and 1906 . . . then his whole library would transform into a chain of the same authors in different languages. A chain of Homers, Virgils, Goethes. This would definitely have a deleterious effect on his work. His attention would shift from his characters to the periphery: to publication dates, annotations, paper quality, bindings. This kind of ranking might turn out to be useful at some point, but not now, when he was working on individual figures. Here sharp lines were needed. At this point one must proceed from things themselves, not from annotations. Annotations must be only an accompaniment, and in order to bring his arrangement to a truly grand scale, Whistlin emptied a shelf, took Gogol's *Dead Souls*, Dante's *Divine Comedy*, works by Homer and other authors, and set them side by side.

"People are just like books," thought Whistlin, relaxing. "You can read them. It's really even more interesting than reading books, richer; you can play with people, put them in different configurations." Whistlin felt he was utterly unfettered.

8. THE SEARCH FOR SECONDARY FIGURES

Whistlin didn't stay sitting at home long. He needed secondary characters for his novel, city locations, theaters. The next day, toward evening, he went out.

He set about translating the city's particularities with great enthusiasm.

Customers were crowding around the amputees.

"Yes, yes," answered a man buying wild fowl. "I am former professor Nikolai Wilhelmovich Kirchner."

The professor was wearing his same old greasy skullcap, the same old loose cloak, the same old galoshes on bare feet, tied up with rope. The same gold-rimmed glasses, the same bundle eternally in hand. He felt it was still necessary to hurry off somewhere and stand in endless lines.

Now the professor received a one-hundred-ruble pension and lived in the Bristol Hotel, but it was all over for him. For him, eternity had commenced. His face was somber and his eyes gleamed with an insane light, while his lips were pursed in a slightly skeptical way.

For ten years he and Whistlin had encountered each other on the city streets and had never spoken. But today the professor was in a state of terrible agitation. He had been rudely driven from the office of the State Philharmonic. He had been taken by the arms and thrown outside, the door slammed in his face. But how could they! After all, his sister had broken her leg while leaving after a concert, on the stairs. She had slipped and fallen.

Having taken leave of this tertiary character, Whistlin headed out to see his secondary characters, the old folks in Toxovo. These old folks were delighted to see him, since they were lonely and eager to chat. And they felt that they could talk with Whistlin about their previous life, make clear to him how much more musicians had once been valued, show him the medal and the card from a highly distinguished official with a handwritten note, and the portraits of highly distinguished students, little boys in uniforms whom Petey, in days of yore, had taught to play the balalaika.

"Oh, Tatyana Nikandrovna, don't make such a fuss over me. I am a simple man," Whistlin was saying. "I took such a liking to you and now I've dropped in on you, just to spend a nice evening. It's so cozy here, Tatyana Nikandrovna. I can feel it. I knew that you'd have jam, too. Of course I'm nowhere near the musician Peter Petrovich is, but I do love music. And sometimes I get a real hankering for music. And I was just hoping that Peter Petrovich might take up his flute and play us something after tea."

"What do you play?" asked the old man.

"Just a little piano," Whistlin answered. "Practically with one finger. I can read music, though, and accompany."

"You must have quit?" the old man asked sympathetically. "Yes, people don't have much perseverance! None of my students ever became a musician either. I remember I was once hired to teach the children of a state councillor. They were delightful boys. Now everyone writes that we were mistreated. Don't believe it, it isn't true. Tatyana Nikandrovna here can attest to that. But what an education they received! They were taught such nice manners. Do anything wrong and they'd get no dessert or be sent to stand in the corner, and their mama would be apologizing, and their papa would come and say, 'I'll be sure to punish them,' and they'd never let us go without a nice dinner. And even though they were such important folks they'd sit you right down next to them; so's not to make you feel bad…"

"And they'd give recommendations," Tanya interrupted. "And set up lessons and find you other jobs."

"Not to mention the gifts," the old man added. "For Christmas and Easter both. And if they found out you're getting married, then they'd be the one to give away the bride; if you had a baby—then the godfather; if your student son turned out to be a revolutionary—they'd go speak with the town governor in person."

Whistlin drank tea and helped the old man tell his story. He asked questions and at the appropriate moment sighed, or kept silent, or shook his head, or mumbled something, or gave a little cough.

"Here, I'll bring in the gifts and show you!" said the old woman. "Petey, what'd you do with the key?" Her voice carried over from the next room.

Petey got up and Whistlin heard the scraping of drawers opening.

"Oh my," Whistlin said affectionately. "Does it still run?"

"It not only runs, it strikes the hour," the old man said, pleased. "Listen here." He took a glass out of the cabinet, turned it upside down and put the watch on the overturned base.

The watch clearly struck eleven.

"And for now, here's a list," Tanya said, "of what was given in what year—" and she handed some yellowed sheets of paper to Whistlin.

It was quite a list: baskets of flowers with accompanying cards, a barometer, a cigarette case, cufflinks, tie pins.

Whistlin read on. The old folks bowed out for a moment and came back bearing their treasures. They said nearly in chorus:

"We saved everything, didn't sell a thing! We were hungry but we didn't sell the things we'd been given." And they laid out the gifts on the table before Whistlin.

Whistlin was quite taken with the old folks. He decided they were not merely secondary. He decided to visit them more often.

Returning along the very same path he'd come by, getting a light and making conversation, Whistlin made friends with a policeman. And the policeman recited his poetry to him:

> Where the tram tracks end
> That's where my Aglaya stands
> When she pulls that lever
> Her eyes stay on me ever
> And when I walk my police beat
> I see her sugar lips so sweet.

At first the policeman was afraid for some reason, but then he saw for himself that Whistlin was really a kind and talkative fellow.

Whistlin would often sit with the policeman, smoking and discussing poetry with him, after which they would set out walking down the street together, hands clasped behind their backs.

Against dark-blue trees, the policeman talked about how fine it was back in his village, what wonderful apple trees he had there and how many poods of dried apples they'd stored away at his house, all the different kinds of winter apples there were, how you could graft branches from one and the same apple tree to a birch, an oak, a linden, and how the apples would have a different taste depending on which tree the branches were grafted. He talked about how they made formic alcohol, how they'd steam ants in sacks and squeeze out the liquid.

Whistlin would ask him about how they did things in the village, what kind of superstitions people had, whether they had a reading hut, and about the sexual habits of the youth. He begged him to remember, said that it was crucial for his book.

Thus they would sit for long stretches on a bench beneath the gates. The policeman told him everything that came into his head, answered Whistlin's incessant questions, and Whistlin would write it all down by the light of the lantern on the building.

And once again a great deal of time passed. One day the spouses were standing by their third-floor window. The sun was shining as if in a picture, the window was open, the old man was holding Traviata by all four paws, the old lady was scratching her little belly and tail with a white ivory comb.

"Come now, why are you squirming, sweet Traviata?" the old lady said. "Why are you barking and whining? We wish you only the best. Let's give your neck a scratch. You can't reach there with your teeth. And here, between your brows."

"Look how they're sucking the lifeblood out of her," the old man said, parting her fur with a free thumb. "No wonder she's so sad."

"I wish I could see Nadia's soul!" the old lady suddenly burst out, apropos of nothing. "Her soul must be lovely."

"Yes, she's a gentle girl. Scratch here. You can tell she's from a good family. So do you think Ivan Ivanovich will marry her? Stop fidgeting, Traviata!"

"Look, look outside, Traviata, who's coming. See that great big dog. She's being walked on a chain. Look, Traviata, look."

"It would be a shame if he doesn't marry her…" said the old lady.

"Look how many there are. Wait, don't move, one jumped on you!"

"Well, how're we going to catch it now?"

"Remember how that jacket used to suit you? And now you're not even clean-shaven. Remember my gray silk dress with the beading? But now you're nice and clean, Traviata. Let her down."

"Look how she's shaking herself out!"

"Hey there, sweet Traviata, give us a dance." And taking the pup by her paws, the old lady began waltzing her around.

The little dog, arching her back, moved slowly and from time to time lifted her snout and barked. Then the old lady gathered her up in her arms, the old pup rested her snout on her shoulder, closed her eyes, and began breathing heavily.

And the old lady began singing in a wavering voice:

> Lullaby and goodnight,
> You're your mother's delight.
> In the night, long and deep,
> I rock Traviata to sleep.

"Oh, my little old girl! My poor little baldie!" And the graying child, understanding that she was being pitied, began whining excruciatingly.

The flautist's wife truly loved animals. She fed all the cats in the stairwell, took home all the abandoned kittens, and was filled with indignation for them.

She had a woodshed in their courtyard. Her real life took place inside this shed.

Every hen, every rooster had its own nickname, either "my little girl" or "my little boy," and they all knew how to peck white bread from her hand. The old lady even had goats.

This was the peaceful family Whistlin barged into. He noticed the old lady's loneliness, and decided it was due to an unspoken longing for motherhood. He began bringing Traviata candies, petting and praising her, and the old lady's heart nearly burst.

"You are loved," she would say to Traviata, "everyone loves you very much, and you're admired all around! Just wait a bit, when it's winter I'll sew you a new jacket and you'll be such a beauty."

"Have you had this little pup long?" Whistlin would ask.

"Oh, six years or so," the old lady would answer.

"She's barely aged at all."

"Of course, she's still fresh as a rose," the old lady would confirm, hiding her favorite's true age.

"Won't you stay to have dinner with us?"

Whistlin stayed.

Tatyana Nikandrovna sat Traviata down at the table and tied a napkin on her.

"Please excuse us," the old lady said. "Traviata is a substitute daughter for us."

They all sat down and began eating soup. Traviata finished first, looked at everyone and whined a bit. She loved to eat.

"You're awfully hungry, Traviata dear?" Tatyana Nikandrovna asked.

Traviata cocked her head and began whining again.

The old lady took her plate, went to the kitchen and ladled in cold soup.

Traviata again began lapping. Tatyana Nikandrovna brought in the roast and, on a separate flowered plate, placed a separate piece with a bone for Traviata. When everyone had tea, Traviata lapped up milk. Then she leapt down from her chair and asked to go out. After dinner Whistlin accompanied on the piano. The old man sat next to him playing the flute.

9. THE STRUGGLE AGAINST THE BOURGEOISIE

In the very same building lived Raspin.

More than anything in the world Raspin feared little vases. Raspin went pale when he heard the word "bourgeoisie." For this reason he would not allow his new wife to bring any of her girlhood pretties, her geranium or fuchsia, into their rented room. Likewise he did not let her hang a photograph of her mama on the wall. Despite his wife's resistance, he pulled the nail out of the wall and hid the hammer.

"If you want to live with me, make an effort to submit to my will. I will not allow you to make a fool of yourself!"

And the next morning Lipochka brought the flowers back to her mama by tram. Her mama was washing Raspin's collars at that moment and threw up her small hands with a splash.

"Ah, these men, they don't like flowers!"

They had dinner. Her mama began laying out curtains for the windows.

Mama and daughter sat gazing in admiration. The curtains were handmade. Grandma herself had crocheted them long ago.

"Look what I've got here, Pava my sweet!"

"I'm not Pava, I'm Pavel. Don't talk to me like I'm a dog, please."

"Just look at the patterns . . ."

"Curtains on windows," Pavel noted drily, "are a sign of bourgeois attitudes. I cannot allow you to do this. This Saturday we'll go to Passage and buy something proper."[45]

Meanwhile, Whistlin was wandering the streets and dropped by Passage for breakfast.

Raspin, despite the crowds, strode along proudly. Clinging to her husband's sleeve, Lipochka was practically running to keep up.

"Get a look at that little vase! Maybe we could . . ."

"Please stop with the little vases."

"But there's a little kitten piggy-bank."

"Stop badgering me," Raspin said in irritation, pulling his sleeve away. "And what's with this bourgeois tendency of clinging to me. Just walk normally."

"Buy us a picture, Pava. We can hang it over our bed."

"I said quit badgering me."

"At least buy a lampshade."

"I won't buy a lampshade either."

Raspin was elevating his struggle to a major creative achievement. He couldn't get enough sleep, lying awake at night thinking about how to stay on guard against this evil. He would be walking down the street and suddenly see a wax bourgeoise displayed in a store window. The bourgeoise was decked out in gewgaws, the bourgeoise wore lipstick, its hair was curled up in the Parisian style. Well, it was one thing for hairdressers, they had always been like that, but co-ops and business corporations!

Raspin felt a pain in his heart at the thought that shops and business organizations had been infiltrated by the bourgeoisie.

"This is kitsch," Raspin pronounced, examining a little Venetian glass vase that was light as a feather.

"Naturally," affirmed Whistlin, who had stopped nearby. "How nice to see a man who knows his way around these things."

"What kind of fish is that?" Lipochka turned to face them.

"A dolphin," answered Whistlin.

"She's always daydreaming about golden fish!" Raspin explained to the man they'd seen fleetingly in the courtyard.

The man they'd seen fleetingly gave an empathetic groan. Raspin, sensing unexpected support, cheered up.

"See, I told you, and this citizen is saying the same thing."

"Yes, we must all participate in the struggle against the bourgeoisie," sighed Whistlin, hiding a grin in his collar.

The man who had just spoken was evidently a well-informed and enlightened person.

"Perhaps you could recommend what to buy?" Raspin asked the stranger. "It seems we've seen you before in the courtyard. I am Pavel Raspin, a cash collector."

"I am Whistlin, a writer."

"Very good," said Raspin. "See, Lipochka? The writer thinks the same way."

Raspin, having loaded Lipochka down—he felt that men should not carry packages—seized hold of Whistlin.

"Come join us for tea."

Whistlin followed Raspin and Lipochka down into the basement. The basement had a narrow red and black woolen carpet of the sort once found in fine entryways, a dining table, and a mirror. Unusual cleanliness reigned in the basement. The windows looked nearly crystalline, the windowsills had been scrubbed to a sheen. The painted yellow floor gleamed.

"Hygiene," Raspin said, "is the first sign of a cultured person. Just look at how our toothbrushes are stored." And Raspin led Whistlin to a little shelf above the faucet. "You see, the soap is also in a little case to prevent bacteria from getting in. I've already triumphed on that front. Now a new front has opened up for me—in the evenings I've been working on my handwriting. Calligraphy teaches a man perseverance and patience."

This literate and cultured man was Raspin's first guest. The host hungered for enlightenment. But in the evenings Raspin did more than just work on his handwriting. He also listened to the radio. The radio filled Raspin with rapture. It seemed to him that thanks to the radio he could find out just about anything in the whole world. He could become educated about opera, he didn't have to waste time on the tram, and it was so economical. He often talked about this with his wife. There was hell to pay if his wife was making noise while he sat there with his gleaming headphones on. And Lipochka was determined not to let him down.

"I am so anemic that my only salvation lies in sleep. I can sleep at any time and for however long," Lipochka told Whistlin, settling down on the colorful sofa.

"How on earth did you learn how to sleep whenever you like?" Whistlin asked, leaning elbows on the back of the sofa.

"Working at a nightclub will teach you anything," sighed his hostess.

"You are so refined," Whistlin murmured sadly. "All of this house-keeping business must be hard for you."

"I do have to run around an awful lot," answered his hostess. "If this goes on much longer, I'll die. The bindings alone were such a nuisance! I was running to the bookbinder nearly every day."

"What kind of bindings?" Whistlin wondered.

The hostess proudly led their guest over to the decorative shelves. "These are my Pavel's favorite books."

Whistlin bent down. *Old Times*, an annual publication of the architects' society.

"You have a subtle grasp of art," Whistlin said, straightening up. "These canvas bindings fit your décor remarkably well."

And at this point Andrei Nikolayevich decided to become a friend of the family.

"Andrei Nikolayevich said, Andrei Nikolayevich recommended, Andrei Nikolayevich got us tickets for a concert today, Andrei Nikolayevich is taking us to a museum"—reverberated in their apartment.

The old folks upstairs were jealous.

"Do you think Andrei Nikolayevich has taken offense?"

Raspin's circle of acquaintances was made up of:

Miss Pluchart, aged around sixty, a retired school matron with a braid twisted into a low bun, and two teeth left on top; a maiden who no longer had anywhere to dance the mazurka.

But how boldly she had once slid across the dance floor in her yellow lace-up boots at the gymnasium balls, the same gymnasium where in the mornings she would sail through with hands folded across her chest, stone-faced: "Long hours for working, mere minutes for shirking."

Jean the hairdresser, an educated man who loved order; now he was compelled to shave and trim all kinds of riffraff! Clients you can't even chat with, you can't tell them anything, and they don't have anything interesting to tell you either! Shaving and trimming used to be a real joy…You'd find out what was going on in the Senate, or abroad, or how Countess Z.'s home theater performance had come off.

Jean the hairdresser used to be a fixture in the best houses of the city. Back then, he had worn a top hat and tuxedo jacket on saints' days. And taking communion had been a real joy. Up front, the uniforms threaded with gold, white trousers, tricorn hats held under arms, bright dresses, the scent of perfume, cologne, and everyone was familiar, familiar. You stand there by the door and barely have time to exchange bows with everyone.

Vladimir Nikolayevich Hunger, proprietor of "Decadence," a photography studio where everyone who had pictures taken would get their eyes pasted in and end up looking wooden.

Former builder Turkeyev, a great drunkard and enemy of the people.

This whole company got along very well and was nearly fun.

Turkeyev admired Miss Pluchart as a well-read and intelligent woman. Miss Pluchart liked Turkeyev for being a positive person, albeit a drunkard. The maiden and the old widower did not feel entirely the same way regarding questions of upbringing. But Turkeyev was sure that their thoughts were entirely aligned and was very glad for it.

Jean, although lower than Pluchart in terms of class origin, had over the course of his life acquired posh manners: he knew a few words in French, such as a hairdresser of his time needed to know, and he knew absolutely everything there was to know about the theater world. Pluchart, albeit late in life, was getting to know life backstage.

Naturally, this group included a former officer, as is the case in nearly every such group, since until comparatively recently who, really, had not served in the military? Malvin had been mobilized as a whiskerless youth and ever since had borne an officer's title. Meanwhile he had become famous for his mazurka while still a first-year student at the Mining Institute. He was an entirely lonely person. This was why he so loved Raspin. Everyone knows lonely people. Everyone knows they are self-conscious and neurotically cheerful, that they love to recall their glory days.

On Sundays and holidays this company would gather at Raspin's place. Whistlin fell in with them. Whistlin never missed a Sunday.

Pluchart valued literature, she believed that literature ought to edify in a straightforward fashion. Jean liked humorous tales. Turkeyev said that he didn't have a head for books. Malvin preferred popular science novels. There was plenty to discuss and argue over.

They got Miss Pluchart a little tipsy. She sat there red and ebullient in her shortened skirt and blouse with its collar buttoned all the way up. Turkeyev became drunk and talkative. Malvin topped off Whistlin's glass from the bottle and asked his opinion about literature. Raspin wanted to show Whistlin his acquaintances in all their glory, so that he would see what kind of company he, Raspin, kept.

"Anna Nikolayevna will now dance a mazurka," he told Whistlin. "She's been shy around you but I think today she feels fine."

Then something picturesque, from Whistlin's point of view, occurred. The guests and their hosts moved the table out of the way. Raspin took up a guitar and plucked the strings. Everyone except Pluchart and Malvin sat down along the walls. Malvin approached Pluchart and asked her to dance. He clasped her around the waist and with a tight spin they took off. Malvin performed a *pas*, trying to dance as he had as a student, squatting down on his knees. Miss Pluchart dashed in circles around him. He would leap up, spin her around once more, and they would take off again.

Whistlin sat admiring Pluchart's disordered braid, and the blue veins on her temples, her slightly scornful and prim expression, as well as Malvin's bald patch and sweat; the colorful figure of bearded

Turkeyev, falling asleep good-naturedly in the corner; the bamboo summer chairs and the sofa made from a mattress, and a long egg box upholstered in calico. For Whistlin people were not divided into good and evil, pleasant or unpleasant. They were divided into those who were necessary for his novel and those who weren't. He had a real need for this company, and among them he felt in his element. He didn't compare himself to Zola, who had even maintained real last names, nor to Balzac, who would write and write and only then go out to meet people; nor with his acquaintance N., who had once taken on a Smerdyakov-like repulsiveness in order to see what kind of impression it would make on acquaintances. Whistlin assumed that all these things were wholly permissible for an artist, and that he would have to pay for it all in the end. But he did not think about what this payment would look like. He lived for today and not for tomorrow—he was carried away by the very process of abducting people and transposing them into his novel.

To an extreme extent, he sensed the parodic nature of the world vis-à-vis any sort of norm. *Instead of a correct meter inscribed in our souls—as a poet might say—the world moves to an idiosyncratic rhythm.*

But Whistlin was no longer at the age when people strive to resolve questions of universal import. He wanted to be an artist, and only an artist. In the poet's view, Whistlin had a certain quotient of Mephistopheles in him but, to tell the truth, Whistlin had never observed this quality in himself. On the contrary, for him everything was simple, clear and comprehensible.

The poet would not be at a loss, the poet would object that these were in fact Mephistopheles-like qualities, that a Mephistopheles-like banality explained this dismissive and fastidious relationship to the world, which was in no way appropriate for an artist. But then, that's why he's a poet, so he can express himself in lofty and obscure words, seek certain correspondences between this world and the next. Whistlin was a sober person and, to all appearances, possessed adequate willpower.

For Whistlin the world had long since become a kind of cabinet of curiosities, a collection of interesting freaks and monsters, and he himself something like its director.

Raspin's workday consisted of going around to apartments. Not to apartments, really, but to the entryways, wherever these were present. His duty was to write down how much electricity had been used up that month. Raspin was a man with an open mouth and close-cropped bristly hair like a hedgehog.

Miss Pluchart's workday consisted in wiping noses, and having conversations in French, and following children and little dogs around city squares, if the weather was fine. She would walk around a square, dragging a child behind her, and say: *"C'est qu'on ne connait le prix de la santé que lorsqu'on l'a perdue.*[46] Repeat, Nadia."

And Nadia would mince along behind her and repeat.

Miss Pluchart loathed children and had no desire whatsoever to look at anything.

Raspin liked debating anti-religious topics with Ivan Prokofievich.[47]

"Your religion," he would say, "is lies and intoxication. You've never read any books, Ivan Prokofievich."

Raspin felt like arguing down Ivan Prokofievich and getting the upper hand of him. But gray-haired Jean would not back down. He recalled an actual privy councillor, a great thinker. The privy councillor would sit in his house before the mirror and tell Jean, who was gently shaving him: "It's not the clergy's vices that matter, but the idea."

On weekday evenings Raspin would treat his guests to the radio. Lipochka would pour the tea, the guests would eat and drink, and all the while a woman's voice would sing Gypsy romances, the languorous sighs of Hawaiian guitars would drift through the air, poems would be declaimed, the music of Danish or other composers performed. Sometimes they would listen to an entire opera.

Raspin himself had constructed a phonograph horn out of paper and lacquered it. The black horn stood on the table next to the jam and yelled, sang, and laughed, piping in the sweetest sounds.

10. THE ADOLESCENT AND THE GENIUS

LITTLE Masha quickly put the lamp on the mirror and opened the door.

"My God, Andrei Nikolayevich, how pale you are! And you're soaked to the skin!

"Do you like milk?" she asked, after a short pause. "We have cream today!"

She tugged Whistlin's coat off and carried it to the kitchen. She dragged Whistlin into the dining room. She dashed, smiling, to the sideboard and charmingly brought a crystal milk jug right up to her guest's nose. Whistlin watched in admiration.

"Is Vladimir Evgenevich not at home?" he asked.

"No, papa went out on business." And she began searching the buffet for the teacup her father had given her on her saint's day.

"Drink up!" she exclaimed, sitting Whistlin down and passing him her favorite teacup.

Whistlin drank it down.

"But don't leave, I'll be afraid here on my own."

"I really just came by for a minute," Whistlin answered.

But when he saw how Masha's face changed, Whistlin stopped short:

"But if you're afraid, I'm happy to stay."

Gusts of wind buffeted the little house with its two illuminated windows. The storm was expected to grow stronger overnight.

"I'm afraid there'll be nothing left of our oak," Masha said and only then remembered that her hair was in newspaper curlers.

She began hurriedly stripping the papers from her hair and throwing them into the fire.

"Sit here a minute, Andrei Nikolayevich."

Masha came back and threw down an armload of wonderfully dry birch logs destined for kindling. She started peeling off the bark.

Whistlin started splitting off bits of kindling with a knife.

"Your socks are soaked through. Would you like me to bring you papa's slippers?"

So Whistlin sat there in Psychofsky's slippers. He had grown unaccustomed to young people and didn't know how to interact with them. It also troubled him that no one was home besides him and Masha.

He breathed a sigh of relief when Masha took charge of the conversation, but noted that he was giving the adolescent empty and vague answers, despite all his good will. He even became a little sad that he had neither words nor thoughts for Masha.

Masha had read somewhere that a writer was radiant and intelligent, that a writer was, on the whole, a proud and contrary spirit, who could reach the secret that lay in plain sight within every person. And Masha wanted very much to reach that secret herself.

She wanted very much for Whistlin to read her his new novel. She knew that her guest carried it with him everywhere, like some kind of treasure.

Psychofsky had moreover told her at some point that Whistlin was a genius, and the word "genius" now had, and was unlikely ever to lose, a particular allure. And so Masha felt like really speaking her mind with Whistlin, having a heart-to-heart with a genius.

Whistlin felt obligated to keep up his end of the conversation.

What a fine thing it would be to marry a genius, to relieve a genius of petty domestic cares!

And Masha decided to fix the taciturn genius some supper.

She leapt from her chair, opened the ventilation window and began rummaging around in the space between the windows.

But Psychofsky's was a meager home, and she only found a lump of salt pork and a small glass tub of shredded cabbage.

Delighted, she ran off for the frying pan.

The salt pork was spitting, the cabbage growing darker with every minute, the tasty smell drifting off, but not entirely, up the fireplace chimney. Masha found some vodka as well.

The genius drank and ate, while Masha sat across from him in utter delight.

The genius had his bite to eat, set his napkin aside and lit up a cigarette.

Whistlin became lost in thought. He thought about how the food had smelled like smoke, and where and when he had had food that smelled like smoke before.

Masha gazed at him and couldn't get enough. She asked the genius to read from his novel.

"No," said Whistlin, "I'd better not, Masha."

But then Whistlin wondered what impression his novel would make on the adolescent and whether adolescents could read his novel at all.

Whistlin went to the entryway and brought back his manuscript, rolled up in a tube. He thought, thought, and began reading.

From the first lines Masha felt that she was entering an unfamiliar world that was empty, hideous and sinister; figures conversing in empty space, and among these conversing figures she suddenly recognized her papa.

He was wearing an old greasy hat, he had an enormous Punch nose. He was holding a magic mirror in one hand...

11. *LITTLE STAR* AND WHISTLIN

WHISTLIN read:

> Birds on branches chanting praises
> To our generous Creator;
> Love brings their songs into concord,
> Love brings gladness to their hearts.
>
> Meek and tender lambs meander,
> Nipping grass upon the meads;
> Bearing love for their Creator,
> So they thank him without words.
>
> The shepherd plays without a care,
> Piping joyful on the lea;
> Nourished by the fragrant air,
> He sings the beauty of the spring.[48]

Finally, Whistlin got around to the draft version of the little old man and little old lady.

How gay it is to look at little old ladies—

Whistlin reworked several pages from the 1842 children's book *Little Star*:[49]

—when they are running around the garden, not thinking

about anything other than flowers and trees, birds and the blue heavens; how gay it is to look at little old ladies, when they have properly tied on their little bonnets and smocks and go leaping around and enjoying the fresh air and green grass, like the Lord's own carefree birdies.

"There once lived—

Whistlin went on reworking—

a little old lady who was loved by everyone who knew her. When they saw her, dogs would begin barking for joy and lick her hands. Cats purred and rubbed themselves against her legs, and little kittens leapt around and played with her. But why did they all love this little old lady so? Because she was good and kind and acted as a mother to them. She would often sit on the carpet feeding her little dog pies, she herself loved pies, but was always ready to give them to Traviata, and Traviata loved her for this. The old lady was called Sasha.

Every Sunday she went to mass, and one could only admire how she would stand there quietly and pray with great fervor. Her little eyes would gaze ceaselessly at the icon in front of her, never straying to the right or left, or even back behind her, the way naughty little boys and girls do sometimes. She asked that she be made good and pious. She asked for health and happiness for her husband, Traviata, and all the people in the world. Lost in these thoughts, she found that time passed so quickly that she was never tired after mass, like other little old men and women, to whom masses often seem very long. How pleasant it is to contemplate such a mild and modest little old lady. She was attentive and solicitous toward those younger than her and affectionate with everyone in her building. If she needed to ask for something, like a soup pot or a clothing iron, she would ask so sweetly and with such humility that it was impossible to refuse. The little old lady blushed at the slightest praise.

A tiny little old lady. Sometimes in the evenings if her husband had gone out somewhere, which happened very rarely, she would open her trunk and get out all sorts of scraps of cloth, bits of embroidery, Easter eggs, pencil ends, old posters and opera programs, old fashion plates, greetings cards, envelopes, calling cards; she would reread pages of old calendars and poems:

Up above the sun is shining,
Warmth is wafting through the air,
On this day good folks are going
To stroll around the market square,
Oh the piles of wondrous treats
On the tables gleaming bright—
Pussy willow, glass, dolls, sweets . . .

and she would remember the Lenten market that used to be held around Gostiny Dvor.

Whistlin closed the book and thought about where to put this excerpt, how to tie it in to the rest of the novel and whether he might be able to put the foreword together today. He once again took up the book he'd set down, opened it up to the marker, and, replacing each word with a different one, wrote out a page's worth:

FOREWORD

How fine it is to read an interesting book. Engrossed, you don't even notice how the time passes. Isn't that right, dear readers? And you, I imagine, have felt this in your own lives, even if you haven't managed to read a great deal. But have you noticed which books you like best? Of course, the ones where everything is said clearly, simply and truly, no matter the topic at hand. For example, if the thing under discussion is a flower, then that flower will be described so well and in such perfect accord with how it is in real life, that if you were to see it, you would recognize it right away from its description, even if you had never seen it before. If the thing under discussion is a little forest, then it's as if you can see every little tree in it, as if you can feel the coolness that its shadows lend to the earth, after it has been warmed by the summer sun; and if this book describes people, then they seem to be alive right in front of you. You recognize their facial features, their physiognomy, and their habits. It seems to you that you'd recognize them right away if they could appear before you.

And however many decades or even centuries have passed since this book was written, these descriptions nevertheless remain beautiful, because they have been traced faithfully from nature.

And thus I begin my tale, which will flow like a peaceful brook, its banks strewn with silvery daisies and baby-blue forget-me-nots.

In the morning, reading through his chapters and materials, Whistlin confirmed that there were no gardens in his novel. Not a single one. Neither new nor old. No workers' gardens or city parks. But a novel cannot exist without greenery, just as a city cannot.

Whistlin went out for work—all the more so as the day was a fitting one. He had gone past the monument to Peter the Great, but turned back when he heard singing: approaching the monument from Senate Square, a gray-bearded man in a long, discolored coat stopped in front of it, shook his fist at Peter, and said:

> We give you bread—
> You give us wigs.
> It's your fault we have pogroms.

Then, hanging his head, he wandered on.

Whistlin stopped and wrote this down, and then entered the Garden of Laborers.[50] He bought some cigarettes and chocolate from an amputee, lit up, and began attentively examining the condition and location of the garden: *What can I take from here? The busts in uniform, the people sitting on the edge of the fountain basin? Should I show the Admiralty with its giant figures? . . . The people crowding and going in circles and courting one another? . . .*

Whistlin leaned up against a tree trunk.

Three a.m. A bar. Whistlin took a seat right by the orchestra. A trio was playing onstage: the cellist was an old man in a velvet jacket, the violinist a Russian man in a gray suit and gaiters, at the piano—a Jewish stutterer.

Do not tempt me for no reason . . .

moaned the sounds.

An old man stood up from his table. An imperious gesture—be silent!—was addressed to his young drinking companion, who wore black leather gloves and a Russian caftan. Then, listening to the mournful romance, the old man put a hand over his eyes and began weeping.

He has the soul of Don Juan, thought Whistlin, and not without impatience remembered that in his pocket there were gardens he had only just secured.

Back at home. The candle was burning down, the wick had drooped, and the flame was touching the sconce.

Whistlin took out a railway candle and fitted it into the candlestick. He lit up, thought for a moment and leaned down over the sheet of paper he'd taken out of his pocket, with the gardens transposed into words. Next he put Psychofsky into one of these gardens:

Having finished his fortune-telling, Psychofsky walked over to the old man's table.

"Your lot in life is dreadful," he whispered in the man's ear.

In the taverns by evening Psychofsky made a little money on the side as a graphologist. Just now he had come over, moved by sympathy. But out of habit his speech apparatus added:

"Will you show me your handwriting?"

The old man removed his hand from his face and looked at Psychofsky.

Music was coming from the Summer Theater. A few acorns fell onto the path. The tops of the trees—darker than the trunks, which were lit up by tiny, colorful electric lights—touched one another.

12. PUTTING THE MANUSCRIPT IN ORDER

PILES of fleeting sketches, clippings, scribblings, phrases overheard in shops—such as: "Lamb like a mirror, snowy little lamb!"; and conversations—"All I really do is drink tea, or coffee"; observations— "An elderly man with a large potbelly began meowing at the table— this was how he expressed his wish for a cup of tea"; genre scenes; sketches of different parts of the city—all of this grew and came together in Whistlin's room.

A mass of characters who were not fully living had to be tossed out. Many characters had to be combined into one for having too much of a certain enrapturement in common, and others, and a third type too, and a fourth type, had to be left as general background decoration, extras in the crowd, sometimes affording just a glimpse of a head, a shoulder, a hand, a back.

Whistlin yawned and laid aside his fountain pen. Layers of dust had already managed to settle on the books after their recent rearrangement, and powdery beetles and watery bugs were gnawing and chewing and drilling their way through the books. The beetles were ticking in eager rivalry with the clocks. To the accompaniment of the beetles, Whistlin straightened up. *What should I do now?* he thought and decided to go out for a stroll. He walked down the street, exhausted by work, with an empty brain and an aired-out soul.

The novel was finished.*

The author had no further interest in it. But the work continued to pursue him. Whistlin began to feel as if he were inside his novel. Here he is meeting Cockadoodle on some strange street, and Cockadoodle yells at him: "Yoohoo, Whistlin! Coo-coo!"†

"You're the Cuckoo, Whistlin," and suddenly Psychofsky leaps out from behind Cuckoo and begins doing magic tricks in a deserted space. "And now," he says, "I will show you how to make a pact with the devil. But for heaven's sake, don't tell Masha about this. What? You're talented? You're a genius? You will show me to everyone in all of my evil potency?" And Psychofsky begins to pronounce the words: "Sarabanda, fluffanda, rassmeranda…" and Whistlin sees himself standing under a green birch-tree, telling Masha about her papa. "Now, now," he says, "Masha. Your papa is not an exalted man at all, he is a despicable and despised figure. He is not a real mystic at all, but the damnedest thing. And he can't see past his own nose. As far as spectacles that allow you to see the invisible world, well, you know… he never had any such spectacles. So there is no way for him to have lost them. He is lying when he says a certain German professor gave them to him. He is lying when he says he used them to watch his ancestors having dinner." But Masha seems to be eighteen and not fourteen. And here come Pasha, and the policeman, and the deaf-mute woman, marching toward him in single file.

Whistlin went out.

*First came the gardens, the typical buildings, mild daybreaks, the hustle and bustle of the streets. Next, here and there last names began to emerge; they came together, shook each other's hands, played chess or cards, disappeared and then reappeared. Under these names figures began appearing. And finally under each name a person rose.

And everything was suffused by a sweet, plaintive, captivating rhythm, as if the author was trying to carry someone away.

†Here Whistlin thought sadly of Cuckoo and recalled the lines from the *Thousand and One Nights*: "You can find another country for yourself / But you cannot find yourself another soul."[51]

Ba-bum ... Oh, my carriage, la-la-la, ba-bum—and parted ways like ships at sea.[52] The house lights lit up the corners of buildings and gates, the sounds of songs and guitars led off into side streets and came back out onto the embankments, melting away there amid stars and their reflections.

Viewed from above in the day, the city gave the impression of being a child's toy, the trees looked as though they hadn't been grown but laid out in a pattern, the houses looked as though they hadn't been built but set down. The people and trams seemed like wind-up toys.

At night Whistlin smoked above the upside-down illuminated buildings on the Fontanka Embankment. The long iron grillwork of the railing swayed; in the water, clouds illuminated by an invisible moon floated past.

Loneliness and boredom were written on Whistlin's face. The lights in the water, which had captivated him in childhood, could not distract him now.

He felt that everything around him was growing more depleted with every passing day. The places he had described had turned into wastelands for him; the people he had known had lost all interest for him.

Each of his characters entailed a whole series of people, each description became something like an idea of a whole host of places.

The more he contemplated his newly published novel, the greater the sparseness and emptiness he felt forming all around himself.

Finally he felt that he was completely locked inside his novel.

*

Wherever Whistlin found himself, he saw his characters everywhere. They had different last names, different bodies, different hair, different manners, but he recognized them right away.

Thus Whistlin passed entirely into his book.

1928–1929

TRANSLATORS' AFTERWORD
A Note on Names

KONSTANTIN K. Vaginov began his writing life as a poet, and in addition to the entire poems and songs scattered through these novels, traces of the poet's exacting relationship to individual words and phrases are everywhere in his prose. Examples abound and are yours to discover; in this essay, we touch briefly on the names of Vaginov's works and characters, both to illustrate some of the difficulties in translating his Russian into English, and also to illuminate some of the historical context for these books.

Goat Song, Vaginov's first novel, was written between 1927 and 1929. The novel mentions the ten-year anniversary of the October Revolution in passing, rather obliquely, yet the shadow of that event and its immediate and long-lasting consequences hang over the entire book (and over his subsequent three novels as well). For Vaginov, the Soviet practice of naming and renaming is emblematic of societal changes that were—paradoxically—wholly superficial yet devastatingly momentous. Like *Goat Song* itself, place names like "Second Rural Poverty Street" or "Victims of the Revolution Square" represent political shifts that are simultaneously exaggerated to the point of silliness and profoundly, genuinely tragic.

The tragedy of names is heralded in the title itself, *Goat Song* (Russian: *Kozlinaia pesn'*): this is a literal translation of the ancient Greek *tragōidia* (*tragos*, goat + *ōide*, song), the source of the English word "tragedy."* The book's two forewords then take up the name

---

*For one in-depth interpretation of the goat-related etymology of "tragedy," see V. N. Toporov, "Some Thoughts on the Origin of Ancient Greek Drama," in *Tekst: semantika i struktura*, ed. T. V. Tsivian (Moscow: Nauka, 1983).

change of Vaginov's home city; the first foreword ends with the declaration: "I have no love for Petersburg, my dream has ended," while the second begins: "Now there is no Petersburg. There is Leningrad." The task of the author—"a coffin-maker by trade"—is to tell the tale of a city that no longer exists. The copious notes to the 1999 annotated edition of Vaginov's novels do an excellent job of marking and tracing the (often multiple) renaming of various central locations in St. Petersburg/Leningrad. Compiled in the post-Soviet period, they add another layer of tragic irony to Vaginov's skeptical attitude toward these wholesale shifts. For example: all four novels refer to Petersburg's central Nevsky Avenue (Prospekt) as 25 October Avenue, as it was christened in 1918 following the October Revolution. This name stuck until 1944, when it—along with many other streets and city landmarks—once again acquired its prerevolutionary imperial designation, in a wave of patriotic fervor connected to the war effort. It is hard to imagine that Vaginov would have greeted this reversion with unequivocal celebration. (Need it be mentioned that the fondness for toppling monuments and updating ideologically problematic public designations is hardly limited to the Bolshevik context?)

In comparison to other chroniclers of the 1920s linguistic landscape (such as Mikhail Zoshchenko or Yuri Olesha), Vaginov gives short shrift to Soviet "newspeak" (most famously parodied by George Orwell in *1984*), a simplified socialist idiom overfond of abbreviation. The names of institutions like Politprosvet ("Politedu") or Domprosvet ("Educenter") pop up from time to time, but for the most part Vaginov's characters are thoroughly prerevolutionary in their speech habits—indeed, this is shown to be their downfall. A different kind of downfall appears in *Harpagoniana*, the novel in which Vaginov subjects his characters' speech to linguistic colonization by the ideologically charged idiom of the Stalinist economic and political system. This novel not only reflects but strikingly embodies the disastrous effects of these policies on both societal relations and the individual consciousness, simultaneously.

*

In addition to the semantic charge attached to the names of places, streets, and institutions in his novels, Vaginov also endows his characters with pointedly "speaking names" (nodding to Nikolai Gogol/ Mykola Hohol, another brilliant chronicler of the denizens of Petersburg but also in a way typical of other contemporary writers like Andrei Platonov). The novel opens with Balmcalfkin, a person whose name is so ludicrous that it elicits a whole philological crisis on the part of its bearer:

> *What would happen*, he thought, *if my last name was not Balmcalfkin, but something completely different. The two syllables "balmcalf" are obviously an onomatopoeia, the word "kin" could be sort of ominous, like "king," but that's prevented by the consonantal "lf" sound, while if I had a syllabic "f," then it'd be Balmcalofkin, which would be terribly doleful.*

It also seems to be the only name appropriate for this absurdly helpless, hopelessly erudite character. Like "Balmcalfkin," the name in Russian, "Teptyolkin," does not exactly mean anything on its own, but the sounds that make it up point in various directions: tep- > tyoplyi, or warm; tyolk- > tyolka, or heifer calf, also with hints of the feminine and doltish. We felt that these strong and meaningful associations, as with most of the other names in these novels, could not be ignored, and thus we elected to "translate" most of them. For overall persuasiveness, and to remind readers that Leningrad is not in Indiana, we kept most of the suffixes vaguely Slavic ("-ov," "-off," "-kin"), but sought to convey the "speaking" roots: to take one example, the immortal pair of Rotikov (root: *rot*, mouth) and Kotikov (root: *kot*, cat) became Kissenkin and Kittenkin. Some names we left alone because they seemed equally as neutral (Dalmatova) or bizarrely evocative (Toropulo) in English. Not all the solutions are equally satisfying: Whistlin, the title character in *The Works and Days*, conveys the happy-go-lucky aspect of the name Svistonov (*svist* is whistle)—but elides the moan or groan tucked into the middle of the name (*ston*).

First names were mostly preserved. Note that in polite or formal speech of this period, Russians addressed each other with name and patronymic, thus "Maria Petrovna" (Maria, daughter of Pyotr/Peter) or "Mikhail Petrovich" (Mikhail, son of Pyotr/Peter). At the other end of the spectrum, informal or intimate speech offers a myriad of variations on a single name: a person named Maria might be called Masha, Marusya, Musya, and so on, with each variation carrying nuances of emotion, greater and lesser degrees of affection, intimacy, irritation, and more. The various protagonists of these novels play around with greater and lesser formality in address. To take one example, the hairdresser, a minor character who appears toward the end of *The Works and Days of Whistlin*, is usually referred to as Jean—the French name clearly tying him to the old world of the French-speaking Russian nobility (albeit as a servant). It is, however, perfectly natural when another character refers to him more formally as Ivan Prokofievich, since "Jean" is the French version of Russian "Ivan" or English "John." Generally speaking, forms like "Masha," "Misha" (Mikhail), and "Volodya" (Vladimir) are casual and informal; the "-ka" suffix ("Pashka," "Seryozhka") contributes a playfully aggressive tone; further variations, like "Andriushechka" or "Lenochka," are tender (and potentially patronizing).

The characters' names do not only speak in terms of etymology and nuances of address—they also reveal subtle (and not so subtle) ties to real-life counterparts, functioning as part of Vaginov's basic orientation toward allusion. Thus Balmcalfkin has been recognized as bearing traits of the literary critic and scholar Lev Pumpiansky; Maria Petrovna Dalmatova echoes Maria Yudina, who dabbled in philosophy and later became a famous pianist; and the philosopher Andrievsky resembles Mikhail Bakhtin in several respects. Only a few of the characters match up perfectly to a concrete individual; most are given characteristics of several people at once. Sometimes the name of the character "speaks" of their connection to a historical figure: the mad poet September, for instance, points to the real-life poet Venedikt Mart (Mart = March), even as other characteristics resemble the quintessential Futurist poet Velimir Khlebnikov. Sometimes even a character's patronymic offers a clue to a point of origin: thus Whistlin is Andrei Nikolayevich, the name and patronymic of Vaginov's friend and fellow novelist, the classicist Andrei Egunov.* (We direct readers interested in a full breakdown of the various characters' origins to the 1999 Akademproekt edition.)

Some of Vaginov's "victims," including Pumpiansky, took great offense at the less than flattering portraits, breaking off relations with the author. Vaginov would go on to lampoon his own practice of writing fictionalized versions of friends and acquaintances in *The Works and Days of Whistlin*, in light of the ecstatic bursts of gossip and scandal following the publication of *Goat Song*:

> From time to time there were eruptions of giggling, whispering back and forth. People recognized some acquaintances, didn't recognize others. Then they would whisper to one another: "Who's that?"—and their faces would start looking worried. And finally, the right guess would hit them like lightning, and they would take up their whispering again.†

Still, Vaginov did not spare himself—the doomed unknown poet, a.k.a. Agathonov, doubles his author (even as the "author" does, too), and most of the poems in *Goat Song* are Vaginov's own. More humorously, he presents himself as the unpopular experimental poet Marya Stepanovna in *Works and Days of Whistlin*.

Vaginov's passion for names extends, of course, to the names of these four novels. *Goat Song*, as we have seen, announces its own essence; the two words in Russian furthermore belong to different

---

*K. K. Vaginov, *Polnoe sobranie sochinenii v proze*, eds. Vladimir Erl' and Tat'iana Nikol'skaia (Saint Petersburg: Akademproekt, 1999), 537. See also Egunov's bizarre masterpiece *Beyond Tula: A Soviet Pastoral* (Boston: ASP, 2019), which was written around the same time as *The Works and Days of Whistlin* and *Bambocciata* (and first published in 1931).

†See pages 247–248 in this volume.

332 · TRANSLATORS' AFTERWORD

registers, as the ordinary adjective "goat" smells strongly of the barn-
yard, while the word *pesn'* points to a lofty sort of singing. In a similarly
baroque combination, *The Works and Days of Whistlin* collides the
Works and Days of Hesiod, a long didactic poem from around 700
BCE, with the decidedly flighty and pedestrian Whistlin. Vaginov's
reference to Hesiod is broad, covering the poem's focus on the everyday aspects of running a farm (recalling Whistlin's—and Vaginov's—
fascination with mundane and trifling details) as well as its
articulation of the "Myth of the Ages."* All four of Vaginov's novels
reflect features of the "Iron Age," which Hesiod associates with toil
and hardship, the decline of morality and spirituality, and the characteristic detail of people being born already gray-haired (cf. the
"balding young men" in *Goat Song*).

Bambocciata is the only one of Vaginov's titles directly explained
by the author, in the pithy epigraph that opens the novel. "Bambocciata" is described as the depiction of scenes from everyday life in
caricatured form; the term comes from an eighteenth-century Dutch
artist's nickname, "il Bamboccio"—the cripple. Here, Vaginov em-
phasizes once more the crucial role of "everyday life"—keenly observed
snippets of speech and other social behaviors—as an artistic device
and investigative method in his novels, but there are two more details
worth noting. First, the fact that he provides an explanation, and that
the explanation includes the phrase "in caricatured form," likely
points to the increased pressures felt by Soviet writers in the early
1930s. Radical formal and ideological experimentation was rapidly
losing currency as "socialist realism"—which purported to depict
"reality in its revolutionary development," i.e., the best possible light

---

*Dmitri Bresler points out that translations of Hesiod's poem in Vaginov's time
used a slightly different construction for the title (*Raboty* vs. *Trudy*) and suggests
that Vaginov may have been more immediately inspired by highly detailed literary
biographies such as N. O. Lerner's *Works and Days of Pushkin* (1910). "Roman
K. K. Vaginova 'Trudy i dni Svistonova: poetika zaglaviia," *Vos'maia mezhdun-
arodnaia letniaia shkola po russkoi literature* (*Proceedings of the Eighth Interna-
tional Russian Literature Summer School*) (Kaukolempiälä: Svoe izdatel'stvo,
2012), 146–56.

—became the only game in town. Second, Vaginov's title highlights the "cripple" (here, an art form associated with a disabled producer), a persona and concept increasingly foregrounded in his last two novels.

While Vaginov's characters all have at least a hint of the grotesque and the inadequate, in *Bambocciata* and *Harpagoniana* their physical agonies and spiritual destitution are increasingly on display. To wit, *Harpagoniana* is named for Molière's odious character Harpagon, from the play *L'Avare ou L'École du mensonge* (first performed in 1668). While all Vaginov's novels feature idiosyncratic, variously obsessive collectors, most of them—from Kostya Kissenkin to the inimitable Toropulo—have been inoffensive eccentrics (and sometimes downright attractive). *Harpagoniana* opens with the utterly repulsive, lank-haired Zhulonbin, maniacally amassing piles of rotting detritus in his crypt-like quarters; he sets the scene for an unequivocally negative view of collecting as capitalist accumulation. Zhulonbin's name carries faint echoes of thievery (*zhulik*), but the combination of sounds alone seemed to adequately convey his repugnance in English as in Russian.

To conclude on an appropriately Vaginovian note of vulgarity, we can explain Vaginov's own name to curious English-language readers. When Konstantin was born in 1899, the family name was still Vagengeim—a version of the Germanic Wagenheim (harking back to ancestors from a primarily Jewish part of the Pale of Settlement, in present-day Lithuania).* In 1915, in an environment of strong anti-German sentiment after the start of the First World War, the family was granted a special dispensation to Russify their name to Vaginov. It should be noted that for Russian speakers in the early twentieth century (and many of them to this day), the name "Vaginov" does not immediately suggest vaginas (probably because the Russian pronunciation of the name—"VAH-ghee-noff"—is stressed differently

---

*For more on Vaginov's family history, see Aleksei Dmitrenko, "K istorii roda Vagengeimov," in *Vaginov, Pesnia slov*, ed. A. Gerasimova (Moscow: OGI, 2012), 348–55.

from that of the organ—"vuh-GHEE-nuh"). In any event, the inevitable resonances of Vaginov's name in the Anglophone world would surely give Balmcalfkin cold sweats—and Kostya Kissenkin a good cackle.

—A.M., G.C.
December 2022

Translators' Acknowledgments

THE TRANSLATORS are grateful to Alex Andriesse, Polina Barskova, Flynn Berry, Dmitri Bresler, Jeff Bruemmer, Ulrika Carlsson, Aleksei Dmitrenko, Alexander Dolinin, Edwin Frank, Anna Gerasimova, Igor Gulin, Ilja Kukuj, Roman Leibov, Igor Loshchilov, Dmitri Manin, Aleksandr Markov, Carl Mautner, Richard Morse, Tatiana Nikolskaia, Eugene Ostashevsky, Valerii Otiakovskii, Phil Redko, Jeff Rehnlund, Anna Shipilova, Ivan Sokolov, Elizabeth Stern, Andrei Ustinov, Maria Vassileva, Emily Wang, Muhua Yang, Matvei Yankelevich.

NOTES

Our source text for both *Goat Song* and *The Works and Days of Whistlin* was the authoritative Konstantin Vaginov, *Kozlinaia pesn'* in *Polnoe sobranie sochinenii v proze*, eds. A. I. Vaginova, T. L. Nikol'skaia, and V. I. Erl'. St. Petersburg: Akademproekt, 1999 (13–146). Many of the notes refer to the excellent annotations in that edition (514–33). We are grateful to Nikol'skaia and Erl' for their scrupulous efforts.

INTRODUCTION

1. C. P. Cavafy, "If Actually Dead," in *Collected Poems: Revised Edition*, tr. Edmund Keeley and Philip Sherrard, ed. George Savidis (Princeton, NJ: Princeton University Press, 1992), 103–4.

2. Anthony Anemone's PhD dissertation, *Konstantin Vaginov and the Leningrad Avant-Garde, 1921–1934* (Berkeley, CA: University of California at Berkeley, 1985) remains an excellent English-language introduction to the poet.

3. Aleksei Dmitrenko, "K istorii roda Vagengeimov," in Konstantin Vaginov, *Pesnia slov*, ed. Anna Gerasimova (Moscow: OGI, 2012), 348–55.

4. Nikolai Chukovsky, in ibid., 338.

5. Philostratus, *The Life of Apollonius of Tyana*, tr. F. C. Conybeare (Cambridge, MA: Loeb Classical Library, 1912), vol. 1, xiii–xv, 11; vol. 2, 484–605; Renaissance reception in Grégoire Holtz, *Paganisme et humanisme: La Renaissance française au miroir de la Vie d'Apollonius de Tyane* (Geneva: Droz, 2021). Vaginov may have read *The Life of Apollonius of Tyana* in Vigenère's 1611 translation.

6. Filostrat, "Zhizneopisanie Apolloniia Tianskogo" [1:4–33], in *Pozdniaia grecheskaia proza*, ed. M. Grabar-Passek (Moscow, 1960), 483–502. For more on Egunov, see Andrei Egunov-Nikolev, Beyond Tula: *A Soviet Pastoral*, tr. Ainsley Morse (Newton, MA: Academic Studies Press, 2019).

7. Mikhail Bakhtin, *The Duvakin Interviews*, 1973, eds. Slav N. Gratchev and Margarita Marinova (Ithaca, NY: Bucknell University Press, 2019), 172–82.

8. Nikolai Chukovsky, in Vaginov, *Pesnia slov*, 345.

9. *Mariia Veniaminovna Iudina: Stat'i, vospominania, materialy* (Moscow: Sovetskii kompozitor, 1978), 346–47. Quoted in Tatiana Nikolskaia, "K. K. Vaginov (kanva biografii i tvorchestva)," *Tynianovskii sbornik* 4 (1988): 73.

10. Lydia Ginzburg, in Vaginov, *Pesnia slov*, 296.

11. Bakhtin, *The Duvakin Interviews*, 182.

12. Boris Bukhstab, in Vaginov, *Pesnia slov*, 292–96.

13. Andrei Krusanov, in Aleksandr Vvedensky, *Vsio*, ed. Anna Gerasimova (Moscow: OGI, 2011), 714.

14. The thesis of the formalist critic Yuri Tynianov that alogical combinations of words push denotations into the background but connotations into the foreground probably influenced both OBERIU and Vaginov. See Tynianov, *The Problem of Verse Language*, tr. Michael Sosa and Brent Harvey (Ann Arbor, MI: Ardis, 1981).

15. For "beyonsense," see page 331 of the present volume.

16. Mikhail Bakhtin, *Problems of Dostoyevsky's Poetics*, tr. Caryl Emerson (Minneapolis, MN: University of Minnesota Press, 1984), 6, 11. Original wording is the same in both the 1929 and 1963 editions.

17. Ibid., 107. Phrasing from 1963, missing from 1929 edition. Bakhtin's interest in carnivalesque genres predates the 1930s, however. See Mikhail Bakhtin, *Sobraniie sochinenii v 7 tomakh*, vol. 2: *Problemy tvorchestva Dostoievskogo* (Moscow: Russkiie slovari, 2000), 472.

18. For *Goat Song* as "carnivalesque," see Tatiana Nikolskaia, introduction to Konstantin Vaginov, *Polnoe sobranie sochinenii v proze* (Saint Peterburg: Akademicheskii proekt, 1999), 9–11.

19. Bakhtin, *Dostoyevsky's Poetics*, 242, 292. The poet Vaginov combines words disjunctively, whereas the novelist projects disjunction from the axis of combination onto the axis of selection, introducing it inside the individual word.

20. Konstantin Vaginov, *Semechki*, ed. Dmitry Bresler and Mikhail Lurie (Saint Petersburg: Evropeiskii Universitet, 2023).

21. Rudakov, in Vaginov, *Pesnia slov*, 311.

GOAT SONG

1. Vaginov refers to the midsummer phenomenon of "white nights." Located a few latitudinal lines south of the Arctic Circle, at the eastern end of the Gulf of Finland, St. Petersburg enjoys nearly round-the-clock daylight during the summer months. The literary dimension is explored in Fyodor Dostoyevsky's novella *White Nights*; the eerie quality of midnight twilight is considered characteristic of the city's unstable, chimeric nature (as described in accounts of the so-called Petersburg text).

2. See remarks on early Soviet naming and renaming practices in the Note on Names. "Second Rural Poverty Street" was changed to "Michurinskaya" (Michurin Street, named after the plant geneticist Ivan Michurin) in 1935.

3. Alexandru Averescu was a Romanian military leader and populist politician remembered for his violent suppression of a peasant revolt in 1907 and for his 1926 treaty with Mussolini.

4. "Politedu" translates "Politprosvet," an abbreviation of "Politicheskoe prosveshchenie" (political enlightenment), a Soviet political education initiative active through multiple government institutions in the 1920s and 1930s. Also see Note on Names.

5. Philostratus does not refer to the historical Philostratuses, including the author of *Apollonius of Tyana* mentioned below. Vaginov evokes instead the generalized image of a refined court poet of late antiquity.

6. Nevsky Avenue was renamed 25 October Avenue in honor of the 1917 revolution. Also see the Note on Names.

7. "English Anna" refers to a character (Ann, not Anna) in Thomas De Quincey's *Confessions of an English Opium-Eater* (1821), published in Russian translation in 1834.

8. Lake Avernus (Lago d'Averno) is a lake in Italy with an outsized role in mythology: its poisonous fumes allegedly killed birds flying over it, its banks housed the grottos of the Cumaean Sibyl and a sacred grove of Hecate, and Homer reportedly entered Hades here. Apollonius of Tyana was a Greek neo-Pythagorean philosopher from the town of Tyana in the Roman province of Cappadocia in Anatolia.

9. The family bookshelves demonstrate a typical reading selection of the late nineteenth-century Russian bourgeoisie.

10. Sergei K. (Creighton), the son of a British architect, was a real childhood friend of Vaginov's.

11. "Zemcity" is an abbreviation of "zemstvo goroda," a prerevolutionary semi-populist municipal government body.

12. The River Neva runs through the center of Petersburg. The poet compares it to the Tiber, which correspondingly runs through Rome. Nero's gardens and the Esquiline Cemetery are likewise well-known classical sites in Rome.

13. Taegio was a sixteenth-century Milanese lawyer and writer. His *L'Umore* was published in 1564.

14. The narrator refers to the second-century CE writer Longus, and to his *Daphnis and Chloe*, an erotic-bucolic novel that became a model for the late Renaissance pastoral. Under the tutelage of his friend Andrei Egunov, Vaginov translated some excerpts from this novel in the early 1930s.

15. The *Zodiac of Life* (*Zodiacus vitae*) is a long poem in Latin by Pier Angelo Manzolli (pseudonym of Marcello Stellato). The book was first published in 1536 but banned by the pope in 1559.

16. Both of these places were famous in ancient Italy for their roses.

17. *Goat Song* contains a number of original poems and excerpts from Vaginov's other poems, sometimes but not always attributed to the Unknown Poet. Translation of this and all subsequent poems by A.M. and Eugene Ostashevsky.

18. Vaginov was an avid collector of anonymous urban folklore and "street songs." This poem, composed for *Goat Song*, is a good example of a borrowing of this kind of romantic ballad.

19. The St. George's Cross was a much-prized prerevolutionary imperial Russian military honor.

20. In the prerevolutionary period the Orthodox Christian holiday of Easter was celebrated through rituals including signs of the cross, Easter greetings ("He is risen"), and special foods including eggs dyed red with onionskin, rich sweet cottage cheese (*paskha*), and sweet brioche with raisins (*kulich*).

21. Sublieutenant Kovalyov sings romantic songs popular in the late nineteenth century.

22. The Komsomol (Kommunisticheskii soiuz molodezhi) was the Communist Youth League, instituted in 1918.

23. The exchange between the narrator and "Tamara" refers to the literary association between that name and Mikhail Lermontov's nineteenth-century Orientalist classic novella, *A Hero for Our Time* (1840).

24. "Victims of the Revolution Square" was the name for the Field of Mars between 1918 and 1944. Also see Note on Names.

25. "Kruzhalov's Corner" most likely refers to the Turgenev corner at 34 Sadovaya Street in downtown Petersburg/Leningrad.

26. "September" refers to the experimentally inclined poet Benedikt Mart (March—real last name Matveyev), but the character also shares characteristics of the full-blown Futurist Velimir Khlebnikov (who spent time in Persia) and Sergei Yesenin, who published the *Persian Motifs*.

27. The amethyst is one of twelve gems meant to decorate the habit of a high-ranking priest.

28. The Russian translation of the first volume of Oswald Spengler's 1918 *Twilight of Europe* was published in 1923.

29. These are the opening lines to the Slavophile poet and philosopher Aleksei Khomiakov's 1835 poem "Dream" (Mechta).

30. The Garden of Laborers is now known as the Alexander Garden. It is located next to the Admiralty, near Falconet's Peter the Great statue.

31. Euphratesky (Zaefratskii) is primarily meant to evoke Nikolai Gumilyov (shot in 1921). Euphratesky's widow, Yekaterina Ivanovna, is based on Gumilyov's second wife, Anna Engelhardt. See Note on Names.

32. The Stock Exchange building (designed by French architect Thomas de Thomon), with its maritime Rostral Columns, is centrally located on the spit of Vasilevsky Island. See map.

33. Peterhof is a southwestern suburb of St. Petersburg, best known for its sumptuous Peterhof Palace complex, with its extensive gardens and fountains.

34. The philosopher Andrievsky is based on the philosopher and literary theoretician Mikhail Bakhtin.

35. The University of Marburg was founded in 1527 and was, in the nineteenth and early twentieth centuries, a major place of study for Russian philosophers and poets, including Bakhtin. Hermann Cohen (1842–1918) was a German neo-Kantian philosopher and headed the "Marburg School" of philosophy.

36. The Babigon Heights [*Babigonskie vysoty*], a park designed around three hills, are located a few kilometers south of Peterhof.

37. Vaginov really did write this poem, "The Year 1925," in 1925. The two lines on the previous page belong to it, as do the subsequent lines "In statues lurks…" Another part of it is given as Agathonov's last poem at the end of the novel ("In our youth fair Florence…").

38. The Belvedere palace was built in the mid-nineteenth century for Nicholas I. In the early Soviet period, it served as a sanatorium for artists.

39. "Gaudeamus igitur" (So let us rejoice), also known as "De brevitate vitae" (On the shortness of life), is a popular students' drinking song, thought to originate in a thirteenth-century Latin manuscript.

40. Vaginov refers to an 1870 romantic poem and song by Alexander Navrotsky; it became a revolutionary anthem in the years leading up to the early twentieth-century revolutions in Russia.

41. Alexander Pushkin's famous 1830 poem "For the shores of my distant fatherland" (Dlia beregov otchizny dal'noi).

42. Konstantin Krayevich (1833–92) was a celebrated physics scholar whose textbooks were foundational for secondary-school and university physics instruction through the mid-twentieth century.

43. General Pyotr Nikolayevich Vrangel was a leading figure in the "White" Russian opposition to the Bolsheviks during the civil war (1918–22).

44. Vyacheslav Ivanov (1866–1949) was a major Symbolist poet, philosopher, and theoretician.

45. Vaginov cites a line from an untitled poem by Anna Akhmatova, "What makes this era worse than those preceding…" (1919).

46. "Trianon" refers to chateaux in the park at Versailles; the "Petit Trianon" was the location of Marie Antoinette's "little mill village" where members of the court would stage theatrical pastorals.

47. "Laughter through tears" is a frequently cited attribute of the work of Nikolai Gogol (1809–52), based on a quotation from his *Dead Souls* (vol. 1, ch. 7): "And it is determined by some strange power that I will go hand in hand with my odd heroes for a long while yet, that I will observe this enormous rushing life, observe life through the laughter visible to the world and the invisible tears unknown to it!" (*Polnoe sobranie sochinenii v 14 tt*, vol. 6, 134). Gogol was a major influence on Vaginov.

48. Here, "beyonsensical" (Paul Schmidt's translation) translates the Futurist concept of *zaum'*, also known as a "transsensical" or "transrational" language based on sounds.

49. The young people sing the "Internationale," also the Soviet national anthem (Kots translation).

50. This is an alternative version of the popular prerevolutionary drinking song "Little Bottle" (Butylochka).

51. Luis de Góngora (1561–1627) was a Catholic priest and highly renowned Spanish Baroque poet. Giambattista Marino (1569–1625) was an Italian Baroque poet, best known for his long narrative poem *Adonis*.

52. This scene refers to Vaginov's brief adherence to the avant-garde OBERIU

group (the "Association of Real Art"), associated with poets Daniil Kharms, Alexander Vvedensky, and Nikolai Zabolotsky.

53. This oblique mention refers to the ten-year anniversary of the October Revolution (1917–27).

54. The reference is to the *Dictionnaire Historique et Critique*, a biographical dictionary compiled by French philosopher Pierre Bayle (1647–1706).

55. See note 5 (Philostratus).

56. A rhyton was an ancient Greek drinking vessel shaped like a horn or an animal's head. Julia Domna was the wife of the emperor Septimius Severus; she sponsored Flavius Philostratus's *Life of Apollonius of Tyana*.

57. French: "Forever this memory awaits and moves me…" Balmcalfkin reads André Chénier's poem against Pushkin's poems inspired by Chénier; most likely the poem in question is Pushkin's "Kogda poroi vospominan'e" (When a memory from time to time).

58. Balmcalfkin refers to his city's prostitutes using terms from ancient Greece: in the sixth century BCE, the lawmaker Solon is said to have instituted *dikterions*, or state-regulated brothels, which would have employed *dikteriades* as well as *auletrides*, or women flute players (also prostitutes).

59. A 1922 poem by Vaginov.

60. Mosselprom (short for Moscow Rural Cooperative Administration) was an NEP-era production conglomerate that combined foodstuffs, tobacco, and beer.

61. *Puppchen* was a 1912 German operetta that enjoyed great success in Russia in 1913–14.

62. Anastasiya Verbitskaya was a popular prerevolutionary writer who advocated for women's emancipation. She is best known for her 1913 book *The Keys to Happiness*.

63. The sistrum was an ancient Egyptian percussion instrument, somewhat like a maraca, used in rituals.

64. Regdip (Regional Division of the People's Education) = Gubono (Gubernskii otdel narodnogo obrazovaniia). Angelo Poliziano was a fifteenth-century Italian poet and humanist.

65. Vladimir Solovyov (1853–1900) was a philosopher, theologian, and poet known for his development of "Sophiology," a doctrine based around a benevolent feminine spirit of wisdom. The poem Balmcalfkin reads is from 1892.

66. Caterina Sforza (1463–1509) was an Italian noblewoman notable for her gender-bending assumption of powerful political roles.

344 · NOTES TO *GOAT SONG*

67. Latin: "Under eternal light."
68. The "wall newspaper" was a hallmark of the early Soviet period; it could refer to major newspapers posted on outdoor booths (a means of saving paper) but was often used by smaller-scale print operations, such as the newspaper of a given factory or institution.
69. Pyotr Konstantinovich Kissenkin is the father of Konstantin (Kostya) Petrovich Kissenkin.
70. The character of Bauer will briefly resurface in *Harpagoniana* (as Dauer, the Portuguese consul).
71. For more on Agathonov's name, see Note on Names.
72. Vasily II the Blind was grand prince of Moscow in the mid-fifteenth century, great-grandfather of Ivan the Terrible.
73. The early twentieth-century Petersburg publishing firm run by Roman Golike and Artur Vilborg operated between 1903 and 1918. They published lavish illustrated editions of classics.
74. A 1927 poem by Vaginov.
75. Petersburg is built on several interconnecting pieces of land; the outermost three islands—Yelagin, Kamenny, and Krestovsky—had few buildings and were popular parks for strolling and recreation.
76. Girolamo Fracastoro (1476/8–1553) was famous for his 1530 poem "Syphilis sive morbus gallicus" (Syphilis or the French Disease) (he gave the disease its name). Auguste-Marseille Barthélemy (1794–1867) wrote "Syphilis, poème en quatre chants" (1851).
77. The Irish poet briefly introduced here is based on Vaginov's friend Douglas Harman.
78. *Chi* is "*x*"; *Akte* is the classical Greek name for Mt. Athos; *urbs* is Latin for city; *palestra* (*palaestra*) refers to a public space in ancient Greece for teaching wrestling.
79. The Petrograd Committee of the Russian Communist Party established "labor concentration camps" for "enemy elements" in July 1918. At this time (and subsequently throughout the "Red Terror" of the immediate postrevolutionary period) whole families were sent to the camps on the basis of their class identity.
80. Samuel Pitiscus (1637–1727) was a Dutch classical scholar known for his commentary on Suetonius.
81. Vsevolod Meyerhold (1874–1940) was a leading Russian and Soviet theater director known for his influential experiments in theater and performance. He was shot in 1940.

82. *Ruslan and Liudmilla*, an opera by the composer Mikhail Glinka, is based on one of Pushkin's most popular narrative poems.

83. What Vaginov refers to ironically as the "Quiet Haven" is Petersburg's Pushkin House (Pushkinskii dom), an archival and literary research center founded in 1905.

84. Charles Leconte de Lisle (1818–94) and Abbat (Jacques) Delille (1738–1813) were both French poets.

85. The little old man refers to Alexander Pushkin, known as the "sun of Russian poetry," in whose honor the library and archive (Pushkin House) are named.

86. Sirin is a Russian mythological creature with the head of a bird and the body of a woman. In most legends she lives in a paradise-like location called Iriy.

87. They are walking in Pavlovsk, a popular park south of the city. See map.

88. "Saxe" refers to a popular, extremely ornate and kitschy style of porcelain made in Germany.

89. The "red corner" was a Leninist institution that first appeared in connection with the effort to "liquidate illiteracy." Reading corners outfitted with propagandistic political literature were established in apartment buildings, institutions, villages, and community centers across the entire newly formed Soviet Union. The phenomenon built on the longstanding Orthodox tradition of a "red/beautiful corner" in peasant huts, where icons were hung.

90. *The Dream of Scipio* (*Somnium Scipionis*) is part of Cicero's *De re publica* (54–51 BCE). It includes an extensive and later highly influential discussion of classical cosmology (the structure of the universe, the meaning of the stars, the music of the spheres).

91. See earlier notes on the three different Philostratuses. *Hetaerae* were a class of highly educated and cultured women prostitutes in ancient Greece.

92. Aviakhim (better known as Osoaviakhim, a portmanteau representing "Society for the Assistance of Defense, Aircraft, and Chemical Construction"), was a volunteer militia club popular in the early Soviet period.

93. Jacopo Sannazaro (1458–1530) was a Neapolitan writer best known for his popular pastoral romance *Arcadia. Il Pastor fido* is a tragicomic pastoral by the Italian poet Battista Guarini (1538–1612).

94. The inscription should read RVRIS NON INFIDA VENVS—"the rural Venus is faithful."

95. The reference is to the fifteenth- to sixteenth-century Venetian Aldine Press, founded by Aldus Manutius (the Elder). The Younger is his grandson, Paolo.

96. Vaginov obliquely describes St. Isaac's Cathedral.

97. Lieutenant Schmidt Bridge was formerly, and is now, Annunciiation Bridge.

98. Tikhon (1865–1925) was patriarch of the Russian Orthodox Church, but was deposed in 1922 as part of a reformist movement (the Renovated Church) that largely took over Russian Orthodoxy in the Soviet Union. The "living church" was one of these reformist groups; it sought to unite Communism and Christianity.

99. Balmcalfkin finds himself by the sphinx statues on the Vasilevsky Island side of the Neva.

THE WORKS AND DAYS OF WHISTLIN

1. Vaginov's description of Whistlin's building precisely reproduces his own.

2. Prosper Mérimée was a French Romantic writer particularly admired for his short prose. The series Collection de l'histoire par le bibelot (The Collection of History through Trinkets) was published in Paris by Henri Daragan in the first years of the twentieth century.

3. Avdotya Panayeva (1820–93) was a Russian novelist who presided over a literary salon that was central to the mid-nineteenth-century literary scene in St. Petersburg. Her *Memories* (1889) provides a riveting portrait of her contemporaries.

4. The character whom Whistlin calls Count Ekesparre refers to Baron Ungern (Nikolai Robert Maximilian Freiherr von Ungern-Sternberg), who began his military career fighting in the Russo-Japanese War, World War I, and the Russian Civil War (as a member of the White Army), but went on to become an independent warlord fighting for the revival of the Mongol Empire. He was executed by the Red Army in 1921.

5. Pyotr Kozlov (1863–1935) was a prominent explorer of Central Asia. His discovery of the ancient city of Khara-Khoto played a significant role in the development of knowledge about the Tangut people and culture.

6. Whistlin's source text is N. F. Dubrovin's 1886 *History of the War and Dominance of the Russians in the Caucasus* (*Istoriia voiny i vladychestva russkikh na Kavkaze*) (vol. 3, ch. 10).

7. The "book bacchanal" mentioned here refers to the wholesale sloughing-off of entire personal libraries in the years of chaos and deprivation following the October Revolution.

8. Dmitri A. Benckendorff (1845–1917) was a Russian painter.

9. The quotation comes from Matvei Komarov's *Tale of the Adventures of the English Lord George and the Brandenburg Marquise Friederike-Louisa* (1782).

10. Before 1918 in St. Petersburg, on Konnogvardeiskii Boulevard, a bazaar would be set up for Palm Sunday (the sixth weekend of Lent) every year.

11. The sources of these quotations are unknown.

12. This scene parodies the experimental OBERIU poets' 1928 "3 Left Hours" performance, in which Vaginov took part. He presents himself as the poet Marya Stepanovna.

13. Penates are household gods; for Alexander Pushkin and his circle of poet friends, *penates* symbolized intimate domestic communication far from affairs of state and the beau monde.

14. The opening line of a 1925 poem by Sergei Yesenin ("Do svidaniia, drug moi..."), which was turned into a popular romantic ditty.

15. Cuckoo and Whistlin meet in Tsarskoe Selo (Tsar's Village), a suburb of St. Petersburg. The town's name was changed to Detskoe Selo (Children's Village) in 1918; it was again renamed as Pushkin in 1937, to mark the one-hundredth anniversary of the poet's death (it bears this name today). The suburb is home to several imperial palaces, one of which housed a prestigious lycée where Pushkin studied as a youth.

16. It is highly characteristic that Cuckoo would visit the haunts of Pushkin's youth holding a volume of poems by Pushkin's friend Anton Delvig.

17. The "Bridge of the Republic" was previously (and is now) "Dvortsovy" (Palace Bridge).

18. The "Palace of the Arts" is the Hermitage Museum, housed in the Winter Palace in central Petersburg. In the first years after the revolution the building was painted brick red (now mint green).

19. The Goncourt brothers (Edmond and Jules) were prominent nineteenth-century French litterateurs known for their gossipy journal and occasionally scandalous literary themes.

20. The "Savage Division" refers to the Caucasian Native Cavalry Division, which was composed mostly of Muslim volunteers hailing from the Caucasus. The Yudenich offensive was an attack on Bolshevik-held Petrograd in October 1919 by White Russian general Nikolai Yudenich.

21. Cuckoo refers to the famous literary pair of Prince Andrei Bolkonsky and Natasha Rostova, from Tolstoy's *War and Peace*.

22. Cuckoo refers to the tavern where Faust and Mephistopheles meet in Goethe's *Faust*.

23. Vladimir Yakovlevich Kurbatov, a Petersburg-based professor of chemistry with a doctorate in art history, founded the Museum of Old Petersburg in 1907. In addition to art history and architecture publications, he wrote several books on the city and its suburbs, including *Pavlovsk* (1909), *Gardens and Parks* (1916), and *Petersburg: An Art-Historical Study and Survey of the Capital's Artistic Riches* (1913).

24. Dropoff quotes the 1907 poem "Devil's Swing" (Chortovy kacheli) by Fyodor Sologub, a major Symbolist and Decadent poet.

25. Psychofsky ironically quotes a famous line from Maxim Gorky's 1902 play *The Lower Depths*, where the "proud sound" belongs to the Russian word for "human," *chelovek*.

26. Line from the Rimsky-Korsakov opera *Sadko* ("Song of the Indian Guest").

27. See note 75 to *Goat Song*.

28. From Pushkin's short 1833 lyric "O gloomy time! Enchantment of my eyes…" (Unylaia pora! Ochei ocharovan'e…).

29. Pushkin House (or the Institute of Russian Literature) was founded in 1905, originally as a collection of manuscripts belonging to the poet Pushkin, and by the time of this novel it contained materials belonging to several major nineteenth-century authors (also see the references to "Quiet Haven" in *Goat Song*). Yasnaya Polyana is the name of Leo Tolstoy's estate outside Tula, which had become a national museum in 1921.

30. Liza is the positive female protagonist and love interest in Ivan Turgenev's *A Nest of Gentlefolk* (1859). Lavretsky is the semi-autobiographical protagonist of the novel, who falls in love with Liza but is thwarted in his efforts to wed her.

31. The "Writers' Pathway" (Literatorskie mostki) is a necropolis for famous writers at Petersburg's Volkovskoe cemetery. Mikhailovskoe is one of the villages associated with Pushkin's family estate, part of the "Pushkin Hills" memorial complex near Pskov.

32. These "electric candles" are most likely Yablochkov candles, a type of electric carbon arc lamp invented in 1876; they later appear as "railway candles" (zheleznodorozhnye svechi).

33. According to legend, after writing his play Molière was told that Philibert de Gramont (brother of Antoine, marshal de Gramont) strongly resembled one of the protagonists; when de Gramont saw the play, he was greatly impressed.

34. Count Alessandro de Cagliostro was the alias of the eighteenth-century Italian adventurer and magician Giuseppe Balsamo (1743–95). The immediate reference for readers in Vaginov's time would have been the silent film *Cagliostro*, which premiered in Berlin in 1929.

35. From the end of a famous poem by Aleksandr Blok (1880–1921): "Of brave deeds, of grand feats, of glory" (O doblestiakh, o podvigakh, o slave).

36. Psychofsky is messing around with ancient Jewish mysticism. Thus the Sefirot are, in the Kabala, the ten emanations of God; Azazel is a demonic desert-dwelling being, equivalent to Satan in Talmudic texts; Haborym is a duke of hell; Astaroth is an evil deity associated with the planet Jupiter.

37. "Eleusis" refers to the site in ancient Greece where the religious rites known as the Eleusinian Mysteries took place. The other words are of uncertain origin.

38. Psychofsky uses a traditional Masonic code that replaces each Latin letter with a number. The first twelve letters are numbered in reverse order (l=1, k=2, and so on), then the letters from n through y are ordered sequentially ($n = 13, o = 14…y =24$), m is 25, and z is 26. The initiation scene that follows resembles a Masonic ritual.

39. Psychofsky has in mind Cato the Younger, a first-century BCE Roman politician remembered for his conservative principles aimed at the preservation of old Roman values in decline. Cato's legacy has been chronicled and interpreted by writers from Cicero to Plutarch to Dante.

40. French: "When the night of that day came, the sorcerer led his companion along mountains and valleys where they had not been before, and it seemed to him that they covered a long journey over a short period of time. Arriving at a valley surrounded by mountains, he saw a great number of men and women who had gathered there and were celebrating a grand holiday…" This is a passage from Simon Goulart's *Thrésor d'histoires admirables et mémorables de nostre temps* (1620).

41. The song is "Little Carriage" ("Sharabanchik," also "Akh, sharaban moi, Amerikanka")—a romantic ditty that became a rallying cry for the Whites during the civil war.

42. LSPO stands for Leningrad Union of Consumer Cooperatives (Leningradskii soiuz potrebitel'skix obshchestv), an organization founded in the nineteenth century that exists to the present day.

43. "Fordism" refers to the system of standardized mass production pioneered by the Ford Motor Company in the early twentieth century.

44. This was a sixteenth- or seventeenth-century Florentine plate with Tritons that Vaginov actually owned (having bought it at the Alexandrov flea market).

45. Passage (Passazh) is an upscale department store on Petersburg's Nevsky Avenue. It was first opened in 1848 and was renamed the Palace of Soviet Trade in 1933.

46. French: "One only learns the value of good health when one has lost it."

47. Jean (= John/Ivan) is Ivan Prokofievich (also see Note on Names).

48. Whistlin reads stanzas 6–8 from N. M. Karamzin's "Spring Song of the Melancholic" (Vesenniaia pesn' melankholika) (1788).

49. Vaginov quotes more or less literally from the 1842 children's journal *Little Star* (*Zvezdochka*), specifically from the stories "Lidin'ka," "Sasha," "Humility and Pride," and "Scenes from the Life of Young Shakespeare."

50. See note 30 to *Goat Song*.

51. The quotation comes from the tale "Nur Al-din Ali and the Damsel Anis Al-Jalis." Cf. a nineteenth-century English translation of the same lines: "For a land else than this land thou may'st reach, my brother, / But thy life thou'lt ne'er find in this world another."

52. Whistlin once again sings "Sharabanchik."

APPENDIX

1. The reference is to the *Dictionnaire Historique et Critique*, a biographical dictionary compiled by the French philosopher Pierre Bayle (1647–1706).

OTHER NEW YORK REVIEW CLASSICS

For a complete list of titles, visit www.nyrb.com.

DANTE ALIGHIERI Purgatorio; translated by D. M. Black
CLAUDE ANET Ariane, A Russian Girl
HANNAH ARENDT Rahel Varnhagen: The Life of a Jewish Woman
OĞUZ ATAY Waiting for the Fear
DIANA ATHILL Don't Look at Me Like That
DIANA ATHILL Instead of a Letter
HONORÉ DE BALZAC The Lily in the Valley
POLINA BARSKOVA Living Pictures
ROSALIND BELBEN The Limit
HENRI BOSCO The Child and the River
ANDRÉ BRETON Nadja
DINO BUZZATI The Betwitched Bourgeois: Fifty Stories
DINO BUZZATI A Love Affair
DINO BUZZATI The Singularity
DINO BUZZATI The Stronghold
CRISTINA CAMPO The Unforgivable and Other Writings
CAMILO JOSÉ CELA The Hive
EILEEN CHANG Written on Water
FRANÇOIS-RENÉ DE CHATEAUBRIAND Memoirs from Beyond the Grave, 1800–1815
AMIT CHAUDHURI Afternoon Raag
AMIT CHAUDHURI Freedom Song
AMIT CHAUDHURI A Strange and Sublime Address
LUCILLE CLIFTON Generations: A Memoir
RACHEL COHEN A Chance Meeting: American Encounters
COLETTE Chéri *and* The End of Chéri
E. E. CUMMINGS The Enormous Room
JÓZEF CZAPSKI Memories of Starobielsk: Essays Between Art and History
ANTONIO DI BENEDETTO The Silentiary
ANTONIO DI BENEDETTO The Suicides
HEIMITO VON DODERER The Strudlhof Steps
PIERRE DRIEU LA ROCHELLE The Fire Within
JEAN ECHENOZ Command Performance
FERIT EDGÜ The Wounded Age *and* Eastern Tales
MICHAEL EDWARDS The Bible and Poetry
ROSS FELD Guston in Time: Remembering Philip Guston
BEPPE FENOGLIO A Private Affair
GUSTAVE FLAUBERT The Letters of Gustave Flaubert
WILLIAM GADDIS The Letters of William Gaddis
BENITO PÉREZ GÁLDOS Miaow
MAVIS GALLANT The Uncollected Stories of Mavis Gallant
NATALIA GINZBURG Family *and* Borghesia
JEAN GIONO The Open Road
WILLIAM LINDSAY GRESHAM Nightmare Alley
VASILY GROSSMAN The People Immortal
MARTIN A. HANSEN The Liar
ELIZABETH HARDWICK The Uncollected Essays of Elizabeth Hardwick
GERT HOFMANN Our Philosopher
HENRY JAMES On Writers and Writing
TOVE JANSSON Sun City
ERNST JÜNGER On the Marble Cliffs
MOLLY KEANE Good Behaviour